# THE PERFECT LIE

*By Emily Barr*

Backpack
Baggage
Cuban Heels
Atlantic Shift
Plan B
Out of my Depth
The Sisterhood
The Life You Want
The Perfect Lie

# The Perfect Lie

Emily Barr

headline review

First published in 2010 by HEADLINE REVIEW
An imprint of HEADLINE PUBLISHING GROUP

1



Cataloguing in Publication Data is available from the British Library

Hardback 978 0 7553 5132 9
Trade paperback 978 0 7553 5133 6

Typeset in Garamond by Palimpsest Book Production Limited,
Grangemouth, Stirlingshire

Printed in the UK by CPI Mackays, Chatham ME5 8TD

Headline's policy is to use papers that are natural, renewable and recyclable products and made from wood grown in sustainable forests. The logging and manufacturing processes are expected to conform to the environmental regulations of the country of origin.

HEADLINE PUBLISHING GROUP
An Hachette UK Company
338 Euston Road
London NW1 3BH

www.headline.co.uk
www.hachette.co.uk

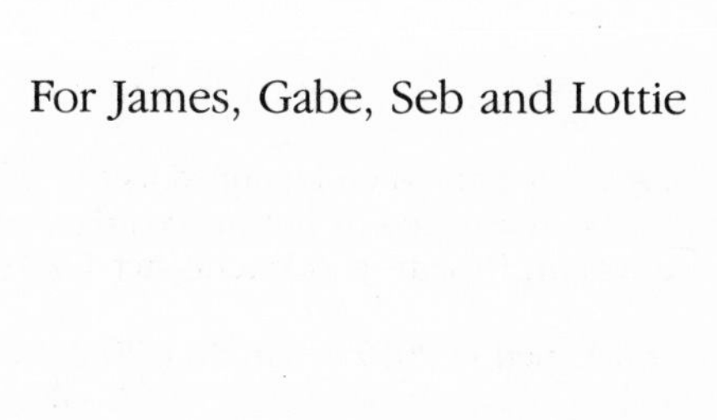

For James, Gabe, Seb and Lottie

## ACKNOWLEDGMENTS

Thanks to Samantha Hawkins, the former [illegible] the staff of [illegible] for providing me with a [illegible] specifically [illegible] Thompson as that [illegible]

## ACKNOWLEDGEMENTS

Thanks to Samantha Lloyd for the fantastic research trip, and to the staff of Caffé Nero for providing me with coffee while I subsequently wrote the book. Enormous thanks to Leonard Cohen for the inspiration, and for smiling at me at Weybridge. Thank you to all the teachers and nursery workers who keep my children occupied, and even teach them things, while I work.

Heartfelt gratitude to everyone at Headline for their unfailing support and for being the most lovely of publishers, and the same to Jonny Geller without whom I would be lost.

And thanks as always to James, Gabe, Seb and Lottie, for everything, and especially for distracting me with real life.

# part one

# chapter one

June 2008

Shortly before I was forced to stop my pretend life, my best friend was telling me about her Saturday night. We had driven to the beach in Eliza's new electric car, me squashed into the back seat with the two girls, Seth sitting in relative comfort in the front passenger seat. Eliza was driving slowly, with enormous concentration, slowing down every time she passed a pedestrian. She was convinced that she was going to knock someone over, because they wouldn't hear her coming and would step out into the road.

The quietness of the car disconcerted me, too, but at least it didn't burn much petrol.

'Don't you just love it?' Eliza had exclaimed, when we were safely out of Falmouth and on the road to the north coast, the dangers of unwary pedestrians left behind for the moment. 'I keep expecting us to take off.'

'Is it a rocket?' Clara whispered to me. She clutched my hand. 'Is it magic?'

'It's not a rocket,' I said, reluctantly, 'but it is a *little* bit magic.' I thought about adding a lesson about the environment, but it was a beautiful day, and I was generally reluctant to burden the girls with the depressing truth about the world they were going to inherit.

The tide was a long way out at Chapel Porth, and the sand was dotted with little groups of people. I looked around. It was a perfect cove, ringed by cliffs. The flat, slightly wet sand stretched out in front of us for what seemed to be miles. The water was a distant line, glinting bright white in the morning sun. I was happy here. Safe, and happy. Today, at this beach, I had everything in the world that I needed. I leaned back on my hands, held my face up to the sun, and appreciated the miracle.

There was barely a single wave: the water was flat, the air still. I felt that, for a moment, we were frozen in time. Afterwards, I would look back on the moment and wish that I had been able to elongate it, to stay in it, to preserve it somewhere: a time when we were all together, all of us safe.

Seth's footprints made a straight line which led from the blanket where Eliza and I were sitting to the very edge of the water. His sandals were on our blanket; they were black Reef ones, trodden down so the shape of his foot was moulded into the plastic. I imagined the waves lapping over his bare feet. He was skimming stones over the motionless ocean, leaving tiny concentric circles skittering across the water.

There were a few surfboards lying on the beach, useless on a flat-calm day like this. The girls were playing nearby, trying to do handstands on the stony sand, falling sideways and giggling. They were miniature versions of their mother, with dark hair, big eyes, and smooth pale skin. Imogen, the elder one, had long tangled hair that reached halfway down her back. It trailed in the sand when she was mid-handstand. Clara had a short bob just like Eliza, because she was averse to hairbrushes. Clara was wearing a sundress over her swimming costume, and Imogen had little purple shorts over hers.

I tore my eyes away from their innocence, and looked back to Eliza.

'So,' I said. 'Go on then. Let's hear it.' Seth had jogged away to throw stones in the sea when he realised that Eliza was embarking on the story of her latest date.

'I don't need to know about these things,' he'd said, holding his hands up, and left us to it.

She stretched her legs out and started to fiddle with the edge of the tartan rug.

'It's one for the annals,' she said. She turned down the corners of her mouth. 'Possibly a classic. OK. It started well. We met in Toast. Which is a cool place but it's full of bloody students, all loud music and people drinking brightly coloured shots that I wouldn't even know how to order. So I spotted him at once, because he was the guy in his forties – fifties, even, maybe, I don't know – sitting in a corner looking out of place, nursing a pint of bitter and ignoring all the young folk in their outlandish clothes. I thought I should have suggested the Chain Locker.' The Chain Locker was a traditional pub, beloved by Seth and by every man who liked a nice pint of ale.

'And he looked like . . . ?'

'He looked fine. Grey hair. Longish, but above his shoulders, and slicked back in that professorish sort of way. A bit Julian Barnes. Nice jacket.' I looked at her. She was squinting into the sun, avoiding my eyes. I was waiting for the 'but'. 'So,' she continued. 'He got me a drink, a glass of wine. And we sat down and started to chat. I was trying on the one hand not to shrink away with terror at the idea that I was in the company of someone halfway presentable, and on the other not to jump ahead to planning when he could meet the girls.'

'Even though he was so old?'

'Even though. We did the awkward getting-to-know-you thing for a bit. You'd think I'd be OK at that by now, but it doesn't get easier.' She tailed off.

'And then?' I prompted. There was a gentle breeze from the sea. It made the little hairs on my arms stand up.

'And then he asked if I was Cornish. I said yes. He said good. He doesn't mind people moving here "from England", just as long as they're not what he calls "the Ethnics". "I'm not racist," he said – he actually used those words. "I just don't think this is the place for them. It's tradition." At which point I wanted to throw my drink down my throat and howl at the moon. Another fucking dud. Can you imagine?'

I sighed. We had pored over this man's emails together, and he had seemed promising. Self-deprecating, charming, funny. 'So what did you do?'

She sighed. 'I fiddled with my wine glass for a bit, without saying anything, and then I thought, fuck it, I can't just sit here because that implies that I agree with him. So we fought. It got heated. I think he was a bit drunk already. He said I'm a crazy PC bitch who betrays her homeland with every breath she takes. I said if he doesn't like seeing black faces around town, that *does* actually make him a racist. I think I said: "You are not just a racist, you are a racist *fuck*."' She smiled. 'All the students stopped drinking and stared at us. I got a round of applause at one point.'

I lay down on my stomach and rested my chin in my hands.

'Well done. Sorry you had to go through that, though. So, who was worse? The racist or the alcoholic from April?'

She considered this. 'The racist was more objectionable, and he has to take the crown for the moment, but the alcoholic chased me down the street until I ran into a pub and locked myself in the ladies'. So it's hard to say.' She looked at me. 'Patrick was every bit as bad, too, because I actually already knew him and liked him, and I thought that we could have a future of some sort.' She narrowed her eyes. 'But all he wanted to do was talk about you. And now I have to see him all the time at school, and I skulk around avoiding him because I'm so embarrassed. He tries to talk to me and I wave at imaginary people on the other side of the playground and stride away from him.'

I swept Patrick away with my hand. That had been stupid of him; a big mistake.

'But,' she continued, 'the ones who are secretly married are worse than any of them.'

I nodded. I knew all about that.

The sky was a perfect light blue. There were a few wispy clouds. The air was getting warmer. It was shaping up to be the most beautiful day of the year.

I passed Eliza the flapjacks and looked at her. She wasn't meeting the right man because it was too soon, in my opinion, but I was not planning to tell her that. She had been on her own for over two years, but in her head she still lived with Graham. His clothes still hung in her wardrobe. There were photographs of him all over the house.

That had to be the reason, because she turned heads wherever she went. Her hair was black without a hint of grey. Her skin was creamy, her features perfectly even. She was small but curvy, and she was three years younger than me.

I looked back at Seth, distant, in his fisherman's smock and long shorts. He and Eliza were the most beautiful pair of siblings. Seth still looked to me as though he had stepped out of a Thomas Hardy novel. He was rugged and gorgeous and I could stare at him all day long. I liked to look at him while he was sleeping. He had faults, plenty of them, but I was as profoundly attracted to him today as I had been at the moment we met.

As I watched him, I deduced that he had run out of skimmable stones, and so had moved on to lobbing the chunky ones into the sea. I could picture the concentration on his face. He stepped back, took a little run-up, and gave it his best overarm bowl. I hoped there were no swimmers or seals in the vicinity.

Seth wanted me to marry him. I should have leapt at the opportunity to snare someone so gorgeous. He kept trying to talk about it, sounding me out, looking at me with a cheeky smile and looking away again, pretending to be coy. He probably still thought that a wedding was every girl's fantasy, and I was afraid that one day soon he would stage a big romantic proposal and present me with a ring.

I was doing my best to fend him off. Whenever talk turned to weddings, I would be as dismissive as I could. 'We're not so bourgeois as to need a piece of paper telling us how we feel about each other, though, are we?' I would say, with a chuckle. Or: 'Think of the carbon footprint!' (an argument which stood up to no scrutiny whatsoever).

The idea that we could get married, have an unconventional wedding and a party on the beach, with all our friends, was something that tore me apart. I could not do it. I would have done anything to have been able to, but I couldn't. It was quite likely that my identity would not even withstand the bureaucratic process. I would be exposed as a fraud. And there was another reason too. I would never be able to tell him why, but I definitely could not marry Seth.

Seth thought I was someone who was uncomplicated, free-spirited, obsessed with the environment. Someone who had moved to Cornwall on a whim, because I liked it. He thought I had had a couple of serious relationships in my twenties and a long period of single life, culminating in my meeting him. He knew there were family issues, and that I never talked about them, and he carefully left them alone because he knew that was what I wanted.

'Was he always like that?' I asked Eliza, indicating Seth with my head.

She nodded and picked up a handful of sand, let it run through her fingers.

'Thirty years ago,' she said, 'he'd stand right there and do exactly what he's doing now. It's a bit freaky, actually. The years pass but nothing changes. It does, of course, and that's why it feels so weird when some things stay the same. Namely, my big brother thinks all the stones should be in the water. It's his version of tidying up.'

'It's the only version he has,' I said.

A family nearby passed foil-wrapped sandwiches to each other, even though it was far too early for lunch. Their teenage boy watched them through his camcorder. I looked at him scanning the beach with his lens, wondered whether he was playing with a new toy. A man on his own, a little way behind Eliza, poured a brown milky liquid from a thermos flask and sipped it with his eyes closed. The sun shone on his face.

'So. More fish in the sea?' I asked. She snorted.

'Yeah. Loads of fish in the sea. Unfortunately for me, they're all those ugly ones with bulging eyes. The ones that live on the seabed and have spikes on their chins. I don't know why I bother. All the good ones leave and go to London, and then they come back when they've got a wife and a baby, and even then only if they can work down here, which most people can't. And anyway, an ageing widow with small children isn't the most attractive prospect in town.'

'Yes she is, Eliza. Because you're forgetting that you're gorgeous.'

'Oh, shut up. Maybe I should try lesbianism. That could be the way forward. Anyway, I'm going to dip my feet in the sea. See if I can bear to let the girls swim.'

She stood up and walked away from me, leaving footprints in the sand as she headed towards the water's edge. I filled my lungs with the bracingly clean air, and smiled. There was no way the water was going to be even slightly warm.

I looked around. The girls had moved over to the bottom of the rock face. Imogen was chatting to a little girl with white-blond hair. I looked around for Clara. Imogen pointed up the cliff, talking behind her hand, giggling. They both laughed. I became aware that a few other people were looking up at the cliff too. I followed their gaze, wondering what they were looking at.

My mouth tried to form a word, but I couldn't make the sound come.

I had no idea what I was doing, but something propelled me to my feet. I was at the foot of the cliff, pushing past Imogen and the blonde girl. Then I was off, up it. I knew I could do this, and I could see that nobody else was going to try. Eliza was far away, now, at the water's edge. Seth was with her. By the time either of them got here, it would be too late. At first the climbing was easy, as the cliff sloped gently away from the beach. Then it became steeper, and finally, vertical.

She was far above me, standing on a ledge. She seemed quite calm, and looked incongruous, halfway up a rock face, wearing a white cotton dress over a pink swimsuit, and canvas shoes. As I watched, she reached up for another handhold and set off again. I could not see her face, but I could imagine it: the determined frown, the pursed lips.

It was a long way to the top, and there was no way she could make it. If she got there, the first handful of grass she grabbed would send her falling straight down, crashing past the rocks, bouncing off the outcrops.

I was getting closer, measuring my progress purely in terms of handholds and footholds. I wanted her to wait, but I didn't call out, because I was terrified of making her look down, lose her nerve, loosen her grip.

I was hardly able to breathe for the last part of the climb.

Then I was alongside her.

Her head turned. She was entirely unperturbed at the sight of me. Her black hair was slicked back from her face with sweat, and her cheeks were pink with sun and exertion. She had a sprinkling of freckles that I had never noticed before.

'Hello, Lucy,' she said. She smiled.

'Hello, Clara,' I replied. I tried to keep my voice steady. 'Where are you going? Can you step back down on to that ledge for a moment?'

She thought about it. The sun was strong now. I could feel it on the back of my neck.

'OK,' she agreed, and she bent her knee and felt downwards with her left foot until she located the flat rock. I watched her lower her weight back down, ready to reach and grab her if she fell, but knowing that if that happened we would both crash all the way to the beach, and there was nothing I could do, no manoeuvre I could perform that would keep us balanced.

When she came to rest, I exhaled. She was on a ledge that was wider than the length of her foot. She was as safe there, for a moment, as she could be. The fact remained, however, that we were perhaps thirty metres above the ground, and that we had a cliff to descend together.

'Clara?' I asked. 'What are you doing up here?'

'I'm going to the top,' she told me, her face determined. 'Because Imogen said I dare you, and if someone says they dare you, you *have* to.'

'No you don't,' I told her, quickly. 'You definitely don't. It's too dangerous up there. You've done some amazing climbing, and now we need to go back down. Imogen's going to be in trouble.'

Her face brightened. 'Is she?'

I reached out and gripped her around the waist. It was precarious, but as long as she didn't fight me, it could work.

'I'm going to try to carry you down. OK?'

She stared at me, and said nothing.

I was shaking as I tried to hoist her on to my shoulder. It was a manoeuvre, I realised at once, that would not work. I began to lose my balance, lurched suddenly outwards, felt our weight being pulled by the irresistible force of gravity. I leaned forward, suddenly, desperately, and held on as tightly as I could with my fingertips. I put Clara in front of me and looked down, willing Seth, or anybody, to have followed me up, to be behind us, ready to save us both.

The beach swam before my eyes. There was crowd of miniature people down there, gathered close to the bottom of the cliff, staring at us. No one was climbing. We were stuck, a thousand miles from anyone or anything.

I swallowed hard. I needed a new plan. Just the two of us, in the sunlight, halfway up a cliff. Sooner or later, we would fall.

'Hold on to my front,' I said. It was the only thing I could think of. 'Pretend you're a baby koala. Can you manage that?'

'Course.' She turned carefully around, and reached up for my neck.

This felt marginally more stable. I reached down with a shaking leg, and found a foothold. Then I found another, and a handhold. Each step that worked, I told myself, was a step closer to sandy beach beneath my feet, to safety.

I could feel Clara getting restless. Her arms were sticky and sweaty, pulling hard around my neck. She was hot and bothered. Our descent was precarious, and seemed endless.

'Shall we sing a song?' she asked at one point. My foot slipped and I had to lean up against the rock to keep our balance. She cried out and burst into tears. 'That hurt my back!' she said, angrily.

'Sorry,' I said through gritted teeth. My foot was bleeding; I could feel it. 'Look, why don't *you* sing us a song?' I said.

'Don't want to now. This is boring. I wish I'd gone up to the top. It was fun before *you* came.'

She carried on whimpering and sniffing and moaning, and I felt like joining in. Our descent continued, and I began to zone out. There was nothing in the world but me, and Clara, and the jagged rock face. Her mutterings and grumblings kept me company. Then, when I was not expecting it at all, my foot found the sand, and I realised we were there. I lifted Clara down to the ground, looked blankly at the crowd that was all around us, and let Seth take me in his arms. I folded up. All I wanted to do was to lie down and cry.

I looked up and saw the lens, pointing at me, the sun glinting off it. I thought nothing of it, nothing at all.

# chapter two

Seth leaned back in his seat, spread his limbs around the chair, and raised his glass.

'To the saviour of the day,' he said, smiling. His face was a little bit stubbly, in an artful way that made him look like the untrustworthy charmer that, I had discovered, he actually wasn't. 'To our heroine. Didn't there used to be something in the old fairy stories where if you save someone's life you own them for ever?'

'Oh, shut up,' I said, and I smiled into my vodka. We were upstairs in our favourite pub, the Boathouse, looking across the estuary to Flushing. The sun was low in the sky, casting elongated black shadows, and the water rippled in the breeze. A few boats were bobbing around. Falmouth was away to the right, and the little village opposite clung around the harbour. 'Shut up,' I said again. 'I don't *own* Clara. Maybe I could have a special bond with her for ever, if you like.'

He nodded. 'A special bond for ever. Yes. That sounds more like it, doesn't it?' He took my hand and squeezed it. I squeezed back, grateful.

From time to time, I would still catch a glimpse of Seth and find myself unable to believe that he was mine. This was inevitably, and properly, followed by the private acknowledgement that although he didn't know it, he was not. Nobody could touch me at all. That was my secret.

When I met him for the first time, three years ago, we were

at a party at Eliza and Graham's house. I knew Eliza slightly, because she was a member of a book group I had attempted to join a month earlier. It met in a bar and was full of intimidating women who gave a cursory nod to the book, then discussed their children, in great detail, for the next two hours. The sole time I attended, I went home drunk on cheap wine and so bored that I had entered a different realm of existence, one where the pattern on the wallpaper and the weave of the carpet was interesting and I could not bear to speak ever again. The only person who had taken any notice of me whatsoever, at the book group, was the small, cherubic woman with the shiny hair, who gave me a party invitation as I left and whispered: 'It won't be full of these guys – don't worry.'

I went to her party on my own, nervous but with nothing else to do, and was instantly enveloped into the family. It was everything that the book group hadn't been: it was warm and inclusive, and the music was loud, and although there was evidence, in the shape of primitive artworks, that children lived in this house that overlooked the sea, they had, according to Eliza, been 'shipped off for the night – that's what grandparents are for'.

She introduced me to Graham, who was tall and happy-looking, with flyaway hair standing up all around his head. He patted it down from time to time.

'And this one's my brother,' she said, happily, grabbing the arm of another passing man. I looked at him.

I had given up men for ever. I knew it was the right thing, because since I did it, life had slipped into place and the sun had come out in my head. No men, and almost no alcohol: it was the only way.

I felt I already knew this man. I looked at him, and a voice inside my head said, 'Oh, it's you.' Although I had given up men, I felt that I could not fight this. I smiled a tentative smile.

He was taller than me, but not too tall, and he had enormous dark eyes in the kind of face that had been thinking good, interesting thoughts for about thirty-five years. I liked everything about him.

Everything, that was, apart from the anorexic blonde on his

arm. She was wearing a lot of make-up, and a very tight pair of jeans, and a plunging top. So, for one thing, I did not do men any more, and for another, he was taken. Besides, if this woman was his type, then I was not. I had made an effort for the party, but my effort involved wearing my clean jeans and a long-sleeved T-shirt that I'd actually ironed, then blow-drying my hair and wearing it loose. I saw the blonde woman looking me over, scorn in her gaze.

Then my eyes met his.

He turned around, towards me.

'Hello,' he said, in a warm, wondering voice. 'Who are you? I'm Seth.'

'Lucy,' I said. The woman pulled his arm, but he didn't take his eyes away from mine for several long seconds, even as he was being steered across the room. My palms tingled; my heart pounded. I did not so much as glance in his direction for the rest of the evening.

Three days later, he called me, newly single, asking whether I would care to meet him for a drink. It was one of the more surprising things that had ever happened to me; and it felt like the first good surprise I had ever had. I quickly rethought the vow of chastity, and as time went by, I altered my other rules too. There was no reason, I told myself, why Lucy Riddick should not settle down with a man. Just as long as she was ready to leave it all behind when the need might arise.

'Yes,' I said now. 'A special bond will be fine. Anyway, I don't want to talk about it any more. It was just one of those things. You know. You do things when you have to, don't you?'

I was embarrassed by my rescue of Clara, and I wished everyone would stop talking about it. It had not occurred to me to stop at the base of the cliff, to ask if anyone else was a good climber, to enlist a partner, to work out a plan. I felt that it was probably some form of reckless egotism on my part that had sent me charging up there. It was not something that Lucy Riddick should have done.

'Stop being bashful,' he said. 'You did great. There must have been a hundred people on that beach, and no one else did what needed to be done. You know, the best the rest of us could come up with was the idea of holding out a picnic blanket to break your fall.' He looked into his pint, and swirled it around.

'Oh, don't,' I pleaded. 'You were throwing stones into the sea. It was important work, and you were miles away. You can't give yourself a hard time for the fact that you were tidying the beach, and facing the wrong way.'

'If she'd fallen,' he said, 'then I would have blamed myself. Completely.'

'Well she didn't.'

He held up his glass, and I clinked it with mine.

'No,' he said. 'Indeed she didn't. So let's drink up and head over to visit my little sister, with wine. I imagine she'll be needing it.' He hesitated. 'Is it bad that this is my automatic reaction? Eliza's needed so much emotional support these last few years. All I seem to be able to do about it is to turn up on her doorstep with booze.'

'You're a terrible brother,' I agreed. 'No, of course you're not. Your parents have been there for the emotional stuff. So have I, so have lots of her friends. Boozing her up is your department. It's fine.' I swallowed. 'It's what brothers are for,' I said, and shut my eyes, briefly, and hoped he didn't notice. I was pretty sure he did, but he never said anything.

'Thanks.'

I pulled myself together, kissed him. He surprised me by taking two handfuls of my hair, pulling me in tight, and kissing me back, harder than he ever had. His stubble scratched my cheek, rubbing my skin raw. He held my long, tangled hair in both hands, as if he were trying to meld us into one being.

As we walked through town, the clock struck seven. The cries of gulls sounded high above our heads, and wisps of pink appeared at the edges of the sky. There were people around: students, workers. People were locking up shop. There was a smell of chips and pasties in the air, and it made me hungry.

Seth put an arm around my waist. I reciprocated. We walked

close together, our bodies warm against each other. This was what I loved about not being single. I loved the comfort of knowing he was there.

'Why don't we get some chips?' I said. I never bought chips, but things felt, somehow, different today. I stretched my foot out. It was still raw and painful.

Seth was pleased. 'Yess!' he said. 'A change from piles of green leaves and home-grown tomatoes.'

'Those things are good.'

'I know. Of course they are. If you're a *rabbit*. And I appreciate that I wouldn't get my five a day if it wasn't for you. I'd be lucky to get one a day, if I was on my own, but now I get at least eight. Look, the chippy. Harbour Lights. At the end here.'

'Yeah, I know where it is,' I told him. 'I may not patronise it often, but I have lived in Falmouth for five years, remember?' I smiled and leaned into him. He pulled me closer.

'And you patronise *me* often,' he said, into my hair. He laughed. 'I can't believe we were in the same town for all that time before we met. It shouldn't have been technically possible, in a place this size.'

'Well, I believe you managed to entertain yourself while you were waiting for me.'

He snorted. 'Just because you were training for holy orders. Pardon me for enjoying my youth.'

We walked slowly together up the steep hill, away from the main street. As we climbed, I reached across from time to time and grabbed a chip. I had forgotten how perfect they could be, when you didn't eat too many. As Lucy Riddick, I had eschewed all junk food. I grew vegetables and ate them raw or steamed them. I ate oily fish twice a week, and I went running. I checked the food miles of all the shopping I did, and I banned both of us from having baths, ever.

Seth often told me that I treated my tomatoes like babies. I ignored the conversation he was attempting to start. It was worse than the wedding one.

Falmouth was a hilly town, and it was impossible to go to the town centre, which was at sea level, without a steep climb back home. I liked that: I liked the fact that there was no option but activity, that leg muscles were used no matter what. I was sometimes shocked at how healthy I had become.

We emerged on a high terrace of white and pastel-coloured houses, which overlooked the harbour, and headed to Eliza's. This was the same house where I had been to the party, had met Seth. This was our part of town too, though we did not have the bewitching sea view. Eliza did: Graham's life insurance had paid off her mortgage, which was the least she deserved.

Seth crumpled the chip paper, looked around for a bin, then pushed it into his pocket. I walked up to Eliza's bright white house and rang the doorbell outside the porch. I had a key in my pocket: I made the long walk to the outskirts of town to collect Imogen from school, twice a week. All the same, it seemed only polite to ring when we were visiting.

Imogen answered. Her dark hair hung over her face, and what was visible of her rosebud lips formed a perfect pout. She was a child whose moods were transparently readable, and today she was cross. She was still in her school uniform, a green sweatshirt over a green and white checked dress. Her feet were bare, her toenails badly painted in pale pink. I loved her in her uniform: she looked so wholesome. I wanted her to stay that way for ever and ever. Without a word, she turned and walked away, leaving the door swinging open.

'Hey, Imo!' called Seth, stepping into the porch and then the house. 'You can't still be upset about yesterday?'

She was already on the stairs. She looked back and scowled. I tried to give her a conspiratorial smile, but she turned and ran upstairs. A door slammed.

Eliza and Clara were in the kitchen at the back of the house.

The kitchen was the hub of their home. It was papered with paintings that the girls had brought home from school. The large table had a bowl in the middle of it that was filled with little toys, pieces of Lego, letters that had come back from school. The window was open, but there was still a faint smell of tomato sauce hanging around in the room. Every time I came here, which was often, I had to quell pangs of regret and longing.

Clara was sitting at the table, swinging her legs and sucking milk through a straw, while Eliza bustled around loading the dishwasher.

'Shouldn't these guys be in bed?' asked Seth, handing her the Threshers bag. She peeped inside it.

'Thanks,' she said. She kissed Seth's cheek. 'Appreciate it. You know I don't drink on my own. Pour us all a glass.'

'Of course,' I said. 'Moral support, that's us. Co-drinkers.'

'But you mustn't mention the rescue,' added Seth, stroking my hair. 'Lucy is too modest to talk about it.' He twisted the top off the chilled bottle of Sauvignon, and took three wine glasses out of the cupboard.

'That's not true,' I complained. I sat down next to Clara at the big pine table, and looked at an orange and black painting that had appeared on the wall since my last visit. 'Nice digger,' I added.

'It's a boat,' Clara said sternly.

I pulled her on to my lap. 'Sorry.'

'OK, we won't talk about it,' said Eliza, tersely. 'But I would just like to say one more time that I cannot *believe* that Imogen ordered her sister to climb a cliff and then stood and laughed at her, and that *Clara*,' she looked meaningfully at her younger daughter, 'Clara did something so *stupid* without questioning it.'

'Yeah, I know.' Seth sighed heavily. 'And I should have been the one scaling the cliffs, James Bond stylee. Not leaving my fiancee to do it. Where did you learn to climb, Luce, anyway?'

'Oh, I had a brief phase as a kid. Used to go to the climbing wall. Prefer doing it with ropes, ideally.' I stopped. 'And Seth? *Fiancée?*'

He grinned, raised his eyebrows, and did not reply. I sighed, and held Clara on my lap like a shield. I wished I could fling my arms around him and accept the implicit proposal. I would have given anything to be able to do that. Almost anything.

Imogen was still sulky in a pair of red and white checked pyjamas, smelling faintly of toothpaste. I sat on her bed and she leaned on me while I read her two chapters of a book about a Viking called Hiccup. A funny golden light edged into the room from the evening sun through her flimsy curtains.

'It was Clara's fault,' she said as I closed the book. 'She shouldn't have done it. I was only joking.'

She was looking at me with big, troubled eyes. I kissed her forehead and tried to say the right thing.

'It's fine,' I told her. 'Everyone's fine. You just need to remember that she looks up to you because you're her big sister, and she wants you to think she's clever and brave. So be careful what you dare her to do in future.' I could hear the question in my voice, because I was on unsafe ground. I had no idea how to tell a child anything about the way the world was.

'Huh. I'm never allowed to dare her to do anything, ever again. Mum says. Even Mr Davidson said . . .'

I cut her off. 'Fair enough.'

'I wish Dad was here.'

'I know.' We looked at each other.

'Lucy!' yelled Seth. 'Get down here! Now!'

I widened my eyes at Imogen, and exhaled with a tiny bit of relief at the abrupt end of our conversation. I smiled at her.

'All right,' I called back. 'In a sec.'

'Now!'

'Can you believe how rude your uncle is?' I asked her. She giggled.

'Can I come down with you?'

'No. Good night.'

I kissed Imogen again, tucked her into bed, and went down the stairs.

Eliza's television was a big solid one that she and Graham had had for years. Seth (who hated television as a rule, and only watched boxed sets of *The West Wing* and *The Wire)* was staring at it, mouth open. His jaw appeared to have dropped without him noticing. He patted the seat next to him without taking his eyes off the screen, which was filled with shaky video footage of rocks.

'Look,' he said. 'Look at this.'

At first I thought it must be one of those home-footage ITV programmes, the sort of thing we never watched. But there was no comedy commentary. As I stared, I began to understand what I was seeing. There was a woman hanging on to a cliff. A woman wearing my blue T-shirt, with a pair of little hands gripping her around her neck, though the girl on her front was not visible.

I watched myself edging down, exploring for footholds with my bare toes. I felt the gash on my foot throbbing. As I sat on the very edge of Eliza's sofa, I was terrified the woman on the screen was going to fall, even though I already knew how this ended.

The only soundtrack was the muffled sound of voices around whoever had been filming. I couldn't make out what anyone was saying; just a general tone of gasping fear and interest.

'You missed the bit where you went up,' Seth said, staring straight at the screen. He was agog. 'And you missed the part where you tried to get her over your shoulder and the pair of you almost fell backwards. Should have heard the gasps on the beach at that one.'

I was attempting to quell the beginnings of abject terror. I stared, willing the teenage boy with the camera to stop filming as soon as Clara and I reached the ground. I did not want to see my face.

We were there, tremulously feeling the soft sand beneath our feet. My bare foot was bloody, but my face was blurred. I disappeared into Seth's arms.

'Look,' I said weakly. 'It's you.'

Clara burst into tears as Eliza swept her up. I hadn't noticed that happening. The camera moved away from me, focused on Eliza and Clara, and then panned around the beach, which was almost empty as everybody was gathered in a knot around the base of the cliff. It took in the crowd, then, with a horrible inevitability, the focus swung back to me. I saw my face. The camera zoomed in on me.

This was the moment I had avoided for twenty years. I had kept to the background, obsessively. I had never gone anywhere near a camera. It was my number-one rule. I lived a quiet, unremarkable life.

Then it was over. The reporter was saying: 'Well an extraordinary piece of footage there, Claire.' The presenters' voices droned on, as they bantered fakely, and then someone else was talking about the weather.

The meaty taste of blood was in my mouth. I had bitten my lip too hard. I pulled my sleeves down over my fingers, which was something I always did when I was nervous, and I fought for breath and did my best not to panic.

It was the local news. It had lasted a few seconds. No one would have seen it. This could not be going to be the thing. It could not.

Seth's phone beeped. Then mine did too.

# chapter three

## Marianne

March 1988

I walk back from school ten paces ahead of Finn, until we get to the corner of our road. Then I stop, and wait for him to catch up. That's the way we always do it.

'OK to be seen with me now?' he says, making a rude face.

'Yeah,' I tell him. 'Only because there's no one to see us.' I ruffle his hair, because he hates it. He pings my bra strap, because I really, seriously object to that. He even manages to do it through my thick coat.

'Oi,' I tell him, shaking him off. 'Stop that or you're not allowed to walk with me any more.'

'Oh, woe is me! My world is at an end!'

I smile at him, briefly, and then I pretend to be cross again. I like the end of school. I like walking with Finn, and going home to Mum. I like it that we bicker like we used to when we were seven and six. It's more comfortable than school with all the 'fuck off' and the 'bloody bitch'. I can't keep up with everyone at school any more. I don't really want to be cool – I don't have it in me – but I have to make a bit of an effort so I am not actively uncool, because I cannot bear the idea of standing out in any way.

Finn is singing, loudly. 'Oooh, heaven is a place on earth,' he croons.

'Oh, very cool,' I say, admiringly. 'Aren't you quite the hipster?'

'You should be so lucky,' he retorts.

'Lucky, lucky, lucky,' I echo. I sing Kylie for a while. He retaliates, as he always does eventually, with a loud blast of 'So Long, Marianne'. And then we are home.

We have lived in this house for ever. Other people's places are bigger, but at least it's a whole house, not a flat. We have a front door that is just ours (I suppose it is, strictly speaking, our landlord's, but as far as we are concerned, it belongs to us). The house is battered, and the green paint on the front door is peeling, and there are patches of mould that grow up the walls at the back, but we don't care. Neither does the landlord. Mum says he's an unscrupulous bastard and refuses to let me meet him, but he leaves us alone and he doesn't charge us much rent, and although Mum keeps saying that one day he'll sell the place to developers, he doesn't seem to have thought of that yet.

'He's just waiting for the right time,' she says, darkly.

Finn puts his key in the lock and turns it, and we race each other inside.

'Mum!' Finn shouts.

'Offspring are home,' I call.

She comes down the stairs, smiling. I can hear Leonard Cohen singing on the bedroom stereo upstairs. She always listens to him: that's why I am called Marianne, because of one of his songs. Sometimes we ask her if he's our dad, and we are only half joking: he is as good a candidate as anyone.

She has been in love with him for ever, and we have a sneaking suspicion that she might have met him once. No one else has even heard of him, but since his new album came out in February, he has provided the constant soundtrack to our home. I like his deep voice, and I like the words he uses, but I wouldn't mind listening to something else from time to time, just so that I could keep up with what everyone else talks about at school. I just nod and say I like Simple Minds, and I laugh about Kylie.

'You know,' she says, 'I kind of heard that happening. But I thought it was a herd of elephants. In fact I'm rather relieved that the door's still on its hinges.'

I roll my eyes. 'Mum! We're not *four*.'

'Yeah, Mum,' Finn agrees. 'Got any cake?'

She nods, and we follow her to the kitchen. Mum is forty-five, but people always think she's about thirty or less. She has light brown hair which is almost down to her waist. She dyes it at home. We help her. She says Finn doesn't have to any more because he's a teenage boy and teenage boys don't like that sort of thing, but he sort of enjoys it. At least, he still comes into the bathroom and sits on the lid of the loo while I make sure every strand is covered. I want to dye mine too, but Mum says I have to wait till I'm at least sixteen. She says she only started doing it when she went grey, and it's true, when she has roots, they are pretty much old-lady coloured. But the colour we dye her is gorgeous, kind of honeyish-brown.

I'm going to do mine auburn when I'm sixteen. I want to see what it feels like to be a redhead.

And Mum dresses completely in stuff she gets from the charity shop, because we have no money, but she looks really good. She's very skinny, and she likes beachy-looking clothes. When she wears jeans, you can see her hipbones poking out above them, and her waist is amazing. She calls it 'the poverty diet'.

'I'm going to write a diet book,' she said, the other day. 'It is foolproof, so it will definitely make our fortune. It goes like this: "Make sure you don't have enough money for food or for public transport. Walk everywhere and eat lentils. Watch those pounds melt away."'

'That might be a bit short,' Finn pointed out. 'For a book, I mean.'

'So it'll suit people with no attention span,' said Mum. 'Which is good. We'll put one word on each page. We'll doodle pictures around the edges.'

'But then you'll make us rich,' I told her, 'and we'll be able to shop at Marks and Sparks.'

'And we'll get a big car with a chauffeur,' added Finn.

'And then you'll get fat, and no one will buy your diet book any more.'

'So they'll have to pulp the book, and we won't have any money, and the circle will begin again.'

I wish I looked like her. I'm poor too, of course (because I have even less money than Mum), but she gives all the nice food to us, and eats our leftovers. That's why she's so thin that she sometimes looks as if she'd break in half if you even looked at her too hard.

'Ta-dah,' she says now. 'Cake!' She produces it with a flourish. It looks gorgeous – golden, sticky, and slightly sunken in the middle. She has sprinkled extra sugar over the top.

'What's in it?' Finn checks, as Mum stands next to it, blunt knife in her hand.

'Well, let's see,' she says. 'Butter – actual butter, I'll have you know. The kind of white bleached sugar that costs twelve pee a bag. Two eggs. Seven-pee-a-bag flour. And a spoonful of golden syrup. Does that meet with sir's satisfaction?'

'A big piece?' he wheedles.

'It's got to last.'

'No it hasn't.'

I watch Mum carefully, making sure she has a slice herself. She does, but she only takes one because she sees me looking, and her piece is so small that it is really just a clump of crumbs.

The kitchen is lined with nasty chipped tiles which have brown and orange flowers on them, and black grime where the grouting once was. The worst of the black mould is hidden by a poster of Venice that we have had for ever. Mum is obsessed with Venice. I don't know why. It's not as if she's ever been there. Two of the cupboard doors have fallen off, and are leaning against the wall, where they have stood for months. We will probably replace them the night before our landlord's inspection, which is going to happen in seven weeks' time (we are always very focused on the six-monthly inspections, and Mum always makes us go out before he arrives). The floor is covered in dirty cream linoleum, which is curling at the edges. Our kitchen table is rickety formica, but last month we got an offcut of red floral tablecloth from one of the textile shops, and it fits perfectly. It is the wipe-clean kind, and it has made our kitchen more cheerful.

We wipe it after our cake, and Mum dries it with a dishcloth, and it becomes the homework table. Mum is totally in charge of what goes on in the house. She forces us to do our homework, and she checks it afterwards, and if we don't understand something, we sit down together and Mum does her best to work it out. She says we have to do well at school so we don't end up like her, and she also says: 'You two weren't exactly born with silver spoons – you need all the bloody work ethic you can get.'

I spread out my history coursework. Finn starts on some maths sheets. We sit in silence. I suck the end of my pen and think about the Second World War. When I glance over at Finn, he is doing long multiplication.

Mum starts cooking: she gets out a tin of beans, some slices of bread. She boils the kettle for a pot of tea. I smile. We don't have much, but this is the way I like things. Mum rules our world, and I know that with her in charge, everything is going to be all right. At home I am so much more comfortable than I ever am outside the house. The world outside scares me, but between our walls, I feel safe.

# chapter four

A surprising number of people watched the local news, it turned out; and that was just the start of it.

Although it was Tuesday morning, I was hung-over, and so was Seth. We'd shared two bottles of wine with Eliza, and now that we were well into our thirties, it turned out that this was all it took to ruin the next day. Drinking was something I could only do in careful moderation these days. Otherwise the throbbing head, the dry mouth, the general protestations of my body made it unbearable. I found the enforced sensible behaviour rather soothing.

I woke up, reached for the water glass that was beside the bed, tipped it back, and found it empty. My body panted in anticipation, and then I moaned with frustration.

'Where's the water?'

Seth rolled over and rubbed his head.

'Oh,' he said. 'Hmm. I have a vague recollection of pouring it all down my throat at some point in the night. Sorry.'

He swung his legs over the side of the bed, and pushed himself upright with obvious effort. He took the glass over to the basin in the corner of our room, held his hand under the tap until he was sure it was running cold, and filled the glass for me. I sat up and took it.

'Thank you,' I said, between gulps. Every drop made me feel slightly better. We looked at each other and smiled rueful smiles.

'Getting too old for this,' Seth said, rooting around for

painkillers. He located them and popped two into my hand, and two into his.

'Why do we forget that?' I asked. 'All the time?'

'Optimism. The illusion of youth. Are you working today?'

'Not till one. One till eight.' I thought about work. Of all the jobs to do with a hangover, pouring endless pints and glasses of house wine was not a desirable one. 'I'd better be feeling a hundred per cent by then. What about you?'

'Mmm.' He took the water glass I was holding out to him, and swallowed the pills. 'I think my boss has just afforded me a morning off.'

'Understanding of him.'

'He's a nice guy.'

Seth was self-employed. He did his best to combine doing what he wanted to do, which was painting pictures of Cornish scenes and selling them through the galleries in town, with doing what he needed to do to earn enough cash to keep himself going. He painted walls, worked on the boats, and, when he was desperate, picked up shifts in the local pubs and cafés. Neither of us had a proper career. Neither of us really wanted one.

I got out of bed, experimentally. 'So,' I said. I felt better than I had expected. 'The morning stretches ahead of us.'

'Go out to breakfast?'

I put my dressing gown on, ready to make a bid for first shower. I knew Seth would let me. He would let me do anything.

'We can't enormously afford it,' I said, trying to be sensible.

'I know,' he agreed. 'But let's do it anyway and put it on Visa.'

I smiled. 'OK. Why the hell not?'

I watched Seth pulling his muscular legs into a pair of jeans, and I tried to believe that all of this was secure, that nothing was about to change.

When we left the house, the sky was filled with every type of weather. To the west there was a black looming cloud. To the east, the sky was a deep china blue. The pavement was wet, but the sun was shining.

'Look,' I said, taking Seth's arm. 'A rainbow.'

He nodded. 'There's always a bloody rainbow,' he said. 'That'll be because it rains all the time.'

'It's cool though. I like it.'

'I know you do.'

'Even when it's raining, there's a silver lining.'

He laughed. 'Nice cliché.'

'Clichés become clichés because they're true.'

'And you've told me that so many times, my darling, that it has itself become one.'

'Which sets up some sort of swirling black hole that the whole world is sucked into, and reality ends. Either that or it makes everything really banal and pointless.'

Seth nodded. 'I'll take the swirling vortex. Let's get breakfast, quick, while the going's good.'

As we walked towards the beach, we were overtaken by several cars that were jammed with duvets and bin bags full of stuff. There were middle-aged parents in the front seats, and sulky-looking nineteen-year-olds in the back. It was, clearly, the end of Falmouth's university term.

I had been careful for so long. I had not put a foot wrong. I came to the west of Cornwall because it was remote, and then discovered, in Falmouth, a place which was close to the far corner of Europe but which felt like anything but a frontier town. As soon as I stepped off the train, I knew it was home. It was quirky and accepting and interesting, and it was far from London, and it was not somewhere that occurred to people. I had settled here easily.

I wondered how the parents of the students in the cars felt about the fact that their offspring had chosen a small town in Cornwall over all the big cities that were out there. Relieved, I imagined. Or else annoyed that they had to drive vast distances from wherever they lived to deliver and collect them.

I was one of life's great blenders-in. That fact had been my salvation. My hair was the world's most boring colour. It was the colour of faux-pine parquet floors, of the bark of the kind of trees that you didn't particularly notice. It was a default setting, not an actual colour. Nothing about me would ever stand out. That was the way it had to be.

'Hey!' called a voice from across the road. 'Seth! Lucy!'

Gareth, one of Seth's surfing friends, was dodging the cars and running across the road towards us. Gareth was the sort of man who had been strikingly handsome until the age of about thirty-two, at which point he developed a beer belly and a double chin, and started to lose his hair. He had passed from handsome prince to ugly sister overnight. Today he was wearing a wetsuit, which strained over his belly, and he had bare feet and a cold-reddened face. What remained of his hair was practically standing up with the cold.

'Friar Tuck!' said Seth, and he patted Gareth's stomach. 'How's things?'

I winced on Gareth's behalf. This was the way Seth and his friends spoke to each other, and none of them ever seemed to take offence. I could not stand it.

'Seth!' I said, admonishing him.

'Yeah, cheers,' said Gareth, unperturbed. 'Lucy, amazing job! Up the cliff, grab the kid, straight back down. Nice one.'

I smiled and looked away. 'You saw it,' I said. 'I can't believe someone filmed it.'

'And then sent it to the local telly,' added Seth. 'It was only a kid. Wanted to pick up a piece of cash. See his work on the screen. Be famous.'

Gareth was picking something out of his toenails. 'Well, that's shite, isn't it? We have no idea about the kid who filmed it. It's Lucy here who's famous, and quite right too. Was it one of Eliza's girls up there?'

'Yeah,' said Seth. 'Clara.'

'Eliza of all people. Nightmare.'

I was desperate to change the subject.

'Are you surfing, Gareth?' I asked. 'It's not one of those days when there's waves in Falmouth? Is it?'

'It is,' he said. 'You have to be quite desperate, but I reckon it can be done.'

'Going to Gylly?'

'Gylly, then work.'

'We'll be watching you from the café.'

He made a mock salute. 'Watch out for me. I'll be the one riding the tubes.'

'Going to take that fat suit off before you go in?' asked Seth.

'Fuck off.' Gareth laughed, and ran barefoot towards the beach.

We stood on the edge of the sand, hand in hand. It was windy and drizzling, though the sky over the sea was the palest shade of blue. There were two dogs running all over the sand, even though they were supposed to be banned in the summer. I counted seven surfers in the water, and four swimmers.

One of them came out of the water, pulled off her swimming cap, grabbed a towel and threw it around her shoulders. She was wearing a black one-piece, and she looked like the sort of hardy woman who swam every day. I recognised her from my yoga class, and waved. She immediately strode in our direction, and I racked my brains for her name. She was in her fifties and had mauve streaks in her hair. I thought she might have been Janet, or otherwise, Anne.

'Saw you on the news,' she called, through the wind, as soon as she was close enough to be heard. 'And I said to my husband, I said, "That's Lucy, oh my goodness! Clever Lucy!" that's what I said. Well done you, darling. What a star.'

'Um,' I said. 'Thanks.' She was looking at me expectantly, so I fumbled for some more words. 'Just one of those things,' I muttered. 'You know, something happens, you deal with it, and then it's over. I had no idea anyone was there with a camera.'

'*And* you're so modest! It's so wonderful to see something positive on the news, you know. A good story. You clever thing.' She looked at Seth. 'Isn't she clever? Are you Mr Lucy?'

He laughed and encircled me with both arms, standing behind me.

'Yes,' he said. 'She is clever. And yes, I would be more than happy to be known to the world as Mr Lucy.'

Janet or Anne's arms were purple with cold, and she was trembling.

'Go and get dressed,' I suggested. 'I'll see you at yoga.'

'There's no escape,' said Seth, when she had gone.

'Tell me that they'll all forget about it soon,' I begged him, as we turned towards the café.

'They'll kind of forget,' he agreed. 'But not entirely. For years and years it's going to be the thing they remember about you.' He looked at my face. 'Which is not a bad thing!' he added. He took me by the hand and led me up the steps to the café's door.

We found a table by the window, and watched the sea, the sky, the castle on the point, as we sipped coffee and ate breakfast. I flicked through the paper. All this would pass. Things would settle down and carry on as they had always been.

I looked at Seth, who was attacking a piece of bacon as though there were lives at stake. He looked up and grinned at me. He loved me. I wished I were free to be able to love him.

I emptied my mind and stared at the waves, coming one after the other, sucking back across the rough sand. I loved to listen to the seagulls and the crashing sea. It was different every single day. Sometimes it was so flat that the clouds were reflected on the surface of the water, dotted about like mysterious underwater forms. At other times, it churned and chopped and tossed pieces of driftwood around, and the wind that came off it could blow a child right over. Today it was unusually orderly, the waves coming in straight lines, the surfers occasionally managing to get to their feet.

'Thoughtful?' said Seth.

I looked at him, and I wanted to tell him everything.

Seth had come into my life at the very moment when I had resigned myself to spending it alone. For more than a year now, I had been wanting to tell him the truth. It turned out I could not do it: I just couldn't make my mouth say the words.

'Just looking at the sea,' I said, with a smile.

'Yeah,' he said, with a grin. 'It kind of grabs the gaze, doesn't it? Do you know which of those bad surfers is Gareth?'

'They all look the same.'

He cleared his throat. I forced my eyes away from the waves, and looked at him.

'Hey, guess what,' he said. 'I've got you a present.'

I tried to smile.

'A present?' I said in a small voice. 'It's not my birthday. It's ages till Christmas.'

'If I'd waited for your next birthday or for Christmas, it would have been too late. Here you go. A present because I love you. Hope you like it.'

I let out my breath in a rush of relief when I saw the shape. The flat envelope could not possibly have contained a ring, unless it was loose, which I thought was unlikely. He had tied a piece of pink ribbon around it, and attempted a big bow, but it had not quite worked. There was something so touching about this that I felt tears prickling my eyes.

I pulled the ends, then unpicked the knot with my fingernails. I slid my finger under the seal, and opened it.

There was an envelope within the envelope. The inner one was white, with a window in it, and Seth's name and address printed inside.

I opened that, too, without a word. I pulled out some stiff card from inside. Tickets. Two tickets to 'The O2 Arena'. All I knew about the O2 Arena was that it was in London. I had not been to London in more than a decade. The furthest afield I ever went for entertainment was Truro. Seth knew that. He hated London, and I said I did too, and we got on well like that.

When I looked again, and saw what these tickets actually were, I stopped breathing until I became dizzy. Seth had no idea what he had done.

A terrifying blast of icy wind blew in from the past and knocked me over.

'Leonard Cohen,' I whispered, and I blinked, because I could not cry at this. I tried to think of a normal response. 'I didn't know he was touring,' I managed to say. 'I didn't even know he was still alive. He must be about a hundred.'

'Yeah, he is,' said Seth. 'Probably.' He smiled at me. I could see the concern in his face. 'You like? You're upset.'

I looked at the dates on the tickets. 'No, I'm not. Just – well – emotional. This might be the best present I've ever had. July the seventeenth? Next month? How long have you had these?'

He grinned. 'Ages. I've been dying to tell you. Best present ever? Really?' He looked pleased with himself.

'We're going to London?' I said. 'You don't even like his music. Or London.'

He smiled. 'But you do. And since I've noticed you listening to him whenever you can, for the entire time that I've known you, it seemed like the least I could do. Eliza wants to go with you.' He saw my face. 'Hey,' he said. 'They're your tickets. I'll come if you like, give him the evil eye if he looks at my bird funny. Or you can take Eliza, since she has the same thing for him that you do, thanks to you. It's up to you. But I think you should take Liza, because she hasn't wanted to do a thing like this for years and it was nice to see her all excited. We can go for a dirty weekend together some other time. Maybe not in London.'

I smiled. 'Venice. Let's go for a dirty weekend in Venice one of these months. More than a weekend. That's where I want to go with you, not London.'

'Venice suits me. Can we have a room overlooking the canal? Can we stay in the room all week, drinking the minibar dry and shagging and looking at the view?'

I smiled at him. 'You give me Leonard. I give you anything.'

Everything was golden, for a while. Seth was happy because he was pleased with himself. I was going to see Leonard Cohen, which terrified and elated me by turn. Nobody else rushed up to congratulate me on my heroism. We spent the morning wandering around, doing nothing in particular. At lunchtime I cycled to work, and got through my shift without mishaps and without nausea. The moment it was over, I rode home again, enjoying the green lanes between Mylor and Penryn, then bracing myself for the main road. Then, even though I had been on my feet for hours and cycled for miles, I went for a run.

I loved to run on the light summer evenings. My foot was still hurting from the cliff, but I took a perverse pleasure in inflicting ever more pain on myself.

I ran beside the sea, which was glowing in the velvety light of the evening sun. The trees were casting golden shadows and the sun was huge and low in the sky. Shadows stretched along the pavements, and when I looked back, I saw an abstracted version of my shape, elongated, a Giacometti figure stretching back on the tarmac.

My foot was bleeding again, inside my trainer. I ignored it. I ran on and on, taking pleasure in the burning sensation in my chest and trying not to limp. I turned my head and ran looking at the sea, which was calming down, as if settling for the night. The seagulls congregated above, squawking and shrieking.

I ran around the headland and up to the castle, and made my way home along the roads. I got in as darkness fell, ready for a lot of water, and a relaxing end to the evening.

When I saw Seth's face, I knew that I wasn't going to get one.

'What's wrong?' I asked, as mildly as I could. I kicked off my trainers and threw them under the stairs. I peeled off my sweaty socks and put them straight into the washing machine. I turned and looked at him, knowing that I was beetroot-red and sticky.

'Nothing's wrong,' Seth said, clearly unsure of himself. 'It's just been a bit surreal around here. You've been at work and out running. I've been dealing with . . . all sorts of weird stuff.'

My heart started to thump, and I sat down on the edge of the table.

'What happened?' I demanded. I dreaded the answer.

'The phone,' Seth said. 'It hasn't stopped ringing.'

'Who was it?' I whispered. I gripped the table so hard that one of my nails broke.

'Look,' he said. He handed me a few sheets of paper. 'Here are some of the messages. There are more.'

The paper was covered with biro scrawls: numbers, and

unfamiliar names. I stared for a moment, completely clueless, before I realised that these people were journalists. One was from the *Independent*, another from *The Times,* and just about all the tabloids seemed to be there.

I closed my eyes as I realised what was happening. This was a step down the road. The rest of it was inevitable.

# chapter five

## Marianne

I love Saturdays. I wake up and the room is already full of sunlight. It seems like the first day of summer. We don't have a curtain in our room, just a sarong that is nailed to the window frame. It is a bright sarong, orange and yellow and green like something from Africa, and it keeps out just about exactly no light at all.

Finn's bed, right above mine, keeps out plenty. I think it is a sign of growing up, the day you suddenly find yourself wanting the bottom bunk; when you realise that it is actually much more convenient and less annoying to be able to swing round and put your feet on the floor.

I stretch out. I am content. I am (today) feeling all right about everything. About myself, I mean. Because it's Saturday, and I don't have to go to school and try to be just the right amount of nondescript, to keep myself invisible. I get to be myself on Saturdays and Sundays.

I am kind of liking the way my body feels at the moment. Sometimes it is horrifying, but at the moment I feel like a woman, and in a good way. I'm waiting for the time when I start to hate my family and scream and shout and get spots. So far, it's better than you'd think. Everything always is. Anyone looking at our life, in a rubbish house in a bad part of east London, with a single parent and no money at all, would think we were miserable, but I am not miserable at all. None of us are.

I pull the sarong aside and sit on the end of my bed, right next to the window. The glass is smeared with grime on the outside, but I can see past it. We have a tiny square of cracked concrete out there. Mum is an expert at taking cuttings from other people's gardens, from parks and from anywhere at all (she often carries secateurs in her back pocket, which sometimes get painful when she forgets about them and sits down). So we have a large number of cheap plastic pots, all filled with lovely plants. Lots of them are starting to bud and even to bloom. The sunflowers look promising.

Beyond the yard it gets a bit more bleak, but on a morning like this I can see some lovely things in it. The pale sunlight makes that possible. There are the backs of the houses behind us, and they are streaked with black and grey, industrial and grim. But if I look diagonally, there is a house with geraniums in window boxes. The buds are just opening. There is always something, if you look hard enough.

Finn starts to stir. I hear his mattress creaking. Then his head appears, up close to the ceiling, looking down at me. His cheeks are pink, his hair tousled. Nobody at school knows that, at fourteen and fifteen, we still sleep in bunk beds. They never will.

'Morning,' he says, and loses himself in an enormous yawn. He farts loudly. I ignore it.

'Lovely day,' I tell him. He grunts, but I know Finn well, and I can tell that it is a happy grunt.

Mum is sitting at the table with a cafetière of coffee in front of her. She cradles a mug in her hand. It is a lilac one with polka dots on it that I found in the 50p shop for her last birthday.

'Marianne, sweetie,' she says. 'You're up. Coffee?'

I nod. I am still trying to like coffee. I can manage it half-and-half with milk. Mum drinks it black. That's one of the reasons why she doesn't weigh anything.

'Toast?' I ask her, as I sniff the milk in the fridge.

'Nah, I'm fine. Get some for you and Finn.' She looks at me. 'Hey,' she says. 'Come here, you gorgeous girl.'

I sit next to her, and she starts fiddling with my hair. She pulls it up, experimenting. She makes her fingers into blunt scissors, and pretends to cut it. 'Jaw-length bob,' she says. 'You want one?'

I shake my head. 'I like it long. Like yours.'

'But yours is different from mine. I'd have given anything in my youth for straight hair like this. You could carry off a Louise Brooks cut, you know. I'm not sure I could quite manage to cut it impeccably, but I could give it a shot. I could definitely give you a straight bob. With a fringe. You'd look amazing.'

I stare at her. I want to look like she does, but she is right. My hair would never get that long, and it would never, ever have that sort of body to it. At the moment it is straggling below my shoulders, in a pathetic imitation of hers.

'Go on then.' I reach for the kitchen scissors, and pass them to her. She throws them in the air, spinning them, and catches them by the blades.

'Have I got my dad's hair?' I ask her, as casually as I can, before she starts cutting.

She doesn't answer for a few seconds. 'I guess so,' she says, eventually. 'Probably. But yours is nicer.'

We take a picnic to the river, and sit on a bench. The wind is blowing off the Thames, and the air smells strangely fresh. Finn is listening to music on his headphones, on the second-hand Walkman that we managed to get him for Christmas.

I can feel the warm breeze on the back of my neck. I keep touching it, the place where my hair used to be. I think I like my new haircut, but am worried that Mum might have made me look too striking.

Mum passes me a sandwich. As I take it, I look at her.

It is a lightning flash. One moment everything is fine and normal and I am thinking about my new hairstyle. Then I realise that she is ill. Not with flu or a cold, but properly ill. She is not just thin: she is emaciated, and her skin is yellow.

I gape.

'You're ill,' I tell her, and I can hear the urgency in my voice.

She frowns, and shakes her head.

'No,' she says, and I can hear that she is lying. 'I'm your mother. Mothers are always all right. They're not allowed to get ill.'

'They are,' I object. 'When you have tiny babies, maybe not, but when your children are big enough to look after themselves, and to look after you too, then it *is* allowed. It's OK to rest for a while and let us look after you. Or to go to the doctor.' Panic begins to rise in my chest. 'Have you been to the doctor?' I demand.

She laughs. 'Honestly, Marianne, I'm fine. Don't worry about me. My job is to worry about you.'

'Well, we're certainly fine. But you don't eat.'

'I do too eat. I just don't have much of an appetite at the moment.'

Finn pulls his headphones off his head and puts the thick plastic band on his lap.

'Have a bloody sandwich,' he says. He takes one from the Tupperware box, and holds it in front of her.

'Less of the language,' she says, but she takes it and nibbles it. 'Stop looking at me!' she complains. 'How did I manage to have two such eminently sensible offspring? Hey? Who's the parent around here?'

We sit in silence, and watch a little speedboat zooming past.

Late in the evening, I pour her a glass of wine, and Finn runs a bath. I put *I'm Your Man* on the stereo for her and turn it up so that the house is filled with Leonard's voice, the way she likes it.

Everything has changed, and when it falls apart, it falls fast, a tower of bricks felled by gravity. She sips the wine, though I can see that she doesn't really want it, and smiles at us, but her arms and legs are shaking.

She can barely make it up the stairs to the bathroom. I walk next to her and force her to lean on me, even though she doesn't want to. I put a pair of clean pyjamas and her dressing gown on the stool next to the bath, and check the temperature. The water is hot, but not, I hope, too hot, and the bath is filled with cheap bubbles that we have been saving for a special occasion of some sort. I help her into the water, and leave the room and close the door.

We go downstairs and pour ourselves a glass of wine each, even though Mum is strict about us not drinking. We don't discuss it, but we both know that normal rules do not apply tonight.

'A night's sleep, and she'll feel better,' Finn says, though he doesn't sound convinced.

'We'll get her to the doctor in the morning,' I add. 'We'll find the Sunday doctor. Or we could call someone out tonight – let's see how she is.'

'We should sleep on her floor, maybe,' says Finn.

'I will. There's no room for us both.'

We go upstairs and drag my mattress into her room. Mum has always looked after us, magicked up everything we need at the very moment we have needed it. We have no idea about our dad, or our dads. We don't even know if we are brother and sister, or half-brother and half-sister. She just calls our father (fathers) 'the impregnator'. Neither of us has a name on our birth certificate. This is why we choose to believe it's Mum's favourite Canadian singer; because the idea of Leonard Cohen, with his warm voice and his poetry, is a thousand times more palatable and comforting than any reality could be.

Mum has only ever worked as a dinner lady or a cleaner, luckily never at our school. It's not cool to have a dinner lady or a cleaner as a mum, but more than that, I wouldn't want her to see me in my invisible school life. She has always been at home when we get back from school, has always been there to wave us off in the morning, has always spent the evenings and weekends with us. We never felt any need for a father. The three of us have each other and we are good like that. I don't want anything to change.

When my bed is set up, we wait a bit longer. I make three cups of tea, and knock on the bathroom door.

'Mum?' I say. 'Are you OK?'

She doesn't answer.

'It's OK, Mum,' I say. 'We're not trying to hassle you. We just made a cup of tea. I can bring it in if you like.'

No reply. I picture her lying back, her ears underwater, her hair spread out, her face under the water, like Ophelia in the painting that hangs on the wall of the art room at school.

This image is disturbing. I tap again, and try to open the door.

She has locked it. She never locks it. She must have got out to do that, and got back in again. I have no idea why she would have done it. It could not have been for Finn's sake. He keeps well away from any place where Mum or I might be naked.

'Just let us know when you're ready to get out,' I say, lamely. The water must be cold by now, and she hasn't run any more, because if she had, the boiler would have been shaking and juddering and letting us know about it.

We break the lock.

She is not lying in the water like Ophelia. She is sitting up, curled over, her back touching the back of the bath. Her head is bent forward, the ends of her hair in the water.

'Mum,' I say, and everything slows down and becomes weird.

She does not move. Her naked body is shocking, her ribs jutting out like in the photographs of concentration-camp victims I was looking at for homework yesterday. Her skin is yellow, her body absolutely still. The bath water is cloudy and most of the bubbles have gone.

We stand and stare. I don't look at Finn. I want to prolong this moment of not knowing.

# chapter six

The next morning, it was everywhere. It was worse than I had feared. The piece of footage, twenty minutes on a beach, was apparently fascinating to the entire world. I had staked everything on the hope that it would be only of local interest. I calculated that I could live with a little fleeting notoriety in south-west Cornwall.

I did not think I would be able to live with this. I sat up in bed, looking at the sunlight that was pouring through the very fabric of the blinds, and realised that, after tossing and turning for almost the whole night, I had slept late. All night long I had made and cancelled plans.

Seth's side of the bed was empty. I wondered whether he was downstairs, or whether he had escaped to work.

As I was deciding that he had probably painted half an exterior wall by now, the door handle turned, and he strode into the room and flung himself down on the bed in one long movement. He handed me a stash of newspapers, with a broad grin. His cheeks dimpled, and his eyes crinkled. He had no idea.

'Look at this,' he said, kissing my forehead. 'Quite the global superstar. This is fucking surreal, I tell you. You are *amazing*.'

I screwed my eyes tight shut.

'I don't want to see it,' I told him. 'I mean it. Take them away.'

'No – look. You're on the front of almost every paper. You're all over the internet.' He looked at me closely. I could feel him, through my eyelids. 'There's no reason not to enjoy this, Luce,' he said, his confusion showing in his voice. 'You may be in the tabloids, but they're not slagging you. Quite the opposite. Also, I unplugged the phone because they were all ringing the house all the time asking for an interview. Seems you could pocket a nice little sum. An unbelievable sum, in fact. If you just talked them through what happened. We could have a fucking great week in Venice, for a start.'

I opened my eyes. 'Absolutely no way.'

'Lucy, they were starting at ten K. For tomorrow's chip wrappers.'

'I just don't want to.'

'Or you could talk to a nice woman from the *Guardian*. No cash, but lots of cred.'

'No.'

He stared at me. I stared back. I looked at Seth, the man I thought I would never meet, the Cornish artist, the man who made the future brighter than the past.

But when I closed my eyes, I saw someone else.

'Sorry,' I added. 'It's just. You know.'

He looked at me for a long time. We gazed at each other. I wished I could tell him.

'I don't know,' he said, in the end. 'You know I don't know. Because you know that you haven't told me.'

Eliza took me aside once, soon after Seth and I got together, and warned me off him.

'Lucy,' she said. 'Look. I've never liked Seth's girlfriends before. They've been all legs and hair and acrylic nails. They've all looked on me as the dowdy little sister. So I've never particularly felt the need to say anything, even when I've known that he's going to mess them around and waltz off with the next Beach Barbie who crosses his eyeline. But you're not like them.'

'Why, thank you,' I told her, with a laugh. I hated the very existence of a band of women called 'Seth's ex-girlfriends', especially since they all seemed to fit the Beach Barbie template.

'That didn't sound bad, did it?' she asked anxiously. 'I meant it in a good way. Whatever you do, don't tell my brother I said this. But be careful. I hate to say it, but if I were you, I'd run from him, as fast as I could, as far as I could.'

I was grimly fascinated. 'Because . . . ?'

'He has a modus operandi.'

'Like a serial killer?'

'Yes. Not quite so dramatic. But, yes. He is charm personified. He does everything he can to make the woman fall in love with him. He makes sure he himself is not in deep. He keeps a bit of distance by being mean. He makes sure he never gets hurt. I don't know why he's like that, but he is. I don't want him to do it to you. Give him a kiss goodbye and go and find someone who'll be nice.'

I laughed again. Eliza had no idea of my history. I was a long way beyond heartbreak.

'I'll have to take my chances,' I told her, as lightly as I could. 'Thanks, though.'

'Mmm,' she said. 'Well, good luck, and maybe, since you're different from the others, maybe you'll be the one to change him. You won't ever tell him what I said, will you?'

I never had.

I had kept my distance from Seth for as long as I could. That seemed to draw him in, and suddenly we were not having a fling. We were closer and closer, and then he loved me. He said so. And he was intrigued by me. He knew there were things I wasn't talking about, questions that I deflected time after time until he stopped asking. He did not walk away, and I would never walk away from him. Not through choice.

I could not help glancing at the *Daily Mail*, which was on the top of the pile of newsprint that Seth had bought for me. The right-hand side of the front page was taken up with a long picture of my back, with Clara's feet and hands clearly visible on either side of me. I stared at my arms and legs, reduced to dots of newsprint. They were slightly less muscular and more wobbly-looking than I would have liked. All the same, they were clearly fit enough for the job in hand. I did not look bad, considering.

'At least it's just my back,' I murmured, as much to myself as to Seth. He said nothing, but took the paper and opened it at page seven, and passed it back.

There it was: the full sequence of stills from the footage. In the last one, I was facing the camera, wiping my brow, displaying a little armpit stubble. I was entirely recognisable. Even more so when I read the caption: 'Friends identified the heroine as Lucy Riddick, of nearby Falmouth, who is related to the rescued tot.'

I managed a smile. 'Tot? Clara won't like that.'

My name, and the town where I lived, were all over the national press. I saw the face again, heard the words he had whispered at me.

I leapt out of bed, vaulting right over Seth, grabbed his dressing gown from the hook on the back of the door, and did it up as I took the stairs three at a time.

When I was in the shower, and it was running, and as hot as I could bear it, I felt a little better. I felt the top layer of my skin turning pink and then red, almost scalding. The steam filled my lungs. I could have stayed there for a long time. I squeezed a huge blob of shower gel on to a flannel, and scrubbed at myself, the way I used to do it. I scrubbed and scrubbed, until I felt I had made it all go away, for a while at least.

I was relieved when Seth went to work, and I thought he was too. This week he was painting the outside of a house next to Kimberley Park. He looked at me hard before he went. I smiled and tried to look reassuring, but it was hard, because my heart was breaking with all the things I could never tell him.

He kept staring into my eyes, waiting for me to tell him what was wrong. I said I had a headache, period pains, that I was worried about Eliza, that things were difficult at the pub where I worked. I babbled. I listened to myself. None of it made any sense, and we both knew that.

I stood at the sitting-room window, and watched him leave, walking slowly down the street towards the car. He turned and looked back at me for a second, and I raised a hand, then stepped back from the window and looked away.

* * *

Seconds later I was upstairs. I knelt down beside our bed and pulled out the bags that were stuffed under there. There were bin bags of clothes that were destined, one day, for the charity shop. There was a winter duvet, crammed into an IKEA bag, and all kinds of random odds and ends that had needed to be shoved out of the way.

I pulled some of it out, lay down on my stomach and reached through the dusty tunnel I had created to the far corner. The backpack was still there, where it always was.

I yanked it out, and sat on the bedroom floor and spread its contents out around me. There were a few clothes, some toiletries, a purse containing a wad of cash, and an emergency credit card I had applied for a couple of years ago, when credit was easy to come by. Deep at the bottom corner was an illegal pepper spray I had bought online, and had delivered to work where I knew Seth would not see it. I took out most of the cash, folded it and put it into my back pocket. I changed the clothes slightly, to make them more seasonal. I added some other bits and pieces that I thought I might need, and packed it all back up again.

The bag was a plain black backpack. It was as unobtrusive as it could possibly be. I replaced it, but squashed the other bags together, so that the tunnel was left open and the bag would be accessible.

# chapter seven

## Marianne

We close the bathroom door. I feel weightless, and there is a loud ringing in my ears. A part of me, a big part, is floating, somewhere by the ceiling. I have split in two, because there is no way in the world that I can really have seen that. That would not be possible. I hover on the damp-stained ceiling, and I look down with impassive eyes. Finn is there, and he is staring at the cheap white door with an odd look on his face.

I am down there too, just standing still, like a statue. Both of us are useless. My mum. Our mother, in the bath. Her ribs were jutting out. We couldn't see her face. She wasn't moving.

Down on the ground, I swallow, and it hurts my throat. The on-the-ground shell that looks like me looks at the door, like Finn, and waits. We are waiting for the sound of her splashing out of the bath, pulling the towel down from the rail. We are waiting for the door handle to turn, for our mum to come out with her usual happy energy, for her to say: 'What are you two doing lurking out there?' We are waiting for her to tell us to go to bed.

Time passes. I lurch back into my body and reach for the handle again. I feel sick as I touch it. This is it: the last chance. This time, it could be all right. I look at Finn. He nods. I open the door slowly. It creaks. The broken part of the lock is on the floor.

She turns her head and looks at me. Her eyes are sunken, but she is still there.

'Marianne,' she says.

'Mum!'

We are both at her side in a second. 'Mum, you're OK! Mum, what happened?'

The relief that flows through my veins makes me so happy that I don't notice that, even though she is alive, she is struggling to breathe. Finn passes me the towel, and I try to help her out of the bath.

'We'll look after you,' I assure her. 'We will. I'm sleeping on your floor tonight. You don't have to worry about anything.'

She nods, and mutters something. I catch her with the towel as she stumbles. I look at her body, which is not slim, not slender, not willowy, but emaciated and wasted. I try not to think about what might be going on inside it.

'We'll get you to a doctor.' I am trying to say what an adult would say.

'Let's phone 999,' says Finn.

'No,' she says, with a gasp. 'I'm fine. No doctor.'

Her breasts have almost gone. The tops of her arms are a lot thinner than her elbows. Her knees look enormous, but they're not. They are just thicker than the rest of her legs. Her bum is hardly there.

I get her into her threadbare dressing gown, the greyish-pink one that she has had for as long as I can remember. She puts one little arm in it, and then the other. I tie it in front, fastening her brittle body out of sight. I pull her hair back, and tie it in a long ponytail with an elastic that I find on the windowsill.

Finn puts an arm around her waist and leads her to her bedroom. We settle her into bed, give her a glass of water, and put the light out. She appears to go straight to sleep.

Then we look at each other.

'We have to get a doctor,' I say. 'Look at her. She's . . .'

'Maybe we should let her sleep,' says Finn. 'We'll sort it out in the morning.'

I lie on her floor, and I hardly sleep. I listen to her funny breathing, and in the light that comes around the edge of the blind, I see the outline of her body, shifting around. Early in the morning I offer her some paracetamol, but she can't swallow the tablets.

She sits up in bed, and I see her making the most enormous effort for us.

'It's just flu,' she says, and I almost laugh at what a massive lie she is trying to tell.

'No it's not,' I say, in the most gentle voice I can manage. I take some deep breaths, pull myself together. I try to think of something practical, something that will allow us to continue to ignore the bigger picture. 'Shall I grind these pills up and put them in a drink or something?'

She shakes her head. 'Soluble ones. Behind the kettle.'

When I look behind the kettle, I discover that there is more than soluble paracetamol stashed there. There is a wide variety of painkillers of various strengths. All of them are generic ones, the cheapest ones possible. Paracetamol, aspirin, ibuprofen, and other ones I have never heard of: codeine, cocodamol, special ones for period pains.

I dissolve some random ones in a glass of water, make her a cup of tea, and put some bread into the toaster, even though I know she won't eat it.

# chapter eight

I did not run. I should have run, but I could not do it.

I lay next to Seth every night, and I felt the black bag, my escape pack, pulsating in the dark corner of the room. Its very existence was a betrayal. It made a mockery of everything. I wished I could really be Lucy Riddick, could really own this life. Then it would all have been so easy: I could have committed myself to him properly, and I would not be lying awake every night, secretly plotting and planning, trying to work out where I would go. Trying to pull together the strength I needed to walk away from him.

I had changed the cash to a different currency, and put it back. I had added my passport, and a guidebook. I had made a plan.

The media fuss died down as quickly as it had blown up. It was nothing, a collective passing fancy that gripped the nation's newsrooms. When I declined all the offers and requests, they quickly stopped bothering and moved on to the next thing. On the surface, I was normal again. I was old news.

One windy morning in July, I woke up at five o'clock. I could hear something downstairs. Seth was next to me, a hot slumbering body that filled me with such tenderness that I could hardly bear to look at him. I held my breath. He snored and rolled over, reaching out a sleeping arm for me, grabbing me around the ribcage. I stared at the ceiling, which was already a light grey from the daylight outside. The plaster rose around the light fitting was casting murky shadows.

I listened.

There it was again. A bang: a sharp, deliberate knock.

I edged away from Seth's grip. He muttered. I lifted his hand, as gentle as the tooth fairy, moved away from him and put his arm down again. It was heavy and unknowing.

I had to climb over him to get to the door. I did it lightly, then took some pyjamas from the top of my chest of drawers and quickly dressed myself. My heart was pounding in my chest. I told myself to be brave.

The stairs were lit by the skylight. I looked up and saw clouds blowing around, above the house. I tiptoed down, everything slightly different because it was light, but still night.

It came again. A deliberate knock on the back door.

I walked slowly to the back of the house. The kitchen was murky, our plates and glasses from the night before piled up by the sink.

The back door was solid wood. The key was in it. I turned it slowly, dreading everything that was about to happen. I stopped, and swallowed. I had known this was coming. I needed courage, but I had none.

After a few moments I pulled the door wide open, a sudden movement, an impulse. I stood and stared.

I almost wanted to laugh, but it was not at all funny. The day was lighter, already, than it had been when I woke. The distant treetops were blowing in all directions. And the wind was channelled down the little courtyard outside our back door. Seth had hung a paintbrush on a string from the door handle to dry, and every now and then the wind was seizing it, and banging it into the door.

I cycled to work again to clear my head and to make my body hurt. I had kept meaning to find a job in town, because that would be convenient, but I found it hard to leave the peaceful surroundings in which I slogged away pouring drinks and cleaning loos. A morning shift at the pub was a good thing because it was not busy, did not get busy until well after eleven. I arrived at half past nine, red in the face, sweaty and fighting to hold myself together.

Was I going to be paranoid for ever? I supposed I probably was: and that was the best possible scenario.

There were three of us there that morning: Ash, Alex and me. Ash was female, Alex male. Ash was younger than me, but she was the sort of thirty-year-old who had always been middle-aged. She called everyone 'my darling' and 'my little love', and she was impressively stern with disorderly drunks, though the Passage House was far too posh for drunks to be much of a problem. Her father lived in France, and she dropped French words into her conversation as much as she possibly could. I always smiled to myself when she called the restaurant 'the rest-au-rong', but I had never been anywhere in Europe, so I was mainly jealous.

I stood outside for a moment and caught my breath. I pulled off the helmet that Seth made me wear, and shook my hair loose. It was damp with sweat, but I was exhilarated.

No one had come for me. I had thought they had, that very morning, but it was just the wind. Perhaps no one ever would. If no one came, then I would be free for ever.

The wind blew my hair around as I stood at the edge of the water. The Passage House stood on the banks of a tidal creek, across the harbour and round a corner from Falmouth. At high tide the water was deep, and a significant number of customers arrived by boat. I watched them, sometimes, with envy, wondered at the kind of life that went with a private yacht. It was easy to tell the amateurs in their rented boats from the rich: the amateurs often made a hilarious hash of mooring up on our jetty, tying rubbish knots that slipped off and sent the boat drifting away while they were mid-lunch, or forgetting about the tide and emerging from the pub, two pints later, to find their boat grounded on the stony riverbed. The yacht-owners generally knew exactly what they were doing, because they had been sailing since they were children, and often sent their own children to jump on to the jetty, throwing ropes back and forth, doing what they had already done a thousand times before.

The wind was still blowing, and the water was rippled with little lines that blew to the shore and vanished. There were no boats on the jetty. The tide was high, and there was only a small expanse of stony, seaweedy beach. Across the water, the expensive houses, with their paths that led down to the water's edge, stood proudly against the elements. Several of them had huge plate-glass windows, and they must have shared an astonishing view, but I preferred the more cottagey ones. Seth and I had picked one out, one of these million-pound homes, as the place we would buy when we became rich, the house in which we would grow old together. It was over to the right, a white house that had surely been there for several hundred years, that must have seen smugglers and pirates as well as an awful lot of tourists. I imagined a log fire inside it.

Something caught my eye in one of the other houses, and I waved. Jasper, a man in his sixties, lived in one of the mansions with the huge windows, and monitored the comings and goings in the creek through his binoculars. He was watching me now, and raised a hand to return my greeting. I would have found him creepy, except that most evenings he got in his rowing boat and rowed himself across the water to drink a pint of Doombar, and I knew he was both harmless and lonely, and a widower with nothing but binoculars to get him through the days.

The clouds were scudding across the sky. Although the school holidays had not yet started, this was still tourist season, and a bleak day meant a busy pub.

I went inside, ready to work, a spark of cautious optimism in my chest for the first time in years.

# chapter nine

## Marianne

Mum won't let us get a doctor. She refuses, completely, to allow it.

Finn and I have no idea what we should do. We talk about it all the time. We have always done what Mum tells us, and we have never done things she has told us not to do. Now she is incapacitated, and it turns out we have no idea how to handle it.

'We just have to go and get someone,' I say on Monday morning. We have both skipped school to stay at home with her, and we are sitting at the kitchen table while the rain falls heavily outside. We are alert for any sound she makes, but she is quiet, and sometimes we have to go upstairs to check that she is still breathing.

'But she said we mustn't,' says Finn. His face is screwed up. Neither of us quite dares to overrule her.

'But she's ill,' I remind him. 'That might be making her irrational. We have to get her better, Finn. She needs medicine.'

'But what if . . .' His voice tails off.

'When she wakes up,' I say quickly, 'we'll tell her we're getting someone. We won't give her a choice. But we won't go behind her back, either. So we'll tell her, and then we'll do it. It's not like it was before, is it? Things are different now.'

He nods. 'OK. Shall we make her some more soup? What have we got left?'

I look in the cupboard. 'An onion. Some slimy mushrooms.'

'Can we make onion and slimy mushroom soup?'

'I don't think it'd be very nice, you know. Or nutritious.'

'It'd be gross, is what it'd be.'

'We need to do some shopping.'

'We need to find the money.'

We sit by her bed and watch her until she wakes up. It is a strange feeling, our mother being so ill. Our world is on its head, and we long for her to get back to normal. She is all we have, apart from each other. The ground is falling away beneath our feet, the walls of our house-for-three crumbling down. Although I still have Finn, I have never felt so exposed, so terrified, so alone.

'What?' she says, suddenly. She is almost smiling. We both shift on to the edge of the bed and look at her.

'Stop staring,' she says. Her voice is quiet, but it is firm. 'You should be at school.'

Finn looks at me. I feel my responsibility as the eldest very strongly.

'We didn't go because we needed to stay with you,' I say quickly. 'Mum, we're going to get a doctor. We all need you to be better. You have to get well again. And you can't stop us, because we're going to do it anyway. We're going to call the GP, and I bet he'll get an ambulance. And then you can get sorted out.'

We look at her. She shakes her head from side to side, as vigorously as she can manage to do it.

'You mustn't,' she says. The rain is beating against the window, and for a random second I hope that it is cleaning the city grime off it.

'We must,' Finn says in a wavery voice.

'Mum,' I say. 'I don't understand. Why wouldn't you want us to get a doctor? When you're so ill?' I blink hard, but I know that they both know that I am crying.

'I'll tell you why,' she says, and she closes her eyes for so long that I start to think she has fallen asleep. Then they open wide, and she takes a deep breath.

'Right,' she says. 'Guys. I need you to be very, very strong.'

And she lies in bed and speaks to us, and the whole world cracks and falls to pieces, and Finn and I are the only ones left in the universe, standing in the ruins.

# chapter ten

I had started to play Leonard Cohen in the pub, whenever I could get away with it. I was psyching myself up for the concert. For twenty years I had listened to him when I was feeling strong, ready for the secret emotional surge that his music brought me. When he had new albums out, I bought them and played them until I was word perfect. In the pub, I always made sure 'Hallelujah' came first, because everyone loved that song. Normally he got through one, or possibly two more before someone realised what I was doing, and changed it for something more upbeat.

'Not your doom-and-gloom merchant again,' Ash would complain, tapping the 'stop' button, inserting Norah Jones instead. 'Who wants to listen to this while they drink a lovely pint of Cornish ale? No one, is who. They're not exactly going to throw caution to the wind and order the seafood platter, are they? If this is the soundtrack? They'll be asking for directions to the ladies' so they can slash their wrists in peace.'

'He is not a doom-and-gloom merchant,' I told her. 'He's a poet. He's funny. He's brilliant. I would order the seafood platter.' No one but me could, apparently, appreciate this fact. When he was singing, I half closed my eyes and let the music go through me. I thought of him, absurdly, as an old friend.

The days had passed, and I was beginning to believe that I had got away with it. The bag was still accessible, but I had not taken it out for checking or for tweaking for almost a week.

The summer was unspectacular. Cornwall had filled up with

people, who sat in cafés listlessly eating cream teas and waiting for the rain to stop. Children in thin cagoules ran around the plaza outside the Maritime Museum, and looked at the boats in the harbour. Their parents peered at the sky, pointed to clear patches, tapped their feet and waited for summer.

Patrons arrived at the pub in such numbers that there were far too many cars for our little car park, and they had to execute precarious three-point turns on the water's edge and head back up the single-track lane, where they parked half in the hedgerows. Wing mirrors were knocked off on a daily basis. The boats were three abreast on the pontoon. Children in raincoats caught crabs and put them in buckets. I poured pints of local bitter and glasses of house wine all through my shifts, and delivered so many food orders to the kitchen that they had to take on extra seasonal staff. The population had taken a collective decision to eat and drink its way through the rain.

The concert was four days away. I was tentatively excited. I was strong enough, I had decided, to go back to London. I would, after all, be in a stadium along with thousands of other people. I could face Leonard and his music. I was starting, in my better moments, to see it as a celebration.

The alarm went off. My shift was not until the evening, but Seth had to be working by half past eight. I felt him about to get out of bed, and stopped him by grabbing him around the waist and pulling him back. He spun round and looked at me.

'Well, hello,' he said. 'Nice to see you.'

'Nice to see *you*,' I told him.

'Nice to have you back,' he said quietly, looking at me with the unasked questions in his eyes.

I pretended not to know what he meant. 'I haven't been away.'

He looked into my eyes. His eyes were dark brown and gentle. He looked so vulnerable, so terribly vulnerable.

'But yes,' I added. 'If I had been away, I would now be back.'

I leaned forward, and kissed him. He put a hand on my waist. We stayed like that, locked together, for a long time.

'I love you,' he said.

'I love you, too,' I told him. It was the first time I had ever said those words to him. It felt like a new beginning.

I was going to go for a run. I walked with Seth as far as Kimberley Park, kissed him goodbye as he unlocked the garage of the empty house he was painting, and then set off. I was going to run up the hill to the other side of town, and then follow the water's edge around, and loop back home.

As soon as I set off, I was exhilarated. It was satisfying, the way my feet pounded the pavement. I liked feeling myself exercising, knowing that I was fit enough, healthy enough, to carry on for miles and miles. I liked being this person. I liked it a lot. Perhaps now I could keep on being her.

I crossed the main road, and set off up the hill.

I ran for a mile, forcing myself to keep going even when I wanted to stop, and my chest was burning when I got home. I was going through the day in my head. Quick shower, get dressed, walk to town and do some food shopping. The sun and the wind would dry my hair on the way. After lunch, I was going to pick up Imogen from school and walk home with her, a brisk half-hour's hike, each way, up and down hills.

I looked at our row of terraced houses, each little house a different pastel colour. Ours was blue. It was tiny but it suited us. Next door was cream. Two students came out of the house that was two doors down from ours, pulling motorbike helmets on to their heads.

I slowed down and reached to the back of my neck to unclasp the silver chain that held my door key while I ran.

A man was standing on our neighbours' doorstep. He was wearing a trench coat. I stopped dead in my tracks. The way he held his broad shoulders: I had seen that before. The hair, thinner than it used to be, greyer than it used to be, but still his hair. I watched him reach up and ring the bell. I imagined the sound inside the house, the innocent 'ding dong'.

The students revved up their bike and roared off up the road. He had not seen me. I was still too far away for him to have heard my approach. I turned and ran, back down the street, around the corner, and into the Spar. I made my way to the back corner, where the milk was, and stood and tried to catch my breath. I leaned against the side of the fridge. I was sure it had been him. He had found me, as I had known he would.

# chapter eleven

## Marianne

Our mother is dying, and she won't let us tell anyone. She has known about it for months and months.

'I thought I might have been able to carry on until you were old enough not to need me,' she says, as we sit on either side of her and stare in total horror.

'Mum!' I don't dare look at Finn.

'Marianne,' says Mum, and there is a reproof in her voice. 'You can't tell anyone about this. Nobody must know I'm ill. You have to carry on until Finn's done his GCSEs.'

I don't know where to start objecting to this plan.

'We have to pretend you're fine?' I say, weakly. She nods. I see her rally, summon some strength from somewhere. 'I've been saving all the money,' she says. 'We've lived off fresh air because I was saving for you. It's in the post office account. There's a book for it. Under the loose floorboard. The money from your dad, Finn, goes in there too. And child benefit and housing benefit. That will keep coming. It'll all keep coming in.'

Finn's voice is almost a whisper. 'While you're ill?' I try to cling on to the same shred of hope.

She looks at him, and then at me. 'After,' she says. 'Listen. This is the important part. I'm sorry, but as you can see, I'm going to die. You can't tell anyone.'

'Mum!' I am dreaming now, I am sure of it. This cannot really be happening.

'What do you mean?' Finn manages to say.

Our mother would not say anything so mad. I am swamped with relief when I realise that this is not real, that I will wake up and everything will be normal. She cannot possibly have just said that.

'We'd have to,' I add, 'if that happened, which it won't because the doctors will make you better. When they take you to the hospital.'

'No. Marianne. Finn. I'm so sorry. This is a burden for you, I know. It's only eighteen months. Until Finn's GCSEs. Then you can report me missing and you'll be all right. But until then, it's really, really important that you let everyone think things are normal. Use the money sensibly. Keep up with your school work. Do well in your exams. I'm sorry you have to grow up so quickly. There's no other way.'

'Er, Mum?' says Finn. 'There is in fact another way. We could just tell the truth. You know?'

He is as baffled as I am. I can see that he is humouring her.

'You're going to promise me that you won't do that.' She looks at us both with the hard stare that we know so well. Neither of us can defy her when she fixes us with this look. 'You can't go and live with your dads. Not an option. You'd be taken into care – fostered, or else sent to children's homes. I couldn't bear that. You'll be fine here. I know that, you know it, but the state would not believe it. You can look after each other.' She closes her eyes, takes a few deep breaths, and opens them again. 'And,' she says, 'the main thing. Most important of all. Don't tell the landlord. Don't let him know there's anything wrong.' She looks at me.

'Why?' I ask.

I see her open her mouth to reply, and then think better of it.

'Because I say so,' she says, as firmly as she can manage.

'But . . . ?'

'Don't tell him. You can't. Pretend things are normal.'

Finn and I sigh and look at each other. We have never even met our landlord.

'OK,' Finn says, humouring her. But she has not finished.

'If he comes over,' she says, 'tell him I'm out, or asleep, or in bed with flu or something. Finn, you deal with him, and stand your ground – he has no right to come into the house without arranging it in advance. Marianne, you can be me on the phone when you have to. Finn, you need to practise my handwriting. You can write letters and cheques. You can take occasional days off school and write notes to the office from me, but only sometimes. Not enough to get yourselves noticed.'

Finn and I stare at each other. It is too surreal. We both know we will not be able to live like that.

She closes her eyes and draws a deep breath. 'No doctors,' she says. 'I told the one who diagnosed me that we were moving to France, and he gave me copies of my notes and said we'd get great treatment there. No one's looking for me. No one's wondering where I went. If there's the merest hint of a doctor, I will be very, very angry with you both and I will still die, and you will have to live forever with the knowledge that I died disappointed in you. Instead of proud of you. Now, go get the cash out of my purse and buy some food. Get me some soup and stock up on soluble painkillers. You can get yourselves chips or something. Go on. Skedaddle.'

Whenever I look at Finn, I see my feelings reflected on his face. We cannot take this in, and sometimes we cannot take it seriously. After a few minutes we stop our faltering attempts to talk about it. I cannot bring myself to make Mum's mad plan real. I can't speak the words. I am still harbouring a hope that I might wake up tomorrow morning and find that things are back to normal.

Only a week ago she was baking cakes from cheap ingredients, and cutting my hair, and we were making do with less than nothing. Now she is hardly here. Finn and I are on our own.

Neither of us sleeps. We sit up all night, without speaking. All the same, we both go to school the next day. We check on Mum in the morning. She is sleeping. We leave iced water by her bed, and a cup of soup. Then we pack our bags, and walk out into the world that is completely changed, that cannot know our secret. We walk side by side, shoulder to shoulder.

'What do you think?' I ask Finn, just before we get to the corner.

'I don't fucking know what I think,' he says, and he blinks a lot, quickly. 'You?'

'Yeah. I have no idea. We can't go against her. But we could, you know? I mean, what's she going to do, if we get an ambulance?'

'She's going to die hating us. She said so.'

We stare at each other. It is the first time either of us has said the word. The phrase: *she's going to die*. Now that Finn has articulated it, I want to say it too. I am compelled to say it.

'Not hating,' I say, rushing. 'But she would be furious with us, and then she would die. And we'd have to live with that for ever, that we'd made Mum die in hospital, that we'd be taken into care, that after she's spent all this time saving up thousands of pounds for us, we did the thing she told us not to do. She's going to die and we are planning to betray her. I don't want to live with that, do you?'

'So, sit tight for the moment, I guess. Fend off the landlord.'

'He can't be that bad. It's probably the illness making her brain mad.'

'We don't even know what the fucking illness is.'

As soon as we get around the corner, we will be in the world of school. We know that, and so we hang back, to put the moment off. I don't want to leave Finn, to go back to the world of the other teenage girls, where hair and boys and homework are the most pressing matters. We stand still for a couple of minutes. Then I put a hand on his shoulder.

'We've got each other,' I tell him. 'Have a good day. We'll work it out.' I am trying to say the things that might make him feel a tiny bit better; the things that Mum might say. He does the same back to me. He gives me a quick hug, even though there are two boys from his year on the corner.

'Yeah,' he says. 'Us against the world, hey? We can do it. She might not be that ill. People get better, sometimes, even without treatment. And we'll soon work out what we need to do.'

We don't. We never work it out.

# chapter twelve

'Morning, sleepy-head,' said Seth. He was smiling.

'Hello,' I said back. I yawned and stretched, looked around. The blind was still closed; this was good. I made myself look into his eyes and smile back.

'How are you feeling?' he asked, looking anxious.

I blinked a couple of times, and put a hand to my temple. 'Better!' I announced, with a big fake smile.

'Brilliant. Then I imagine you're ready for coffee,' he said, putting a cup down on the bedside table. It was the largest cup we had, my favourite one. Seth had painted it for me with swirls of red and yellow, at the local pottery painting shop, and had it glazed by them. He gave it to me on Valentine's Day last year. I knew that if I turned it over it would say 'Seth loves Lucy' in messy painted writing on its base.

'It's great to be feeling so much better,' I said. 'Can I take this mug to London, do you think?'

'Well you could,' he said, with a smile, 'if you were completely mad. I'm not sure it's entirely de rigueur to take a piece of pottery to a concert. But what do I know about city fashions?'

I laughed, stretching, and forcing myself to try to appear normal. 'I'm not actually planning to take it to the concert,' I said. 'The hotel will only have rubbish cups, won't it, because that's what hotels do. White ones with saucers. If I'm going to have to drink horrible tea with UHT milk, it may as well be out of my favourite cup.'

He reached out and stroked my hair, a gesture that nearly induced me to break down and tell him everything.

'I would be honoured for the humble cup I decorated for you to be taken on an outing to the big city.'

'Thank you.' I looked into his face. He returned my gaze. I tried hard to pack it full of apologies and love. He held my eyes. He always did.

I took a deep breath. 'What's for breakfast?'

'You're hungry again – that's great. Toast?'

'With peanut butter?'

'I've just bought some crunchy.'

'Perfect.' I looked at him. 'Thanks,' I told him.

I could see him hesitating.

'Thanks for what?' he said.

*Thank you for everything.* I tried to project it at him without saying anything. And sorry. Sorry for what is about to happen. My betrayals were mounting up, and the big one was yet to come.

'Thanks for the coffee,' I said. 'And the toast, if you're making it. And for looking after me yesterday, when I was ill.'

'That's OK.' He leaned forward and kissed me. 'And now you need to get ready for your big day.'

I forced a smile. 'Yes. Leonard. I can't wait. Sure you're not coming?'

'Nah,' he said. 'You'll have a better time without me. I'm rubbish at London.'

'Me too, really,' I said, and I couldn't think of anything else.

'Lucy?' He looked at the floor. We still had a nasty old carpet in the bedroom. One day we were going to rip it out and sand the floorboards.

'Mmm?'

'It's so nice that you're happy and relaxed. And that your headache's gone. I was worried you were going to have to miss your trip. That's all.'

I took a deep breath, and forced another smile. I wished I were not fooling him. It was turning out to be horribly easy.

* * *

Twenty-four hours had passed since I saw him standing on the neighbours' doorstep. Since then I had been rigorously disciplined. I had been doing such a good job that Seth had no idea that anything was wrong. I had barely left the house, having been stricken down by an imaginary migraine, and Seth had not even mentioned the curious fact that I had never had a migraine before. I had thus avoided both going to work and picking Imogen up from school. I closed the bedroom curtains, and lay in the dark, waiting.

Everything had fallen apart, and he had not noticed, because the darkness that I brought with me was so alien to his world. He did not have the tools to notice it. This was the part that made my heart break. I had already left him, detaching myself for his own good, and he had no idea.

We sat together at the kitchen table, and, miraculously recovered, I ate toast and drank coffee. I leaned back in my seat and smiled at Seth. Then I looked hard into his face, attempting to imprint him on my brain. His dark hair was wet from the shower, and it was slicked back from his face. He had just shaved and his face was pink and tender. I wanted to reach out and stroke it with my fingertips; I lifted my hand, then lowered it again.

'Nice day,' he said, nodding out of the window. 'I'll finish the job today, I reckon. Might head over to Porthtowan after.'

'Good idea,' I agreed.

'You'll have a good time, won't you? Eliza was talking about wanting to hit the shops tomorrow. Don't overdo it – remember you've been ill.'

I smiled and looked down at his hands, resting on the table. 'Don't worry,' I said. 'I'll be fine. I'll steer your sister round Covent Garden and then steer her onwards to a café.'

He nodded. 'I know. I know you'll have a fantastic time. What are you up to next week?'

'I don't know.'

'Working much?'

'Yeah. Well, the usual amount.'

He smiled and shuffled in his seat. 'There's *The Merry Wives of Windsor* on at the Minack Theatre. I thought that might be fun. Expand the horizons and everything.'

A seagull outside the window made a sudden squawk, and we both looked at it. Its diversion allowed me to wrestle my emotions back into submission. Seth's suggestion was so touching, because it was something he would never have thought of doing for himself. I wished for his sake and for mine that our happy future was possible.

When it was time to go, I did everything I needed to do. I was far too good at this. I put on my mask. I swung my black canvas bag over my shoulder. I pushed my feet into my black ballet pumps.

'Hey,' said Seth, and I froze for a second. I looked at him, and saw that he was frowning.

If he realised that something was wrong, and asked me what it was, then, I decided on the spur of this moment, I would tell him. I would tell him everything and we would work out the future together. I knew, had always known, that I ought to have told him a long time ago.

'Yes?' I asked, and I waited, poised, ready to let him in.

'Is that a new bag?'

'What?'

'That bag. I don't think I've seen it before.'

'Oh,' I said. 'No, I've had it for ages. It was under the bed.' This was possibly the only thing I had ever said to Seth that was true.

I reached up and kissed him. I kissed him far more passionately than he was expecting, and he pulled away from me, laughing, surprised. I pulled him back again.

'You'll be late,' he said, smiling at me. Then he kissed me again.

'I'll be fine. You'll be able to look after yourself, won't you? Without me?'

He smiled fondly at me.

'You're only away for one night. Aren't you? I think I'll manage.'

'Mmm,' I said. 'I know you'll be all right. But I'm going to miss you so much.'

* * *

I looked up and down the street, searching for the figure in the trench coat. Penmere station was only five minutes' walk away, but I took so many diversions, secret footpaths, alleys around the backs of houses that were mainly used on bin days, that I made it take ten. I was certain, however, that he was not following me. I tried not to wonder where he was, instead, or what he was doing

For a moment, I thought I had misjudged my journey, and missed the train. I climbed over railings at the back of a steep slope that had been entirely colonised by buddleia, and paused to listen. I could not hear anything, and I should have been hearing the train arriving at the station. I pushed my way down through the undergrowth to emerge on the single platform.

The train was already there, and the doors were beeping, about to close. I ran and leapt on, my bag catching in the closing door. I tugged at it, hard, and freed it. The doors closed with a rubbery bump. I had made it. The train smelt of stale air and old upholstery.

Eliza was at my side in ten seconds, laughing.

'Lucy!' she said. 'You gave me a heart attack! What happened? I thought I was going to have to go without you. You know this train connects with the London one, and there's no way you'd have been able to get to Truro by car faster than the train gets you there. So I was wondering, what do I do? I was just on the phone to Seth when I saw you. You came out of the trees! Lucy?'

I laughed too. 'Sorry,' I told her. 'Really sorry. I got delayed. I was running late so I thought I'd try a more direct way, but I came out by the railings so I just had to climb them.'

I watched the station disappearing and tried to calm my trembling nerves. Penmere station had one platform, and it was lovingly tended by volunteers. The station sign was shiny and new, but deliberately old-fashioned, brown, with curved edges. The buddleia bushes crowded in from all sides, their purple flowers lending a hint of pollen to the sea air. There was nothing at Penmere but a platform, a shelter, and a view of the hills. We left it behind for the last time. I would miss it.

Eliza shook her head. 'You nutter. There's no more direct way than the road. And those railings back on to gardens, don't they? Did you run across somebody's lawn?'

I shrugged, and followed her to the seats. The train was not busy, and I took a window seat in front of Eliza's and stared hard at Falmouth as it accelerated past the window. It had been good to me. I bit my lip and controlled myself. I looked at the green landscape, the trees, the mundane, safe life going on.

'So!' Eliza said. She passed me a bottle of water over the back of my seat. 'You must need a drink. Look at us, on the way to London!'

I turned and looked at her. She meant more to me than she would ever know. I knew this trip was a milestone for her, and I was desperately sorry that I was going to trash it so comprehensively. I decided that, in the meantime, I would make sure she had fun.

The loss of Seth was lurking around the edges of my consciousness, however hard I worked to shut it out. The fact that we had never been the sort of soulmates that Eliza and Graham were made it worse, not better: we could have been soulmates if I had let him in, and if I had been able to do that, he would have been coming with me. Everything I touched broke and cracked.

I turned my best smile on Eliza.

'You look *amazing,*' I told her, and it was true. She was wearing a summer dress I had never seen on her before. It was black, covered in a pattern of red flowers. Its skirt was gathered, and stuck out around her: she was one of the few people I knew who could get away with that. Her hair was straightened and shiny, in a sleek bob. She had a red ballet-style cardigan pulled around her, tied with a bow at the back, and red ballet pumps on her feet. 'Actually,' I told her, 'you look like a flamenco dancer.'

She squinted at me, the pale sun in her eyes. 'In a good way, or a loo-roll-cover way?'

'Eliza! A good way, of course. I don't think you need to do any more online dating. Leonard will catch sight of you and he'll sweep you away with him and sing to you for ever.'

'Our eyes will meet across a crowded arena. He will somehow pick me out of the crowd of whatever-many thousand. How old is he these days?'

'Seventy-three.'

'I could overlook that.'

I felt rather sick at the idea that, later that day, I would be hearing the very same voice, and looking at the very same man, who wrote and sang the music I had been listening to for most of my life. I knew his voice, every word of every one of his songs, but I had only the haziest picture of the man himself in my mind, the photo of him that was on the cover of the *I'm Your Man* album, the one that resonated with me so much that I had to call on all my steely reserves to be able to listen to it.

He was going to sing those songs tonight. I was scared, sick with anticipation.

Eliza had moved on. 'We can go for a drink somewhere nice before the show, can't we,' she was saying. 'And maybe go somewhere afterwards as well? And I want to do some shopping. Is Covent Garden good for that, or is that just what I think because I'm from Cornwall?'

I tried to focus on this. 'No,' I said. 'You're right, Covent Garden is fine. Busy in the summer, though. But it's Friday so it shouldn't be too bad. We could find somewhere for lunch in Soho, maybe. Though we don't get to Paddington till half twelve, do we, so maybe we should do that first.'

'Let's have something for lunch that you can't get in Falmouth,' she said. 'How about, I don't know, Japanese?'

'Eliza, do you even like Japanese food?'

She smiled. 'How would I know? I live in Cornwall.'

We changed at Truro, directly on to the London train, which was already there, waiting for us. There was a clatter of smart shoes as two thirds of the people from the little Falmouth train climbed the stairs, crossed the bridge, and went down the stairs on to the London platform. I loved Truro station. There was a cafe which sold papers and magazines, there was a ticket office, there was a very rustic car park which filled with enormous puddles when it rained, and that was it. Two platforms plus a smaller one that hosted the Falmouth line.

All the other people who made the connection with us were dressed for London. They had a determined air about them. They pulled little cases on wheels, and they were wearing their smart clothes. The women had make-up on, and the men were in shirts with collars, though no ties. In my jeans and floral cotton top, I felt I was letting the side down.

We found carriage C, and our reserved seats. I made Eliza take the window seat, because I knew she wanted it. I did not think that gazing out of the window at the Cornwall I was leaving would do me much good. I did not want to see, hours from now, the beginnings of London, either.

'You've got your hair down,' Eliza said. 'It looks gorgeous. I wish mine would grow like that. Crowning glory indeed.'

'It's a pain in the arse,' I told her. 'Truly. I wear it down for half an hour and remember precisely why I never wear it down.' I had an elastic on my wrist, and pulled my hair up into a ponytail. I never wore it in a ponytail either, because I thought it looked too schoolgirlish. 'It never used to get this long. It changed when I was an adult. Got all thick. Anyway,' I said, 'when were you last in London?'

She smiled. 'Nearly four years ago. Can you believe that? Graham and I went for the weekend. We left the girls with Anne and Mike. Clara wasn't even a year old. God, we appreciated the break. We had an amazing time. Graham died not long afterwards. Not that we had any idea, of course.'

My heart ached for her. 'Great that you did it, then.'

'Yes, you should never say "next time". Because there might not be one.'

'I went to New York,' I tell her, 'in the spring of 2001. With my friend Rebecca. We stood at the base of the World Trade Center, and debated whether to go up it. I can still remember saying, "The queue's a bit long – we can always do it next time."' I smiled at the memories of that trip. It was my single trip abroad, of my entire life. I had been so terrified to be using my passport, so amazed when it actually worked, so swamped with relief at having got away with it, that I had vowed never to push my luck by leaving the country again.

She smiled. 'And I don't think there's going to be a next time for Leonard Cohen, is there? Not if he's seventy-three.'

'Yes,' I said, 'I guess you need to grab the moment, when you get one, with both hands, because you never know what's about to happen.'

'You're telling me,' she said, and we sat in silence for a while.

Eliza and Graham had been one of those couples who were the linchpins of the lives of everyone around them. They had been together for years and years, and they would have stayed together for ever. They had Imogen, and then Clara, and everything they touched turned to gold. Then, one day, they were all walking on the cliff path at Lamorna, and Graham went on ahead to see if it was safe for the girls. He stepped aside to let a family pass, and took an extra step back. A single backwards step, and the lives of everyone was changed for ever.

Three years had passed. Eliza had been forced to pick up the pieces, to hold herself together for the sake of her girls. I was in constant awe of the way she had carried on with life without her partner. The reluctant dating she was doing was breaking my heart. The men she met in bars for disappointing exploratory conversations were not worthy of her. I decided that if there was a way, I would get in touch with her, later, to try to explain a little of what had happened to me. I owed it to her, not to leave her forever wondering.

London slapped me in the face. I had been away for years, but its energy was just the same. The smell of Paddington station was so familiar that every nerve ending in my body tensed. I was not Lucy any more. I was the little girl who had struggled to do the right thing without any idea of what the right thing might have been. The girl who got it so horribly wrong.

We stood at the top of the steps to the Tube, and looked at each other. People walked around us, purposeful, impatient. Eliza laughed.

'Different pace of life,' she said. 'Not quite Cornwall.'

'Indeed.' I pointed at an indicator board, which was listing the afternoon's departures. 'Look, it looks weird even to see the word "Penzance" written here.'

'Tell me that we can go on the Tube without getting blown up,' Eliza said.

'We can go on the Tube without getting blown up,' I told her.

'Then let's do it.'

By the time we made our way to the arena, we had had two large glasses of wine each, and Eliza was excited and jumpy. I wanted more, wanted to drink myself into oblivion and collapse, and not to have to listen to my mother's music. I wanted to poison myself and be taken to hospital. I wanted to relinquish control.

I had left Seth, and no one but me had any idea. I hadn't left him a note, but I had taken my bag from under the bed. And now I was in east London again.

When the Jubilee Line stopped at North Greenwich, huge numbers of people got out. I didn't want to hang around.

'Eliza,' I said, touching her arm. 'Look! We must be twenty years younger than most of these people.'

She looked. 'Now there's something that doesn't happen every day,' she said.

The crowd shuffled out of the station, following the signs to the arena.

'The O2 Arena, anyway,' said Eliza, as we trooped with the sensible coats and the grey heads. 'I know nothing about it. What did it used to be called?'

'I have no idea. North Greenwich? Nothing's in North Greenwich, is it? We must be somewhere near the Millennium Dome, maybe?'

At this, we stepped out of the station and realised that we were extremely near to the Dome, that the O2 Arena was, in fact, the Dome, finally given a useful job. I felt like a country cousin who had never even been to the city before. I wished I was.

'And to think I used to live here,' I said.

Seth had got us some of the best seats in the house. We were on the floor of the arena, far closer to the front than I had imagined, though there was still a sea of heads between us and the stage. Armed only with a plastic cup of warm white wine each, we took our seats twenty minutes before the concert was due to start, and Eliza kicked back, leaning back in her seat, looking around at the other people, getting excited. I pretended to be doing the same, but all I was doing was checking the crowd compulsively.

People milled around us, the atmosphere hushed. Women of my mother's age made up most of the audience, and many of them had men who had an air of 'being the chaperone' about them following on behind. I stood up, and stared around, trying to look at everyone. The place was unimaginably enormous, and it was full, and there were blurs and blurs of faces. I hoped I was safe here. I thought I probably was, but I had been wrong before.

For the first and last time in my life, I was under the same roof as Leonard Cohen. My mother was at my shoulder. I shuddered, and linked my arm through Eliza's.

# chapter thirteen

## Marianne

Every time the phone rings, we jump. My heart pounds so loudly that I feel it, not just in my chest, but all the way from my throat to my stomach. I am so scared.

Finn and I hardly talk about it. From time to time, we talk about the fact that we don't talk about it.

'I don't think,' I tell him, one day after school, when we are sitting at the table with homework books in front of us, trying to act as though our mother was not dying quietly yet painfully upstairs, 'I don't think it would help us at all, would it? If we sat around discussing the . . . well, the way things are.'

He looks at me, his eyes locking into mine. I have no idea how I would be doing this without him.

'No,' he agrees. 'It would actually be slightly impossible to get on with anything, if we were talking about it all the time.'

'Just the ground rules.'

We agreed the ground rules between ourselves, and we ran them by Mum when she was having an energetic moment (these days, Mum's energetic moments are when she can sit up in bed and focus on us). They are:

1. If the phone rings, Finn is to answer whenever possible. This is so that if it's someone who needs to speak to Mum, I can come on the line as her.
2. Any notes or forms for school are to be signed by Finn,

because he does the best version of Mum's writing, and they need to be consistent.
3. If the landlord calls round, which he shouldn't as long as we keep paying the rent on time, we are always to say that Mum is in the house, sleeping off a shift at work. If I am home alone, I am never to open the door to him. This is one that Mum made us put in. It is the one that she is most determined about. We are due an inspection in a couple of weeks and we have decided to say that Mum has flu and hope that he stays out of her room. I suppose she thinks he is dangerous because he is the only person who has the right to come into the house.
4. It is obvious already, but neither of us is ever to invite a friend home. We haven't spoken about it, but I think that Finn and I have both distanced ourselves from our classmates. Nothing they care about seems to mean very much any more.
5. Both of us are to keep up with school work and maintain a good attendance: to make sure, in other words, that school has no reason to contact home with any concerns about us.

We have fallen into this new way of being so quickly, and have become so completely immersed in it, that when I think back to the way things were only a month ago it looks like someone else's life. It had been an illusion for years, I know that now. Mum was skinny, and she was always sorting things out for us. We lumbered through life complaining about our homework and asking for another biscuit, and all the time she knew she was going to be leaving us, knew she was dying, and she was setting it up so we could carry on without her.

Her plan is mad. It is insane. I know it, and Finn knows it, and if we'd told anyone, they would have known it too. It only makes sense in Mum's head. I am still intending to tell someone what is happening. Every day I tell myself we will do it tomorrow. I am going to be sixteen soon. That means that I won't have to go into care, I am sure of it.

The illness must have got to her brain, because no one in their right mind would plan to die without any treatment, and leave their children to cover it up. We are going to betray her, one of these days. We have to.

We have tried, several times. On the Tuesday of the week after she collapsed, we skipped lunch at school, met in a corner of the playground, and went to see the nurse. Mrs Evans is quite fat and comfortable, and she's always nice, although she can tell very quickly when you're pretending to feel ill and she sends people back to lessons a lot of the time.

We walked together, very scared. We had agreed on the way to school that we had to be sensible, and that the sensible thing to do would be to tell somebody. We thought we had to trust the system to look after us. We were sure it would not work out the way Mum said it would. We thought Mrs Evans would take charge of things, and if she called an ambulance for Mum, the people in the hospital might even be able to cure her.

We stood shoulder to shoulder outside the nurse's room. It was at the end of a corridor, and the air outside smelt of disinfectant.

I swallowed hard. Finn was shaking.

I raised my hand to knock.

I pictured Mum, the way she would look at us as they took her into the ambulance. The heartbreak, the hurt. The betrayal. We had always been a unit of three. Although she wasn't like other mothers, we always knew that she was the one in charge. She set the rules. We followed them. The idea that we were going to turn on her, because she was too weak to stop us, was almost unbearable.

I put my hand down. We looked at each other.

'I can't,' I whispered.

The door opened, and Mrs Evans almost walked into us. She stepped back and smiled. Her cheeks were rosy with too much blusher, and her eyelashes were clumped together with mascara. She was wearing a sensible tweed skirt and a blouse that gaped slightly between the buttons.

'Hello, you two,' she said, eyebrows raised. 'And what brings the Jenkins siblings to the sick bay today?'

I looked down. Finn was still shaking. He was staring at the ground. He looked terrible.

'I was worried about Finn,' I said quickly, because I couldn't do it, simply could not be so treacherous to Mum when we were all that she had. 'He's been feeling a bit wobbly and trembly and he's had a headache. He didn't want to come and see you but Mum said if he still felt bad at lunchtime I should bring him here.'

Mrs Evans looked quickly at Finn, and then at me. I could see at once that she believed me, even though I felt the word 'liar' flashing in neon on my forehead.

'Come on in, Finn,' she said, in her kind voice, the one she uses when she isn't feeling sceptical. 'You don't look good. Why don't you lie down for a bit. Is Mum at home today? Could she come and fetch you?'

'No, she's at work,' I said quickly. 'If Finn can stay here for the afternoon, I'll make sure he's all right on the way home later.'

'You're a nice sister,' she said, in approval. 'It makes a refreshing change for me, to see teenagers who aren't at each other's throats. Come on, Finn. Shoes off. Marianne, go and get yourself your lunch. He'll be fine. I'll tell his teachers.'

Since then, we have kept our heads down and followed Mum's plan in the absence of any other option. If the doorbell rings, we panic, but otherwise we get through the days.

Someone bangs hard on the door, three times.

Finn and I have had half a bottle of wine between us. We drink it because Mum had a stash, under the stairs. If we are behaving like adults, we have decided that, from time to time, we can drink like them too. It is nice to have something to do, and nice to be able to feel dizzy and irresponsible, and nothing much seems to matter these days anyway.

At the sound of the thumps on the door, however, we are instantly sober.

'It's him,' I say. 'It's got to be him, hasn't it? Mum says that if he comes, he bangs on the door.'

'He's a week early.'

'Tell him that. Make him go.'

'You run upstairs. I'll open up. Make sure she's OK, check if she's asleep. Don't come down unless you have to. He's been paid, hasn't he? And the inspection's next week. Not today.'

I am unsure. 'Mum really doesn't like him. Maybe we should just not answer.'

'The lights are on. He knows we're here. And he's probably got his own key. The last thing we want is him just letting himself in. Go upstairs.'

I run up the stairs as he bangs on the door again. I hear the door creaking open, and my insides turn to liquid as I listen to Finn's conversation with our mysterious landlord.

'Hello,' says the landlord, in a friendly voice.

'Hello.'

'You must be the young man of the house. I'm Benjamin Burdett. I own this joint, for my sins. I'm after your mother. Is she in?'

'Um,' says Finn, and I send him thought waves, desperate for him to say the right thing and to sound as if he's telling the truth. 'Um, she is in. But she's been working a double shift, and she's sleeping at the moment. Can I help you?'

'Can you help me? What are you, the receptionist?' He is laughing, but not in a nasty way. 'No, you're all right. I just wanted to see Mary. To check in. It's been a while.'

'But we've paid the rent. The inspection is next week.' Finn sounds jumpy, but he's doing all right.

'Indeed you have, and indeed it is. Hey, don't look so worried, mate. There's nothing wrong. I just want to say hi.' He laughs. 'If you don't let me in,' he says, 'I'll have to start to wonder what you're hiding.'

'But you have to make an appointment in advance.'

'Come on. I can see you're being very sweet and protective of your tired old mum. But enough's enough. I haven't got time for this.'

Mum is, mercifully, fast asleep. I pull the duvet right up to her neck, and nudge her over so she is facing the wall. Then I arrange her hair so it is over her face. I tidy the room a little, draw the curtains tightly shut, and turn the cassette player on, pressing down the 'play' button. Leonard starts singing the wonderful, outlandish lyrics to Mum's favourite of his songs, 'Take This Waltz'. I turn the volume down low. She will seem less dead if there is music playing, I am sure.

I stand at the door, as if I could possibly stop this man called Benjamin Burdett from going exactly where he pleases.

I hear his feet on the stairs. I take a small step back. In no time he is in front of me.

He is taller than I expected, younger, better-looking. I imagined him as an old, creepy man, but he looks younger than Mum. He has thick black hair, longish, Public-school style, and his face is slim and film-star handsome, with high cheekbones and big dark eyes. He is wearing jeans and a white collarless shirt. I see a glimpse of his tanned throat.

He is the sort of man I look at in magazines and films, the sort of man who would never notice a girl like me.

'Marianne Jenkins, I presume,' he says, and he smiles with one side of his mouth, and my heart starts pounding in my chest. I have kissed boys a couple of times, once on a school trip and once at a disco, but I've never been out with anybody. I am one of the least experienced girls in my year. And yet this man is looking into my eyes, and I am forgetting everything, forgetting even Mum. I am thinking about that great unknown: sex. I didn't mean to think about it at all. 'Now I see why your mother has kept you away from me,' he says, and I am rapt. 'So, she's asleep, is she?'

I nod.

'Well,' he says, 'in that case, there's no need for us to go disturbing her. Can I just peek in?'

I nod again, and I open the bedroom door. I don't look at Finn. I just lead Benjamin Burdett into the sick room, and I hope that the slightly open window has allowed most of the sicky stench of terminal illness to escape into the night. I catch a whiff of his aftershave as he brushes past me. It smells like soapy lemons.

'Mum needs to sleep,' I say quickly. 'She's been working all sorts of shifts.'

'Of course. I understand.'

He stands beside the bed and looks at her back.

'Who the hell is this?' he asks, but still with a laugh in his voice. I bite my lip and stop breathing.

'It's Mum,' I whisper.

'Not her! I can see that she's your mum, and I can see that she's flat out. I mean this guy singing about dead magazines. I mean, what the hell?'

'Its Leonard Cohen,' Finn says defiantly, from the doorway. 'Mum loves him.'

He raises his eyebrows. 'And he loves her right back, by the sound of it. Never heard of him.'

I don't want him to leave. As he goes back down the stairs, he says: 'Get her to give me a call when she's slept it off, hey?'

I want to offer him a glass of wine, but I know I shouldn't, so I walk with him to the front door instead. He turns to me, smiling that sideways smile again. My insides dissolve and I make an effort to regulate my breathing.

'I'm sure we'll be meeting again, Marianne,' he says. 'Very soon.' Then, in a gesture so quick that I almost think I imagined it, he takes my face gently in one hand, brushes my cheek with his thumb, and turns and leaves.

'What a wanker,' Finn hisses as we close the door. 'The way he was sliming around you. You did well not to tell him to fuck off.'

I am surprised, but I realise I shouldn't correct Finn's impression.

'No point kicking off,' I agree. 'Best to let him come and go without any trouble.'

No one has ever made me feel like this. Lots of the girls in my year have had multiple sexual experiences, but I haven't. I can't even talk about those sorts of feelings without sounding like an educational leaflet and using phrases like 'multiple sexual experiences'. They would laugh me out of the playground if I said something like that.

Mum has warned us about him. She makes him sound like a monster, without explaining why. Perhaps, I reason with myself, she and Benjamin just don't get on. Maybe they have argued about something. But I know that Mum has not often been wrong about things, or about people, until now.

All the same, I want to run after him and jump into his car. I want to depend on him, to tell him the truth, to let him look after me.

'I'm going to go back to tae kwon do,' Finn says, suddenly. 'Then I could do this.' He attempts an ambitious high kick, and chops his arms around, reducing an imaginary Benjamin Burdett to pulp. 'And then I'd kick him down the stairs.' He does this with a sudden pumping leg movement.

'And then we'll have two bodies to dispose of,' I tell him, and we lapse into silence. This is a part of the plan that Mum has not got an answer for. When she is lucid, she says, 'Oh, just put me in the garden', or 'under the floorboards', but we know we can't do that. The best idea we have come up with so far involves rolling her in the tablecloth, like something from a Carry On film, and making a two a.m. trip to the park and a six-foot-deep hole prepared under the shrubbery. There are so many new office buildings springing up nearby that they will probably end up excavating the park at some point, and finding her. All the same, we can't think of anything better. We cannot keep her in the house.

'Anyway,' says Finn. 'What's for dinner?'

I look at the kitchen. We have rather let the tidiness part of it slip lately. There are dirty plates and cups stacked over all of the surfaces. Nothing has been wiped clean for ages. We have stopped eating cereal in the mornings because all the bowls have remnants of Weetabix or corn flakes glued on to them. Instead, we have toast. We have toast for breakfast, toast, if we are home, for lunch, and toast for dinner.

There are a few tins in the cupboard. I open the door. It comes off in my hand, and I prop it up with the other ones against the wall.

'Beans!' I say, triumphant. I hold the tin up. 'Beans on toast.'

Finn manages to grin. 'Brilliant,' he says. I want to cry.

# chapter fourteen

When I turned and looked behind me, the sheer number of other people in the building gave me vertigo.

I knew that nobody else's screwed-up life could have been quite as punctuated by this particular music as mine had been. I had assumed that Leonard Cohen had a niche following among people who appreciated proper lyrics. It seemed, however, that there were thousands upon thousands of people who thought that the music was speaking just to them.

'Ladies and gentlemen,' said an echoey voice. 'Please take your seats. Mr Leonard Cohen will be on the stage in five minutes.'

Mr Leonard Cohen. This had the surreal quality of a dream. I sat down and gripped the arms of my chair.

I looked at the stage and tried to relax. The band was already there, a group of cool-looking men in hats, and a line up of three women in trouser suits. Two of the women were young and luscious. The third was older, and beautiful. I looked at her face, which was lined and strong, as if she were a survivor of something, and I wondered who she was, how she had got there. I wondered whether I could call myself a survivor. Emphatically not.

Then a roar came from behind me, and a little man ran on to the stage. I leaned back into my chair and stared. He was wearing a suit and a fedora, and he was smiling and bowing. I held my hand to my mouth and tried to make sense of this. Here was the man my mother had loved: here, in front of me. I hoped he was going to sing my song, the one with my name in it. I hoped he was not.

I looked quickly to Eliza, and although she knew nothing of what was going on, she sensed something, and reached over and took my hand. I squeezed hers back, grateful for the contact, and I took strength from her. We stayed like that, hand in hand, breaking off only to clap.

He sang 'Dance Me to the End of Love'. It was a good way to start because it was not a song that had a particular resonance for me.

The moment he opened his mouth, I realised that he was an unexpected embodiment of the fact that things did not have to go horribly wrong, that in spite of everything, they could go right. He was not washed up, not burned out, not an entity known only to me. He was at the peak of his powers.

I stared at him, gazed into his face and revelled in the moment, and felt, for the first time in more than twenty years, that some things were not complicated. He was brilliant, wonderful, spell-binding. Every other woman in the audience was gazing at him in the same way. The air, in fact, was thick with pheromones.

It must have been an odd thing, being Leonard Cohen, having this effect on a stadium full of women at the age of seventy-three. If Mum was still alive, she would have been sixty-five. She would have been here. She would have been next to me, gazing at him, hoping that he might look at her just for half a second, taking in every detail of the night and remembering it for ever.

I pulled my hand gently away from Eliza's, and wiped my eyes.

The interval came too quickly. I stood up and stretched. I was stronger. I had heard those songs, and it was almost the last thing that Lucy Riddick was going to do. I had made a plan, though I had not dared to finalise anything. I had to do it at the last moment. But I had looked up the timetables, and I knew what I was going to do, and where I was going to go.

'Bloody hell,' said Eliza. 'He is the coolest guy I've seen in my life. I'd shag him, you know. Seventy-three and all. Wouldn't you?'

'Oh, I definitely would,' I said lightly. 'If it wasn't for your brother, obviously. Leonard would say *all* the right things.'

'Of course he would. That's the whole point. Another drink?'

'Sure. And the loo, too.'

We wandered out of the stalls and found the nearest bar. There were thousands of people milling around. I left Eliza trying to get served, while I headed to the loos.

I kept walking, away from the crowds, trying to find the furthest ladies' toilet, one that did not have a queue that came out into the foyer. I worked my way around what I supposed was part of the dome before I came to the end, and found it. An almost empty toilet block. I looked at every man I passed, looked behind me, looked up in case there was any sort of balcony above me. I checked every cubicle, peering at the shoes underneath in case any of them were on men's feet.

This was insane. I locked the cubicle door and drew a deep breath.

I came out of the cubicle, washed my hands, didn't bother to dry them, and stepped back into the foyer. I started walking slowly back towards the crowds, trying to think of nothing but Eliza and my drink, and the fact that Leonard had not sung 'I'm Your Man' or 'First We Take Manhattan' yet, and that those two had been among Mum's favourites. I hoped he was not going to sing 'Tower of Song', because that, I knew, would be too much for me. I knew he would, though: it was probably his best song of all.

The hand on my shoulder came as a shock. I spun around. My heart went into overdrive, beating like a bird in a box.

It was a woman. She took a quick step back.

'Sorry,' she said, and she put a hand to her mouth. 'I didn't mean to scare you. I think you've dropped this?'

It was my hairclip. I pushed it back into my bag, and smiled and thanked her, trying to get my breathing back to normal.

'Where did you get to?' Eliza asked, handing me a plastic beaker of wine, as I slid back into my seat. I rested the hand that was holding the wine on the armrest, so that she would not see how violently I was shaking. Her voice changed. 'Lucy!' she said. 'What's happened? You look awful!'

I shook my head.

'I'm fine,' I said. 'I just . . . I thought I saw someone I used to know. It's the music. It reminds me.' I looked at the empty stage set, at the drums and the instruments.

She was concerned.

'What does it remind you of?' she asked, gently.

I shook my head. 'It's OK,' I said. 'I'm fine now.'

I stared at the stage. Summoned by my desperation, Leonard Cohen came bouncing back on, and the arena burst into applause, applause that was loud enough to end our conversation for several hours. I sank back, stared at the man, and tried to think of nothing, to let him wash over me.

# chapter fifteen

## Marianne

I sit in front of the doctor and yawn.

'Just something to help me sleep,' I say. I rub my eyes elaborately and wonder whether I am overdoing it. 'I just can't do it. I go to sleep and then I wake up and I lie there and I can't get back off because I'm thinking about my school work and my coursework and it's so important that I get my GCSEs because my mum's a single mother and she really needs us to do well. She works so hard for us and that shows me that I need to work hard too.'

He is looking at me with a blank face. I scrutinise it, trying to work out if he is sympathetic or impatient.

'Try not to worry about things,' he says. 'Avoid anything with caffeine in before bed – that includes chocolate. Do you drink alcohol? You can tell me the truth.'

'Not really. Just occasionally with my brother.'

'Well, don't. Listen to peaceful music. Try some relaxation techniques. I can help you out with some of them if you like.'

'Yeah, I do all that. I've been going to yoga and everything. I just think some medication would be great as a short-term thing till I get my coursework done.'

He shakes his head. 'You're fifteen years old. I would be highly reluctant to prescribe you the sort of thing you're after.'

'Just a tiny bit? I can come back in a couple of weeks if you like. I just have to get my geography and English coursework finished. Otherwise it's all going to go wrong. You see, I've got it lined up. It's like, you know when you line up dominoes? And then you push the end one. If I screw up these ones, it's all going to fall down. Then I won't be able to do the A levels that I need to do to get to a good university.'

He is wavering. I am sure of it.

'And I know I'm fifteen,' I add, 'but I'll be sixteen soon, and that's old enough for lots of things.'

Unfortunately, this gives him a different train of thought.

'Do you have a boyfriend?' he asks. 'Or man troubles?'

'No,' I say with a smile. 'Not at all. No boyfriend, none on the horizon. I'm not really interested.' And I am not. I am not interested in any boy. I am, however, entirely fixated on one particular man. 'All I want is to do well in my school work.'

He is sceptical. 'What does your mother say?'

I pause. The correct answer would be, she says absolutely nothing because we're pretty sure she's in a coma, and we're glad about that because it means she's probably not in excruciating, unrelievable pain right now.

'She just wants me to do the best I can,' I say, instead, 'but she wants me to be happy, too. She's a bit worried about me.'

He nods, and starts writing on a pad. 'These are the mildest ones I can give you, but they should have an effect, at your age and body weight. When you come back, get your mother to come along too. I'll see you again in four weeks and you can tell me how well you've done with that coursework.'

I grin at him. 'Absolutely. Thank you so much.'

'I got it!' I tell Finn, waving a pharmacy bag. 'He didn't want to. He said they're the mildest ones, so we'll need to give her lots.'

We are stockpiling medicine, because we both feel Mum is going to need it, soon. She has not woken for almost a week. We know she needs to be on a drip, but we are propping her up on her pillow, tipping her head back and dripping water and thin soup into her mouth using a pipette Finn stole from the science room. She has been more agitated lately. I think she is going to wake up, and when she does, I know she will be in a worse state than it is possible for me to imagine, even though the things

I can imagine have changed radically over the past month. She is going to want all the sleeping pills we can gather together, to get her back to sleep. Any sort of sleep.

I take the brown glass bottle out of the paper bag, and jiggle it. It rattles in a satisfying way. I put it on the kitchen windowsill with the rest of the stash. These new pills, these Nitrazepam, are the star of the show. The rest of the haul consists of five small plastic bottles of Kalms, three packets of Nurofen, and some Feminax. All of them have been purchased, carefully, at different pharmacies, one by one.

'I could see a different GP,' Finn suggests.

'Mmm.' I am unsure. 'You could try, I guess. As long as they don't look at our records and realise that we're up to something. I'm not sure it's worth it. I have to go back to this one in a month.' A month is a very long time. I am fairly sure that everything will have changed in a month.

'But how do you get morphine?' he asks. This is a question we have been asking each other, repeatedly. People who are ill need morphine. Everyone knows that. Unless we stage a break-in at the hospital, I don't think we're going to be able to get her any. We have seriously considered breaking into the hospital, and have worked out a basic plan whereby one of us will acquire a head injury that will necessitate a trip to Casualty, and the other will scout around stealing drugs whenever we are left in a room. We have not dared try it yet, but if Mum wakes up, and if she is in a terrible way, then we will.

'Maybe all this lot together,' I say, 'will have a cumulative effect that will be like morphine. Or at least it'll knock her out.'

'Um.' Finn looks unsure of himself, but presses on. 'Um, what about, you know, drugs. The "just say no" sort, I mean. There are people in the sixth form. Even in your year. We could look into it.'

I have no idea why I didn't think of that before. 'That is a brilliant idea,' I tell him, warmly. 'Of course that's what we'll do. So. How do you think we go about it?'

It is a warm spring day, and I am mooching around the playground, trying to look as if I were cool and edgy. I don't think it is working. If there were pockets in school uniform, then my hands would be in my pockets. As it is, I am not entirely sure what to do with them, and I seem to have ended up clasping them behind my back. This, I realise, is very uncool indeed. I try, instead, to emulate the posture of Jessica, the hippest girl in my year. I stand with my toes pointed inwards, heels out, like a reversal of the ballet first position that I used to do, many years ago, when Mum took me to dance classes. I hold one arm straight down my side, and clasp its elbow with the other. It feels ridiculous, but this is the way girls stand, when they are the sort of girl I need to be.

The boy I need to speak to is called Moz, although I remember from when we were further down the school that he used to be called Mohammed. He is wearing skinny black jeans and a white grandad shirt that is hanging down almost to his knees, and he has Doc Martens on his feet. His hair is backcombed into feathery black spikes. He is in the sixth form, and so he gets to dress how he likes.

I pull a strand of hair into my mouth and chew on it. It is only just long enough to reach.

He is sitting at the edge of the playground, surrounded by his gang, leaning back on the fence. I realise that he is looking at me, and smirking.

'Hello, little girl,' he says, in an accent that I know isn't his real one.

'Hello,' I say. It comes out too prim. 'Hiya,' I add, in what I hope is a more 'street' voice.

'You after something?' They are all staring at me now, this gang of unimaginably worldly boys and girls who are only a year older than I am. For a few seconds I envy them ferociously, because their lives have this space in them, the space for them to wear stupid clothes and create new versions of themselves, versions that are quite different from the way their parents would like them to be.

Emboldened by the fact that they would be fascinated and thrilled if they knew the truth about my life, I hold my head up and say:

'Yes. I need to buy some . . . stuff.'

The girls titter. I stare out one of them. Her name is Mandy, and she has recently bleached her hair. It looks terrible. Her skin is pink and scarred, her eyebrows too heavy for her new pallor.

'Some "stuff"?' asks Moz. 'What sort of stuff?'

'You know. Drugs.'

At this, they fall about laughing. I turn to walk away, but then I remember why I am doing this. I think of Mum, and I force myself to turn back.

'Look,' I say, and I am looking only at Moz, because he is the leader and the rest of them will do what he says. 'Look, if you can't help out, that's fine. But don't think you can laugh at me, don't think I'm worse than you are in any way, because you know nothing about my life, and I am not. I can promise you that.'

One of the boys in the gang raises his eyebrows and turns his attention to a cigarette he is rolling. The rest of them look at me, with a few smirks.

'Grab a seat, darling,' Moz says, and everyone shifts up so I can sit next to him. I look across the concrete to where Finn is loitering, and our eyes lock for a split second.

Then I am next to him. I can smell the stale cigarette smoke and chewing gum on his breath. I can smell his slight BO. I can see that he shaves, because he has stuck a bit of tissue paper on to a cut on his neck, but I can also see that he doesn't need to.

'Right,' he says. 'Now, let's see if we can help you out. You're Nicola, yeah?'

'No,' I tell him. 'I'm Marianne.'

'So you are! Coolio name. Marianne. You can be Maz. I'm Moz. We're almost family. What, precisely, are you after, Maz?'

'I am after something that makes you feel different. Something that takes you away from your real life and your real world. Something that can give you a really, really lovely place in your head.'

He is nodding, interested in me.

'Yuh-huh,' he says. 'Well, I guess you may have come to the right place, in that case.'

He tells me to meet him at the far corner of the playing field, on Monday at afternoon break. I stay ensconced in their gang for the rest of the lunch hour, silent but listening, wondering whether everything would be a bit easier, in the future that I know is close, if I managed to become a part of this group. In the time after Mum. They drink and smoke and take drugs. That would, I think, help to take the edge off reality.

On Monday night, we ceremoniously award the title of Star of the Stash to my newly purchased ecstasy tablets. Moz sold me four of them, for a grand total of a hundred pounds, which we took from the post office account. He said they are brand new, the craze that's about to sweep the nightclubs, and that if we didn't live in London there'd be no chance of getting any. 'Or Manchester,' he added, after thinking for a moment. He said they make you feel happy, and that's why they're called ecstasy.

'I can't believe you did it,' Finn says. 'Before this, you'd never have spoken to Moz and that lot, would you?'

I force a smile. 'Yeah,' I agree. 'It's funny, isn't it? It was easy, because nothing really matters. You can do anything when nothing matters, can't you?'

'Yeah,' he says. 'You can.'

We are contemplating the meaning of this, trying to think of new projects to occupy ourselves, when Mum wakes up.

She wakes up with a terrifying, soul-rending scream that doesn't stop. It goes on, and on, and on. I have no idea how she is even breathing.

We reach her side in a few blurred seconds. She is sitting bolt upright, and her mouth is wide open, and she is like a cartoon character screaming.

I put my hand on her shoulder, and Finn touches her head. She screams and screams and screams, and then she stops, and slumps back.

'Mum,' says Finn, and I say it too: 'Mum. Mum. Mum.'

We are both crying.

'Help me,' she whispers. She looks at me, and then at Finn, and then at me, and then at Finn. This is the last time we will see her lucid. Even at the time, I know it. Everything about her,

her aura, her very self, is woven together with the stench of death.

'I love you,' she croaks. 'Look after each other. Help me die.'

I stare at her. We always do as we are told. This is what she is telling us to do. I put the thought from my mind.

Finn runs downstairs, while I stroke her hand, and when he comes back he has the whole stash balanced in his arms. I refill her water glass. We are not helping her die, not now, because we cannot. But we are going to do whatever we can to make her feel better, for a while.

We look at each other. Finn still looks so young. I suppose I must too. He looks like the sort of boy who should be into *Star Wars* and computer games. Not the sort who would grind up an illegal ecstasy pill to alleviate the suffering of his secretly dying mother.

He pounds it into a powder, using the base of the glass on a piece of paper, and then he tips the powder into the water. We stir it, but it doesn't dissolve. In the end, we fish out the lumps with the teaspoon and deposit them on her tongue. She used to do that for us: feed us with a spoon. She used to be so strict, so much in control. The moment when she obediently opens her mouth for what she thinks is a tablet to make her die is the worst moment of all.

She lies back and shuts her eyes. Silently Finn breaks one of the other pills in half, and we swallow one piece each. We wait for a few moments, and then we float away in blessed, blissful relief.

# chapter sixteen

When the second half of the concert began, I knew that the dam I had built for myself so painstakingly over twenty years had burst. It had been breached the moment the camera pointed at me on the cliff. For years and years I had lived comfortably in the haven I had created, but now the haven no longer existed. The torrents had come in, and they were sweeping me away. I was not safe any more. I was not Lucy Riddick any more.

'Now I don't want anyone to get alarmed – I know you probably haven't seen one of these before,' said Leonard Cohen drily, indicating the keyboard in front of him. 'It goes by itself.'

He pressed a button, and the opening strains of 'Tower of Song' sounded. I sat so still that I was not sure I was even breathing. I could not allow myself to move, could not react, because if I did, everyone would know. I had not been able to listen to this song for twenty years. I had always stopped that album before its last track. And now the man himself was singing it to me.

I was back in the house. I was sitting by her bed. Everything was squalid and wrong. The smell hit me in the face, though I only allowed myself the tiniest of winces as I remembered. Finn and I had spent months doing our pathetic best for her; and the only thing that held all of us together were the words of Leonard Cohen, constantly soothing Mum's pain from the cassette player. I looked at him, in his suit and his hat, standing in front of the microphone, and I felt that he understood, that he had been there too, even though I knew he had no idea about any of us, no interest at all.

When he got to that line, the line about the voodoo doll, I clenched my fists and surrendered. The tears poured down my face and I didn't make even a token attempt to wipe them away. I was Marianne. There was no way I could carry on pretending. I was Marianne Jenkins and I had lost my childhood, lost my innocence, lost my protector, lost everything that mattered.

I had never, in all this time, allowed myself to miss her. As soon as she was gone, the fact that we missed her had instantly become the least of my problems. It had been swept aside.

I remembered the long hair halfway down her back, the short skirts that showed her perfect legs, the way the corners of her eyes crinkled when she smiled at me. I remembered the cakes she would bake for us. I could, suddenly, recall the comfort of her embrace, as if it were yesterday.

I pleaded with him, silently, to swoop down from the stage and look after me. I begged him to take me away, to rescue me from the thing that was about to happen. I would follow him on tour, pour his drinks, tuck him into bed at night. I could fit in. I would want nothing in return but protection. His eyes were closed but I thought he understood.

After that I was wrung out. I pushed myself as far back as I could into my seat, and let the music take me away. I never wanted it to end. He sang my song, the song I was named after, and I let it wash over me, lost myself in it. Even when he sang 'Closing Time', a song I had discovered when I was living in Bristol, a song that had instantly reminded me of my past, I clung on to it. He was singing about me: the words sent a jolt through my whole being. A song about debauchery and sex, and the end of the world.

Then, suddenly, it seemed as if it were all over.

This could not end. I would have given anything, everything I had, to be able to slip into a time loop which meant I could stay here for ever, between lives.

Leonard Cohen said: 'Closing time, friends – thank you so much,' and skipped off the stage. I tried to draw a deep breath and gather my strength. He would be back for an encore, but this was it. We had been here for two and a half hours, and it was over.

There was an encore, and then it really was the end.

I turned to Eliza, and saw at once that, while my very identity had changed, she had noticed nothing.

'He is incredible!' she said, and my heart broke again at how unaware and how happy she was. 'He looked at me, you know. In "First We Take Manhattan". He actually winked at me when I was yelling out the chorus. I think he did, anyway.'

'Of course he did,' I told her. I tried to look like Lucy Riddick, though already she was dissolving and her essence was slipping away from me. She was nice, uncomplicated. She had ideals and morals. Lucy Riddick cared about the environment and believed there was hope for the future. Marianne Jenkins, on the other hand, knew that we were all fucked and doomed, and she didn't care. I had loved being Lucy. I tried to think of anything else I could say.

'To the hotel?' I suggested.

She looked slightly disappointed. 'Is that what you want? You do look tired. Are you OK? Is it that person you mentioned?'

I arranged my features into what I hoped was an appropriate expression. I had no idea any more. I was dissolving.

'I'm fine,' I said, and I took her arm and made myself smile.

People were streaming out of the arena, but it was big enough for everyone to move freely. We shuffled along in the crowd. I saw him everywhere, in the back of every head, in every tall man, every imposing stranger. I was losing my grip.

It was all I could do to make the journey to the hotel, and as soon as we got in, I locked the door and pushed a chair up against it. I stood at the window and pulled the curtain aside. There was no one there, but it was only a matter of time.

Eliza took ages to go to sleep. She was on a high, and she chattered away, sitting on her bed, a glass of extravagantly expensive minibar wine in her hand.

'You know, when Graham died, I never ever thought this day would come,' she told me, and I was happy for her, even though she was from my old life, and I could feel our connection fading with every second that passed.

'You never thought that what part of this day would come?' I asked.

'This,' she said, with a gesture that took in everything. 'Me. Happy. Me leaving the girls – I never thought I would let them out of my sight for a second, now that I know how fragile it all is. It could just as easily have been them as Graham. We know that. I can't even think about Clara climbing those rocks. But I've changed. I wish I could go back to the then-me, and tell myself that it was going to be all right, that it would start to heal. Today is the first time in years that I've been able to look someone in the eye, to look myself in the eye come to that, and say "I'm happy". I think about Graham all the time, and I know that I always will, but I can just about begin to get more philosophical about it. We're all born and we all die, and Graham's lifespan was shorter than anyone would have wanted it to be, but I'm trying to be grateful for the fact that I got to meet him and fall in love and have our beautiful girls. Even if we'd known what was going to happen, I wouldn't have done any of it differently. And,' she added, 'I just *loved* that concert.'

She fell asleep at one o'clock. I sat up in bed and watched her, in the dim light of night-time London that lit the room in the dingiest of greys. She was by far the best friend I had ever had, although she did not know it. She, not me, was the survivor. She had survived, and I had not.

I took out my phone and wrote a text to Seth.

*Concert amazing*, I typed. *I love you so much*.

I looked at Eliza's flushed cheek, her perfect little nose, her black hair tangled on the pillow. I wanted to remember her, almost as much as I wanted to remember Seth.

'Look for me,' I said, quietly. 'Look for me. Tell Seth. Look for me. Find me.' She stirred in her sleep. I held my breath. 'Look for me,' I whispered again.

Then I sat down and wrote a note that said exactly the opposite.

# chapter seventeen

## Marianne

I don't care about anything, and neither does Finn. We drink. We let domestic life fall apart around our ears. I spend my free time at school slouching against a wall with Moz and his gang. I use the family allowance to buy drugs, and Finn, Mum and I share them.

I start to find out what I like. I like speed, because it gets me through. I like ecstasy, but only in moderation. I hate spliff. I want to try heroin, particularly when I discover that it is related to morphine. I ask Moz to get me some. He says no.

I meet Moz one Friday night, in a pub. I thought I was meeting the whole gang, but it turns out it's just the two of us. We sit at a table, him seventeen, me fifteen, and we drink five shots of tequila each. Then we take some speed, without even bothering to go and find a private place. It is a small, dingy pub and nobody could care less. I rub it into my gum, and allow the artificial energy and happiness to take me over. The relief is immense.

'So, Marianne,' he says. He leans forward. I can smell him: I think he's wearing some sort of aftershave.

I lean towards him. 'Yes, Mohammed?' I ask.

'You kind of sprung from nowhere, you know? I don't even think I ever looked at you for years, and then suddenly you're marching over demanding some drugs. What happened?'

I look away and bite my lip. 'Nothing,' I say, but it is a lie and we both know it.

'Just curious.'

He stares at me. I look into his eyes. They are big and brown and gentle.

'Look,' he says. He puts one of his hands over mine. 'My dad hates me. He hates me for slacking. He wanted me to go to Oxford. But he's not one of the hard-core fathers and he's not going to try an arranged marriage or anything like that. But he'd have liked me to bring home a nice Muslim girlfriend. Anyway, he knows now that that's unlikely.'

I look at him, interested. I have no idea where this is going.

'Right,' I say.

'So what I'm saying is, perhaps, well. Maybe you'd go out with me? I think he'd like you. Even though you're not a Muslim.'

I look at him and I want to laugh. The coolest boy in the school wants to go out with me. He wants to take me home to meet his parents. A couple of months ago, I would have loved this. I would have been over the moon at the outlandish idea that one day it might be possible for me to become Moz's girlfriend.

Now I shake my head. I cannot get close to him, and I don't want to. I like him and I'm grateful to him, but I will never be going home with him. If he invited me to his house, he would expect me to invite him to mine. This is so far from the realms of what is possible that I smile.

'Oh, Moz,' I say, and I try to say the right words. 'I would love to, but . . .' I stop, completely at a loss for words. In the end I resort to a formula I have read in magazines in waiting rooms, have heard on the rare times I have seen a soap opera. 'I'm just not looking for a relationship right now,' I tell him, hating myself, knowing that I sound ridiculous. 'I'd like to keep hanging out with you, but that's all,' I add. 'Sorry.' Then I try one more familiar line on him. 'It's not you. It's me.'

He takes his hand off mine and pretends that it's all right, that he doesn't mind and that he wasn't serious anyway.

# chapter eighteen

I closed the door as quietly as I could behind me. It clunked shut and I stood in the corridor for a moment, listening. Eliza did not stir. Half of me wanted her to open the door, to ask me what I was doing, to pull me back.

We were staying at an absolutely generic chain hotel. The corridor was thickly carpeted in a blue and gold pattern. I remembered reading somewhere, long ago, that hotels chose patterned carpets because they did not show stains, and I wondered what this corridor would look like if it were carpeted in white. Not pretty, I supposed.

It was lined with closed doors. Many of them had Do Not Disturb signs hanging on the handles. I pictured sleeping people behind them, innocent people, people with ordinary uncomplicated lives. Much as I knew that ordinary lives were generally complicated, I assumed that mine was worse than most of them. I wondered what illicit liaisons were being conducted here, behind these doors, what scandals were playing out.

In spite of myself, there was a quiet thrill in walking away. I wondered if I were slightly addicted to it, to leaving a life when it became compromised, and going somewhere new, starting again, becoming a different person.

The lift arrived silently, and its doors opened with a quiet ping. I pressed the 'G' button.

There was a bored-looking man sitting at the reception desk, who looked about twenty, and a large amount of foyer between me and the door. I hitched my black rucksack on to my back, and kept looking ahead. I assumed he would not question my leaving in the middle of the night, since we had paid for the room and given a credit-card impression for the minibar.

I was right. As I drew close enough to the main doors for them to open automatically, I heard him say, 'Thanks, good night,' in some form of Eastern European accent. I lifted a hand to wave, without looking round. Then I stepped out into the night.

# chapter nineteen

## Marianne

In a sickly fug of illness, hallucinating and rasping, she dies. We sit on either side of her, waiting for her next breath. She is a skeleton, a half-person. Her eyes are sunken, her face not like herself at all.

We gave her all the pills. We ground them up and fed them to her on a spoonful of jelly, because that seemed to be the easiest way for them to slip down. She knew what we were doing and we could tell, from the effort she made to swallow them, that it was still what she wanted.

She kept asking for them, even though she couldn't talk. She did not need to be able to talk: she demanded them with her eyes. We had held out against obeying her for weeks. Then we gave in. It suddenly seemed that there was no point at all in prolonging it.

We gave her the pills less than ten minutes ago.

She has made us play the *I'm Your Man* album without stopping, for days and days. She has issued the instruction solely by lifting a finger in the direction of the stereo. As she dies, Leonard Cohen is singing 'Tower of Song', the last track. The seconds tick by as we wait for the breath. We stare at her face, wanting her to breathe again, and not wanting it. I look at her chest, wanting it to heave up, and not wanting it at all.

Leonard is singing the line about the voodoo doll. I liked that line. I won't any more. Finn stands up and switches it off with a click. The silence is shocking. The absence of Cohen is almost weirder than the absence of our mother. That album has been the wallpaper in our house, the soundtrack to the end of everything.

After a while, we look at each other. Finn's face is blank. He doesn't look fourteen any more. It is his birthday next week. I suppose I will make him a cake, carry on the family traditions.

Less than three months have passed since she told us. The world will carry ruthlessly on and we will do whatever we can to carry on with it, to stay in our places, to stop anyone asking what's wrong. We must show the world the faces they expect to see. We sit on either side of the lifeless husk of the only parent we have ever had.

But we have stopped questioning the wisdom of Mum's decision, and started to follow her wishes. We have got this far: there is no way we can let ourselves be taken into care now. We know we can manage by ourselves. *They,* whoever they are, would not appreciate our abilities.

She looks entirely unlike herself. I pull some strength from somewhere.

We have to deal with her body. After that, we will be able to do daily life. We will carry on by ourselves until Finn is sixteen. That will be the easy part. Then we will report her missing, in exactly the way she told us.

I close my eyes and remember her, just for a second. I remember her reading to us, when we were much younger, with an arm around each of our shoulders, both of us snuggled into her. I can remember the way I felt, encircled by her, entirely safe. I have never needed a dad. He is no one, whoever he might be. Mum was more than enough for us.

I look at Finn. He is staring at her. I know we should close her eyes, because that is what people do. I reach out and do it. Her skin is still warm. Yellow, taut, and warm.

'What now?' I say.

'I wish we could have a proper funeral,' says Finn. 'You know. Like normal people do.'

'So do I.'

'We should do it tonight.'

'We can do it tomorrow.'

'It's going to get worse. You know it is. The longer we put it off.'

'One day. We need one day.'

We go to school the next day. It feels wrong, leaving her in bed like that, but there's not much else we can do. We discover that death is nothing at all like the way it looks in the movies. Her body goes completely stiff. I have heard of rigor mortis, but I had forgotten about it, and I'd never had a clue that this would happen, that she would tense up like a person made of hard plastic. We are wondering when it will start to rot.

I sit in my lessons, staring at the sheets of paper in front of me. GCSEs start in ten days. Katy used to be my friend. She is sitting next to me, but we don't talk to each other. I don't want a friend. I only hang out with the sixth form, so now my class are a bit impressed and a bit pissed off with me. I don't care. I can't play any part in normal school things. I only want to spend time with Moz and Mandy and the rest of them, because through them, I can access the drink and the drugs that make me feel different, and a bit better.

After registration, Mrs Barry wanders across the classroom towards me. She is so fat that she keeps impaling bits of her flesh on corners of furniture. Her face is all squashed, and I don't know what she would look like under the fat. I start to amble away, pretending I don't know that she's after me. She changes course until she has cut me off.

I look at her, pull a strand of hair across my face, chew it, stare at her.

'Marianne,' she says, in her funny spiky Scottish voice.

'Hi,' I say, and I look away from her.

'Marianne, I'm concerned about you,' she says. I get ready to protest, and she stops me with a hand. 'Are you eating properly? Are you getting enough rest? Do you want somebody to talk to?'

I say it in my head, am tempted to say it aloud just to hear the sound of the words. 'Well,' I don't say, 'last night we sat up until Mum died at quarter to two, and then I took a valium to get me to sleep. Tonight won't be much better because we're somehow going to get rid of her body in a deep hole. But I'll be OK for the exams.'

'I'm fine,' I say. 'I'll try to eat better. I haven't been sleeping great.'

She looks at me, her head on one side. 'Shall I have a word with your mother?'

All of a sudden, I want to cry. But I don't. I keep rigidly in control of myself.

'No, honestly,' I say, and I manage to smile. 'I'm doing all right in my work, aren't I?' I focus on a bit of graffiti on the wall. It says TJ 4 Matt. I try very hard to concentrate on working out who TJ is.

'Yes you are. I hope you're going to have a very impressive set of grades. That's why I don't want to see you do anything to jeopardise that.'

'I won't, I promise. I'm actually not sleeping well because I'm studying so hard.'

She is sceptical. They have all seen me slacking around with the bad crowd. I hold her gaze and try to look bright and keen.

She lets it go. 'Well, take care of yourself. There are plenty of us around if you need anyone to talk to. And Marianne? Be careful of the company you keep.'

I decide that I must do everything in my power to stop Mrs Barry from phoning home. She, I feel sure, would notice if I got hastily into character as my dead mother. I go to the library at lunchtime, instead of hanging out and smoking. I revise my history. It feels like the right thing to be doing. I hear Mum's voice: 'You need all the work ethic you can get.' She is right. I have to do well at my exams, and stay around for A levels, so that Finn can get through his GCSEs too. Only then will we be free.

Since I turned Moz down, anyway, I am not feeling so welcome in the lunchtime crowd. It is a relief to be away. I sit and work, chew the end of my pen, force myself to think about Hitler, because that is infinitely preferable to thinking about my real life.

Moz appears behind me, touches my shoulder.

'Maz?' he says. 'I was wondering where you'd got to.'

I shake him off, ignore him. After a while, he wanders away.

We wait until two in the morning. Then we set off for our macabre, stupidly risky mission. It would be easier, in many ways, to keep her in the house. But the smell, we can tell, will soon become overwhelming, and then she will rot, and that is not really an option. She suggested, once, that we might stick her in the freezer, but our freezer is tiny – we would have to cut her into hundreds of pieces and shove them in the ice compartment. The back yard is small and concreted over. We would need a pneumatic drill.

So we have to leave the building.

The tablecloth was too small. We have pulled up the carpet from her old bedroom and wrapped her in it. That was not straightforward: it was unwieldy and much more difficult than it looks in films. We have left her on the hall floor, ready to go. I grabbed a few flowers from gardens, and growing out of cracks in the walls, on the way home from school. We will throw them down after her. We lie her down next to the front door. I run ahead to open it. We have planned the route, practised it. We know that this is going to be the worst part of all. Once we have done this, everything else is going to seem easy.

'Don't think about it,' I advise Finn.

'I know,' he says. We are not speaking very much at the moment. I know I can only get through this by keeping it bottled up. I think he probably feels the same way.

I open the front door. Then I scream.

He is standing on the doorstep. He does not look surprised when I scream in his face. He smiles at me.

I run away, all the way through the house into the kitchen. I curl in a corner and put my arms over my head. I can hear the sound of voices, raised, Finn's and Benjamin's. I do not want to know what is going on. I want to shut myself away and make myself so small that I disappear altogether.

Finn pulls my arms away from my head.

'It's all right,' he says. 'Marianne! Listen to me. It's all right.

Benjamin knows what's been going on. I think he's been coming in when we're at school. Anyway he's cool. He's not going to tell anyone. He's going to help us. He says he has a better idea than the park. Come on, Marianne. It's OK.'

And so, with our landlord's help, we put our mother's body into the back of a car, and sit in silence as he drives us to one of the huge building sites that are all over the City.

He leads us past barriers and dire warning signs to a place where there are enormous holes that have been excavated for foundations. I try to stay detached, and barely manage to register what is going on. All I know is that by the time we leave, we no longer have her body, and Benjamin is promising us that it will be all right, that no one will ever know what we have done.

As we make our way back to the car, I lose the ability to walk. I step over the last of the barriers, and my head fills with a high-pitched ringing tone. My legs give way. I feel myself sinking to the ground, but there is nothing I can do about it.

Strong arms pick me up, and I black out.

I wake up stretched on the back seat of the car. It is dark outside. We are moving, but not very fast.

I try to sit up. Finn and our landlord are sitting in the front. I try to talk. Finn looks round.

'Hey,' he says. He looks terrible.

'Hey,' I say back.

'Right, you two,' says Benjamin. He sounds as if he's making an effort and being a bit too jolly. 'No one's sleeping tonight, are they? Let's go out and get some breakfast.'

Finn eats fast and urgently. I push some beans around my plate.

'Are you going to shop us?' he asks, looking up.

I look at Benjamin. I am not swooning at him today. Swooning is the last thing on my mind. But I note how well put together his face is. I wait anxiously for a response.

'No,' he says, and he cuts the crusts off a piece of white toast. 'No, of course I'm not. I can see why you've done it this way and you're the bravest kids I've ever met. Who am I to hand you over to the authorities? And quite apart from that, I'm in it with you now, aren't I?'

The table is circular: we are all sitting next to each other. Benjamin shifts his chair towards mine, puts a hand on my shoulder and pulls me close to him. I succumb at once, and lean into his bulk, so touched by the fact that there is someone to comfort me that I dissolve into hysterical tears.

I try to separate myself from him a bit. Mum was so certain that he was dangerous. But how can he be? I decide, for the first time, to go against her wishes. We have done a lot for her. Now we are on our own, and I am going to do the thing that I think is right, and trust him.

When I pull back, I look into his face. He is staring at me so intensely that I want to look away, but I cannot. I see salvation in his eyes.

'You need someone to look out for you,' he says. 'Both of you.'

'We can keep up with the rent,' I tell him.

'And I won't bother you,' he says with a nod. 'In fact, you can have a big discount. A youth discount. How old are you?'

'I'm fifteen,' I tell him. 'I'll be sixteen in July. I've got GCSEs coming up.'

He looks at Finn.

'Fourteen,' Finn says. 'Nearly fifteen.'

'Close together,' he says. 'Sorry about your mum, by the way.' He looks at me. 'Hey, don't cry! I was trying to be nice. Do you prefer not to talk about it?'

I nod, and wipe my eyes with a flimsy rectangle of scratchy tissue that is masquerading as a napkin.

'We don't talk about it,' I manage to say. 'Not at all. It's the only way.'

'Then don't. I've got the basic gist. I knew it the moment I saw her that time, in her bed. Nothing could be more obvious. I knew it before, too. She looked dreadful. So, we won't mention it.'

'Cheers,' says Finn. His voice does not sound the way it normally sounds, not at all. I wish I was able to look after him properly.

As we walk across the floor of the cheap café, on our way back to the car, Benjamin pulls me back. Finn does not notice, and walks on ahead.

'Marianne,' our landlord says in a low voice. He takes my hand and plays with my fingers. 'Look. Let me take you out at the weekend. Take your mind off it. Treat you. Show you that you're going to be all right.'

I look at him, at his handsome face. Before I was swooning. Now it goes a lot deeper than that. I have shared the unimaginable with this man, and he has come through it with me.

But Mum never wanted me to see him. She did not want me to have anything to do with him. She insisted. And now she is dead. I cannot bring myself to go against her wishes.

'Thank you,' I say quietly. 'But I'd probably better not. Maybe another time.'

He looks into my eyes. I try not to look at him, but it is difficult to tear myself away. I long to change my mind. Just as I am opening my mouth to say the word 'actually', he nods at me.

'That's fine,' he says. 'Of course you won't feel like it. When you're ready.'

# chapter twenty

London by night was less frightening than I had expected it to be. I hardly saw another soul as I walked from Canary Wharf, the scene of so much of my past, to the Euston Road. The few people I did see took no notice of me whatsoever. I walked around the yellow patches of light made by the street lights, sticking to the dark as far as I could, with my pepper spray in my hand, and I took care to stay well away from any streets that I had ever known in the past. There were many places around here that I did not care to revisit.

Most of the cars that passed me were taxis. A few lorries thundered by. The windows were blank, and although I knew that there were people everywhere, all around me, most of them sleeping, all stacked up on top of one another, I felt entirely alone. I felt I was walking the pavements of a world that I had just created.

A cat jumped off a wall as I approached. I forced a smile at it.

I looked behind me, often. I never heard footsteps.

In the centre of town, I took as much money as I could from a cashpoint, using my normal bank card, then as much as I could with the emergency credit card. I had never had a credit card before. In Cornwall, I had been too sensible for things like that.

King's Cross was busier, and although I had planned to check into a hotel round here, the ones I passed looked seedier than I would have liked, and so I kept going.

I looked at a woman who was cadaverously thin. She was wearing fishnet tights and a tiny skirt, and tottering heels. She was a parody of a street hooker, and I tried to smile at her in solidarity, because I could so easily have ended up the same.

She looked back. 'Good time, darling?' she said, in a listless voice.

I shook my head. 'Good night,' I said.

'Well, fuck off then!' she yelled, suddenly animated. I lifted a hand and waved, without looking round. I wanted to cry for her.

Then I stopped. I was standing next to a sturdy black bin. I bit my lip: I knew what I had to do. I took the mug, my huge, flamboyant, favourite mug, out of my backpack, and pushed it through the slot. There was no room for 'Seth loves Lucy', not any more.

I found a Thistle hotel up a side street by Euston station, and checked in. I used my normal bank card: here, there was no harm in being traceable. By the time anyone caught up, I would be far away. The receptionist did not look in the least bit surprised by my early dawn arrival. I took the lift to the third floor.

It was exactly like the room in which I had left Eliza; but here I was alone. I did not bother to undress. I lay down on top of the tightly tucked sheets, and closed my eyes. To my surprise, sleep overwhelmed me at once.

When I stirred, it was light outside, and there was a steady hum of traffic. I lay and looked at the ceiling. My new life had begun. I tried hard not to have any regrets. I tried not to succumb to the bleakness that was hovering around the edges of everything. I tried particularly hard not to articulate the words 'What's the point?'

I switched on the television, anxious to check that I was not being touted around as a missing person, but it was just the financial news.

It was ten o'clock. Time to pick up my bag and vanish.

# part two

# chapter twenty-one

## Eliza

The room is very light, and the first thing I notice is that I have a hangover. That is the trouble with being a grand old dame in her thirties. When you're my age, you always get a headache, even after a couple of drinks.

And I was positively expecting it. I drank the wine at the O2 without even registering it and we had a couple of glasses beforehand as well, three beakersful at the concert, and one of those small minibar bottles each afterwards, back at the hotel. At least, I had one of those minibar bottles. I'm not sure Lucy did.

Urgh. I feel grim. When I roll over and prop myself up on my elbows to check the time, the blood vessels in my head start to pulse, and my stomach heaves, lurching between announcing impending vomit, and demanding a full English breakfast.

I have poisoned myself. I reach for the water glass, and take a big swig. This is when, quite forcefully, I notice the second thing. I spit it all out. It sprays all over the pillow. There is nothing more vile than a mouthful of slightly warm minibar wine when you wanted water. It makes me gag and tremble.

I always, *always* sleep with a full glass of water beside me. It's a total compulsion (there are others: I cannot, for example, go to the loo in a bathroom with a closed shower curtain in case someone's lurking behind it ready to leap out and stab me when I am at my least dignified. There are many more). Graham used to huff and roll his eyes about the water, and laugh about the shower curtain, and tell me I was neurotic. I would send him downstairs for more water if he drank mine, or if he took the glass to the dishwasher without warning me.

No one has taken my water glass to the dishwasher for years. I exchange it on occasion, when it gets disgustingly smeary. Sometimes I try to see this as a positive aspect to my life, but it is tricky to pull that off.

So I have a headache, and I fell over unconscious into my little hotel bed without fetching a glass of water. This does not bode well.

I yawn and decide to postpone the moment when I get up to hydrate myself. I am not sure how good I would be at walking. Then I remember everything else.

I had the best night! Leonard Cohen! I have pretended to Lucy that I share her passion, because it was sweet that she was so intense about his music. But now I really, completely get it. It was a spectacular show. And something changed for me while I was there. I moved on in some way. I can't really describe it, but I hope it lasts. Life looks better than it has for a long time.

I know what it was: last night was the first time I have truly enjoyed myself and been happy since Graham died. He was speaking to me. He said that if I wanted to sleep a moment on the road, he would steer for me.

That is my favourite line of any song, ever. Graham said exactly that to me once. I never forgot it. He didn't use those precise words, but we were driving down to Spain, through France, and we were sharing the driving, and I said I was getting sleepy.

'Pull over at the next services,' he said. 'Until then, don't worry. I'll steer.' And he did: the road was empty and he took the wheel, just for a minute or so. I had, perversely, never felt so safe.

Leonard made me remember my darling lost man, and he made me feel happy that I had something like that in my life, even though it was ripped away. That spark of being-OK is still there, buried beneath layers of hangover. At least I don't feel remorseful today. Beneath the nausea, I feel good.

I look over to the other bed, ready to compare notes with Lucy. That is when I notice the third thing.

I yawn. She is probably in the bathroom. I can't see the bathroom door from here, but I know that her guilty pleasure is a bath, and I know that she doesn't have them at home because she and Seth say they can't justify it because of the environment. They are both like that. If Lucy's away or working a night shift, Seth immediately runs the deepest, hottest, most bubbly bath he can. I don't think Lucy does, but now that she's in a hotel, I bet she's gone and run a bath and tipped in all the bubble stuff she could find.

I listen for splashes, but I can't hear any. I close my eyes. I might just sleep a moment longer, in fact.

When I wake up, she is definitely not in the bath any more. She is not in the room, and all the toiletries are untouched, so she hasn't had a bath at all.

I catch sight of myself in the mirror. It is not a pretty sight: bags under eyes, blotchy skin, terrible hair. I start the bath running to try to sweeten my horrible self a little.

I try to imagine her going down to breakfast without me. I cannot see it. The only thing I can imagine is that she woke early, probably hung-over like me, and went for a walk.

I decide to do some sleuthing, to find her shoes. Obviously they're not there. She would hardly leave the room with bare feet. At least that means she's definitely gone somewhere, as opposed to, I don't know, rolling off the bed, and under it, without waking up.

I cannot see her backpack either, but some of her stuff is still here.

I send her a quick text. *Where are you? Want breakfast?* (Much as I can see the convenience of writing 'u' instead of 'you', I cannot bring myself to do it. I am definitely too old.) I send it and stare at the phone, waiting for the reply.

Then I look around a bit more, for a clue. I feel silly and Famous Five-ish. But when I pull back her sheet, trying to work out whether she even went to sleep at all, I find an envelope. It is on her pillow, but the sheet has been pulled up to cover it. My name is on the front, so I open it.

I read it. I read it again. Then I sit on the bed and take a deep breath. I cannot process what I am reading. It makes no sense whatsoever.

Dear Eliza,

This is really hard to do. I have to leave now. It is for the best. Please tell Seth I love him, and try to stop him looking for me. This is not easy, but it's safer for everyone this way. I've always known it was going to happen one day – everything has been an illusion. I beg you to trust me, and to believe that this is the only option there is.

I love you lots. Big hugs and kisses to my lovely girls. I will always remember you all as the only family I have.

Until one day, I hope.

Your friend,

Lucy xxx

# chapter twenty-two

The station was busy, which was good. I had changed my clothes, and was dressed almost entirely in black. When I was Lucy Riddick, I had never worn black. I had clothed myself in colours, because I was that sort of person. Now I was in black footless tights, a very short denim skirt, and a black vest. I was dressing young, because I needed to get that old energy back, that strength that had taken me to Bristol and then onwards.

If Eliza was looking for me here, now, which was unlikely, she would never recognise me from a distance, at least. But she would have missed me by now. She was probably missing me this very instant. I put the thought from my mind. I was not Lucy any more, and so there could be no Eliza in my life.

I wove through the crowds, slipping around groups, dodging past bulky suitcases. Everyone was too wrapped up in their shopping, travelling, reuniting to glance at a random woman dressed like a teenager in clothes she had bought from the Falmouth Dorothy Perkins a week ago. I clutched my bag and stared around, looking at signs and shops and queues, and in the end, I saw a glass door that said it led to the ticket office.

I stood in a snaking queue, the sort of queue that had an indicator at the front and an electronic voice telling you which desk to go to. It was very modern, with bright lights all over the ceiling, bare brick walls, and a shiny floor. I shifted my weight around, impatient. The line moved quickly, and soon I was at the front.

The man who was serving was about my age, and he looked bored.

'Hello,' I said, in my poshest voice. If anyone asked, he would remember a posh woman. 'When is the next train to Paris, please, and could I buy a ticket for it?'

'Next train? Thirteen thirty-two. I'll have a check for you.' He tapped at his keyboard a bit, and winked at me. 'Yes, I've squeezed you on. You should buy in advance next time if you can. Much cheaper.'

I smiled a big fake smile.

'Absolutely. Thank you. How much is this, then?'

'One way or return?'

'Definitely one way.'

'One hundred and seventy-eight pounds fifty.'

He looked at me, waiting for a reaction. I nodded, pleasantly surprised, and counted out a load of notes.

'And I'll need your passport.'

It seemed to take him for ever, but eventually the ticket was printed, the passport details noted.

'Enjoy your trip, madam,' he said. 'Security closes in ten minutes, so you should make your way through right away.'

'Fabulous,' I said. 'Thank you so very much.'

I ran to the security desks and threw my little backpack on to the conveyor belt. I smiled at the man and woman in uniform, and waited for my backpack to come out of the other end. When it did, I felt safer. There were hundreds, probably thousands of people milling around, waiting for trains, and I scanned them and then made an effort to contain my paranoia. I bought a newspaper and a couple of books, and a bottle of water and a sandwich.

Then I found the ramp that led up to the platform, waved my ticket around, and suddenly I was beside my train. There was a huge glass roof, and a train that went on for ever.

I decided not to go to my booked seat, so I went to the dining car and sat down there instead.

I was breathing like someone who needed to go to A and E. My whole body was shaking. When a man wearing a blue raincoat came to the window, and put his hands to the glass to cut out the light and peered in at me, I felt the blood drain from my head, and for a few seconds I thought I was about to faint. I was trembling so violently that I sat on my hands, because that was the only way I could control myself.

I looked away from him, but I knew he was looking at me. He could see me. I screwed my eyes tight shut and waited for him to appear, to grab me, to drag me off the train.

And at that moment, the train started to move. I looked at the window, startled, and I saw the man in the blue raincoat, standing on the platform, waving and smiling. He was not waving at me, was not interested in me. Because he was a complete stranger to me, as I was to him.

I knew what I was going to do. I had spent years thinking about it, working out my plan. I had taken advice from the internet, but mainly I had worked it out by myself. Since I was easy to follow, I was going to have to leave a few decoys for anyone who might be trying to come after me. I had to concentrate, just do what I had to do for the immediate future, and I was not going to think beyond that. At some point I would have to work out who I was going to be next.

I found my seat and sat in it, annoyed with myself for being so hysterical. I was only going to make this work if I stayed calm, I knew that.

I had a seat at a table. There was a woman opposite me, a sensible-looking woman with short square hair and a navy business suit. She was probably about the same age as I was, but she looked far more grounded.

She looked up from her *Economist*, raised her eyebrows, and then smiled. I smiled back, and slid into the window seat. I took out one of the books I had bought, but I could not focus.

I stared at the Kent countryside, and then the blackness of the tunnel, and then the wider landscape of northern France, and all the time I thought about Seth.

It had been a charmed time, my life in Cornwall. It was a dream come true. I was lucky to have had it, to have escaped my sordid life in London. I had never really thought that the Lucy Riddick business was going to work. I had vaguely remembered reading about a way of getting a new identity, and had tried it out because I had no other options. I had spent a morning in the public records office in Bristol, looking at birth and death certificates until I found someone who suited me. Lucy Riddick was born a year before me, and died at the age of three, and I often thought about her and felt horrible for the way I had stolen her identity. I felt that I had somehow been responsible for her death. As Lucy, I was older than I had been as Marianne.

I had been astonished when it actually worked. I had expected to find myself arrested, but I figured that at least in a women's prison I would be safe. Instead, I ordered a copy of her birth certificate, got a man in the pub to certify the photographs and say he was a lawyer, and sent off the application. Three weeks later, my new passport arrived. With that, I could do anything.

The woman put her magazine down on the table, and sighed. I looked at her.

'Paris,' she said. 'It sounds so romantic, doesn't it? Are you going for pleasure?'

I bit my lower lip. 'Yes,' I said. 'Well, not exactly. I'm an actress. We're doing some improvisational theatre on the Left Bank.'

'Oooh,' she said. 'Lovely. Sounds much more romantic than anything I'm doing. What's your show called?'

I hesitated. 'It's called *The Show With No Name*,' I told her, imagination failing me. 'How about you? Business?'

'Oh, of course. Straight in, back-to-back meetings, and straight out again tonight. Not even a hotel to show for it.'

'And they don't let you travel business class?'

'You'd think, wouldn't you?'

'What sort of business?'

'Banking. Can you imagine? The whole world now hates bankers, and France has never exactly been at the forefront of the financial world because of all that socialism and what have you. And yet they keep sending me over to sit in rooms and talk to our French colleagues. Of all the ways I could be spending my days.'

'Do you at least get taken out to nice restaurants for lunch?'

'Exactly! That was always the great thing about working with France. They had proper lunch breaks, with wine and three-course menus. But not any more. These days they're going all American on us, and grabbing a sandwich at the desk. So, what about you? Where do theatrical performers get to sleep?'

This was easier. 'In a hostel,' I told her. 'A really shitty little place and we're all on top of each other, but we don't really care.'

'Sounds like heaven,' she said, unconvinced, and we grinned at each other again. 'I love the Rodin museum,' she said suddenly. 'That's where I would go, if I had any time to amble around. I'd go to the Rodin museum and sit in the garden with a Camembert baguette and an apple. That's all I ask.'

'It doesn't sound like much,' I agreed. 'I've never been to the Rodin museum. Maybe I'll get there this week.'

'Do it. Please do. It's heavenly.'

Northern France was whizzing past the window, and I was beginning to relax. Clearly, I seemed normal, because otherwise this woman would not have been talking to me. I made an effort not to let my eyes dart up every time someone walked past us.

As the suburbs began to appear, adrenalin started to pump through me. I dug the *Guardian* out of my bag and stared at it, but I didn't dare open it because of my trembling hands.

I could not stop in Paris for more than a few hours. I had to keep going. I would get out of there as quickly as I possibly could.

# chapter twenty-three

## Marianne

Every day is almost impossible. Finn and I can't be bothered to tidy up and keep the place clean, and since no one ever comes over, we just let it settle into a general squalor. The dishes are all dirty, and we give them a rinse in cold water before we use them. There are mouldy remnants of toast and baked beans in various stages of decay all over the kitchen. There are cups with green mould in them, growing up the sides. Everything is filthy. Everything is foul.

I make an effort with our uniforms, because that is the thing that will get us found out. So I wash them in the washing machine and dry them on the radiators, and sometimes I even iron. We have clean clothes, and I have a shower every day (Finn doesn't). Everything else – the sheets, the house, everything – is disgusting. I don't want to tidy it up. I like it like that.

Then, one night, I can't take it any more. I am in the middle of my exams, and I know I am doing all right, when suddenly it appears like something new, the realisation: Mum got ill and died and all we did was feed her ecstasy. She died after we gave her all the pills. That means that we killed her. It was what she wanted, and she was almost dead anyway, but I cannot get it out of my head. We are killers. We dumped her body and now a tower block is growing up as if we had planted her. Benjamin knows. He will tell someone, who will tell someone, and the police will catch us. It is bound to happen. You cannot get away with a thing like that. If we hadn't done it, she would still be alive, probably, in her way.

Finn is doing some English homework. I am sitting across the table from him, revising my music, and suddenly I can't do it any more. I put my head down on the table and feel some sort of old food creeping into my hair, and I open my mouth and howl.

I stay there, like that, for hours. Finn doesn't try to comfort me. He doesn't say anything at all.

A few days later, Benjamin is waiting on the doorstep when we get home from school. Finn sighs when he sees him, and mutters, 'Oh, bloody hell.' He turns round and starts walking away.

'Finn,' I say, to his back. 'Come back!'

He turns. 'I can't hang out with him. Don't make me. See you in the morning.'

I watch him walking away. He doesn't look back.

I know what it is. He cannot bear the fact that Benjamin knows what has happened. I feel a little bit the same way myself.

'Fucking hell,' Benjamin says, when he sees the state of the place. 'This is my bloody house, you know.'

I look at it through new eyes, and it looks even worse. I never noticed the flies before. I had not noticed the smell, either.

'Sorry,' I say, in a small voice.

'No, don't worry. Look, I'd send someone over to take care of it, except that this is a bit extreme for that. It would raise a few difficult questions. You can sort it out, can't you?'

I nod. I can't speak. He is looking at me, and I remember the way I felt the first time I met him. I want him, desperately, to look after me.

'You need to get out of here,' he says. He puts an arm around my shoulders. 'Sweetheart,' he adds, and he kisses the top of my head. 'Well, your hair smells clean, at least. Thank Christ for that. Come on. Much as I love you in your school uniform, you'd better get out of it or people will talk.'

I look at him. 'Get out of it?'

He laughs. 'And into some normal clothes! What did you think I meant? Get changed – we're going out. I promised you a treat, and this is it. You have clearly not been looking after yourself. You need a break.'

'I shouldn't,' I say, in a very lame way indeed, and I look to him, waiting for him to contradict me, which he does.

For a few hours, all my troubles melt away. He takes me to Regent Street, and buys me a dress in Liberty. It is a beautiful dress, silky and black, and it fits me like nothing I have ever worn before, and makes me look like a new person, a person who could actually be somebody. He buys me shoes with heels and ankle straps, and a handbag. He looks at me in it all, and when I see the approval in his face, I am suddenly happy. This is such a strange feeling that it takes me a while to give it a name.

Then he takes me to dinner at Joe Allen, and he orders a bottle of wine.

'You shouldn't be drinking, of course,' he says, with that crooked smile. 'But judging by the empties in your kitchen, I won't be corrupting you any more than you've already corrupted yourself.'

'Considering the situation,' I say, 'you'd drink underage too, wouldn't you?'

'Of course I would.'

And the evening passes by, and I find I can chat to him, can say anything at all. The relief in being able to talk is immense, unimaginable. When he squeezes my knee under the table and says, 'You're going to be all right, you know. I'll see to that,' I believe him.

All the same, I should not be doing this. At every moment of the evening I have a nagging voice, which sounds spookily like Mum's voice, asking me exactly what I think I am playing at. It keeps on and on at me until, at last, I have to ask him.

'Why did my mum never let me meet you?' I say, quietly, looking at the table. 'That was one of her rules. If you came over, I was supposed to go out. I would have done that night you came round when she was ill, if there was a back gate.'

'I'm glad there wasn't.'

We look at each other. I wait for the answer. In the end he sighs.

'Why do you think?' he asks. 'I've known Mary a long time. I knew her for a long time, I mean. She knew me well. She knew that I would find you adorable. She didn't want me corrupting her little girl. Fair enough, and all that.'

'You're not corrupting me,' I tell him. 'You're saving me.'

I look at him. I feel it is true. I think it is true.

'I hope so. It's the only thing I want to do.'

The restaurant is filled with people, and none of them takes much notice of us. I thrill to the idea that we look like a couple. I wonder how old I look, whether I could pass for nineteen. I drink my wine and eat my food and feel, for the first time in a very long time, almost normal.

Afterwards, we go back up the stairs to the outside world, and as we walk down the street together, towards the Aldwych, he strokes my waist. Then he stops, and he pulls me round, and he kisses me.

I have never been kissed like this before. The world spins, and I want to be with him for ever.

I wake the next morning in a king-sized bed, in a huge warehouse apartment that is geographically close to our home, but a million miles away. I am naked. Benjamin, next to me, is naked too. I do not feel entirely comfortable, and what we did last night was not comfortable, nor, if I am honest, was it something I would have chosen to do. But it was what Benjamin wanted, and I would happily have done anything for him. A bit of physical pain is nothing, absolutely nothing, if it means he looks after me.

I stretch out, and he rolls over and takes hold of me. He pulls the duvet back, exposing my body, and he stares at me. I wriggle, uncomfortable with his gaze.

'Don't,' he breathes, stilling me with a hand on the stomach. 'Marianne. You're perfect. You have no idea. You know, this is your peak. This is perfection. Enjoy it.'

I lie there for a while, obediently, and let him look at me. When I think it has been long enough, I look up at him.

'I've got school,' I remind him. He bursts out laughing.

'Of course you have,' he says. 'Can't keep you off your GCSEs. You haven't got an exam today, have you?'

I nod. 'French oral. This afternoon.'

He smiles to himself. 'I must teach you a bit of French oral myself, at some point.'

'Oh that's OK. I already know it.'

He laughs, and runs his fingers through my hair. 'Do you?' he says. 'We'll see about that. I'll take you up to A-level standard.'

# chapter twenty-four

## Eliza

I don't want to have to tell Seth.

We have both known all along that there were a lot of things Lucy was not telling us, and we both tried to tell her that, for one thing, we weren't going to care about anything that happened to her in the past, and for another thing, she didn't have to tell us anything if she didn't want to. But she blanked the subject so completely that we could never even say that. The shutters came down totally. I've always been scared that it would catch her up one day, but I was thinking more in terms of her having a bit of a breakdown than her actually vanishing.

Seth was desperate for her to open up to him. He always thought he would lose her one day.

He wants to marry her. He wants them to have children, but that's something Lucy does not entertain to the point where he doesn't dare mention it. He, I think, has been hoping for a 'happy accident'.

I sit on my bed and stare at the letter in my right hand, and my phone in my left. I have to do something, and I have to do it now. He needs to know. I try to think what I would say to the police. I cannot get it all straight in my head. I need to speak to Seth before I do anything.

At first I thought she was playing a really clever game with him. My big brother was always a handsome boy, and he always had girls falling at his feet. They used to call the house: 'Hello, is Seth there please?', said quickly, nervously, all in one breathy exhalation.

He used to put me in horrible positions. I had to respond with: 'I'll just go and check, who is it please?' and then, if he was next to me, I had to write down her name on the pad that was beside the phone. He would nod or shake his head. I would try to convey the 'no' in a convincing way: I would walk away from the phone and then come back and say, 'I'm sorry, Sarah, I think he's just gone to the shop.' Sarah would ask me to get him to call her when he came back. I would pretend that there was any chance at all of that happening.

When he grew up, he was just as lazy. He always had women flocking around him, so he made no effort and went out with Page Three girls (they looked like Page Three girls, that is – they weren't, as far as I know). At school, those sorts of girls pretended that they wanted to be my friends so they could get closer to Seth. Later, when we grew up, they despised me, those women, because I was not at all like them, and because I was close to Seth in a way they would never be. I despaired of ever having a sister-in-law, let alone one I would actually want to speak to.

And then Lucy came along. I met her at the godawful book club I used to go to because I thought it would be good for me (had I known – had I only known – I would have spent every single evening cuddling Graham on the sofa, making the most of him, being part of him while I still could). She looked so miserable that I invited her to our party, and that was where she met Seth, and he changed, completely, beyond all recognition.

I thought she was being elusive and hard-to-get on purpose, to reel him in. But she did reel him in, completely, and she was still elusive. And now she has gone.

I scroll down to his number. My thumb hovers over the 'call' button.

I change my mind, and get Lucy's number up instead. When I call it, it goes straight to voicemail. I leave her a garbled message that I hope she will hear.

'Please come back,' I say at the end. 'Please. Please.' I tail off, and then hang up.

Then, finally, I ring him. It has to be done.

# chapter twenty-five

At the Gare du Nord, a cluster of French police scanning the crowds made my heart stop. They were more frightening than the British police: their unfamiliar uniforms were terrifying, the guns on their belts worse. Their faces were set, uncompromising. While I was watching, from a distance, one of them caught my eye. He stared at me and I had no idea why. I modified my course and walked in a loop, as far from the police as I could. I looked back up. The man was still watching. There were hundreds of travellers on this station, and I moved with the crowd, trying to blend in. I had always blended in, and I ran through the reasons why he might have noticed me. I supposed I must have guilt and fear all over my face.

I looked up again. He had broken away from the group, and was heading towards me, on a course that would cut me off, no matter which way I tried to go. I had no idea what on earth he could want.

I considered turning and heading back to the train. He would know, if I did that, that I had something to hide, and he would run after me.

He had a tanned face, his mouth set in a line. He did not look like a man who compromised. His eyes bore into me as he came closer and closer. Hundreds of people separated us, but they were a mirage: there was no one on this station but me and this man.

I forced myself to keep walking. The crowds parted before

him. Then I heard a shout behind me. The other officers started heading my way too. I looked back. There was a man, a black man, behind me, and he was starting to run. The officer I had thought was after me was on top of him in a second. The rest of them piled in. They had him on the ground. He was fighting back. I watched the policeman I had thought was coming after me raining blows down on this other man, and then I looked away and hurried on.

I stopped as briefly as I could at the tourist information, found out what I needed to know, and ran, finally giving into my impulse, to the shops in the station concourse.

By the time I stepped on to the Metro, I was still wearing my skirt, but my top was in my bag, and in its place I was wearing a tight white T-shirt which proclaimed *J' ♥ Paris* in red and blue letters. There were bright yellow Crocs on my feet; I hated Crocs with a vengeance, but I was trying to change my appearance, and me wearing Crocs was definitely a change. They were shockingly comfortable, and suddenly I understood their appeal.

Not only that, but I was also in possession of all the euros the cashpoint had allowed me to withdraw. The wedge was folded over in the pocket inside my little rucksack. The cash I had amassed was barely going to cover the next stage of my journey, and I knew I was going to have to find a bank and convert the Visa card into as many euros as I possibly could.

The Paris Metro was, it turned out, a good place to be paranoid. It was dark, grimy, and thickly populated by men with swept-back black hair and expensive coats. I hurried through, keeping my head down.

I had never heard of the Gare de Bercy, but apparently it was the place I wanted. It was in an obscure part of Paris, somewhere that seemed devoid of landmarks and views. There were odd modernish facades, crowded apartment blocks, Asian restaurants and a dodgy-looking shopfront offering 'Relaxation Massage Asiatique'. The station itself was small, ugly and hot, and thronging with groups of young people with backpacks.

There was a long, stultifying queue in the ticket office, winding obediently between blue cordons. I shifted my weight from foot to foot, trying to look normal. In fact, in this environment, more than anywhere else I had yet been, I could merge into the crowd. Everyone was dressed in weird, dirty-looking combinations of outfits. All the youngsters near me looked wide-eyed and baffled. In their cases, it was because they had been travelling randomly around Europe for weeks and were not quite sure which country they were in.

I was torn between obsessively checking everyone who came into the vicinity, and staring at the back of the man in front of me. He was so acne-scarred that it extended to the back of his neck, and I felt sad for him. That took my attention, at least, for a few moments. Then I went back to looking around. It was agony: I was standing still, a sitting target, and I had no idea if anyone was watching me.

It took twenty-three minutes for me to reach the front of the queue. I knew because I watched the clock behind the desks. The black hand jumped forward every time the minute changed.

When I tried to ask for my ticket in clumsy, long-forgotten French, the woman, who had lustrous black hair and pretty eyes, immediately dropped into English. She tapped at her keyboard.

'Only first class,' she said. 'Only one place left.' I shrugged, and paid a lot of euros, and suddenly I was holding my ticket. I had the last compartment on the train. I now had fifteen euros to my name.

The train was leaving at half past eight. Sitting on the station for three hours was an unbearable prospect. Bercy was far from the airy, romantic Parisian station of my imagination and I had to get out of it. Now that I was leaving, I had to be the steely runaway again, the teenage girl who depended on no one. The only way I could do this was to be as paranoid as I could possibly be.

I had to keep following the plan I had been dwelling on for years. I had to make sure that once Seth, or anybody, realised that I had gone to Paris, they would not be able to track my next step, because there would be too many paths to follow.

With the ticket safely at the bottom of my bag, I went back to the Metro, caught a train to the Bastille, because I had heard of it, and set about looking for a bank. It took a while to find one; Paris appeared to be filled with clothes, souvenirs, and expensive fruit shops. Eventually, however, a branch of Crédit Agricole loomed up at me.

The interior was shiny, cream, fake-marble. There were posters with pictures of houses on them, and cartoon families holding the keys to their new car.

'*Oui, madame?*' asked the girl at the desk, who looked about eleven.

I handed my card over, and wondered just how bad my French was going to be.

'*Je voudrais de l'argent*,' I said. I want some money. '*Combien de l'argent est-ce que je peux avoir?*'

The girl giggled, put a hand to her tiny mouth.

'You would like to withdraw money on this card?' she checked, in excellent English.

'*All* the money from the card,' I said.

Phone calls were made. I had to hand over my passport, which was photocopied and certified. The girl had to summon the manager, and together they pored over the paperwork. They asked me over and over again whether I was sure. I stood there for well over an hour, but in the end I walked out of the building with fourteen thousand euros in my scruffy black bag.

I practically ran to Austerlitz station, where I queued again and bought a ticket to Avignon, for a train that left at half past five. I paid for it with my normal British bank card. Then I went to an internet centre inside the station and bought a Eurostar ticket back to London. For good measure I also purchased a third-class sleeper ticket to Madrid, which would leave that night. Now it would take any imaginary pursuer a while to work out which train I had actually taken. I felt bad about the money I had taken from the account we both used, which was not exactly overflowing with funds, and promised myself that I would pay it back when I could.

I had an hour and a quarter before my train left, and a lot of things I needed to do.

The big Galeries Lafayette was such an enormous shop that I felt defeated the moment I stepped in through the door. I took a deep breath, and marched to the escalators.

I tried nothing on. I picked things up, held them over my arm, and then went and paid for the whole lot. It took fifteen minutes, and then I was armed with a wardrobe of lovely new clothes. They were neutral: I did not want to be recognisably English. I had tops and T-shirts in black and beige. I bought jeans that looked as if they might fit, and two pretty but forgettable cotton skirts. I got three pairs of flip-flops and some nail polish. I paid for it all in cash. Then I decided that finally, after all these years, it was time for me to lose my hair. There was, I hoped, just about time.

I had a strange relationship with my hair. For years I had kept it as long as I could, even though I knew it would look better short. It had thickened as I reached adulthood, and although it was a pale imitation of my mother's, it was all right if I brushed it. Mum had cut it on the day we found out that she was ill: for some reason this fact had made me keep it long, as if long hair would stave off other disasters.

Ten minutes later, I was sitting in a random Parisian hairdresser's, in the seat furthest from the door. I pointed to a picture in a magazine and waited for the woman to laugh at the very idea that I might have a haircut like the one belonging to the model, but she simply nodded and led me to the basins to get my hair washed. I didn't try to converse. I just sat there and watched, as the strands I had maintained as some sort of pathetic tribute to the woman I could not think about were cut away and dropped on to the smeary white tiles of the floor.

I made an effort not to convulse with long-repressed emotion as I recalled myself sitting at the kitchen table in Mile End while my mother did exactly this, while she gave me this very haircut, this precise slanted bob. 'Jaw-length bob?' she said, in my head, as if she were actually there.

When it was done, I smiled at myself, and at the woman, and touched the back of my neck. It felt odd, and I looked completely different. I looked like someone who had somewhere to go. I did not look like someone who was so scared of a confrontation that she left an entire life to avoid it.

I looked radically different, astonishingly so. With my new hair and my new clothes, perhaps I would be able to merge into Europe.

The entire haircut had taken half an hour. I paid with cash, and tipped her handsomely, then set off back to the station. I wished I had a moment for the Rodin museum, as the woman on the train had suggested. I wanted to go somewhere peaceful, to try out my new persona. However, I barely had time to catch my train. I set off to dash back to the Gare de Bercy.

The station was still crowded, still hot and frustrating, but this time I was going straight through it. I pushed my way into a crowd of Italian students and stood there for a few minutes, scanning the concourse. People pulled suitcases behind them, and backpackers wore overloaded rucksacks. A woman scooped up her tiny dog and put it carefully into her handbag.

My train was waiting at platform U, and it was going to leave in eight minutes. I took a deep breath, shoved a few students aside, and strode to the platform. I could see my train, kept glancing up to read the intoxicating name of my destination on the indicator boards. It was somewhere I had always wanted to go, the place in Europe that was pulling me.

I had memorised my carriage number (92), my berth number (56). I kept my head down and marched along the platform, kept going and going and going until I feared the train was going to leave before I found the right door. There were a few clusters of people further along the platform, but almost all the doors were closed, and the train was finally ready to go.

On the other platform, on my left, there was an apparently endless Motorail train, loaded completely with cars. That looked full, and so did this train. The holiday season was in full swing.

When I reached coach 92, there was a gaggle of people at the door, and a woman and child leaning out of the window, saying farewells that were both lengthy and tearful, in French. I coughed and tapped and said, '*Excusez-moi*,' until the departure party moved resentfully out of the way, and I managed to wrench the door open and step on to the train.

A uniformed guard, wearing a maroon waistcoat and a peaked cap, materialised in front of me and asked for my ticket. He laughed and said something in Italian, then flipped into English.

'Just in time,' he said, and the train pulled away.

My compartment was small and perfect, with three seats, a hand basin tucked into a cupboard, and what looked like two more beds folded away into the walls, ready to be flipped down. Out of the window, the Motorail train and a concrete building behind it went on and on. The evening light was shining on to everything and making it glint and glisten. I stretched my legs out and held my breath. I kept the compartment door open so that I wouldn't have to worry that someone was loitering outside. Nobody was out there: no one was interested in me. I was anonymous, and it was suddenly, briefly, perfect.

I was in a double or triple berth, and because I had paid so many euros, I had clearly booked the other bed too. I sat down heavily on the seat, my alertness suddenly vanishing, overtaken by fatigue and by the motion of the train. As I stared at the urban landscape of Paris giving way to suburbs, and then nothingness, in the dusk, there was a purposeful rap on the open door.

My head jerked around. I was on guard, heart pounding, fingers clenched into palms. I was trapped. There was nowhere to go.

The carriage guard had taken off his cap, and his hair was black-grey and springy.

'For breakfast?' he said. 'In the morning? Cappuccino and croissant?'

I smiled. 'Yes please,' I said. I closed the door behind him, and locked it.

Ten minutes later, a woman terrified me by knocking again, so I had to stand up and unlock the door. She asked whether I would like to eat in the restaurant (answer: no). Instead, I stood in the corridor for a while, while the guard transformed my row of seats into a bed. I changed into one of my new T-shirts and clean knickers, brushed my teeth, and climbed between the sheets. I stared at the ceiling, and ate an apple. The train man came by again to tell me to lock the door, and I locked myself in, and I was safe.

# chapter twenty-six

## Marianne

I buy a lot of cleaning products, and scrub the kitchen as hard as I can. I run hot water into the sink, and fill it with bubbles. I spray the surfaces, scour them, spray them again, scour them again. I bleach all the cups and plates overnight, and then wash them and rinse them. I open the windows and let the air in. It turns back into Mum's house.

Finn doesn't comment. He is not speaking to me, because I am spending so much time with Benjamin. He knows what I am doing. He detests it, and he despises me.

He is focused on his social life, while I have let mine drop, and I see no one but Benjamin. I can cope with this now. I can get through the months. I make Finn do his work. Sometimes I do it for him. I am doing my exams, and I think I am stumbling through. I will not be emerging with the row of As that I was meant to get, but it will be respectable.

I don't want to carry on with my education after this. All I want is Benjamin. I would do anything for him. When I am with him, it all feels possible. He knows our darkest secret. I told him about the pills we gave her, and he still wants to be with me. This is the most amazing thing in the world.

Finn does not see it that way.

'He owns us,' he says. He is sitting at the table, watching me clean up. He would not dream of helping.

'It's not my fault,' I tell him. I am trying to stay calm. It would be so easy to turn on Finn, but I am responsible for him, and I mustn't. 'It's not my fault he turned up that night.'

'No, but he can do what he wants now, can't he? Because if we piss him off, he'll tell on us.'

'Tell on us? Is he five?'

'Shut up.'

'You shut up.'

We glare at each other. Finn stands up and gathers his things together.

'I'm off,' he says.

'Bye,' I say cheerfully. I have no idea whether he is off out of the kitchen, or out of the house. He wants me to ask, so I don't.

He pauses in the doorway. 'We could have done this, you know,' he says, as a parting shot. 'We could have stuck together. If you hadn't gone and thrown yourself at that creep.'

'Yeah,' I tell him. 'Right.'

He stamps away. I hear the front door slam.

# chapter twenty-seven

It was morning, and it was undeniably Italy.

There were snow-specked mountains just visible through the haze, far away. There were houses with terracotta roof tiles. There were cars and there were people walking, some with baskets. There was washing hanging out of windows. No one of those things, individually, would have signified Italy, but somehow the whole collection of details did. Perhaps it was just because I knew that was where I had to be when I woke up this morning.

We were at a station. That was what had woken me: the cessation of the cradling motion. I sat by the window, the blind open, and stared. This was so completely random. I was in Italy: not London, not Cornwall, not even Paris. I was, this morning, in Verona.

I dressed quickly. There was a knock on the door, and the man in the dark red uniform appeared, checked I was awake, then smiled and handed me a breakfast tray. All of a sudden, I was hungry. I tore open the plastic wrapper of the croissant, and dipped it into the coffee, and although the pastry was lumpy and too sweet, it was the best thing I had ever eaten. There was a carton of generic fruit juice, which might as well have been sugar-water, but that was nectar to me.

I dressed quickly in a short cotton skirt that was patterned with blue flowers, and a black T-shirt, and I felt good, though I could have done with a shower. The sun was shining, and I was heading to a place I never thought I would actually see. I had forgotten how addictive it was, running away. I had, I thought, pulled it off so far.

I gazed, rapt, out of the window as we stopped at Padua. I kept my compartment door open, so I could see people walking down the corridor, and listen to conversations in the vicinity.

The next compartment was occupied by an English man and his son, a boy called Richard, even though no one called little boys Richard any more. He was, I thought, about eight, a little bit older than Imogen. I shook my head and tried not to think of Imogen and Clara.

'Can we phone Mummy?' Richard asked.

Seconds ticked by. His father did not reply. 'Maybe later,' he said after a while. 'Now, what can you tell me about Italian politics?'

'Berlusconi,' the boy said.

'Yes. First name?'

'Silvio.'

'Good! Anything else?'

'Japan is Fukuda,' the boy offered.

'Good lad.'

I thought of Eliza. I knew she would have had a few comments to make about this man's parenting style. I could hear her voice, too clearly, in my head. She would have been sharp, then understanding. 'Oh, he's probably a weekend father,' she said now. 'Poor thing. He's doing his best.' I felt a strange, brief envy of the boy: at least he had a father. I had no idea what that was like. I had lost my father before I even took my first breath, and then my mother, and my brother, and now I had lost Seth and Eliza, my new family, as well. I could not think about that.

We were on the causeway, heading out over the water to the world's most unlikely city. The last thing I saw on the mainland was a car park.

There was water outside my window. There was going to be water everywhere. It was magical. And suddenly my heart leapt, because I was going to the place that had haunted my dreams for ever, the city that had long been my imaginary haven, the place in which I was trusting I was going to be all right. The place that Mum had stuck on the wall of our little house in east London.

I had to be all right in Venice. I held on to that instinct, and craned my neck to see the city itself, across the water.

# chapter twenty-eight

## Marianne

The first time I say 'my boyfriend', the world shifts on its axis, and it is never the same again. I am fifteen years and eleven months old. Benjamin, it turns out, is thirty-six. I am an adult. I understand the world now. I have a place in it. I am no longer sheltered. I find myself looking down on the way I used to be, sneering at the absurd innocence of the girl who used to come home from school excited about the possibility of a home-made cake. I thought I was grown up when I managed to drink a cup of coffee. I had only been wearing a bra for three years. To me, the cheap white BHS ones that Mum had bought me had been the height of sophistication.

Now I drink champagne. I wear scratchy bits of funny-shaped underwear that Benjamin gives me. He likes me to put on a bra and some knickers that go up my bum, and suspenders and high heels, and stand in front of him while he takes photos. I don't mind, because if I do this for him, he does masses more for me. He looks after me and makes sure I do my exams and he even helps me revise. I think about the way we would have been, Finn and I, had we kept this secret from Benjamin the way we were supposed to, the way we were trying to do it. I can see us now, descending into squalor in our filthy house, the two of us desperately trying to keep the world away from us. It would not have worked. This way, it does work.

I can relax with Benjamin. I can talk to him. He takes care of me in a way that I would never have imagined possible. He makes me feel interesting and irresistible. He makes me sexy. I rarely admit it to myself, but I would not have chosen to go straight into a sexual relationship like this. But that is what Benjamin wants me to do, and so I do it, because I would do anything for him. It's not too bad, anyway: I am getting used to it, and although it leaves me sore, he treats me like a goddess the rest of the time.

I am sitting on the grass outside school, after an exam, on my own. I avoid the company of everyone at school. I don't even think I really live in the same world as them. I see them through a pane of glass, a smeared one at that. I am sore and chafing from Benjamin's attentions to me last night, and I have just sat an English literature paper and I think I did well enough. I managed to spew out the standard answers about *Macbeth*, *Great Expectations* and *Of Mice and Men*. I know it was fine.

My head is pounding with a slight hangover. I really, really want to sleep.

The grass is scraggly and a bit muddy underneath. I stretch my legs out in front of me. They still look like schoolgirl's legs. I wear my uniform properly these days, so that no one from school can try to ring Mum and complain about me. So my legs, today, are wearing white socks and a school uniform dress, which is blue and white checked. I know that the mud will stain the back of my dress, but I don't care. In fact, I want that to happen. I want to be soiled and filthy. I lie back and look up at the sky. There are more clouds than there ought to be. They are arriving quickly, scudding in from all over the place, congregating right above me.

I put my hand over my eyes, and tell myself again that I am happy.

Katy comes and sits down next to me. She is much taller than I am, these days. She is tall and skinny, with heavy black hair and round glasses. When I look at her, I imagine the way Benjamin might react to her. I think he would be a bit scathing about her, because she is neither particularly pretty nor girlish.

I don't talk to her much any more. I remember us, the way

we used to be, but I can't do it any more. Sometimes I miss having her as a friend. I know that the things that have happened to me have pulled me away from all my friends. My friends are grown-ups now. Even Moz is too young for me.

When I stop, though, I wish and wish and wish that things could be the way they were, just for a day, just for an hour. Then I stop wishing. There is no point in wishing. I look up at the sky. The only thing to do is to get on with it. Life, I have discovered, is hard and nothing works out the way you want it to.

I don't think about Mum, don't remember her, and I don't long for her. I try not even to think about the fact that I don't think about her. I have erased her. This is bad, but it is the only thing that gets me through the days.

Katy smiles at me. It is hard to be friends with someone when they don't know that your mother's dead. All the same, I try to smile back.

'You all right?' she says.

'Yes,' I tell her. 'Yes. Fine. You?'

'Oh, I'm doing OK. It's a relief, isn't it? The exams are nearly over. Freedom! I'm going to Florida with my family afterwards. What are you doing?'

I had better say something. 'Going to Italy,' I improvise. 'If we can afford it.'

I manage a small smile. The pictures of Venice are still on the walls at home. Mum always said she would take us there one day. She was fixated by the place, enraptured at the idea of a city whose streets were made from water.

'Mum's taking us to Venice,' I add.

'Brilliant. Lucky you. I'd love to go on a gondola. *So* romantic!'

'Are you staying for sixth form?'

'Yeah, of course. You're not, are you?'

'I'm going to college,' I say quickly. The sun goes behind a cloud.

She looks at me uncertainly. 'That sounds good,' she says, but she is not sure.

'I might move in with my boyfriend,' I add, and I see her relax. I watch as she understands why I have been so distracted, why

I have stopped bothering with her company. It is, in Katy's eyes, the age-old story. Girl gets boyfriend, girl dumps friends.

'I didn't know you had a boyfriend,' she says, and she smiles and shifts closer to me. 'Tell me about him, then. He's not from school, is he, or I'd have known. Unless it's Moz? Is it Moz?'

My head is still spinning. I called Benjamin my boyfriend. I am his girlfriend. We are a couple. I grow two inches taller, sit up straight, shoulders back. I see Katy across an impassable gulf. She does not have a boyfriend, and even if she did, it would be a boy of our age, someone who had no clue.

'No,' I say. 'It's not Moz. His name is Ben. And he's a bit older than me. He's not at school any more.'

His name is not Ben. He is adamant that he will never answer to 'Ben'. And I will never tell Katy exactly how much older than me he is. I will let her think he's nineteen, because she would never understand the truth.

# chapter twenty-nine

## Eliza

Seth came to London straight away. We are going to find her. We have kept the same hotel room, in case she comes back, and we have texted her to say we are here.

It is hard, beyond that, to know where to start. London is enormous. More people live here than in the whole of Cornwall, and I would never expect to stumble upon someone in Cornwall, let alone here.

I met Seth's train at Paddington. He hates this city, but he is so terribly worried about Lucy that he seems to have forgotten about that. When he came through the ticket barrier, he looked terrible. He looked the way I think I used to look, in the weeks after the accident. His eyes were darting around everywhere, as if there was a chance that she might actually have been on the station.

I took his arm. 'Come on,' I said. 'She's OK, you know. She's alive. She's just gone off to sort something out.'

'Where's the letter?'

I handed it to him. It was on creamy hotel stationery, written with a cheap hotel biro.

Seth stopped. People carried on walking around us. I watched him reading it. It was definitely her handwriting.

He stared at it for ages. Then he said: 'This is fucked.' He was so angry. 'Dear fucking Eliza? She's my partner. My fiancée. Where's the letter to *me*? I get a text: concert was amazing. She forgot to say P.S. Goodbye.'

* * *

We went to the police. Just walked into a police station and said that our friend had gone missing. We sat in a little room with the world's most junior policeman, whom I suspected of being the work experience boy. He kept looking at his watch and I could see that he wanted to smile.

I told him about the concert, about how she came back after the interval looking white as a surrendering flag, and how she said she thought she saw someone from her past, but that it hadn't been them.

'So if I hadn't got those tickets,' Seth said in a quiet voice. I could only ignore him. I went on to say that she'd seemed fine afterwards, and we went back to the hotel and had some more wine, and then in the morning she wasn't there any more. I showed him the letter and Seth showed him his text.

'Sorry,' the policeman said, when he'd read it. 'I'll take a copy of this and keep it on file. But it clearly states that she went of her own accord. There's frankly sod-all we can do. We'll keep an eye out, and if you hear anything that makes you think she is in trouble, by all means get back in touch.' He was looking through the open door, and when a woman in a cheap suit came past, he leapt half out of his seat and called: 'Hey, Helen, get us a biscuit!'

So we are back in the hotel room. Seth will sleep in Lucy's bed tonight. He keeps smelling the sheets. He is sitting on the bed now, calling round all the hospitals. I am staring at my phone, waiting for her to text. I called the O2 management earlier, and asked them to look through their CCTV footage to see if they could spot Lucy meeting this mystery stranger, the one who wasn't the person she was scared of, just in case we could get any clue from that, but they said no. They said they would do it if the police asked them to, but otherwise they did not give a shit (I am paraphrasing), and they added that there were twenty thousand people in the arena last night. So that plan seemed like a bit of a non-starter.

Then I went down to reception and asked the woman there if she could tell me what time Lucy left. She said: 'Of course, I have no idea,' but she said that Robert was on reception last night and we could ask him when he came back on at ten tonight.

'But he might not remember,' she warned, and then she looked at me all sternly, until I left.

I look over at Seth. He is saying, 'Right, fine, thanks, yes. Well, in case you do get a woman who could be my fiancée, could I leave you my number?'

Lucy pulled him up every time he called her his fiancée. I don't think, however, that this is the appropriate moment to correct him.

The girls are still with our parents. They will be fine there for a few more days. It will be an adventure for them. I told Seth that we would be going back to Falmouth with Auntie Lucy in tow, that we would all go to pick the girls up together, but I know that we won't. We have no idea where in this city, or out of it, she might be. She told us she grew up here, but she never said where.

I am going to have to tell the girls that Auntie Lucy has gone away. She will be in touch when she can. I have to believe it.

# chapter thirty

I stepped down from the train, and the smell of the water hit me in the face. The station was like many other stations, but for that smell, and for the signs that proclaimed *Venezia Santa Lucia*.

Santa Lucia: St Lucy. I forced a smile at that. Lucy was in the past, and it was true, she had been good while she lasted.

I stood still for a moment, letting everyone else flow around me. The heat of the morning seeped into my body. The warm salty air filled my lungs. I closed my eyes.

In one hand I held a black rucksack that was filled with cash and papers. In the other, an enormous Galeries Lafayette carrier bag, with my new identity inside it. I could feel the slight breeze on the back of my neck. I knew I looked different, but I also knew I did not look different enough.

I pulled the backpack on to my back and quickly joined the throng of people heading down the platform towards the station buildings. There were backpackers and tourists pulling suitcases, old people, the very young, and everyone in between. I became one of them, just like that.

The world felt new. Even the recent past faded away. The woman who had been to the concert, the one who lived with Seth, the one who buried her mother. All of them had died.

I had stepped from a first-class rail carriage on to the platform. That was it.

* * *

The platform was crowded. I could hear Richard and his father, walking somewhere behind me.

'What are we going to buy?' asked the father.

'A three-day Venice Card,' Richard answered.

'Good lad.'

There was a babble of languages: English, French, Spanish, and lots and lots of Italian. I let the crowd carry me along. I regulated my breath, closed my mind, and thought about nothing. I started to feel as if I were invisible.

In the interior of the station, I caught a glimpse of shimmering water through thick glass and brass doors, and I kept my face away from it. I queued at the tourist information office, still listening to Richard and his father as they bought their three-day Venice Card:

'There will be a phone at the hotel, won't there, Dad, so maybe I can phone Mummy?'

'Hmm, we'll see.'

I bought a seven-day vaporetto pass. Then I pulled one bag on to my shoulder, hoisted the other one up from the floor, and set off, through the heavy doors, and down the steps.

This city was absurd. It was a heightened, more extreme version of the way I had expected it to be. It was a painting, an illusion. The light glinted off the water, and made me screw up my eyes. The buildings on the other side of the shimmering expanse of turquoise were flat-fronted, dignified, standing looking over the canal. The light bleached out their colour, and dazzled me.

The station's steps were wide and smooth, trodden down by hundreds of years of travellers' feet. Groups of people sat on them, idling the time away, talking, laughing, reading guide books and newspapers in languages I did not recognise.

I made my way down quickly, and, taking lungfuls of the hot air, followed the crowd to the vaporetto stop. A boat arrived, number 42, and I pushed hard to secure my place on it. A woman in uniform, with long curly hair, pulled a barrier closed just as I got on. The boat pulled away, out into the Grand Canal. I forced my way to the railing at the far side, where I used my elbows to create a tiny space for myself. The people next to me were speaking French. Further away, I could hear Spanish, and Italian. There was no English.

I held my bags close, and leaned over so the wind was in my face and in my hair. On a balcony on the front of a building across the water, a man and a woman were sitting on wrought-iron chairs. They were looking out at the city. The woman's hair was in a short bob with her neck exposed, like mine. The man, from here, could have been Seth.

I stared at them, craning backwards to keep them in sight until we zigzagged to a stop on the other side of the canal, and they were gone.

Every time the boat stopped, I listened to the shouty woman yelling in Italian, getting people off, getting people on, getting them to move down the inside of the boat, where the seats were, even though almost everybody was a tourist and no one wanted to be indoors. They all wanted to stand on the deck and lean over the railings and look at the city, with the wind in their hair.

Luckily she was authoritative. I watched her as her hair flew around in the hot breeze, as she barked instructions in irresistible Italian, caressing the words. I liked the sound of Italian, the way it dipped up and down in a manner that flat, sensible English could never imitate.

With my bag full of money, I would be able to stay here for a while. I could learn the language, go into churches and look at art and architecture. I could ride the vaporetto up and down the Grand Canal, around the island. I could stand on the deck and lean on the railings and watch. If I stayed here long enough, I might be able to settle in. If I learned to blend into the mass of humanity that this island hosted, I might never have to run away again.

The sun was getting hotter. The sky was a deep and implausible blue. There was an underlying scent of salty water, but mostly I could smell other people's sweat, mingled with deodorant, occasional strong perfumes, and European men's cologne. People crushed up against me, and pushed me farther over the rail, but

I refused to engage. I stood my ground and carried on occupying my small part of this city.

Other iconic places, I thought, were not like this. Other places had traffic and corner shops and tower blocks, and you had to seek out the beauty, the thing that would take your breath away.

Venice was different. Every detail was perfectly Venetian. I stared and stared, as we chugged past palazzi and Renaissance churches, and hotels, and more palaces, and terraces and tiny courtyard gardens. We passed gondolas, and restaurants with canal-side tables and awnings, and people seeing it all through lenses, in every conceivable spot. I knew that I could travel this same stretch of water again and again, and see different details each time. A building that was leaning to one side, visibly crumbling. Another that was covered in scaffolding, mid-restoration. The front of the Peggy Guggenheim Foundation, whatever that was. The façade of the Accademia. The Rialto Bridge – here, finally, was a mild disappointment, because the doors of the little buildings on it were covered in graffiti and it was crowded with so many people that they looked as if they were part of the architecture.

I tried to edit out the people. They were my camouflage, nothing more. I saw the marble church, the yellow palace, the distant shape of the cupola, of the spire. I knew, even as I felt this overarching amazement, that it was a brief reprieve. I was running in a dream from my past, and it all felt like a hallucination. It would become real at some point. I had walked out on the people I loved, the people who loved me, my chance of a normal life. I knew that I was being foolish by coming here and imagining that I could start again. All the same, I was enraptured, and I tried hard to postpone the moment when I would have to acknowledge the cold reality.

The boat stopped every few metres, on one bank and then the other, to disgorge and take on passengers. Nearly an hour must have passed before we arrived at St Mark's Square. I recognised the Doge's Palace and the bell tower from far away. The whole area was heaving with people: it was hard to get a single glimpse of the paving slabs that I assumed covered the ground. There were just heads, and brightly coloured T-shirts, and endless, endless flesh. It all moved up and down, shifted around in the sort of complex patterns that, if viewed from above, would probably sort themselves into geometric shapes according to chaos theory. From here, it was simple chaos.

Everyone got off the boat. Very few people got on. I took a deep breath, and stretched my arms above my head. This was the end of the Grand Canal. I was going to have to set foot on land, to engage with this city.

I stepped on to a worn paving stone and looked around. I could not face the huge crowds of St Mark's Square, so carried on along the bank. I walked until I felt I had left the square behind. When I saw a hotel on my left, looking like an old palace, I went into it without hesitation. Its outside was a rusty colour, with gothic pointed windows looking out over the lagoon. I looked up at the name over the door: HOTEL GABRIELLI SANDWIRTH. The 'Gabrielli' was properly Italian, the 'Sandwirth' baffling.

The interior made me stop and almost laugh, and then it made me think of Seth with so vivid a pang that I had to stand still for a second. He would have adored it. It was pure seventies kitsch, and looked as if no detail had been touched for thirty years. There was a long, boardroom-type table in the middle of the huge foyer, with a green baize top, and dusty flowers. My new footwear flipped and flopped as I crossed the room. A Japanese woman sitting in a small armchair looked up from the postcards she was writing, saw me, and looked down again.

The man at the concierge desk stared resolutely at a piece of paper, even when I was standing across the desk from him. I bent my knees to try to force myself into his field of vision. He looked up, then rearranged his jowly features into a smile. He was a heavy man in his late forties, entirely devoid of hair, although he had luscious long eyelashes.

'*Buongiorno*,' he said. '*Signora*.'

'*Buongiorno*,' I said, savouring the first word I had spoken. 'Do you have a room?' It seemed like a reasonable thing to do, speaking English, here in the middle of touristic Venice.

He smiled again. '*Si, signora*,' he said. 'You are lucky.' He started tapping at a computer. I didn't want to be a *signora. Signoras* were married women with responsibilities, not stupid runaways. I was a *signorita*. I did not, however, correct him: I supposed that I was going to be forty at some point in the foreseeable future, and that this fact was visible to the outside world, however young and lost I might feel. 'I have two rooms available,' he said, in excellent English. 'For you I recommend room 513.'

'OK,' I agreed. 'Room 513. How much?'

He looked amused. 'You don't want to know the size of the room? The view?'

I shook my head. 'No.'

'OK. How long you want to stay?'

I was buoyed up by the illusion of liquidity in my bag, the wedge of borrowed cash.

'Six nights,' I said, at random.

'So, six nights, I can do you a better price. Saturday night is more. But six nights: eight hundred and seventy euro.'

I bit my lip, then nodded. There were no rules at the moment, and I had the money. I had already decided to stay in this place. I started to count out the cash.

'No, no. You pay when you leave,' he said, quickly. 'You just give me a credit card now.'

I couldn't risk it. 'Please can I pay you now?' I said. 'Truly, honestly. I want to. Then I won't need to give a credit card, will I?'

He shook his head. 'For security, I need a card number.'

I hesitated. 'I won't have anything from the minibar, I promise. In fact, take the minibar away. If there is one. Is there a minibar?'

'Yes. But I'm sorry, *signora*. I am obliged.'

'If I gave you a card number, you wouldn't charge anything to it?'

'No.'

'Will it show up on the statement?'

'No. Not when I use my old machine.' He took one of the antiquated machines that worked with carbon paper, and made an impression of my card.

I paid a huge amount of cash, up front.

'Passport?' he asked, holding out a hand.

I tried to look appealing. The effect was doubtless nauseating, but there was nothing much I could do about that.

'Do you have to have it?' I asked. I saw that he was about to say yes. So I added: 'I'm running away from someone. He's violent. I don't want him to be able to trace me.'

The truth of my words hit me in the solar plexus. I screwed my hands into fists and swallowed hard. I forced it all back into its box. I realised I was going to be running for ever.

He looked at me. I stared back, desperate, unblinking. Seconds ticked by. Someone dropped something, a knife on a marble floor, in the distance.

He leaned forward.

'You show me your passport,' he said, quietly. 'I will write the number down wrong. Tell no one.'

I put a twenty-euro note on the counter, but acted as if I hadn't. It was a clumsy manoeuvre, but I thought it might have been the right thing to do. He covered it with his hand, casually, and then it was gone.

'Thank you,' I whispered. '*Grazie, signor*.'

When I stepped into room 513, I gasped. Then I forgot myself, and jumped up and down on the spot.

'Oh my God! Look at the fucking view!' I shouted. The minion whom the bald man had instructed to take me up in the pistachio-coloured lift laughed too, and I didn't think it was in a bad way.

I had a room in Venice. It was small, with barely enough space to walk around the bed. It was on the top floor of the old palazzo hotel, on a bank of the lagoon. It was decorated entirely generically, with some bland artworks above the bed and an apricot bedspread. And it had two windows.

One of them looked directly over a wide expanse of water towards a white church with a simple dome. The other faced along the wide stretch of paved walkway, towards St Mark's Square. The campanile, the bell tower, rose in the near distance. Between me and it, the row of buildings curved around, following the waterway. They were hotels, restaurants, probably galleries, possibly private homes. My side window was at the top of a sloping roof, and the terracotta tiles stretched below me. I was in the attic.

The people moved around, far below. I turned to the porter and handed him a five-euro note. He looked surprised, and thanked me four times in quick succession.

'Good stay, miss,' he said, and the door closed behind him with a heavy clunk.

I opened both of the windows, and leaned out. A gentle breeze ruffled my hair. I turned my face towards the sun. I had no plan, none at all, but I was here, and that was all I could ask for.

# chapter thirty-one

## Marianne

On the day of my last exam, I walk out of school and I know I am not going back. School thinks I am going to sixth-form college, so they are happy to send me on my way to do my three A levels and go to university. Mrs Barry thinks that they have done a good job with me, that I will do all right in my GCSEs. They have no fucking idea at all about just how much they have missed this year. So much for pastoral care.

I slip away without saying goodbye to anyone. They are having party after party in the next few weeks, and I am going to none of them. As I leave, I see Katy coming up behind me, trying to catch me up. I pretend I haven't seen her, and increase my pace. My education is over.

Benjamin refused to wait for me at the school gates.

'What would that look like?' he demanded this morning. 'Your friends would think I was a dirty old man. Not to mention your teachers. They'd think I was your dad. Or else they'd call the cops.'

I laughed and kissed him. 'No they wouldn't. You're much too young to be my dad.'

He sighed. 'Marianne. I *feel* too young. But technically speaking . . . Anyway. I'll be waiting around the corner, in the car. Come and find me, and we'll celebrate.'

I have a bag over my shoulder, a big heavy bag that contains everything that belonged to me that was in the school building.

I am going to be sixteen in four days' time. My childhood is over. It ended a long time ago, but now the rest of the world is catching up with me.

I don't talk to anyone. I see Moz at a distance, walking arm in arm with Mandy, and I raise a hand in farewell. He waves back, but doesn't stop. He has not forgiven me, will never forgive me for turning him down. He is the way my life could have been, if things had stayed the way they were. Although I would never have dared to speak to him if things had not changed, so I suppose that cannot be true.

The younger children swirl around me, all of them leaving on what is, for them, just another Thursday. I look around for Finn, hang back at the gates for a second watching for him. I don't see him. Katy is close to me now. I turn and jog away from her.

Benjamin is waiting two streets away, exactly where he said he would be, impossible to miss in his BMW. He sees me coming, and grins, and leans over to open the passenger door.

'Sweetie! Congratulations! How did it go?'

I smile and get in. I lean over and kiss him. I feel very grown up, behaving like this.

'Fine, thanks,' I tell him, although it was geography and I was too tired to concentrate. 'Well, I'm glad I had good marks for the coursework, anyway. So, what are we doing?'

I look at him, amazed all over again that this man, this older, sophisticated man with the film-star looks, this man who could have picked any woman in the world, has chosen me for his girlfriend. I never suggest anything for us to do, because I know nothing. I am happy to go where he takes me, to do what he wants us to do.

He smiles, that lopsided smile that I love so much.

'We'll ditch the car,' he says. 'Drop it back at the flat. Then we'll get a cab to a bar. We'll celebrate with champagne, and then there are some friends of mine I'd like you to meet. You'll like them.'

I nod, a bit wary. 'OK. But won't they think I'm a silly little girl?'

He laughs. 'Believe me, that is the very last thing in the world they're going to be thinking.'

I change into one of the outfits Benjamin keeps for me at his house. He is very particular about the way he likes me to dress when we go out. I am just happy that he buys me so many new clothes. It feels amazing to step out of my normal self and into someone else's.

'Here you go,' he says. He is holding up a blouse that buttons almost to the neck, and a short skirt. It is not my favourite, because I prefer it when he lets me dress like more of an adult. This outfit is almost like school uniform, except that the skirt is so short that even my crappy school would have noticed.

'Really?' I ask, reluctantly.

'Yes.' He is firm. I don't argue when he's like this.

'Are there any tights I can wear with it?'

'You don't need tights,' he says, and he turns away, pulling off his jeans. I hope he is changing too. I watch for a second. He is. This is a relief, although I would never tell him so. 'It's summer,' he says, doing up the belt on his suit trousers. 'You don't need tights.'

'The skirt is so short, though,' I say, in as meek a voice as I can manage.

He grins at that. 'I know. It looks brilliant. You can wear it with your school shoes. No need for heels. And just a bit of make-up.'

There is a full-length mirror beside the front door. I look at us just before we leave. My legs are not tanned enough to be bare like this, but if Benjamin likes it then I suppose they must look all right. The skirt is patterned in dark blue and grey, and the blouse is cream and silky. I am wearing a black cardigan with it, and my hair is in a ponytail, as it's grown enough now to be put up. I don't recognise myself. Still, I admit that I look good with Benjamin on my arm. He is wearing a loose suit without a tie, and he looks like a film star.

The bar is quiet, as it is only half past five when we get there. Benjamin steers us to a booth at the back, and sits me in the corner. He disappears to the bar, and arrives back followed by a waiter, who is carrying a bottle of champagne, an ice bucket, and four glasses.

I keep finding myself wishing that Mum could see me. In a way, I know she would hate this as much as Finn does (which is to say, a lot), but all the same, I am making something of myself, moving in sophisticated circles. I have pulled myself out of the desperation thing. I am no longer on the poverty diet.

The waiter looks hard at me for a few minutes. I start to feel uncomfortable, and shift in my seat. I look down at the table. I look at my fingernails, which are painted with a clear varnish, a bit chipped.

'Excuse me,' he says. He is much closer to my age than he is to Benjamin's, and he has longish, shaggy hair, but in a cool way. 'How old are you?'

'Eighteen,' I say, too quickly. I can feel him continuing to stare at me.

'Got any ID?' he asks.

Benjamin moves into action. I look at him, watch him deal with this situation.

'She's eighteen,' he says in his firm voice. He reaches out a hand, and I think he's trying to shake hands, which is odd. The barman shakes his hand and shrugs. He opens the champagne and pours us a glass each, then he leaves.

'How did you do that?' I say, when he's gone. 'How did you make him stop asking?'

Benjamin rolls his eyes. 'How do you think?' he asks.

It dawns on me. 'Did you pay him?' I feel so stupid.

'Of course. You're worth it.'

'Am I?'

'You know you are.'

'Why don't you have a girlfriend who's, I don't know, twenty or thirty or something? It would be better for you, wouldn't it?'

He puts an arm around my shoulders. 'Marianne, I *adore* the fact that you're fifteen. You have no idea. And you're not a silly teenager. You're a sensible girl. You've been through the mill with your mum, and you deserve a treat. And you're almost legal now.'

'What am I going to do, now I've left school? I guess I should get a job.'

'I can get you something.'

I look at him, unsure whether I should say this or not.

'Or I could go to sixth-form college?' I venture. 'I mean, not back to school, but I was thinking it might be quite good to do A levels. Because I wouldn't mind going to university. It might be fun.'

He stretches out and puts a hand on my naked thigh. 'University of Life, sweetie. That's where you want to get your degree. I'm not having you off on some campus being pawed at by sweaty students. Not my girl.'

I smile at this. 'You mean you'll still want me as your girlfriend?'

He winks. I assume that means yes. My heart soars.

By the time his friends arrive, I am spinning with the alcohol. I feel like this almost all of the time when I'm with him. I like it. It makes things feel easier, makes me woozier and happier.

These men are older than Benjamin. They are both wearing suits too. One of them has lost most of his hair, and his face is a perfect oval, and he looks like a boiled egg. The other is thin with a sharp nose, but his face is quite handsome.

'This is Tim,' Benjamin says, indicating the egg man. 'And this,' he points at the other one, 'is Pete. Guys, this is Marianne.'

They both smile at me. 'Heard a lot about you,' says Tim-the-egg.

'None of it's true,' I say, because I have noticed that this is what adults reply in that situation. They both burst out laughing.

'Marianne,' Benjamin says, 'why don't you move over there and sit next to Pete. It's annoying for other people when a couple sit together all the time.'

'Sure,' I said, and I slide out of the booth, notice all three men checking out my legs, and slide in on the other side. Pete sits next to me, and moves in close.

They talk about boring, adult things for a while. I drink too much too quickly, and twiddle the stem of my glass. I zone out completely from what is going on, as the room begins to rotate around me. When someone touches my knee, I think at first that it's Benjamin. I lean on him, but he feels different, shorter and spikier and with the wrong smell, and then I remember that it's Pete.

He hooks his arm around my shoulders and pulls me closer towards him. I try to pull away and look at Benjamin, waiting for him to step in and stop this. Benjamin is watching, and doing nothing.

'Hey,' I manage to say. 'Stop it.' I take the hand that is on my left shoulder and try to unhook it. 'Benjamin!' I plead. 'Make him stop it.'

'Marianne,' he says. 'It's OK. You can loosen up a bit. Have another drink. The guys have heard all about you. It's only fair that they get to share my luck.'

I frown. This does not sound right at all. But all of them are looking at me as if I am being stupid and annoying. I try to get away again.

'I'm your girlfriend,' I tell him. 'Not his. You shouldn't let him do this.'

Benjamin sighs and shakes his head, as if indulging me.

'Oh, Marianne,' he says. 'You have a very, um, teenage view of things, which I suppose is to be expected. Look, Pete. Hands off, yeah? We'll all go back to mine. How about that?'

All I hear are the words 'hands off'. I am so relieved that I drink everything from the glass in front of me, which I don't think is even my glass, and I lean against the wall and close my eyes.

# chapter thirty-two

## Eliza

We are eating breakfast, but all I am really interested in is the coffee. Seth is on his third cup, and is shovelling in his eggs and bacon with a look of intense concentration on his face. I am glad to see him eating again. His face is haggard and jowly and he looks nothing like himself.

He puts his knife and fork down for a moment, yawns and stretches. Watching him sets me off in an enormous yawn too.

'So,' he says. 'What the fuck do we do now?'

I shake my head. I have no idea.

'Go back to Cornwall?' I suggest, after a while. 'She's not in hospital, the police aren't interested, and we can't just walk round London hoping to spot her. You could walk round for ten years and never run into someone.'

'I know.' He reaches across and picks up a copy of the *Evening Standard* from the next table. He starts flicking through it.

Seth has sat up for the past two nights, waiting for Lucy to come back. I have woken both times, having slept badly myself, to see him sitting in the hard armchair, his head lolling sideways, dozing uncomfortably. I have never seen him like this. He has barely eaten anything, until now, and he has even refused alcohol. 'Got to stay alert,' he says. He doesn't want to believe that she has left him. He wants her to have been forced, needs there to be a dastardly plot of some sort. He is trying not to be angry, but I know Seth. It will come. I am angry already, but I am trying not to show it. She could have told us. Whatever it was, she could have told us. I am angry with her for that, but I am desperately sad and scared too.

'She'll get in touch when she can.' I must have said this twenty million times over the past couple of days. 'You're going to have to give her time. She'll explain it when she can.'

He flicks through the pages of the paper, concentrating on the little stories, hunting for a throwaway paragraph that might contain a clue.

'You reckon?' he demands, without looking up.

'Yes. Anything in the paper?'

He shakes his head, still not looking at me. 'Policeman stabbed. Guy shot in a car at King's Cross. Someone saw a UFO. Maybe that's our answer. It's as bloody good as every other idea we've had.'

Lucy's departure has floored us both. I am trying not to let my brother see how much this reminds me of the worst days of my life. It is, though, precisely the same. A central figure, yanked away. At least I was certain, with Graham, that he wasn't coming back. It was the most terrible, bleakest certainty there has ever been, but there was no room for doubt. At least he didn't choose to go.

I desperately want to see my girls.

'Let's go home,' I say, and he looks up at me, with big, defeated black eyes, and I see him acquiesce. 'I'll send Lucy a text,' I add. 'Tell her that's what we're doing.'

We both know it will make no difference. I wonder how long we will keep it up.

We have passed through Reading when Seth becomes animated again.

'She never told me anything about herself,' he says. 'Except that she grew up in London. She never even said where in London and I never asked because one part of that place is much the same as another as far as I'm concerned. Stupid twat that I am. But we can start to find out, can't we? We can track her back. She came from somewhere. She must have family out there. Friends.'

I nod. 'People trace their families all the time, don't they? It's all on the internet.'

He sits up straighter. My brother is bereft, but he has a plan. We will turn detective, and find out everything we possibly can about Lucy's life before we met her. Because somebody out there must know where she is.

# chapter thirty-three

I stayed in my hotel room for two days, and looked out of the open window without stopping. I breathed the air and watched the people. I was there when the souvenir stalls were wheeled out and when the bag sellers spread out their merchandise at the start of the day. I was watching when the day-trippers' boats blasted on their horns and summoned their passengers back on board at the end of the afternoon. I watched the boats heading across the lagoon, down the Grand Canal, out of the end of it. I observed the tourists heading in both directions, maps in hands, ticking things off their itineraries.

I did not set foot outside the building. Each morning I went down in the lift to the breakfast room, and I filled my bag with fruit and rolls and slices of cheese. Then I ate the biggest breakfast I could stomach, forcing down croissant after croissant, asking for more coffee and refilling my wine glass with juice over and over again. I ignored my fellow guests, did not even glance at them. I stared down at the table, waiting, just letting the time pass.

Then I went back to the room, and I sat on the chair by the window. I read the books I had bought, and the old newspaper, and after that I just looked. Sometimes I knelt on my chair and leaned over the window frame. Sometimes I stood up. I watched early-morning joggers going by, ponytails swinging from side to side, watched them skittering up and down the steps on the little bridges. Sometimes I would look at the clock thinking that half a day had passed, and it would turn out to have been half an hour. Other times it felt like five minutes, but it turned out to be almost nightfall.

I wanted to be a part of it all, but I held myself back. I had a long, lukewarm bath every day, and when the chambermaid came round, I stood in the corridor for as long as it took her to make the bed and clean the bathroom. I dozed, and when I woke I threw croissant crumbs to the pigeons on the tiles of the sloping roof outside the side window. No one ever asked me why I was the only tourist in Venice who skulked around indoors. I thought the bald jowly man might have put it around that I was running away from someone; or perhaps they just didn't care.

At the end of the second day, I looked at the golden evening light on the white church across the water, and I decided that now it was time for me to do something. The two days' seclusion and rest had done their job. I knew why Buddhists did this. It worked.

All the same, I only made it as far as the roof terrace. It was a surprisingly big space, covering the hotel's entire roof. There were three big swing seats, as well as a sprinkling of tables and chairs, and a strong barrier all around the edge. Everything cast a long shadow. Every seat was occupied by someone, by a little group or a couple, but all I wanted to do, anyway, was to gulp down the cooler air and to lean on the railing.

I could see more, from up here. The perspective was different, broader. There was a boundless expanse of blue above me, for one thing.

I accepted the fact that I was never going to see Seth and Eliza and the girls again. I knew that this was a good thing, for their sake, but my heart ached for them. My life was such that I must always be ready to leave, but actually doing it was like losing a limb.

I would stay here for a while, and then if I still felt unsettled, I would find another place to go. Perhaps I would go much further afield. I was contemplating the idea of moving ever eastwards, until one day I might find myself in Asia. There were some war zones to be skirted on the way, but I thought it could be done.

I thought I might avoid Iran and Afghanistan by making my way to Moscow and taking the Trans-Siberian express. The only thing to remember was that I must stop going east at some point, or I would arrive back where I had started.

This was how it was now. I could not look back, or have any regrets. I was not going to put down roots anywhere, ever again. That, I had discovered, could lead only to heartbreak for everyone.

# chapter thirty-four

## Marianne

I wake up, and the first thing I notice is that I am far more sore than usual, and I feel bad. I have vague memories that the night did not go well. But I am, at least, in Benjamin's bed, and he is next to me, and no one else is around. I cannot remember much beyond the stand-off with Pete in the bar. I recall Benjamin telling him: 'Hands off'. That was good. Things must have been all right.

His arm is around my waist. I roll over, and look at the clock. It is twenty-five to eight. There is a vein in my head that is throbbing, and I think I might be about to be sick. I don't think I ate anything at all last night. I can picture the table in our booth, crowded with empty bottles. No plates, just bottles.

The thought of the champagne, with its thin, acidic taste, sends me leaping out of bed and running to the en suite. I am sick three times, heaving uncontrollably. Foul liquid fills the bowl.

When he finds me, I am sitting on the bathroom floor, naked, hugging my knees and trying to blank out the memories that are forcing their way through. The images. Benjamin telling me what to do, shouting when I didn't do it. The man called Tim reaching out for me, again and again. The man called Pete grabbing me, pawing at me, his fingers everywhere, in places they should not have been.

'Morning, beautiful,' he says. Then he kneels next to me. 'Hey!' he says, his voice and face full of concern. 'Hey, Marianne! What's the matter? Feeling rotten this morning?'

I open my mouth, without any idea of what I want to say, and

I hear a wail, a howl, an animal sound that tears the stillness of the flat and rips the world in half.

Benjamin pats my shoulder. I think he is smiling.

'Look,' he says. 'Get yourself together. Brush your teeth, have a shower. We'll go for breakfast and then I have something I want to talk to you about.'

I look up at him, full of terror. He hooks an arm around my head and pulls me close to him.

'Don't worry,' he says, into my hair. 'It's something nice. Truly. Come on, sweetheart. You can do it. A hot shower, put on your jeans and a nice comfy top, and come downstairs. I promise you. You're going to love it.'

I look away from him. I know that I shouldn't trust him, but there is nothing else I can do.

# chapter thirty-five

## Eliza

No one has any idea how many tranquillisers I used to take. It's ridiculous, but I wanted them to think I was coping. And they did. I would hear them saying it when they thought I wasn't listening. 'Eliza's coping so well.' 'She's amazing.' 'She seems to have put it behind her.' I would hear it in the playground, when, after a few weeks, they realised that I was still 'normal'. When they stopped looking at me aghast from a safe distance, and started talking to me again.

I was living in a fugged-up world, and through the fog I could chat about the school fete and swimming classes. I could be normal, entice people back into my company who were otherwise too scared to go near me. I could even go for coffee with the other mothers, and after a while one of them would feel able to lean forward and say, 'So how are you *doing*?', in a meaningful way, and I would say, 'Oh, you know . . .' and there would be a little pause before we went back to talking about our little girls' ballet lessons.

That worked, because it kept people talking to me. It didn't work with the girls, and it didn't work with Mum and Dad, or with Seth and Lucy. Seth and Lucy used to come over with wine and feed it to me until I broke down, and thank God they did because otherwise I would probably have lived the rest of my life as a semi-person, always half spaced on temazepam and trying to say the right, bland thing so as not to alarm anyone. Anyway, I got through it and things were getting better. I forced myself to go on those dreadful dates because I was so fucking lonely. Nobody in the world had any idea about the loneliness. No one.

I went on dates with fuckwits and losers and creeps because there was the tiniest chance that there might have been another person in the world who could complete me like Graham did, and then there was an even tinier chance that he might live in or around Falmouth. It was *infinitesimal*, but it existed, and so I made myself give it a shot, because I was just so bloody lonely.

Obviously I haven't met him. At one point I thought I might have found a spark, but that went nowhere. In fact I felt a fool, and so the one person who has given me a glimpse of a possibility is now someone I find myself avoiding.

Patrick has heard about Lucy disappearing, because obviously no one is talking about anything else. We are a one-family soap opera. When he heard, he turned up on my doorstep, looking all concerned, asking what had happened. I did not invite him in. Everyone wants to be a part of it while things are still exciting and new. If she is still not here in three months, nobody will even bother to mention her.

So even though Patrick was pale and agitated and his hair was standing up on end, I did not invite him in. I said I would call him if we heard anything, and then I shut the door. I did not need to be reminded of his feelings for her, the ones he thinks are so secret but which are written all over his face. I've been half-heartedly ignoring him when I see him up at school, though cold-shouldering Patrick is the least of my concerns, in the scheme of things.

I am still lonely, and now that Lucy has gone, it is just about as bad as it has ever been. The girls go to bed earlier than I would like, because if they don't, Imogen is exhausted at school the next day and Clara's behaviour is a nightmare, since they seem to be hard-wired to wake up every morning at 6.33. I spend the evenings on my own, and the only word that really describes it is *bleak*. Nobody talks about Graham any more. It feels as though he never existed, as if I imagined him and got the girls from a sperm donor.

Even Seth and Lucy rarely mentioned him, of their own accord, but if I did, they would happily talk about him with me, and listen while I went over the same old stuff, again and again. I have to keep talking, keep telling the same old stories about him, because otherwise I will forget, and then he will be truly gone.

Lucy has gone, and Seth is lost to me at the moment. I reach for the pill bottle. Then I remember the way it really made me feel: the trade-off that was involved, the fact that I could make my way through the day and hold conversations that sounded normal, but that came at the expense of myself. When I was taking them, the real me, Eliza, no longer existed. I have got through that: I am not going back.

The girls are with Mum and Dad this afternoon. I flush the pills down the loo, put on my flip-flops, and march over to Seth's house.

It is a glorious day, which seems like a bit of a mockery. I stand on his doorstep, their doorstep, and feel the sun on the back of my neck. There is nobody around: Seth and Lucy's street is almost entirely populated by students, and today it is blissfully devoid of carefree youngsters with loud music and little summer dresses and no fucking idea of what the world is actually like.

When he doesn't answer, I let myself in. I half expect to find him drunk in a corner, or shouting incoherently on to Lucy's answerphone. The hall, however, is quiet. It is tinged with a smell of stale alcohol and unwashedness that belies the fact that he has only been alone for a few days.

There are glasses, cups and dishes piled up in the sink. I open the dishwasher: it is filled with clean stuff that I am certain has been sitting there since the day of the Cohen concert. I wonder whether to sort out the kitchen while he is out, or whether I ought to leave him to it.

One of the glasses in the sink has a lipstick kiss imprinted on it. As I am staring at this, the back door, the one that leads from the kitchen into the little garden, swings open, and my brother falls in through it.

He stops, stares at me, frowns in the way that means he is so drunk that he cannot compute my presence in his kitchen. His reactions slow down, almost to a halt, when he is drunk, and I hate it when I am sober and he is not. I hate to see him disabling himself like this. I watch his thought process playing out across his face. He sees me. He looks back into the garden. He edges back out of the door. I follow him. Sure enough, there is a woman there.

I think I have seen her around the town. She is not a Barbie doll like his previous girlfriends: she looks more like a student, with a fresh face and a little sundress and gladiator sandals. Her hair is light and silky and falls to her shoulders.

She looks aghast to see me, and turns and walks quickly away up the garden. Her gait is unsteady too, and I see a rug on the square of grass outside, with two empty wine bottles, two empty glasses, and what I presume is an empty Pringles packet strewn around it.

'Hey!' Seth calls after her. He must be extraordinarily inebriated to be able to do something like this and live with himself. 'Hey, s'all right. This is not *her*! This is me sister!'

The woman lifts a hand, waves goodbye without looking around, and leaves through the back gate.

'Seth!' I say.

He stares at me, as defiant as he used to be when he was a moody little boy. I stare back, trying to channel our formidable mother, until he crumbles.

'Sorry,' he mutters. 'But I didn't *do* anything. I just wanted someone to . . . Oh, Christ.'

'Oh, Seth,' I tell him. 'Don't say sorry to *me*. It's nothing to do with me. What you do is your own business.'

He looks as if he is going to speak. I wait, but he changes his mind. Instead, he turns to the fridge and takes out another bottle.

'Drink?' he asks, unscrewing the cap of an Australian Sauvignon. 'Liza, I think she's not from London at all. I found a Lucy Riddick with the same birthday as her.'

I get out two wine glasses, against my better judgement.

'Great?' I say tentatively, and I look at him carefully.

'Yeah. She's from Bristol. Luce sometimes talks about Bristol, doesn't she?'

'Did you find her family?'

'I've got an address.'

'Are you going to write? Or call? Do you have a phone number?'

He shakes his head. 'Yeah, but no. I think I'm going to go there. It's the only way not to be fobbed off, innit?'

I look at him. He pours the wine, right up to the top of the glasses. I take mine and slurp a bit off the top so that it won't spill.

'Can I come with you?' I ask.

'Yeah. Can you stay around? Now? We could get a pizza later. If you like.'

'OK.'

We spend the evening slobbed out on the sofa, watching *Curb Your Enthusiasm* on DVD, talking about all the little things, resolutely avoiding the bigger picture. It is surprisingly comforting, and for a few hours I forget about all of it.

# chapter thirty-six

I stopped. It was night, and I was in a little square, although it wasn't square. It was a sort of triangle. The buildings loomed up on three sides, tall, dark and forbidding, all their shutters closed. Far above, I could see a slice of night sky, dotted with stars.

There was a dim light on the side of one of the walls, and I could vaguely see the shapes of pieces of clean washing hanging on a line a few storeys above me. Little things like socks at one end, big things like sheets at the other. This was Venetian laundry. It was part of my Venetian life.

I was on my way back to the hotel. I had sat in a restaurant by myself, and eaten a pizza. Once, that would have made me nervous, but now I could not care less. People glanced at a woman eating alone, and then looked away. I looked at them, or didn't look away. None of it meant anything.

I had surprised myself by mechanically eating a whole pizza, even though it was enormous. I had sipped at a glass of wine and drunk an entire carafe of tap water. My table was inside, but by a window, in a pizzeria that seemed to be at least half filled with local people. The atmosphere was lively and happy, and even the background music was funky. All of this was meaningless. It had been a place to sit for an hour or so. Seth would have loved it, but Seth was not here.

I stopped in my tracks and, just for a moment, let the idea of him wash over me. I told myself that I was remembering him as perfect, when in fact he had been as flawed as anyone. I told myself, fiercely, that I had never felt able to trust him with my reality. I should be able to walk away from him. I should not be regretting walking away from him so much that I had to stop and bite my lip and allow the tears to leak out of the corners of my eyes, just for a few seconds, just for a brief reprieve.

Seth used to see food as fuel, and he ate too much of it, and he did not care about having a balanced diet. Now that I was on my own, I could eat well. It was not much of a consolation. I remembered him eating, relishing his food. I loved him.

I heard distant footsteps, echoing in the night. There was a path at each corner of the triangle. One I had just come down. That left two options: right or left. Both alleys were small, but the left was smaller, barely wide enough for a body, so I chose the right. The footsteps were coming closer. I drew a deep breath, and stepped back into the darkness. I walked, trying to look purposeful, wanting to find my way back to the crowds by myself, not wanting to meet anybody.

I paused. This was a silent place. The other footsteps had stopped. Either whoever it was had gone the other way, or he had stopped too. I kept my eyes fixed on the place, up ahead, where the alley turned a corner. If I took my eyes off it, a figure would appear there, waiting for me. As I drew closer, my pace grew slower. There was something bad around the corner, something menacing. This was not meant to happen. I was meant to be sticking with the crowds. One wrong turn, and I was utterly alone, walking towards a dark corner, terrified but unable to turn my back on it.

I smelt the water before I heard it, and heard it before I saw it. Around the corner, the alley stopped, and there was a canal. It smelt, like all the parts of waterside Venice I had visited, like a dirty version of the sea: a salty tang, permeating the city. The air of stagnancy suited this city, which had something satisfyingly sordid about it. The water in this little canal was dark, and it splashed gently. There was no bridge: the path just stopped. A boat bobbed up and down. I considered, for a moment, untying the boat, pushing off from the wall, sculling along with my hands until I found the Grand Canal. Then I turned and retraced my steps. I was braced all the way for someone who was waiting for me, but he was not there.

Back in the triangular square, I took the other path. As I squeezed through a space that felt as if it were closing in above my head, pressing down on me, I realised that I was going to be wandering around Venice, increasingly lost and desperate, all night long. I had strayed into a labyrinth. At least no one would find me here. Years from now, somebody would peer into a corner of a long-abandoned alley and find my skeleton, its mouth wide with a terrified scream.

And then it opened out. There was a church, a proper square, a bridge. There was a sign on the wall that I couldn't read in the dark, but I could just make out its arrow, pointing to the right. I followed it. A group of people was up ahead of me, and they were chatting in some European language or other. They did not look lost, or worried. I fell into step behind them, far enough back so that I didn't look like a stalker, and I followed them to the Grand Canal. I was found. In as far as I could ever be, I was home.

I had always known that, after Cornwall, I would follow Mum's dreams to Italy. If I tried hard, I could tell myself that this was a positive side to my kind of life: I could think of a place and call it home, and by doing so, I made it my home.

I stood by the edge of the canal and tried to make myself focus. I must not flounder. I must keep active, and stay alert. I would stay in the Gabrielli for the rest of the week, and then I would think of something else to do.

I was not even articulating his name to myself. I was particularly not remembering his figure, the glimpse I had caught of him, in Cornwall. That was the way of madness. If I started down that path, I would see him skulking around every corner. Every footstep would be his, and every stranger would be threatening.

But it had been him, and so I knew he was alive, and he was everywhere. I was inextricably tied to him. Everything I had done from the first time we met, I had done with him in mind. Sooner or later he would catch up with me, and our entwined destinies would play out in one bad way or another.

I shook my head, banished the thoughts, and walked into the hotel.

'*Buonasera*,' called the jowly man, with a grin.

'*Buonasera*,' I replied.

I didn't close the shutters or the curtains. I lay on the bed and stared at the blackness outside, the blackness that was the city of tourists and water.

I had had three years of happiness with Seth. It was more than I had deserved, but even now, I could not think of it as a mistake. I wondered what he thought of me now. I wondered what he was doing. An image flashed into my mind: Seth, lying on the sofa, legs stretched out, feet up on the arm. He was leaning back on a cushion, yawning.

That had been a different life. It had always been an illusion. I could feel Seth's hurt and confusion from hundreds of miles away, but he had wanted to marry someone who had been a mirage. He had come too close, and I had evaporated.

A boat horn sounded outside. Water swished around. Everything else was still.

# chapter thirty-seven

## Marianne

He drives me across town, to a café in Notting Hill, for breakfast. It is miles, and it takes ages, and I am still feeling horrible but trying to pretend I am happy. I don't want to make him angry.

'I've lived in London all my life,' I tell him, with a please-like-me smile, 'and I don't think I've ever been to Notting Hill.'

'So your education continues,' he says, with a smile that clutches at my heart and makes me sure that I do love him, no matter what.

'How long have you lived here?' I ask. 'Were you born here?'

'I wish I was,' he says, with a little chuckle. 'It would be much cooler than being a Stevenage boy.'

'I've never been there, either.'

'Well, in this case, you haven't missed anything. No, I moved here when I was eighteen, so I've lived here half my life. Eighteen years.'

'That's longer than I have,' I remind him.

'So it is! You youngster.' And he reaches out and squeezes my knee. I lean back. I am beginning to feel better.

The café is full of slim young people in messy, but cool, clothes. I wish I could be like them.

'Trustafarians.' Benjamin says, dismissing them. He looks different from everyone else, in his expensive jeans and his Ralph Lauren top. 'Actually,' he tells me, 'you blend in pretty well. You just need to muss your hair up a bit and pretend you've just got up, when in fact you've spent hours in front of the mirror perfecting the artless look.'

I nod and pretend I know what he's talking about. The walls inside are bright yellow, the music is loud and chilled, and there are big pot plants dotted around the varnished floorboards. I decide that I like it here, a lot.

'This is really nice,' I say, and I know that a big breakfast will complete my recovery.

Thirty minutes later, I am shovelling the last of the eggs and baked beans into my mouth, and drinking my second glass of freshly squeezed orange juice, when Benjamin takes my wrist.

'Look,' he says. 'You've finished, haven't you? And you feel better? Because there was something I wanted to ask you.'

I bite my lip. I probably don't want to know. I think it is going to be something to do with his horrible friends.

'Mmm?' I say, and I finish my mouthful and put my knife and fork side by side on the plate. I wonder, with a fierce dread, what might be coming.

But he surprises me. In fact, he astonishes me. He takes something out of the pocket of the jacket that is hanging on the back of his chair, and then he leans forward.

'Marianne Jenkins,' he says. 'You are the most beautiful and adorable girl I've ever met, and so even though I'm so old, I'm asking you whether you would do me the very great honour of becoming my wife.'

I look around. The music is still pumping. The other people are passing sections of the newspaper across the table and lounging prettily on their chairs. A thin waitress is standing at the next table, notepad in hand. None of them take the slightest bit of notice of the astonishing thing that is happening.

I look back at Benjamin. I look right into his deep blue eyes.

'I want to take care of you,' he adds softly. 'For ever.'

He becomes blurry as my eyes fill with tears. He wants to take care of me. He loves me. I love him. I realise that I imagined the bad things that I thought happened last night. That was just a dream; this is real.

'Yes,' I whisper. 'Thank you. Yes.' I laugh. 'Completely, yes.'

He pops open a black velvet box. There is a silver ring inside it, with a row of three diamonds. It is the most beautiful thing I have ever seen. He slides it on to the fourth finger of my left hand. I hold it up, look at it, look at myself, engaged.

I hold both his hands across the table. I don't think that I have ever been so happy in my whole life.

# chapter thirty-eight

## Eliza

It takes three hours to drive to Bristol, even with Seth at the wheel. There are four of us in the car: I have had to bring the girls along because Mum and Dad are in France. They didn't want to go, but I told them they had to, because it was their holiday and they deserved it. If they'd protested one more time I would have caved in gracefully and dropped the girls off with them again, but wisely they did not.

We leave Falmouth at half past three, straight after school, and at exactly half past six we pull up outside a house in a commuter village five miles from Bristol. It is a bungalow covered in pebble-dash, with a big green garden and a red car in the drive. Seth parks on top of a road marking that says NO PARKING.

'Right,' he says. His mouth is set and he is focused. 'You girls wait here. Move the car if any traffic wardens come by, but I'd be surprised.'

There is a steady stream of commuter cars coming down the hill, but there are no pedestrians around. I watch my brother marching up the drive, and up a set of stone steps to the front door, at the side of the house.

The girls have taken their seatbelts off. Imogen climbs into the front of the car and puts the hazard lights on. Clara scrambles on to my lap.

'I need a wee!' she announces.

'No you don't.' I look around. I don't think anyone is looking.

I could, perhaps, let her wee in what might or might not be the Riddicks' garden. 'You should have done one when we stopped at the services,' I tell her, pointlessly.

My daughter twists around on my lap and I pull her close and kiss the top of her head. I don't want them to grow up. I wonder how old a child needs to be before you have to stop smelling their hair.

'I didn't need one then,' she tells me. 'I need one *now*. Or I will do it in my *pants*.'

'Me too,' says Imogen. 'I need a wee too.'

I open the car door. While I have been distracted, Seth has vanished, so I suppose he had been admitted to the Riddick household. I take Clara to the edge of what I see is an immaculate lawn. I start to get her ready for as surreptitious a urination session as is possible, in broad daylight on a strangers' lawn, when I notice Imogen. She has run up the steps, and has her finger on the doorbell.

'Imogen!' I yell. 'No!'

It is too late. The door opens. A woman stands there, and I see her look at Imogen, and then at me, suspending a semi-naked girl over her garden.

'Hello,' Imogen says to her. 'Please may we use your toilet?'

The heating in the house is on, even though it is July. The air is stifling and chemically scented. The woman's face is lined, and her mouth is so tightly closed that I only know it's there because of the lipstick that is creeping up the skin above it in thin lines. Her hair is blond and bouffant. She is wearing slacks and a cardigan, and she looks nothing like Lucy. She seems like a very old woman, but when I look at her properly, I think that she is about sixty.

Our mother is sixty. She is lively and well dressed and she goes for long walks through the countryside all the time. I should not compare.

Lucy never spoke about her family. Now we might be in her family home. There must be a reason for the estrangement: no wonder this woman doesn't look happy to see us.

'At the top of the stairs, dear,' she is saying to Imogen, while I am still apologising.

'No, that's quite all right, love. But please, will somebody tell me what is going on? Is this your husband?'

'My brother.'

I follow her into a sitting room, which has a velvety sofa and chairs, a television and a gas fire. Seth is sitting on the edge of the sofa, glaring at me. I look around. There are a few family photographs, and a couple of them feature a baby, or a little girl, about Clara's age. I cannot tell whether or not she is Lucy.

I try to apologise to Seth, without saying anything. Clara runs forward and sits on his knee. He fights her off, and sits her next to him. All of this takes a few seconds.

'And you want to talk about Lucy?' the woman asks. She sits down in a chair, clearly tired. 'Really?'

'We're so sorry to disturb you,' I say.

'Lucy Riddick is your daughter?' asks Seth.

'Well, yes,' the woman agrees. 'Lucy. She was my daughter. Yes. Who are you?'

'We're friends of hers,' I say.

'I know you haven't seen her for a long time,' says Seth, 'but we were just wondering – have you heard from her lately? Because she's disappeared and we are worried sick about her. She's been living in Cornwall, and . . .'

He breaks off when he sees Mrs Riddick's expression. 'What?' he asks. I see the panic in his face. 'What's happened?'

'Is this a joke?' the woman demands. She sounds angry, but she looks exhausted.

'No,' I tell her. I stand up and go to her side, but she pushes me away, hard.

'You know that my Lucy is dead?' she demands. 'She died. She's dead. She is *not alive* any more.'

I gasp. Seth puts his hands to his face, and is silent. I don't look at him.

'We didn't know that,' I say. 'No. I'm so sorry. What's happened? She has only been gone for a few days.'

'No,' says the woman. 'A few days? What are you talking about?

Thirty-three years. Now, please will you get out of my house and leave me alone?'

We drive into Bristol and take the girls to McDonald's. They run off into the play area, and Seth and I look at each other.

'Well, that went well,' he says.

'That poor old lady isn't going to sleep tonight,' I say. 'God, I feel terrible. So that one can be crossed off the list. How many others were there?'

He shrugs. 'So far, none. Dead end.'

We sit in silence. I try to eat something, but I hate fast food. The girls shriek and laugh and throw plastic balls at each other. Time ticks by.

# chapter thirty-nine

I ordered a fish and salad platter for lunch, and stretched my legs out. I tried to sit still. I put a hand on my leg to try to stop it jiggling. All that happened was that my hand started jiggling with it. My tongue explored the inside of my mouth: there was a little line there where I kept biting the inside of my bottom lip, where it never quite healed before I did it again.

But I had not planned anything beyond getting here. I thought about jumping off one of the bridges and losing myself in the water, many times every day. I looked at things and looked at people, but they might as well have been made from pixels. Sometimes I thought they were; thought that the whole of Venice was a figment.

It was late on Sunday morning, and the square ahead of me seemed to be heaving with people. These were real people, in their proper context: Venetians, who had just spilled out of the church. The older generation defied the weather in their Sunday best: two ladies standing in the shade of a tiny tree were wearing heavy woollen dresses and cardigans, all of it black. A man on his own, a little way away, was wearing a suit, complete with waistcoat.

Even the children must have been hot, the boys in shirt sleeves, the girls in stiff dresses, but they ran and shouted and threw a ball around the square, released from the rigidity of the musty church service.

The ball came close to my table, and I thought I ought to stand up and pick it up and throw it back. It would be easy: first, stand up. Then reach for the ball. Then throw it to the nearest child. By the time I had decided that I would do it, a little girl had darted for it, smiling shyly at me, and run away again.

When I looked up, a woman was watching this girl. She saw her retrieve her ball and run back to the game, and turned back to her conversation. The parents, my generation, stood around laughing and chatting. The weeds that had pushed their way up through the cracks between the paving stones had turned brown and withered away, but the people were acting as if it were a mild day in April, rather than the blazing, dripping, sweaty middle of the summer.

I sipped my drink. I had ordered a glass of prosecco, because I hoped that the alcohol would make me giddy. I was drinking at lunchtimes, and I was visiting churches, mingling with the crowds, tramping the streets of Venice. Anything to tire myself out, anything to avoid standing still, anything to avoid the temptation of the bridges. I had already visited the church in this square. Although the interiors merged with one another in my mind, I remembered a wooden ceiling and a nice San Sebastian, apparently untroubled by the arrow sticking out of his side.

Every time I stepped into a church, I felt a tiny bit better. Sometimes it was negligible, and sometimes it seemed that the musty atmosphere reached out and pulled something within me back upright. I might seek out a convent that would take me in. I pictured the peace of that existence, the idea of surrendering myself to a higher power and living a life surrounded by art and incense. Every detail of every day would be controlled.

Instead, I was making my way around a list of sixteen churches that were included on the Chorus Pass I had bought at the first one I visited. I looked at altars and frescoes. I dropped money in collection boxes. I charged myself, in particular, with the task of seeking out representations of St Sebastian, my favourite saint because he was always depicted in a loincloth with arrows sticking out of him. He was said to ward off the plague. I found him reassuring.

I had decided to call myself Lucia. I knew it was pretentious, but I didn't care. I was no longer Lucy, but I had liked being her:

mainly, however, I was naming myself after Venice's train station, where this new life had begun. My name was a purely academic question, anyway. I did not introduce myself to anybody, ever. I hardly had a voice with which to speak. It was all I could do to order drinks, or food, to keep myself going.

'Salad with fish,' said the waitress, and she put it down in front of me with a smile. I tried to return it. She was cheerful and manly-looking, with short hair and denim shorts.

'*Grazie*,' I said, tentatively.

'*Prego*,' she said, stifling a chuckle.

The plate was enormous. It was square and white, and it was covered with slices of smoked fish, a few prawns, and improbably bouncy green lettuce. I stared at it. I was not hungry. I had forgotten what it was like to feel hungry. All the same, fish and salad were good for me, and I was going to sit here and plough through it, to give myself the strength to carry on existing. I picked up a prawn, and nibbled it.

I was managing to make eye contact with the other hotel guests from time to time. They changed each morning, but they stayed the same too. I sat and watched them. I felt I was invisible, so I could stare as much as I liked.

My favourites to watch were the smattering of Japanese visitors. Eliza and Graham went to Japan once and came back wide-eyed at the fact that 'it was so, well, just so *Japanese*'. 'There was raw fish for breakfast,' Graham explained. 'Seriously. We weren't at the five-star posh hotels or anything, and that meant there was no toast. And no coffee. Truly, there was miso soup and sushi for breakfast.'

'And sashimi,' Eliza added. 'Do you know what that is? Actual raw fish, like sushi but without even the rice. Hardcore stuff. I quite liked it, but not for breakfast. It always looked to me as if it was going to start wriggling.'

I remembered that conversation whenever I watched the Japanese tourists at the Gabrielli queuing up at the breakfast buffet. Were the croissants and jam, the muesli and the choice between coffee, cappuccino, hot chocolate and tea as much of a culture shock for them as the miso and green tea had been to Eliza? I supposed not: they looked thoroughly at home, and Western culture had too much of a grip on the world to allow such innocence to exist.

I thought of Eliza often. As the days passed, I was beginning to realise that she was probably much more worried about me than I wanted her to be. It was unforgivable that I had abandoned her in London with a stupid little note. In a week or so I was going to send an email. I was fairly sure I could set up an account that would be untraceable.

She was the best friend I had ever had, and Seth was still the centrepiece of my mental landscape. They were the first people since Mum died to whom I had been able to get properly close, and I had, inevitably, walked out on them. I knew they were better off without me, but they had probably not worked it out yet.

I felt someone's eyes on me. I turned, instantly alert, and stared at the people at the other tables until I found the culprit. He was about my age, dark-haired, dressed in a dark-red T-shirt. When he saw me looking, he raised his prosecco glass. I looked away, scrunched my eyes tight, shutting it all out.

The church that I was visiting after lunch was Santa Maria Formosa. I crossed the steep wooden bridge at the Accademia, and pushed my way through the streets behind St Mark's Square. I got lost for a while, crossing random bridges and choosing what felt like the right alleys but often turned out to be the wrong ones. I loved the sudden silence when that happened, the way the hot sun was abruptly cut off by high walls. I loved the obscure doorways with doorbells next to them, the hidden little courtyard gardens. I loved the weeds that pushed through at the edges of the paving stones, the occasional yellow signs with black arrows promising S MARCO or RIALTO.

I found myself stepping out of the shade and into the warm light of the square. There was a coffee shop with tables out in the piazza, with an awning to keep off the worst of the sun. There was a hotel and a cashpoint. There was a funeral director's and a table where a shaven-headed man was collecting signatures for something or other, and there was a church.

My second-hand guide book translated its name as St Mary the Buxom, after a vision that had occurred to a sex-starved young monk hundreds of years ago. The building was as curvaceous as the vision must have been.

A sharp-eyed woman with impeccable lipstick eyed me with suspicion as she stamped my pass. I smiled back at her, in a disconnected way, and walked into the dark church. I stood still, waiting for my eyes to adjust, and smelt the musty smell of old paint and old paper and faint traces of incense, and the peaceful feeling came upon me again. I clung to it.

Mum never took us to a single church service. Occasionally one of her friends would get married, but they all had registry-office weddings, the women wearing little coloured suits, the men with carnations in their lapels. Mostly, Mum, Finn and I just went to the parties afterwards. It only occurred to me as an adult that she carefully jettisoned her friends once she knew she was ill.

She had no time for any sort of church, but it was the Catholic Church that she truly hated. Even all these years later, I felt the weight of the weird guilt that it had inspired in her, that she had unknowingly transferred. Her family, she always told us, were devout Catholics, and had sent her away at the age of seven to be 'bullied by evil nuns' at a boarding convent. She had never spoken to her parents again, from the time when she was able to walk away from their money at the age of seventeen. I supposed I might still have some ancient Catholic grandparents somewhere out there, but they had never contacted us, not ever. I doubted they had any idea that Finn and I even existed, and since we didn't any more, that was probably just as well.

All the same, I loved the quiet, even at the height of the tourist season, and the fact that these buildings existed at all, that someone had actually had them built in honour of an imaginary power. There was something enormously comforting about the idea that the people of Venice had thought that whatever it was that created the world deserved these monuments to be built as a thank-you. I loved the flickering candlelight, and the paintings. I loved being enclosed in someone else's world.

I did, however, feel that I had seen all the crucifixions I needed to see. There was torture everywhere, the more graphic the better. This was an odd, but I presumed effective, method of keeping people subdued.

I preferred the virgins and babies, but even they seemed like a fail-safe method of keeping women in their places. I longed to see a representation of a man doing the nurturing, a woman being heroic.

I stepped out of my flip-flops, on impulse, just for a moment, to feel the cold floor slabs under my bare feet. I closed my eyes. I drew a deep breath of cool, incense-perfumed air.

I found the painting around the next corner. I looked, and looked again. She was definitely a woman, and yet she was painted as a hero. There was no question about it. I had stumbled upon a heroine. I looked at the laminated sheet in my hand. This, apparently, was St Barbara. She had been painted by Palma il Vecchio, and she was standing proudly, just like the men. She was not shrinking or simpering, her eyes were not downcast. As I gazed at her, I realised how excluded women were from this sort of iconography.

'I love Santa Barbara,' said a voice next to me. I turned and saw a small, dark-haired woman standing next to me. I took a step away from her, and looked back at the painting.

'Yes,' I said. 'She seems unusual.'

'I think this is the only female hero in Venice.'

'Mmm.'

I did not want random conversation. I nodded, and started to move away.

'George Eliot remarked on her, you know. Said she was "almost unique".'

I looked back at her.

'George Eliot said that?'

'Yes. You know, George Eliot? She was a woman?'

'I know.'

'Not only that, but there is actually a painting in this very church by a woman, Giulia Lama.' The woman smiled and nodded at the laminated sheet in my hand. 'I thought you look French,' she said. 'But then I saw that you speak English. Are you a tourist?'

'Yes,' I said. I started to walk away, again.

'From London?'

'No. From . . .' I hesitated. I did not have a persona yet. I had no idea where I came from. 'Actually, yes,' I decided. 'From London.'

'How long are you here?'

'I don't know.'

'You speak Italian?'

'Not really.' I looked at her. She was small and slim, a little older than me. I was wary of any stranger trying to speak to me. All the same, she seemed harmless. *'Un peu?'* I tried.

She laughed. 'That is French. *Poco* will do. You're staying at a hotel?'

'Yes.'

'But you don't know how long you're staying?'

'At the hotel for two more days. After that, I'm not sure what I'll do.'

'Go home to London?'

'No. Stay around here.'

She smiled. 'You can take a room. Learn Italian. Then you get a job. You speak Italian and English, you can work with the tourists, in a restaurant or in a hotel. Or who knows what.'

'Right,' I told her, in my non-committal voice. I had been trying to plan what I would do in two days' time, but I had not got very far with it. 'Yes, I suppose I'll do something like that.'

I was edging away, but she was keeping up with me, and together we had moved a couple of metres away from St Barbara.

'I can teach you Italian,' she said.

I shook my head.

'Why? You need to learn. Come on. Have a coffee with me. I lived in London. I like to meet English people.'

I looked around. The woman in the booth by the door was frowning at us. We were being too loud and not respectful enough. I shook my head, but all the same, I followed the Italian woman out of the church. I did not want to go for a coffee with her: I would shake her off. I would disappear into Venice, vanish without a trace. It would be good practice.

As soon as we were outside in the glare of the afternoon sun, I started to walk away, ignoring her, being as rude as I could. She set off in a different direction anyway. I took my list of churches out of my handbag, and slowed down while I scrutinised it. The next one was in the Ghetto. I had not been to the Ghetto yet. Then she was beside me, stopping me with a hand on my arm. I jumped. The last time anybody touched me, I had been at the Leonard Cohen concert, arm in arm with Eliza. The contact, now, was so unexpected that I felt I had been violated or burned.

'What?' I asked her. I was rude. I was glad to be rude.

'Where are you going?' she demanded, laughing.

'To the Ghetto,' I said, and regretted it.

'I thought you were coming with me? For a coffee?'

I shrugged. There was something liberating about behaving this way. I had spent my whole life trying to be liked and now I didn't need to be like that any more. I actively wanted nobody to like me, so that everyone would leave me alone.

'Look, I'm sorry,' I said, 'but I don't know you. I'm not really in the business of going for coffee with strangers.'

She laughed again. 'Oh, come on. You are being ridiculous. You are alone. Me too. I have some time, I want to help you. Come on.'

And she tucked her hand into mine and started pulling me to a corner of the square, in the opposite direction from the one I was taking. I pulled back, but her grip was strong.

'Come on,' she said again. 'Come on, you want to see a real Venetian flat, don't you? To meet a real Venetian? There are not so many of us about. What is your problem?'

She was beginning to raise her voice. That was when I discovered how strong the people-pleaser in me was. I looked at her tanned face, and suddenly I smiled.

'Fuck it,' I said. 'OK then.'

She laughed, and let go of my arm, and took my hand instead like a little girl. Her hand was smaller and stronger than mine. Everything about her was small, and I felt ungainly in comparison.

Her hair was long and her dress clung to her little body. She looked like a weird doll.

Together we plunged into a dark alley, and without speaking, she led me around corners, in and out of little courtyards, through spaces that didn't even look as if they were made for people. I knew it was a hot, bright day somewhere out there, but I felt that we were stumbling around half underground, where the path ahead of me was illuminated by the greyest of half-light, and corners and doorways were completely hidden. My hand was sweaty and I tried to pull it away, but she would not let go.

I was entirely disorientated by the time we arrived at a bright green door set into a wall in one of the tiny alleys. She let go of me to unlock the door.

'*Benvenuta*,' she said. She laughed. 'At last you are here. I warn you, there are many stairs.' She looked at me and frowned. 'You're scared! Please, don't be scared of me.'

'I'm fine,' I said. I had no idea whether I should go to her flat or not. 'But I don't trust anyone,' I added. 'Nothing personal.'

She shook her head. 'Oh, come on, you are being stupid. Come on up, and you'll see that you can trust me.'

We set off up a narrow staircase that was lit by an electric light, on a timer. She hit the switch just before she set off. She was a woman, I reasoned, and she was being good to me for unspecified reasons. The chances of my being ambushed by anyone at all were small. All the same, my hand was closed around my pepper spray.

We passed a landing with two doors opening from it. She hit another light switch, and we carried on walking. The same happened again, and again. My legs were aching, and I was lagging half a staircase behind, wondering whether to turn back, cursing myself for being so biddable, when I noticed the daylight. Then we were at the top landing, which was flooded with sunshine from a tiny skylight, and she was waiting for me, laughing at my laborious progress, and unlocking a bright pink door with a Yale key.

'You need coffee and cake.'

I shrugged. My thighs were trembling. As she pushed the door open, I tensed. Then I followed her in.

For days, I had been assuming that there had been no real Venetians for a hundred years, and now I had met one. The rooms in this woman's flat were tiny, with low doorways and sloping ceilings, and all the windows were in the roof. There were geraniums and little trees in pots, and herbs growing in trays. There was a tiny kitchen, a little sitting room with a table in it, and a bedroom with a minuscule bathroom attached. On the table, an expensive-looking Apple Mac appeared oversized next to its surroundings, and so cool that the whole scene looked like an advert. There was clutter on every surface, and that, somehow, added to the charm.

I sighed with relief. This did not look like a trap.

When the woman stood in the kitchen fiddling with a complicated-looking espresso machine, there was no room for me, so I lurked in the doorway, still feeling too big. In fact I felt like Alice in Wonderland.

'So,' she said. 'You don't like to go home with strangers?'

'No,' I said. 'I really don't. You have a nice flat, though. Thanks for inviting me.'

'I'm Gabriella. So I am not a stranger any more.'

She was looking at me, expectant.

'Hi, Gabriella,' I forced myself to say. 'I'm Lucia.' It sounded ridiculous, hilarious in its pretension. She did not laugh in my face. She just smiled, in what I thought was a friendly way. The machine spluttered noisily into life, and she held two shiny blue cups under the stream of black liquid, then handed me an espresso.

'Thank you,' I said. I shifted my weight from foot to foot, unsure what to do with myself.

'You're welcome.'

'Do you often make strangers come home with you?' I asked her.

She shrugged. 'If I want – sure.'

'How did you come to speak such good English?'

She smiled and tossed her hair back.

'Oh, you know London,' she said. 'You know it's full of foreigners? That was me. I went to do a masters. It was hard work. My English was not at all good when I started it, and I imagined that foreigners on the course would be treated a little differently, but it turned out not to be the case. No special treatment. Straight into writing essays: corporate governance and financial markets. In English. By next Tuesday. No excuses. So I cried and cried and stayed up all night with a dictionary, and that way I learned to write academic essays in English. Then, of course, everything else became easy.'

'Where were you at college?'

'The London School of Economics. LSE. You have heard of it?'

I was about to protest that everyone had heard of it when I noticed that, once again, she was laughing at me.

'You must be very clever,' I told her, and although it came out in a barbed way, I meant it sincerely. 'I am the least educated person in the world. I wasn't even sixteen when I left school. I never did anything else. I worked in pubs and shops and bars. In fact, you're lucky I'd even heard of George Eliot, and to tell you the truth, I had a vague idea that he was a woman but I wasn't completely sure.'

She sat on the sofa and patted it, for me to sit down.

'Why?' she asked. 'Are you not very clever? How could you not know about George Eliot?'

I laughed, and stopped, to be certain I was choosing the right words. 'I had a controlling boyfriend,' I said carefully. 'When I was young. He said I should not bother with education. He said I would be OK if I went to what he called "the University of Life". I left him, but it was too late. I never got around to educating myself. I've always felt bad because of it. I meet someone like you, with millions of amazing qualifications and loads of languages, and I feel really, really crap.'

'Don't. We can educate you now. In the Italian language.'

'Go on then.'

'*Buongiorno, Lucia*,' she said. '*Mi chiama Gabriella*.'

I sipped the coffee. It took the skin off the inside of my mouth, and poisoned my breath for the rest of the year.

'*Buongiorno, Gabriella*,' I said, in a meek voice.

She shook her head. 'No,' she said. 'No, no, no. *Buongiorrrrrrno*.'

* * *

It was late in the afternoon when I left her flat, filled with cake, jittery with coffee, and in possession of a few new Italian phrases and a geranium cutting for which I had no home.

The darker part of me had been expecting that I would feel woozy after drinking her coffee or eating her cake, and that I would then wake up in a brothel, or at the very least in an impenetrable alley, stripped of all my belongings, probably wearing only my underwear and possibly with a kidney missing. Yet the only thing wrong with her coffee had been, I thought, its super-charged caffeination, and the fact that I had not quite liked to ask for milk because I was fairly sure that, to an Italian, that would have been sacrilegious.

Gabriella had told me she moved back to Venice a couple of years earlier, after growing up here.

'It's a good place to be,' she said. 'It's not just tourism any more. You find there's quite a scene. Design agencies, anyone who can work freelance, web companies. They're all starting to set up here. There are some great little bars these days, places to go. Of course you need to have a good income just to afford a place to live. *That* is not straightforward. Not at all.'

'So what do you do?' I asked.

'Oh, I work freelance,' she said. 'I design websites. It's easily done from here. I mean, who cares, really, if you're in Venezia or if you're in Clerkenwell or San Francisco? And this apartment, it belonged to my father, so I am lucky with that. Otherwise I could not be here.'

'So what,' I asked her carefully, 'are you doing lurking around churches talking to people like me?'

At this, she grinned broadly. 'Procrastination, of course,' she said. 'Not working when I should be working. What else?'

I wanted to believe her. I almost believed her. Maybe I really could learn enough Italian to get by. Perhaps I could become Lucia-the-waitress. Maybe there was, after all, the possibility of a bit of a life for me here. Perhaps it would actually be all right for me to trust somebody.

I set off in what she had said was the right direction, glad to be alone. We were meeting again the next day, because Gabriella wanted to show me something that she said was amusing, in a different church. The morning after that, I would have to move out of the hotel. I had asked the jowly man if I could keep room 513 for a couple more nights, but he had cringed with regret as he said no, I couldn't: it was fully booked and the only reason I'd had that room in the first place was because of a cancellation. Gabriella had said she would find me a place to live, but I did not want to bank on that. I was going to call in at every hotel I passed, and ask. My afternoon speaking to Gabriella had, at least, given me back my voice.

I walked and walked. I tried to focus on the fact that I had a friend, even if it was an odd and unconvincing sort of acquaintanceship. I tried not to think about the past, but the tide of loss seemed to be rising up from the very canals beneath my feet.

I walked faster and faster, desperate not to let reality catch up with me. The people I had loved and lost were waiting around each corner. I told myself fiercely that Seth was better off without me, that his life was simpler this way, without my complications. The banality of conversation with someone new, someone who was the best friend I had in this city at the same time as being a stranger, was too stark a contrast. I joined a main tourist route, randomly, and in every head of long brown hair I saw my mother. In every gauche teenage boy I saw Finn. Seth and Eliza were everywhere. Every little Italian girl was Imogen or Clara. Ghosts stalked me at every turn. It was unbearable.

I walked into a hotel that had two gold stars displayed outside it. A clerk looked up at me.

'Do you have a room for tomorrow?' I asked.

She shook her head. 'Sorry, madam, fully booked,' she said. 'This time of year? Better to try the mainland.'

# chapter forty

## Marianne

It turns out that you can't dash into a registry office and get married, just like that. You have to wait for four weeks, and the office has to stick it up on their noticeboard to give people a chance to object. I hope Finn doesn't know about that part.

I cannot find the strength to tell Finn that I am marrying our landlord. I know he will hate it when he finds out, so I cannot really make a grand announcement and await congratulations. I see him looking at the ring, but he says nothing either, so we don't talk about it. He doesn't get it at all. He has no idea that Benjamin makes me feel safe again.

We go to the registry office on Thursday. Benjamin makes me change into the most sensible clothes I have before we go, and we fill in the paperwork. We both show our birth certificates, and Benjamin hands over a divorce certificate. I am surprised by this, but I don't like to ask him about it, not in front of the registrar.

The registrar is a smiley man, quite old but very friendly. I think he looks a bit surprised to see us there, but he doesn't say anything. When he looks at our birth certificates, he sucks his breath past his teeth, and then glances up at me. He looks into my face very hard.

'Miss Jenkins is under eighteen,' he says. 'And so she will need written permission from her parent or guardian, before the marriage can take place.'

I am horrified by this, but Benjamin just smiles.

'Not a problem,' he says. 'What do you need? Her mother's signature?'

'Written consent from her parent or guardian.' The registrar stares at me until I look at him properly. 'You're very young,' he says gently. 'Are you sure that you are aware of the commitment you are about to enter into? Are you sure that this is something you are entering into willingly? It's not just about the wedding, if I may state the obvious. This is a commitment that should last for the rest of your life. You are, if I may say so, very young indeed to be making this sort of decision.'

I can feel Benjamin bristling and giving the man his worst scary glare, but I don't look at him. I need to answer this myself.

'Yes,' I say, looking into the man's kind eyes. 'It's the thing I want most in the whole world.'

Benjamin reaches across and takes my hand, and gives it a squeeze that lets me know I have said the right thing. I bask in his approval.

Six weeks later, I stand in front of the same man, and I say the words I have heard on TV and in films.

'I, Marianne Jane Jenkins, take you, Benjamin Godfrey Burdett, to be my lawful wedded husband.' My eyes fill with tears. Since we got engaged, everything has been magical. My sixteenth birthday was wonderful. Just Benjamin and me, at a West End show and then a Thai restaurant in Soho. I have not seen Tim and Pete again. I have felt like the most precious girl in the world. It has been perfect, apart from Finn, who has barely said a single word.

I have to stop speaking when I get to the part about 'so long as we both shall live', because I am making the biggest commitment I possibly could, and I could not be happier about it. My eyes are full of tears, but the registrar helps me through it.

I listen to Benjamin making his vows, and I feel I have stumbled into a perfect world. This man, who noticed me when he came over when Mum was still alive, who made my heart thump while I gazed at him, is actually committing himself to me, forsaking all others, for ever. It does not seem possible.

We sign the register. The witnesses, who are a man and a woman Benjamin rustled up from somewhere, congratulate us, and sign it too, and leave. We will never see them again.

He produced written consent from my mother, and it satisfied the registrar. I have no idea who wrote it, and I do not want to know.

I look at the two rings on my hand. I am married. I am Benjamin's wife. He is my husband. I am an adult. We haven't discussed it, but I suppose I will move in with him when I can leave Finn. I imagine myself being a wife. I will look after the flat, and make sure I am well dressed and have good hair. I will make Benjamin proud. I will cook for him, keep the place clean for him. I will do whatever he needs me to do.

Meanwhile, he has promised that we will go on an amazing honeymoon in Thailand, later in the summer. I have never been abroad. I don't even have a passport. Now I am going to apply for one in my new name, my married name.

Outside the registry office, he turns and sweeps me up into his arms. I giggle. The sun is shining on us, blessing our union. My husband kisses me.

'Congratulations,' he says, 'Mrs Burdett. Shall we go to our wedding reception?'

The reception turns out to be a suite at Claridges. Life, I tell myself firmly, is definitely getting better.

# chapter forty-one

## Eliza

I arranged a date with a man from the *Guardian*'s Soulmates section. I needed something to take my mind off everything else, and there was always the tiny voice saying that this time, this man, might just be the one.

I had never tried the *Guardian* before. It was, I imagined, dating for nice lefties, and so I was possibly less likely to meet a racist than I was on other sites, and more likely to meet a vegetarian (though the two things were not mutually exclusive, as evidenced by Hitler). He was called Jethro, he said. I wondered what his real name was, and whether it was a bad idea to set up a meeting with a man who was clearly lying about his very name. 'Jethro' looked, from his photo, as if he had a friendly face and he wasn't ugly, and was probably less than ten years older than me. Such were my criteria these days: I could no longer afford to be fussy. He was interested in cycling and swimming and cinema, and he lived on the other side of Truro. He was, however, coming to Falmouth, and meeting me in the Tap Room, a cocktail bar that was less of a student hangout than the other venues I had tried.

Seth was coming to sit with the girls. He came round early, and let himself in.

'Hey! Girls!' he shouted, and I could hear from his voice that he was making an effort to be cheerful. Imogen and Clara dashed from different parts of the house to converge on him. I stood at the top of the stairs and watched as he scooped them up, one in each arm (which was quite a feat), and I bit my lip and remembered the way Graham used to do the same thing. He would sit one of them on each of his shoulders until I begged him to put them down. They were a lot smaller then.

At least, I reminded myself, they had their uncle Seth. At least men were not going to be an entirely alien entity to them. I sighed, called out a greeting to my brother, and went back to my wardrobe crisis, throwing everything I owned on to the bed in a quest for exactly the right outfit for a drink with a *Guardian* reader called Jethro.

My heart was not in it. I was not going to see Jethro sitting in the bar and experience anything other than weary resignation to another evening spent scrabbling around for conversation and trying not to look at my watch. I was searching for some sort of fairy godfather, who would sprinkle magic dust all over my life and make it right again. I knew for certain that that person was not going to be Jethro. The only person who was capable of doing that was myself, and I couldn't do it.

I put on some newish jeans and a burgundy crossover top I'd bought from White Stuff, and brushed my hair. That would do. The minimum of make-up, a bit of unobtrusive lipstick and a squirt of perfume, and I was ready.

I looked at the photograph of Graham and me on the bedside table. We were in Scotland, on a hilltop, with the mist rolling around us. I was smiling at the camera, with a cheesy photo-smile, but he was looking at me. The way he was doing it made me grieve all over again, every time I looked at it. I'd had no idea, when it was taken by a random passer-by, that he was looking at me as if I were the most precious thing in the world. I had been, once. Now I was a washed-up widow, a grumpy mother, a woman whose good days were behind her, whose best friend had skipped out on her in the middle of the night without a word, without a clue.

Seth had put a balloon modelling kit on the coffee table. He looked exhausted, but he was overcompensating, getting the girls wound up and overstimulated. I didn't bother to complain.

'OK!' he shouted. 'We're ready to go! Who wants a poodle? Who wants a butterfly?'

They both wanted both. They clamoured to have the first one.

'Seth.' I was almost impressed. 'Do you actually know how to do this?'

He picked up the little pump that came in the packaging. 'There's instructions,' he said. 'How hard can it be? Have you seen some of the guys who do this stuff? If *they* can do it, I think *I* can do it.'

I shook my head.

'It's going to end badly,' I warned. 'Have you eaten? I'm going to have something before I go because I just know I'm not going to want to go to dinner with Jethro. I always end up telling these guys I've already eaten even when I haven't, and then I end up eating toast and honey in the middle of the night, and that's wrong on so many levels.'

A pink balloon sprung up in front of Seth, as he pumped. I stifled a smile, and saw that he was doing the same.

'Haven't eaten,' he admitted. 'Would like to. What about you girls? If you didn't have this, um, meeting planned, Liza, we could chill out together and I'd rustle something up for you all for dinner. Now, what do I do next, do you suppose, to make this into a dog? But since you're going out, why don't we just all have whatever's in your fridge? There's always something worth tucking into in there.' He looked at me, and said quietly, 'She went to Paris. I got the bank statement.'

'No way!'

Seth was silent, looking at the balloon in his hand. Imogen took the instructions from him. She was pink-cheeked, excited. I was glad: she had been withdrawn lately, and I realised that Lucy's disappearance had been far harder for her than I had expected. She had thought we were going to visit Lucy's mother when we went to Bristol, and the total disaster that that mission had proved to be had hit her hard.

But if Lucy was in Paris, there was hope. Paris was smaller than London. We might have a chance of finding her there.

'You needed to leave ten centimetres at the end,' Imogen told Seth.

'Bollocks,' Seth said, and both girls giggled and looked at me.

'Seth!'

'Sorry. Right, then. Start again.'

I sat down. 'I'm not going,' I told them. 'Sod it. I don't care. I'm not going to like him. He's not going to like me. I'm sick of wasting my time and money when I don't even want to meet anyone, not really. I can barely cope with what I have got, without needing to lob an extra complication into the mix. Can I join you guys for an evening's balloon modelling?'

I sent Jethro a text, overwhelmed with relief. He replied with enough petulance to quell any regrets I might have had.

# chapter forty-two

It was my penultimate hotel breakfast. After tomorrow, I would be fending for myself. I didn't care. I was still disconnected from everything.

The waiters wore white tuxedos and black bow ties. They were unflappable, however many people they were trying to seat in a limited space, and unfailingly courteous. They asked what I wanted to drink, every morning, even though I always wanted white filter coffee. They noted my room number. They were beginning to call me *signorina*, as a flirtatious courtesy, a pretence that they thought I was much younger. I was beginning to try to talk to them in Italian. No one ever asked why I was there on my own. I imagined they had seen weirder travellers than me before now.

I tried to pretend not to be English. I did my best to speak to the waiters in a generic European accent, which was (I hoped) lost on them, and I listened in on English-speaking tourists talking to each other, unaware of their nosy audience.

There was a couple on the next table, he short and squat with a froggy face, she taller and slimmer, and I had noticed when they arrived that she had her dress tucked into her knickers. They were a little younger than me, and I had been stalking them for two days, trying to work out what their relationship was like.

She opened the guide book. 'Where shall we go today?' she asked, in a too-bright voice. 'Maybe the islands? Apparently the glass-blowing on Burano is amazing!'

'Murano,' he corrected her. 'Burano's lace. Murano's the glass one. It's also a tourist-infested hellhole at this time of year, but suit yourself.'

She was undeterred. 'Well, the rest of Venice isn't exactly *not* a tourist-infested hellhole, is it?'

'Mmmm.'

After a few moments' silence she said: 'When you came here before?'

'Mmm?'

'Were you with your wife?' She said it quickly, not allowing herself a chance to change her mind.

I stole a glance. He looked annoyed. He was wearing a khaki T-shirt that was too tight at the neck and arms. It did not suit him.

'What if I was?' he muttered. 'You can't expect me not to have a past. You knew the score.'

'I know.' She was chastened. 'I know you've got a past. Fuck it, I know you've got a *present*. I just wish we could have gone somewhere that was new to both of us. Does that make sense?'

'Oh stop being ridiculous.'

'Sorry.'

They ate their breakfast in silence for a while. He caught me looking, and glared speculatively at me, while I pretended to avert my gaze and watched him from the corner of my eye.

'Honeymoon,' he said, after a while. 'We came here on our honeymoon, if you're so desperate to know.'

I stole a look at her. Her head was turned away from me, and from him.

I ploughed through an enormous plateful of pastries, as I always took enough breakfast from the buffet to see me through until dinner time, picked up the floral handbag I had bought on impulse from one of the street sellers, and slipped an apple and an orange into it. I did this discreetly, though I was sure that the waiters could not have cared less.

'*Ciao*,' I called to the man on reception, and he looked up and waved.

'*Ciao, Lucia*,' he said. That small interaction was enough to set me off with a spring in my step. It could be worse, I told myself. I would rather be all alone in the world than be that woman.

It turned out that Gabriella wanted to show me a severed foot. It was an ancient foot, brown, crispy round the edges, with deep-mustard-coloured toenails. Once upon a time, apparently, it had been attached to the leg of St Catherine. It was presented in an ornate golden holder, behind glass. I stared at it, repulsed and fascinated.

'That is the most disgusting thing I have ever seen in my life,' I said, though when I thought about it, it wasn't at all. It was, however, among the more interesting things I had seen.

'This is the Catholic Church!' said Gabriella. 'Everything is weird. Fetishised. I love it.'

'So, do you go to church?'

'To services? No, never! Apart from Christmas Eve and Easter, when I go with family. But I go into churches all the time. I missed them when I didn't live here. They are a part of my landscape. And I love, love, love the artworks in this city.'

'Do you have the guilt? The one that lapsed Catholics normally have?'

She shook her head. 'I do, in a way, but I fight it. I win most of the time. On Christmas Eve, I have it, and ten times more at Easter, but the rest of the time, no. In fact, I get angry at the Church. Which is normal as well, I think.'

I looked around. This church, Santi Giovanni e Paolo, was not on my list, and so I would never have come through its doors were it not for Gabriella. It was a cavernous building, without the side chapels the others had. There was something airy and refreshing about all the space. Footsteps echoed around, and there was a low murmur of amplified whispering. I watched Gabriella light a candle. Then I paid a few coins and lit one myself.

And although I had been to church a handful of times in my life and it had no spiritual relevance for me, the act of dropping a coin into a metal slot with a clank and taking a candle and lighting it from one that was already burning was imbued with such significance that I could not help but be transported back to the time before it all went wrong, beyond the day we realised that our mother was ill, back to the happy times when there was Mum and there was Finn and there was Marianne, and we were normal and happy.

I lit the candle for my old family, for the three of us the way we used to be. It brought peace, of sorts, peace that I knew would wither and die as I left the building.

'Right,' I said, when we came out into the square which was heaving with people. 'I'm off.'

I was still feeling disconnected from reality. I was still existing from one moment to the next. The church had been beautiful. It did not matter whether there was actually a God or not.

I stood in the sun, and looked around. There was a game of football going on over to my left, and a little humpbacked bridge in front of me, tables in the square, a gelateria, a couple of souvenir shops.

Gabriella looked at me, searching.

'Now,' she said, after a few seconds. 'I have found you a new home. Do you want to hear about it?'

I looked at her, laughing. 'Well, yes, I do. Really? I was thinking about moving to a hotel on the mainland.'

She started walking across the square. I was unsure whether we were about to plunge back into the mysterious maze that led, eventually, to her flat. I hoped not.

The paving slabs underfoot were bleached out by the sunlight, and I could feel the heat rising, reflected by them. Groups of people were crowded together in the sparse patches of shade.

'But then you wouldn't be in Venice,' she pointed out.

'I know.' She was still walking, purposeful. I grabbed her arm.

'Let's have an ice cream,' I suggested, and I pulled her to the end of the lengthy queue. The ice-cream shop here was framed with dark-green painted wood, with GELATERIA painted in old-fashioned writing on it.

She acquiesced, and stood beside me in the queue, jumping from foot to foot.

'So,' she said, beaming at me. 'It is perfection. My friend, Antonio, I know him from school. He is an artist, from a very good Venetian family. He has a studio near San Polo. There is a little side room. He used to sleep there sometimes. You can have it for a month, for five hundred euros. It's not luxurious, not like your hotel. But I think you'll like it.'

She looked at me, waiting for a reaction. I made a conscious effort, and smiled. I was going to move into a studio. That was good. It was a bit weird, but I did not care. Gabriella might be odd, but she had nothing to do with the man from whom I was fleeing. I ordered us the biggest, best ice creams I could see.

'Could I move in tomorrow, do you think?' I asked.

She nodded, and took out her phone.

'Let me speak to Antonio,' she said. 'But I am sure you could, yes.'

I listened as she spoke in Italian so rapidly that I had no chance of even picking out words that I knew. All I recognised was my name, Lucia, from time to time. I licked my strawberry ice cream and felt my hair become damp with sweat. Gabriella's conversation became more and more animated, and then she started laughing, and hung up.

'Right,' she said, smiling at me. 'Yes, you can move in tomorrow. You have to meet me and Antonio and some other friends tonight. Then you can talk to him and we can all help you settle in, become a Venetian. Come to Mondo DiVino. Just go to Campo Santi Apostoli, which is easy to find because it's very touristy. Ask the guy at the sweet stall. He'll show you the way. Come at about seven. Now I have to go home and do some work.'

I smiled. 'All right.'

'We will make you speak Italian. All night long.'

I shrugged. 'OK.'

I wandered off, following a group of sightseers over the little bridge, and drifted around the alleys until I found a handwritten sign in a café window promising INTERNET 2€ 30 MINS. I stood outside, stared inside at a free computer, and swallowed hard.

Just a quick email to say I was all right. That was all that was needed. A tiny bit of reassurance for Eliza and Seth.

I couldn't do it. Something stopped me short, and made me turn around and carry on walking, shoving my way into the crowds until I dissolved.

# chapter forty-three

## Marianne

I sit across the table from Finn, in our crappy little kitchen, and I smile at him. He hates this. He knows why I am smiling. I'm smiling because I am a married woman.

I am Benjamin's wife. It makes me feel outrageously grown up. I am more grown up than my mother ever was, because she was never anybody's wife. I am sixteen, I have left school, and I am married. I am a woman now.

Finn hates that.

'Stop smirking at me,' he says, and he shifts his chair noisily backwards and puts his feet up on the table, his heavy Doc Marten boots still on his feet. Then he looks at me, challenging me to say something.

'Feet off the table,' I tell him. He laughs, but not in a friendly way.

'Oh listen to you. Fucking hell.'

'Language,' I say, purely to annoy him.

I am happy. I have a husband who is handsome and rich, who loves me and cherishes me. But I still have to live here, still have to be some sort of guardian to my little brother, even though he's only a year and a bit younger than I am. As soon as I can, I am going to move into Benjamin's apartment and let Finn fend for himself. I wanted to bring him with me, just until he could leave school, but Benjamin hated the idea of a teenage boy moving into his lovely flat.

'Girls are one thing,' he said, stroking my cheek. 'Boys – well, I've been one. I know what they're like.'

So I am still living at home, in the crappy little house which I suppose I now partly own.

Finn glares at me, and I smile sweetly back. I twist my rings on my fingers. An engagement ring and a wedding ring. I am going to wear them for ever, because I am going to be with Benjamin for ever.

It is lucky that I spend so much time reminding myself how happy I am, because otherwise things would feel a bit uncontrollable. Finn and I fight, but that is almost all right. When Benjamin and I argue, it feels completely different. It happens more and more, and then I get scared that he's going to divorce me, and so I cry and say, 'I'm sorry, I'm sorry, I'm sorry,' over and over again, until he pulls me close and tells me to *shhh*, and strokes my hair and promises that he will never, ever leave me, that marriage is for life and that he will take care of me for ever.

We argue about Benjamin's horrible friends, and we argue about Finn. I don't want to see his friends, because I hate the things that happen when we see them, and he doesn't want me to look after Finn any more.

'I don't know why you think you're above everyone else,' Finn says now. He is still in his school uniform, because he just got home, but he has grown huge over the summer. He is far taller than I am. We need to buy him some new clothes. 'You're really not. In fact, you're pathetic.'

'Cheers.' I smile at him. 'You know I'm only here because I have to look after you.'

'Yeah. You really, really have to look after me, because it is so great for me to have you around. I have no bloody idea what I would do without you. Why don't you bugger off and screw your darling *husband*?'

'He's your brother-in-law.'

'Mmm, lucky old me. Marianne, I can look after myself. One day I won't come home. Then you won't have to break off from whatever it is you do with that slimy git to come here and tell me to take my feet off the table.' We both look at his feet. He slowly takes them down. 'What time's *hubby* coming?' he adds.

'He's not. Not today. I'm here with you.'

'Well hurrah!' He says it in a *Blackadder* voice, the voice of Hugh Laurie. We only have a little black-and-white TV, and it has a shitty little antenna, but occasionally we manage to be in the same room for long enough to watch something together. Secretly I think that the times when that happens are the best times of my life, at the moment.

'I've got a cake,' I say, and we both know this signifies a truce.

He nods. 'Let's have it then.' He looks at me, suddenly suspicious. 'As long as it's not wedding cake.'

We sit at the table, the same table where we always used to sit, covered with the same floral tablecloth, and we each eat a slice of a cake that Mum would never in a million years have put in front of us. It is bought from a shop, decorated with cream and unseasonal strawberries. Inside there are layers of sponge and jam and cream.

I bought it with the money that Benjamin has started giving me. We never quite talk about where that money comes from, not Benjamin and I, nor Finn and I. There is a very dark place in my mind, somewhere I will never be able to go. As long as I keep it shut off, I can get through the days. He is my husband, I remind myself when the voice starts up deep in the recesses of my brain. He looks after me. And I shut all the rest of it away.

I make tea in the rubbish teapot that Finn made at school, when they did pottery, and pour it quickly before the liquid starts to seep out of the base. This means it comes out weak, but we don't mind, because this is the way we always drink it. We sit and eat, and for a moment I feel so sad, so broken, that tears come to my eyes for no reason. Finn sees them, but for a long time he says nothing.

After he finishes his second piece of cake, he wipes his mouth on his sleeve, and says, 'You should bin him. Divorce the fucker. Get half his money.'

I nod. I open my mouth to say, 'No, I love him,' but instead I find myself saying: 'I can't. He knows what we did. With the pills.'

'He couldn't shop us. He was there. He helped us bury her. That's got to be a crime. Don't you think? It doesn't exactly make him look good, anyway.'

I shake my head. 'I'm scared.' Again, that is not what I intended to say, and it surprises me. I had thought I was going to say: 'I love him.'

'Yeah.' He reaches for my plate, and I hand it to him. I have only eaten half my piece of cake, and even that feels like too much. He finishes it, picks up the plate, and licks it. I watch my brother while he does this. He could never imagine how tender he makes me feel. Finn hangs out with the cool crowd these days, and he drinks and smokes and goes out on school nights, but he is, all the same, so innocent that he makes me cry. His shaggy hair. The freckles across his nose. His clear white skin. I look at him and I see our childhood, the way it was before Mum got ill, and I realise how much she protected us from the world, and I miss her so much that I am burning up from the inside, and I want to hurt myself as much as I can, just so that I can feel something else.

'Sorry.' It comes out choked.

He looks up, eyebrows raised, waiting for more. I take a deep breath.

'Sorry that I've fucked up so much. We could have been all right, but I screwed it up, I guess.'

I shouldn't be saying this. This is not what I meant to say at all.

He shrugs and pours some more tea, then uses a dirty tea towel to mop up the pool of tea from under the pot. 'You didn't, Marianne. It was when he found us trying to dump a dead body. After that you were his, no matter what. He knew about Mum, and so he owned us. Now he knows about the pills, he *really* owns us. So he could marry you if it took his fancy. Which it did.' He bites his lip and stares out of the window. 'I'm going to get out of here,' he says. 'I really mean it. I can't do this.'

'No you're not! Where could you go?'

'I've got a couple of ideas. It's my business. Perhaps I'll marry a rich older woman and move into her pad by the river.'

'Shut up.'

'Well I mean it. I'm going to go my way and let you go yours.'

'No you're not! Finn – I'm sorry. I said I was sorry. Don't leave.'

'Why not?'

'Because . . .' I swallow hard. 'Because I'd miss you so much.'

He shrugs. Then he gets up and crashes noisily up the stairs. I stay at the table, finishing the weak tea I don't even want. I wait until Finn comes back downstairs, wearing his baggy jeans and a hooded top, and I look at him expectantly.

'Going out,' he says. 'Don't worry. I'll be back.' And the door slams noisily behind him.

I feel so terribly alone. I concentrate hard, and try to enter a world where, just for a second, I am still a child. If I try, I can convince myself that Mum is upstairs, that in a minute she will come down and start cooking carrot soup for dinner. I close my eyes, and for a few blissful seconds I am there.

Then I open them, and everything is real again. I cannot bear to sit here on my own. I get myself back into the right frame of mind. I love Benjamin. I do. I truly love him. I say it over and over again in my head, until I acknowledge that it is true. Then I sigh with relief. I need him. I pick up a bag and my keys, and decide to go to him. I run to the Tube.

I am wearing jeans and a sweatshirt, and I don't look sexy or pretty or interesting at all, but I love him, and he loves me, and so that will be all right. You don't always have to dress nicely for your husband.

He only lives three Tube stops away, but when I get out at West India Quay, it is, as it always is, a different world. There are men hurrying around in suits, looking important and busy. I have met a few of these men, I am sure, over the past couple of months. I shudder, and keep my head down, and walk through the middle of the crowds.

His apartment block is right by the river. I tap in the door code – 1315 – and take the lift up to the top floor. I knock on the front door of the flat and smile, ready for him. When he answers, I will throw myself into his arms, and it will all be all right.

The door swings open, and I make sure my smile is as bright

as it can possibly be. He won't like me in jeans but he will let me change into one of the outfits I have here. I look up.

Then I look down. I twist my rings around. I look up again.

Benjamin's door has been opened by a girl. She is wearing a silky dressing gown that belongs to me, and I can see that she is naked underneath. I tell myself quickly that she must be one of his friend's girlfriends, but the thing that keeps me staring is her age.

She is drunk and swaying slightly, and she is looking at me with glassy eyes, but however much she may be dressed and acting like someone older, she cannot possibly be more than twelve. She is a child.

I hear his voice from inside. 'Who is it, doll? Is it Pete?'

Then I turn and run.

# chapter forty-four

## Eliza

'I'm not in the dating game at the moment,' I warn him, as I kick my shoes off and tuck my feet underneath me. We are at an outdoor table at the Gylly café, sitting opposite each other on wicker sofas with a table between us. It is almost dark outside, and the sea is shining gently with the last of the day's light. A tea light on the table flickers in the breeze. The waves suck the stones on the beach.

Patrick asked me out for a drink. I am wary, because I suspect he just wants to talk about Lucy, but I agreed anyway. It was an excuse to come out and sit by the beach.

'That's OK,' says Patrick, and he smiles at me. I grin back. For some reason I am comfortable with him in a way I am not with any of the other men I have met since Graham. I have, however, been on a 'date' with him once before and it was disastrous, because he spent two hours grilling me about Lucy. 'It's not really a date,' he adds. 'I just thought it would be nice to see you, that's all.'

I smile at him. That is possibly the nicest thing anyone has said to me since Leonard Cohen promised that if I wanted to sleep a moment on the road, he would steer for me.

'Well, that's nice,' I say. 'To be honest, it's great to have an excuse to get out of the house. I'm not exactly inundated with invitations these days.'

'I guess there's been no word from Lucy?'

I knew it.

'No,' I tell him. 'Nothing at all.'

'Not a single word?'

I wish I had stayed at home. I was stupid to hope that Patrick might want to see me for my own sake.

'Nothing. She was in Paris the last time she used her bank card, but she used it at a railway station, somewhere called Austerlitz. We can't get anyone to tell us what she bought, but the trains from that station go to Spain and south-west France, so we think she's probably somewhere over there.'

'Right.'

'We tracked down this woman who we thought was her mother, but it was an absolute catastrophe. Let's just say it was the wrong person.'

Patrick puts his hand on mine. 'She's going to be all right,' he says. 'I bet she is. She's a strong type.'

'Well, who knows? She could be at the bottom of a lake, or she could be sunning herself on the Med.'

Patrick has always had a thing for Lucy. He's tried to hide it, but I know that he has loved her from afar for years.

'I think she's probably pretty resourceful,' he says, and I can hear that he's trying to convince us both. 'She'll be back if she can.'

'Yeah.'

I look at him. His hair is a lovely chestnut brown. He is wearing a red fleece that is open at the neck, and a leather necklace he always wears, with a polished stone on it.

'Anyway, let's not be maudlin,' he says quickly. 'How are your girls? Imogen's got a birthday coming up, hasn't she?'

I am surprised. 'Yes, she has. How clever of you to remember that. She's going to be eight. When she goes back to school, she'll be in year four. She seems so grown up. The past few years have dragged by, because it's been such a huge effort just getting through each hour. But now, all of a sudden, things are starting to fly. Graham's been gone for nearly three years. Immy's almost eight. I guess Stephen Hawking could explain it. Time slowing down and speeding up and all that.'

'Yes,' he says. 'I expect he could.'

I tell myself to stop talking about my children and all the dull minutiae of my life.

'Sorry,' I say, looking down. 'People with children are pretty bloody boring, aren't they?'

He looks up, surprised. 'No,' he says. 'Eliza, you're not boring at all. Nor are your children. Far from it. When I see Imogen at school, it always makes me smile because she looks so much like you. I hope I get her in my class when the time comes.'

'Really?'

'Yes. And I know you've been avoiding me in the playground.'

The waves start to crash louder and I feel the air suddenly become heavy with rain. He leans forward. I look into his dark eyes and my stomach lurches. I am plunged into the grip of dormant forces that have left me alone for years. I think quickly of Graham. I don't think that he would mind. I am fairly sure that, much as he would hate me to be feeling like this about another man, he would, under the circumstances, give me his blessing on this one.

Then I make a huge effort and put Graham from my mind, and focus on the man in front of me.

'I'm sorry,' he is saying, but he could be saying anything. It is the way he is looking at me. 'When we went out together before, it was a bit of a write-off, and that was my fault. I'm sorry . . .'

'Come and sit next to me,' I say, on impulse, because it feels right. I pat the cushion next to me. 'It's getting all windy.'

As he moves to sit close to me, the first drops of rain begin to fall.

# chapter forty-five

The evening was cooler than usual, and a gentle breeze was channelled down the wide street as I asked the sweet-stall owner for directions. He was a heavy-set man with jaw-length curly hair and a dark tan.

'*Mondo DiVino, per favore*,' I said carefully.

He nodded and pointed out the way.

'Down this one,' he said, in English, pointing to a well-trodden walkway over a little bridge. 'On the right.'

I set off, but when I found myself in a square with a church in it, I felt I should turn back. There was a nice-looking wine bar on the other side of the little street, and I put my head in and said '*Mondo DiVino?*' hopefully, but the woman shook her head, pointed across the road, and said something quickly. I gathered that she was not delighted to be asked directions to a rival establishment.

Back at the sweet stall, the man looked into my eyes for five long seconds, laughed, and shouted something to the man at the neighbouring handbag stall. Then he took me by the top of the arm and marched me back the way I had come, along the same stretch of paving stones, weaving quickly between the people, all of whom seemed to be moving in the opposite direction, against us.

We stopped outside a tiny place that had escaped my notice before, a little doorway, a window. He gestured to it, ruffled my hair, and ran back to his stall.

Gabriella was not there. It was ten past seven. I took a deep breath, and walked through the open door.

The tiny room was full of people, although this only meant that there were perhaps fifteen people there. The sound of impenetrable Italian conversation filled the air. No one turned to look at me, so I pushed my way to the centre of the room and stood still. The walls were lined with bottles of wine, most of them lying on their sides in wooden compartments. There were a few bottles of liqueurs on a shelf. I wondered whether to leave. I longed to leave, but if I did, I would have to move to the mainland in the morning.

I did my best to look nonchalant, but still people started turning to look at me. A man nearby said something to me in Italian, and I smiled, shook my head (with no idea of what it was I had just said no to) and made my way to the bar. A very young, very happy-looking woman turned towards me, pushed her hair behind her ears, and grinned expectantly.

Young people, I thought, and I envied her. They have no idea of the things that can happen. I did, when I was her age.

'*Vino bianco?*' I asked.

When Gabriella and her friends pushed their way into the throng. I was sitting on a high bar stool with a large glass of Pinot Grigio in my hand. The woman at the bar was keeping an eye on me, and speaking to me when she got a second in Italian that was slowed down so much that even I could understand it. I had told her, in a mixture of languages, that I was waiting for friends. She had asked how long I was in Venice for, but had to rush off and discuss fruity reds with a customer before I'd been able to answer.

'*Ciao, bella!*' called Gabriella from the doorway. She must have shouted at the top of her voice to make it carry above the ambient chatter. I turned in relief. She pushed through the room with a cluster of people following her, and took me firmly by the shoulders and kissed me hard on each cheek.

'This,' she said, turning to her little crowd and gesturing grandly at me, 'is Lucia. And here is Delfina, Giorgio, Alberto, and there, at the back – Antonio.'

I froze. These people were intimidating. In front of their

confidence, their homogeneity as a group, their lovely clothes and perfect skin, I shrank inside myself. I wanted to step into the shadows, to disappear. Instead, I had to smile, so I made my mouth turn up at the corners and looked at Antonio, the man who was, perhaps, going to let me move into his studio.

Gabriella's friends were all looking at me. They were assessing me. I could imagine how I looked to them. Ungainly, inelegant, English. Then the other woman, Delfina, stepped forward and kissed me on each cheek, speaking in such fast Italian that although I knew I ought to be able to understand her, it washed over me. She was very tall, and very skinny, with hair cropped closely to her head in a style that, were I to try it, would make me look seriously ill. On her it was chic and gamine and made her almost otherworldly. She leaned down to speak to me, and I nodded, too shy to tell her that I didn't understand.

Then Alberto, who was short and stocky with curly hair, came to kiss me, and then Giorgio, who was thin with long hair slicked back from his head, and finally there was Antonio.

When he came closer, I almost laughed. I had imagined Gabriella's artist friend to be bohemian and scruffy. In reality I appeared to be about to rent a room from George Clooney. Antonio was ridiculously good-looking, with an olive complexion and perfect even features. He was wearing a white linen shirt and a pair of expensive-looking trousers.

He kissed me on both cheeks. He smelled of cologne.

'You don't look like an artist,' I told him. He looked at Gabriella, who translated. He said something in reply, and she laughed and hit him on the arm.

'He says you don't look like a penniless backpacker,' she told me. 'Which, you must believe me, is not how I described you, but all the same, it seems to be the impression he took.'

I looked at Antonio. He was in his early forties, I thought. Around the same age as Gabriella. The other three looked younger, although it was hard to tell in this busy room with its dim lighting. He looked back into my eyes, held my gaze for a moment, then smiled and joined Gabriella at the bar.

* * *

Several hours later, I had lost count of how many times my glass had been topped up. I was sitting precariously on a bar stool and doing my best to speak Italian, while the others were trying out their English. Only Gabriella was able to bridge the two.

Someone put a hand on my shoulder. When I looked up, it was Antonio.

'Lucia?' he asked. 'I want to ask you.'

I looked up, watching him frowning slightly as he struggled to find the words in English.

'*Si?*' I said, trying to be encouraging.

'I like you to live in my studio,' he said slowly. 'You like . . . ?'

As he seemed to have ground to a halt, I put a hand on Gabriella's arm and drew her away from Alberto, into our conversation. She and Antonio spoke for a few seconds, and then she turned to me.

'He says, would you like to earn some money by helping him sell some of his and other people's art?'

I nodded. 'Of course! I'd love to earn some money.'

They both smiled. 'Good,' Gabriella said. 'His studio – from time to time he transforms it into a gallery. When he and his friends have some work to show. It's completely normal. When collectors come from abroad, we all join in, make the studio look beautiful so there is a place for them to come and see the work.'

I smiled. 'And maybe it pushes the price up a bit too?'

She raised her eyebrows. 'Well, of course. That is the main reason.'

'So he'd like me to help him?'

'Yes. Some collector is coming from America. He met them at the Biennale. They are coming this week. Antonio says an English receptionist would be a very good thing. If you will be the receptionist for two days, you could live there free of charge for a month.'

I nodded at once. 'Sure. That sounds like fun.'

I tried not to smile too brightly. I was feeling warm and fuzzy inside, feeling wanted. It was surely a short step from being a temporary gallery receptionist to actually living here.

Antonio leaned forward. 'You speak English,' he said. 'For the Americans, this is good.'

I nodded again. 'And just for two days?'

He said something to Gabriella. She answered.

'Americans don't stay long,' she said. 'Always rushing. But he has various visitors of this sort. It could become a regular thing, if you liked.'

I nodded, and started contemplating what I would wear in my new role. I would need to make myself very chic. It would be an interesting project.

'Does he do that often?' I checked with Gabriella.

'Yes,' she said. 'He does it from time to time, if need be. He maintains a gallery website for such moments. I make it for him.'

I looked around the room. Things seemed to be panning out all right. I caught Delfina's eye for a second. She was looking straight at me, in a way that made me briefly uncomfortable. Then she looked away, and I did too, and everything was normal again.

# chapter forty-six

The next morning I checked out of the Gabrielli Sandwirth, with two small bags bursting at the seams with my paltry worldly goods. One was the black backpack I had stored under the bed in my other life in Falmouth. The other was the handbag I had bought from one of the street vendors. It was fake Prada and I was rather fond of it.

The jowly man shook my hand across the reception desk, his chins wobbling with the vigour of his handshake, and confirmed that I owed him nothing.

'You leave Venice this morning?' he asked.

'No,' I told him. 'I'm staying around. I have a room to move into, but I haven't even seen it yet. Near San Polo. I'm learning Italian. I might even have something that is almost a little bit like work.'

He raised his eyebrows and nodded. I sensed that not many of his guests stuck around to do things that could be classified as work. Most of them probably left in an expensive water taxi to the airport.

'Your friends,' he said. They had come back with me last night, had a final drink in the hotel bar, loudly and with no consideration for the other guests, as he had told them several times.

'Sorry about that,' I said, at once. 'I'm really sorry.'

'No, is OK. It was not you,' he said. 'But these people. How well do you know them?'

'Well enough,' I said. 'I'll be fine.'

'Well, if you very much need work,' he said. 'Although the money is probably not what you want. We sometimes have work for waitress or chambermaid. At least you know this is good job.' He picked up a hotel card, and scrawled something on it. 'Here you are. Luigi. Call me, Lucia, if you need to. For any reason.'

I was unexpectedly touched. In fact, I was so touched that I had to pretend to cough, to disguise the tears in my eyes. I nodded, and blinked hard, and thanked him. I saw him noticing my weakness. I hurried away, stroking the card in my pocket.

It was oppressively hot. There were clouds high in the sky, moving in quickly, and the air was electric. I set off, walking through the city towards the next little room that I would call home. It was still early enough for the streets not to be overwhelmingly busy. I looked at the façades of the hotels I passed, the Metropole, the Danieli, the Locanda Vivaldi, and I imagined the amount of breakfast-eating that was still going on inside them, the random people from the rich countries of the world stuffing their faces with croissants and coffee and bread and eggs, just because it was included in the hefty price they were paying for a lagoon-side room.

A few local-looking men and women were out jogging, singly or in pairs. I watched a woman's tiny body with muscular, shapely legs, and I envied her confidence, her fitness. If I was staying here, I decided, I would get myself some trainers and start running again. I walked all the time because it was the only way to get around this mad place, but running would be something different altogether. Running would be purposeful.

I rarely used the vaporetti, and when I did, I often fare-dodged, after Gabriella had shouted at me when she caught me paying for a ticket.

'They never check tickets!' she yelled, when she saw me handing over two euros to cross the Grand Canal. 'Never! If you see inspectors waiting at the stop, you just get off. That's it. Seriously, don't be scared.'

'But,' I tried to say, 'it's a good service, and if no one bought a ticket, the vaporetti wouldn't be able to function.'

She shook her head. 'No, no, no. This is all wrong. Yes, they are useful, often essential. So they should get their fucking act together. They know everybody travels for free. But they don't bother to put in turnstiles, or check tickets. They don't bother with any of it. Because they don't care. They could take so much more money if they wanted, but they don't give a shit. It's them. Not me. In fact, by *not* buying a ticket, you're taking a moral position. Let them sort themselves out, get off their fucking arses, if they want your money.'

So now, as I was trying to be a Venetian, I did not buy a ticket when I travelled on the boats. All the same, unless I was going a long way, I preferred to get around on foot. I had worked out where the worst of the bottlenecks occurred, and attempted elaborate detours to avoid the area around St Mark's Square and the Rialto bridge. It generally didn't work: I got lost and wandered aimlessly until I saw a sign for 'Rialto', then followed its trail until suddenly I would step out of a dark alley into the full flow of tourist Venice, and take my place in the crowds moving at a shuffle amongst the stalls selling the same souvenirs, endlessly, as each other: the T-shirts, the tapestry bags with *Venezia* written on them, the plastic gondolas, the masks. I hated the masks. They freaked me out more than they ought to have done, with the elaborate carnival aesthetic, the harlequin pattern, and, worst of all, the elongated nose that had once been a representation of the plague doctor. I imagined cloaked figures in carnival costumes jumping out at me from around corners.

But today I was on a mission. I was going to cross the Rialto bridge, normally something I avoided, and follow the paths more or less straight ahead until I reached Piazza San Polo. There I would wait for Gabriella, and then I would follow her to my new home.

The crowds in Piazza San Polo were much thinner than elsewhere, and there was a higher ratio of Italians to tourists than there was anywhere around San Marco. This was a huge square, the second biggest, and the thing I loved most about it was the fact that it was so bare. There was a church at one corner, a gorgeous church that I had visited on my Chorus Pass. Like almost every church in Venice, as far as I could tell, it contained works by Tintoretto and Tiepolo, and while I was visiting it, I had listened enthralled to a French couple who were holding a vicious argument in whispers. I had barely understood a word, and yet I had understood it all.

I scanned the area for Gabriella, and when she wasn't there, I went to the café and took the furthest-out table, the closest to the square.

'*Cappuccino, per favore*,' I said to the waiter, concentrating on my accent, pleased with myself. He nodded and disappeared. I stretched out my bare legs, and tipped my head back, and felt the sun on my face.

I was conscientiously not thinking about the life I had left behind in Cornwall. I was trying to shut down, to nail everything I had left behind into a sturdy box and bury it deep underground, or to throw it into a hole in the ground and wait for an office building to appear on top of it. This, I knew, was the only way to cope.

My new lodgings would be obscure, and much safer than a hotel. No one would look for me in a room off an artist's studio, and a tiny pseudo-gallery would be more obscure still.

I sipped the coffee, and forced myself to breathe deeply.

She appeared beside me, and I realised I had closed my eyes, because I hadn't noticed her approaching.

'Hey there, Lucia,' she said. 'It's a big day!'

I sat up straight and made myself grin. 'Yes,' I agreed. 'A very big, very exciting day. You want a coffee?'

She shook her head. 'No, I want us to go. Come on.' She was carrying a large bag, and she pulled it up her shoulder expectantly.

I left the money on the table, and we set off.

'Did you get your work done?' I asked, as we walked.

She laughed and waved an arm. 'I did not go to bed! I came home drunk and I worked for four hours. I drank coffee all night and slept in a chair for two hours! I cannot have any more coffee today because I'm already jittering like . . . like . . .'

'Like a jittery thing?'

'Yes, like one of those. I am frantic with this project. I need to sleep later but I can't because of all the coffee. Why didn't I start it sooner? Next time, make me start sooner.'

I skipped along in my efforts to keep up with her. She led me straight out of the square, round a few corners, down an alleyway.

'Gabi!' I complained. 'I'm supposed to be remembering this. Slow down!'

She laughed over her shoulder, supercharged with caffeine. 'I'll mark it on the map! You'll be fine. The only way to learn it is to work it out for yourself. Keep a map with you, and you can't go wrong.'

'Yeah, right.'

After a few minutes, she stopped. It took me a moment to realise that we were there. We were beside a little canal, though I had been told firmly that only the Grand Canal, the Giudecca and the Cannaregio were actually canals, and that everything else was a *rio*. The building on my left was a smaller version of the palazzi that lined the Grand Canal. It had large, grand windows, and its plasterwork was cream and crumbling. I stepped back and looked up, wondering which would be my window.

Gabriella was fiddling in her big basketwork handbag.

'Keys!' she said, triumphantly, and she handed me a key ring with three keys on it. One of them was big and old-fashioned. It was ornate, and very slightly rusty. When I touched it, it left oil on my hand, and I was grateful that Antonio had done that for me, because the last place I wanted to be was standing in an alley beside a little canal at night, unable to open my front door.

The other two were standard Yale keys. I put the big key into a huge lock in the big black door. It turned easily. One of the smaller ones opened the top lock, and I stepped into an entrance hall, Gabriella right behind me.

The hall was tiled with old cream tiles that were dirty and chipped and which suited the building perfectly. The sun shone through the open front door, a black line of shadow cutting diagonally across the floor. There were doors off to the left and right, and a staircase went up in front of us. The hall smelt a little musty, with top notes of cleaning products.

The door slammed shut, and suddenly the only light was the ghostly half-light that came down the stairs from the landing.

'Up we go,' said Gabriella, gesturing for me to go before her.

There was only one door on the first-floor landing. I stopped and waited, and Gabriella pointed to it. The second Yale key opened it, and I stepped into my new home.

I had imagined somewhere that was poky and cramped, in the manner of anything that is described as a 'studio' by an estate agent. Instead, Antonio appeared to own a banqueting hall that took up the whole of this floor. There were huge floor-to-ceiling windows on three sides, and light poured in from all directions. There were acres of empty floor space, and abstract canvases were displayed around the edge of the room, leaning against the walls and windows. A smell of oil paint permeated the air. It was messy: the floor was stained with paint despite some splodgy sheets that were spread around in places. There was a jam jar in the corner with a screwdriver and a hammer in it, and many more that were full of brushes of every size. This could be transformed into an amazing gallery. All it needed was a desk by the front door, a bit of a clean, and some price labels.

There was a chunk taken out of the huge room, where the stairwell was. On the other side of this, three little rooms opened up off the main studio. All of them were tiny. One was a washroom, which had a basin with cold water and a tiny shower cubicle. Another was a storeroom packed to bursting with painting supplies. The third contained nothing but a mattress on the floor. This, it transpired, was my new bedroom. The window was bigger than the mattress. I was moving into a pool of light.

'You like it?' asked Gabriella. I stared at her.

'It's amazing,' I told her. 'Incredible. But why does Antonio want me living here? Will I need to keep out of the flat while he's painting?'

'You've met him,' she said. 'He is very easy-going. He likes having someone here, especially if you can help him sell his paintings.'

I put my bag on the mattress, and opened the top section of the window. If I stood on tiptoe, I could lean out. The canal, the *rio*, was narrow, and it glinted in the light. On the other side, there were other people's windows. I could see a bridge if I looked to my right. To my left there was a little boat moored on one side of the water. That was all. I took a deep breath of hot salty air, and I swallowed hard.

I turned to Gabriella. She was already unpacking her bag, spreading a sheet on the bed for me, adding a sleeping bag on top of it.

'Thank you!' I said. 'Look, Gabi, you've done so much for me. Getting me this place. Lending me bedding. Being my friend. Just . . . everything.'

She shook her head. 'It's a pleasure.'

'Well, any time I can do anything for you . . .'

She smiled and sat down on the bed she had just made for me.

'When I was in London,' she said, 'one of the girls on my course did this for me. She looked after me, helped me round the city, showed me where to go for food. I was panicking so much to start with, desperate to go home. She made it OK for me. I always said I would do the same for a Londoner one day. Now I have the chance.' She produced a bottle from her bag with a flourish. 'Here we are! Now we celebrate your new life.'

I looked at the prosecco. 'Are you sure? Don't you have to work, or sleep, or something?'

She shook her head. 'Later.'

I found some clean-looking jam jars in the store cupboard. Gabriella popped the cork out.

'Thanks for not asking me anything,' I said quietly, as she poured the bubbling liquid into the jam jars.

'That's fine,' she said. We sat on the floor, and drank prosecco from jam jars in my new, wonderful home.

'Tomorrow,' she said, 'we make this place look smart. And then we make you into someone new.'

# chapter forty-seven

## Marianne

I run out of the building and along the river front for a bit. I don't stop until I am far enough away from the building. No one is coming after me. Of course he's not coming after me. He has someone else to entertain him.

I keep trying to tell myself that it is all right. She cannot have been naked for him. That is not possible, because I am his wife. He is married to me. He has forsaken all others. She must have been there for Tim and Pete and the rest of them. But she is too young. She was naked under my dressing gown, I could see that, and she was too young.

I duck into a doorway, which takes me into a courtyard. It is a newish block of yuppie flats. There are a few doors into the building, each with a lot of doorbells next to it. The yard itself is planted with the sort of plants that wouldn't really grow there: yucca and things like that. Mum would have taken a cutting from a couple of them, and grown them at home.

And all of a sudden it is too much for me. I am sixteen. My mother is dead. I have failed my brother. I am married to a man who is more than twice my age, and there is a naked child in my husband's flat. Although I have done everything in my power not to admit it to myself, I know that he spikes my drinks and lets his friends have sex with me.

Those are the facts. This is the moment I have to face them. The horror of it is so enormous that I don't think I can carry on living.

I have known it all along – of course I have – but I have tried to pretend that I have been imagining it all, because if I face up to it, I will have nothing. The world will be worse than it has ever been. My husband only likes me because I have a young body, one that he can sell.

I crouch down beside a wall, and I curl up and screw my eyes tight shut and wait for it to go away. Then I am hiccuping, and then the tears are coming, and then I cannot control myself, at all. I want to hurt myself. I want to be away from all of this.

A man and a woman are looking at me. They are standing up, and it seems that I am lying on the floor, curled up like a foetus.

'I'm calling the police,' the man says. At this, I twist myself around and sit up. They cannot do that.

The woman crouches next to me. I look at her. She is only about twenty-five, but she is wearing expensive clothes, and she probably lives in one of these flats. I like her blue raincoat. Her hair is glossy and styled and she is wearing nice make-up. I wonder whether anything like this has ever happened to her. She doesn't look as if her world has ever fallen apart around her.

'Are you OK?' she asks. I nod. 'No,' she says, with a little laugh. 'You're not all right. It was a stupid question. What's the matter? Have you run away from home or something?'

I shake my head and wipe my face with the sleeve of my sweat-shirt. I'm glad I'm not wearing the sort of clothes Benjamin gets me to wear, or they'd think I was a prostitute.

'No, I'm fine,' I say. I say it as firmly as I can. I look up at the man. He has a suit on, and he is looking at me as if he can't be bothered to deal with me. He is holding a mobile phone in his hand. Benjamin has one of those.

'No, I'll call the police,' he says. 'They'll take you home, sort you out. Come on, Linda. Leave it to the pros.'

I am on my feet. 'No, honestly,' I say quickly. Linda has her hand on my arm. I let it stay there for a few seconds because I like the feel of her touch. Then I pull away and start walking backwards towards the gate. 'I'm sorry I'm in your garden. I didn't mean to be. I just had a bit of . . .' I bite my lower lip. 'Boy trouble.'

Then, before either of them can say anything else, I turn and run.

I run all the way home. It takes me ages but I don't care. Running takes up part of my brain, and it lets me put off the moment when I have to deal with this.

When I get home, my chest is burning and I am almost feeling strong. I am not, however, strong enough. I will never be strong enough.

I burst in through the front door. Finn has to be home. I don't know what I will do if he is not.

'Finn?' I yell.

There is silence for a few seconds. Then a faint cry of 'Up here!' comes from upstairs.

As soon as I see him, sitting on his bunk bed cross-legged, a book in front of him, a cigarette in his mouth, a saucer functioning as a makeshift ashtray in his hand, my lip starts to wobble again. Snot gathers in my nose, ready to drip, and my eyes sting with tears.

He stubs out the cigarette and leaps down. I cannot say anything. He puts an arm around me, and then pulls me closer. I cry into his shoulder. He holds me close and waits. I sob and gasp for breath. Tears and snot soak Finn's sweatshirt, but he does not push me away. In the end, it stops, and I feel empty. I pull away. I feel Finn looking at me.

'Can I kill him?' he asks. 'Say yes.'

I sit on the bottom bunk. I don't sleep here any more: I moved into Mum's room a few weeks after she died, when I felt we had aired it enough, when we had washed her old bedding enough times for it to feel healthy again.

'We can't kill him,' I say, wiping my face with my sleeve. 'But I tell you what, Finn. I am fucking done with this. We can bloody well shop him.'

I climb under my old duvet and pull it up to my chin. I curl into myself, and I tell him what I saw.

# chapter forty-eight

I slept badly in my new home, tossing and turning on my mattress, constantly aware that the security of the hotel, with its twenty-four-hour reception desk, its concierge, its CCTV, had gone. The only security I had now was a heavy door with a big lock, and the studio door, which was flimsy in the extreme. And obscurity: obscurity was my greatest friend.

I listened to the water, occasionally lapping against the sides of the *rio*. From time to time there would be voices, disappearing as quickly as they arrived, accompanied by the approaching and then the receding of footsteps. Otherwise, there was silence.

I told myself that it was all right. I was going to be comfortable here. If I helped Antonio sell paintings, I could live here free for a month, and that gave me a month longer before my cash would run out. Then there would be return visits by the art collectors, the people who would be reassured by my presence behind a desk. Perhaps I could find a job in an actual gallery. I was fairly sure I could be a waitress, with a bit more Italian practice.

I was so horribly alone. None of it meant anything. I felt the loss of Seth with a physical pain that I had no right to feel. Seth was everything I could never have, everything I did not deserve.

I drifted off to sleep as it was beginning to get light, and dreamed of waves and beaches and Cornish drizzle. When I awoke to the blazing sunshine of a Venetian August, I wanted to close my eyes so tightly that it would all go away. Someone was moving around in the studio. I checked the time: it was half past ten. I had not slept this late for years.

I stood in front of Antonio wearing an oversized T-shirt and knickers. He did not react to my state of undress, just smiled and carried on shifting paintings around.

'The Americans,' he said. 'Tomorrow, they come.'

'OK,' I told him. At least this meant there was something to do. 'I'll have a shower and I'll be there to help you.'

The chilled water made my skin tingle all over, but it woke me up more effectively than anything else could have done. I luxuriated in the unfamiliar feeling of coldness. Then I dressed quickly in my most practical clothes and presented myself to Antonio, my hair still dripping.

I was soon sweating, as we moved his paintings around and cleared the floor. He explained (or I thought he did) that it did not have to look like a polished commercial gallery, but like a studio that sold works that were achingly authentic. There were already nails in the walls, and using two stepladders that he dragged out of the supplies room, we hung his huge abstract canvases on them. He Blu-tacked some labels next to them, and I peered, interested, at the prices.

'Three thousand euros!' I marvelled. He grinned, and stuck a red sticker on to the corner.

'Sold,' he said, and he winked.

I enjoyed the distraction of this work. I imagined that a lot of the art world was about smoke and mirrors, that it was all illusion. We flung the windows wide, and the salty air of Venice came in. If I were rich, I would have bought his paintings. They shimmered in the light. Although they were abstract, they captured the essence of this city. The very brush strokes cast tiny shadows.

Finally, I got down on my hands and knees and scrubbed the paint stains off the floor. It took some time, because the only way I could get hot water was to put cold water through the coffee machine, but soon I had it looking fairly presentable. Antonio watched in approval from his position up a ladder, tacking a nail into the wall. He was sweating, but he still looked impeccable. I watched him standing there with three nails in his mouth, and wondered where he lived, whether he was single, and why I found him so aesthetically pleasing but felt no spark of actual attraction.

We sat down together and leaned on the wall, each cradling a cup of black coffee. Although our communication was very limited, I enjoyed the companionship.

'*Quando?*' I tried. 'Tomorrow. *Domani?*'

He said '*Undici*.'

'Eleven?'

We smiled and nodded at each other.

Gabriella, Alberto and Delfina arrived soon afterwards, carrying a desk between them. It was heaved up the stairs on its end, and made a presentable reception desk for the English-speaking gallery assistant. They laughed and joked throughout the process, and did their best to include me. I focused on the work in hand, glad to have something to think about.

I imagined that if Antonio's paintings were actually good, in an art-world sense, they would be on display at a real gallery, but that was none of my business. I wanted to sell as many as we could.

I stood up and took a deep breath.

'Right,' I said. 'While we work, who's going to teach me to say something nice in Italian?'

The desk was covered with a white cloth to disguise the fact that its surface was chipped formica. There was a glass vase on it that was going to be filled with roses in the morning. Delfina had brought some white china cups and saucers with her, and they were exquisite. The whole scheme was coming together. I stood by the window and looked at the scene.

'*Vuoi ballare con me?*' I said. They had taught me to say this, made me repeat it again and again until I had the swooping intonation almost right.

'*Si!*' said Antonio, and he took me in a proper dancing hold, one of his hands on my waist, the other holding my hand, and waltzed me around the room. We spun together, faster and faster, until I was dizzy and out of breath. Antonio stopped and pulled me to him, hugging me tightly. He nuzzled the top of my head, then abruptly let go.

I looked around. Gabriella was laughing behind her hand.

'This,' she said, 'is what happens when you ask an Italian man if he would like to dance with you.'

I smiled around the room, savouring the brief sense of belonging. Then I yawned. It was a huge yawn, the result of a terrible night's sleep catching up with me.

'Lucia,' said Gabriella. I looked up, shaking myself out of my reverie. 'Lucia, did you sleep? Go and have a rest.'

Antonio said: 'I sorry! I . . .'

'You have worn her out.' Gabriella finished his sentence. Delfina and Alberto smiled, and went back to the work they were doing on Alberto's laptop.

I yawned again, and stretched. 'Mmm,' I said. 'Is that OK? Does anyone mind?'

'Of course they don't! Go on. Sleep!'

As soon as she said it, I was heavy with exhaustion. I smiled at everyone and stumbled to my little room, and lay on top of the mattress. There was just enough of a breeze coming through the window. I closed my eyes.

When I woke up, it was to the sound of the door banging. I yawned and stretched and checked the time. I was groggy and disorientated, after sleeping too deeply.

It was the middle of the afternoon. I waited for a moment, listening. The studio, I thought, was empty. I got up and went to stand in my doorway. This was unrecognisable as the place I had moved into yesterday. It looked every inch the independent art gallery. There was headed paper on the desk. There were a few more artworks, by different artists, around the walls. They had put up white curtains at the windows, and they were blowing gently in the breeze. There was a note pinned to the back of the front door.

*Lucia*, it said. *Come to the pizzeria in San Polo and have lunch with us. Love from your Italian friends. xxx*

That warmed my heart. I clung on to the idea that I had Italian friends. I could work with them, dance with them, eat and drink with them. For the moment, I could patch up the enormous hole that I had ripped into my life. It stopped me throwing caution and sense into the canal and following my heart back to Cornwall.

I ran my fingers through my hair, and set off to meet them.

# chapter forty-nine

## Marianne

We both know the stakes are every bit as high this time as they were with Mum. We messed up with Mum, left a trail that Benjamin was able to follow. This time we cannot afford to set a foot wrong. We sit up late at night, sitting on my old bottom bunk, planning. I am drinking water, overtaken by a thirst like nothing I have known before.

'Sure you don't want a beer?' asks Finn. I shudder. The shock of what has actually been happening to me is too much. I was drunk every time he let the men at me. I never, ever want to drink again.

'No,' I tell him. 'I would hate a beer.'

'Fair enough.' He looks pleased. 'So, what do we do?'

'There's only one thing we can do,' I tell him. 'This is the way we have to play it.'

He is nervous when he goes off to school the next morning.

'You will do it,' he says, for the fourth time. 'You will see it through? You won't let him scare you back to doing what he wants?'

I shake my head. 'No, I can't.'

'Too right you can't.'

'So I won't.'

'Good.'

Benjamin comes over late in the morning, as I knew he would. I hear his rap at the door, and my insides turn to liquid. A bit of sick comes into my mouth, and I spit it into the sink before I open the door. I think, briefly, of my old friend Katy. She is still at school, studying for her A levels. I could be with her, I should be with her. I should be studying. I should not be trying to trap this man.

He knocks again, and I walk slowly down the tatty hallway to the front door, and open it.

'Hey there, gorgeous,' he says, smiling his brightest, most charming smile.

'Hello,' I tell him, and I make myself smile too. For a moment I hope my smile looks genuine, and then I realise that he doesn't care if it's genuine or not. He only cares that girls do what he wants them to do.

I step out of the way, and he comes into the house and kisses me. Then he looks me up and down.

'That dress suits you,' he says, and he pats my bottom. I pretend I like it. I try to put a lid on the swirling emotions. I make myself shut down and play a part.

'How are you?' I ask him. 'Shall I make some coffee? What are we doing?'

'Look at this crappy carpet,' he says, kicking it where it has come loose. 'You should get your landlord to do something about it.'

'Oh, my landlord's a busy man,' I tell him with a horrible flirty smile. 'Are we going out tonight?'

'Marianne,' he says, and he puts a hand on my shoulder and turns me round so I have to look at him. 'Marianne, did you come to my place yesterday?'

I try to look innocent. 'Did I what? No, of course not. Why?'

'You look tired. You look as if you haven't slept, in fact. You can tell me.'

'No,' I say firmly. 'I'm fine. I'll make it in the cafetiere, shall I?'

'Well, if you had come by. And come to the front door. That would be fine, because I know I do that to you all the time, turning up without warning. Plus you're my wife, you have every right to come to our home. It's your home too, you know that. Well, Pete's girlfriend was at the apartment. She's about your age but she looks much younger. If it had been you who came to the door, and remember I do have a camera out there, and if you'd been wearing a pair of jeans and a sweatshirt, say, then I would be hoping you hadn't got the wrong idea about Tricia, which is what Pete's girlfriend is called. She's sixteen. And she's Pete's girlfriend.'

I swallow hard. The kettle is boiling noisily, filling the kitchen with clouds of steam. I am standing close to it, and I feel it opening the pores on my face.

'Well, if all those things had happened,' I say into the steam, 'I would really think it was none of my business. And I wouldn't be stressed about it.'

'Sure?'

I nod. 'Sure.'

He grins. 'That's my girl. You're a good girl, you know.'

I think about that other girl, whose name, perhaps, is Tricia. She was definitely not sixteen. I don't know where they found her, but she should have been at home with her parents, doing her homework, watching a bit of telly, being looked after. I have to go through with this, for her.

'So, I guess I should wait for an invitation,' I say casually. 'Which nights are good for you? Or not good?'

I hand him a cup of strong black coffee. I'd like to drug *his* fucking drink, I think suddenly, viciously. I'd like to throw *his* body into a hole on a building site. Instead I smile and offer a piece of cake.

'Thursday,' he says. Today is Tuesday. 'I'm a bit knackered tonight, as are you. Tomorrow I'm playing poker with some of the guys. Thursday we can go out. Let me really treat you. I'll take you to Bibendum. How about that? Champagne and oysters all right for you? Come to the flat at seven or so, and we'll take it from there.'

'That would be brilliant,' I tell him. 'What would you like me to wear?'

Finn comes home for lunch. I open the front door before he even reaches it.

'Thursday,' I tell him. 'That's the one. I'm going to fucking screw him over.'

Mum would have been horrified to hear the amount of swearing I have been doing lately. However, I think that, all things considered, she would have understood.

# chapter fifty

I checked the clock again. The Americans were due in twenty minutes.

There was no mirror in the apartment, so I had relied on Gabriella and her friends to tell me that I looked all right. When I looked down, I did not recognise myself. Gabi and Delfina had, between them, provided my outfit. They had dressed me up in a grey silk blouse with a bow at the neck, a black pencil skirt with a slit at the back, and a pair of high-heeled, schoolmarmy shoes that were a couple of sizes too big for me, as they belonged to the very tall Defina. My hair had been conditioned to the point of slipperiness, and rinsed in cold water, and it was pinned back in some form of chignon which had been sprayed into place. I was forbidden from touching it.

Gabi had done my make-up, and while I had no idea what it looked like, I imagined it was understated but skilled. I felt every inch the gallery assistant. This really was like becoming someone else. I walked differently, carefully, in my new shoes. I held myself differently. I was in disguise.

The front door was propped open, with a sign on it announcing GALLERIA DI FIORI ROSSI. Deep red roses were spilling out of the vase. The room was glowing in the sunlight. We were ready.

Delfina had run off to work an hour ago. There were just three of us left: Gabriella, Antonio, and me.

'So,' Gabi said. 'Antonio and I will wait in your room, with the door shut. If you need anything, we will be there.'

'I'll be fine, though, won't I?' I asked.

'Of course you will. They will come. You will say . . . ?'

I knew my script. 'I'm so sorry. Antonio sends his deepest apologies, but he's been called away as his mother was taken ill suddenly this morning. If you'd like to come back later, he will be happy to see you at three.'

'Meanwhile?'

'Meanwhile, please have a look around. Can I get you coffee or cookies?'

'Very good.'

'Then Delfina will call, and I'll have a discussion in English about all the interest in Antonio's art and how quickly these works are selling. The longer we can spend persuading them to buy, the more likely they'll snap up some paintings.'

Antonio grinned. '*Molto bene*,' he said.

'And if they want to leave any things here while they go away, I give them a receipt for them. I am as accommodating as I can possibly be.'

I sat behind the desk and tried to look normal. There was an Apple laptop in front of me, hooked up to the wi-fi belonging to the flat downstairs. Antonio and Gabi went away and hid. There was classical music playing gently in the background. Now all I had to do was to wait.

I tapped at the keyboard. I was online.

I had kept away from the internet, because that was the way it had to be. It had not been long enough. I was terrified of throwing everything away if I went online.

I sat still. Vivaldi's Four Seasons, good Venetian music, was playing softly in the background. Delfina and Antonio were silent. I strained my ears for the sound of footsteps on the stairs. Nothing yet. Antonio said the Americans would probably be late, because they would get lost on the way, and they were not even due for another fourteen minutes.

There was no harm in accessing my gmail account. Surely there could be no harm in just clicking on it, to see if there was anything in my inbox. No one would know. I would not write anything to anybody.

I held my breath, and typed 'gmail.com' into the box at the top of the screen. I knew this was a bad idea, but I did it anyway. I entered Lucy Riddick's email address and her password, which was imogenclara. The very act of typing their names gave me a sharp pang. I looked around at the beautiful studio, and reminded myself that Imogen and Clara lived in a different world, that I was unlikely ever to see them again. They were better without such a shifting, unreliable character as me in their lives. I took a deep breath, pulled my shoulders back and concentrated. Maybe if I stayed here. Maybe if I settled and felt safe. Then perhaps, one day, they could come out and visit me.

At the very least, Finn could come over. I needed to contact him. I knew that he would be waiting, that he knew I would be in touch as soon as I could.

I was pulled up short by the sheer volume of messages in my inbox. There was a whole page of new ones, and when I clicked through to the next page, that was full as well. They were from Seth, and Eliza, and a few other people too. I stared at them. I could not open a single one. I did not want to engage with that world. I could not engage with it.

There were footsteps on the stairs.

I looked at the screen one last time. There was a green spot at the side of it, announcing that I was online. There was a list underneath of other people from my contacts list who were online. One of them was Seth. I shut the page down quickly. It had only been open for a few seconds.

Someone was standing on the threshold of the studio. I composed myself. Shoulders back. Distant smile. Deep breath.

I looked up. A tall woman in a wrap dress and heavy glasses. A man in a white shirt and navy shorts. Somehow, there was no doubt that these people were the Americans.

'*Buongiorno*,' I said, in my best accent. I smiled in what I hoped was an engaging manner.

'Hello there,' said the woman. 'Do you speak English?'

They walked in and looked around. I thought they looked appreciative.

I followed my script to the letter.

'I'm terribly sorry,' I said, welcoming them in. 'Antonio has had a bit of an emergency this morning. His mother's been taken ill, and he's had to rush to the hospital.'

They looked at each other. They were clearly annoyed about this, but they quickly hid it.

'I'm sorry to hear that,' said the woman. 'In that case I guess there is no point—'

'But,' I interrupted. 'He called me not two minutes ago, and said that she's stable now, and that if you are able to come back at three this afternoon, he will be delighted to see you. He sends his most humble apologies. You know how it is. Italian men and their mothers.'

They smiled at this, instantly mollified, and introduced themselves as Nancy and Paul. I said I was Lucia, and pretended to be half-English, half-Italian, hoping that I would not be caught out on the Italian front. I could see that they liked me. I made them coffee, gave them a plate of *zaletti*, and chatted about Venice and the crowds and the heat. I offered to look after their things until they came back. They admired the paintings, the space, the gallery.

'It's funny,' said Nancy, smiling at me. 'We'd not heard about this gallery in our dealings with other parts of the art world.'

'Yes,' I agreed. 'We are fairly exclusive. We like to keep ourselves apart from the herd.' I was saying any old thing. I was thinking about the green dot next to Seth's name.

They were cheerful when they turned to leave.

'Why don't you leave your packages?' I said. 'Seriously, I'll give you a receipt for them. You don't want to drag them around Venice for three hours in this heat. And it's our fault that you have to come back.'

Paul nodded. 'Sure,' he said. 'That would actually be great.'

'And there's no need for a receipt,' Nancy added.

'No, let me. Honestly, I have to, it's part of my job.'

I carefully wrote it out on gallery headed paper, and handed it over. Nancy folded it and put it into her handbag. I went to the door and pressed the switch to light their way out of the building. I stood still and listened to them descending the stairs, wondering if I could have a sandwich for lunch without spilling any of its filling down my silk blouse. I needed to keep myself presentable for three o'clock, when I hoped to sell at least one expensive painting.

They tumbled out of my bedroom, laughing.

'*Bravo, Lucia*,' said Antonio, kissing me.

'You did a perfect job,' said Gabriella. 'Better than we could imagine. Well done.'

'It was fun,' I told them, stretching. 'I wouldn't mind doing that as an actual job. If only I really could speak fluent Italian.' I stood at the window and looked down the canal. Nancy and Paul had vanished into the city. They could be anywhere. The sun was shimmering on the narrow *rio*, and the boat outside bobbed up and down gently. As I watched, a speedboat shattered the peace, tearing up the canal, stopping outside the building.

I looked around.

'Hey,' I said. 'What are you doing?'

Antonio was up the ladder, taking a painting off the wall. Gabriella was throwing the headed paper from my desk into a box. She waved a hand at me.

'It's OK, Lucia,' she said. 'You can put your normal clothes on and go.'

'There's no point. I have to be back here at three.'

Antonio looked up. '*Si, ma* . . .'

'We won't need your help this afternoon,' Gabriella said, finishing his sentence in English. 'You can change your clothes and go away into the city. In fact, go to the mainland, like you said.'

They were dismantling the gallery, quickly and efficiently. Gabriella chucked the flowers into the corner, wrapped the vase in the tablecloth and put it into the box. The telephone went in there too, the cafetière, all the bits and pieces that had transformed the room. Antonio, meanwhile, was going through the packages that the Americans had left, taking out a selection of prints, quickly examining each one, smiling, and replacing them.

I closed my eyes. I could not believe that this was happening.

'Gabi?' I said. My voice came out small and pathetic. She did not respond.

'Gabi?' I said again. I was pleading with her.

'Lucia,' she said. She was at Antonio's side, looking through the Americans' packages. 'Please, go away. We are done here. Go on.'

'Antonio?'

'*Lucia*, go,' he said. He did not even look up at me. He said a lot of things in Italian, and laughed.

I stared at them both, and started to walk towards the door. I paused on the threshold.

'The things they left,' I said. 'They're valuable?'

'Sure,' said Gabi. 'Now, go. Here, have some flowers. To say thank you.'

She threw the roses to me. I caught two of them, and a thorn stuck into my hand. Then I went to my little bedroom, changed into my own clothes, and packed up my things. I left the studio without another word, my two bags over my shoulders.

# chapter fifty-one

## Eliza

I wake up early, wondering sleepily why I am naked. I never sleep naked. No one who is the only adult in a house containing children can sleep naked. You need to be able to jump out of bed and hit the ground running if someone is sick or if you think there's a burglar downstairs.

Then I look around, and remember that for the first time in a long time, I am not the only adult in the house. It all comes back to me, and I gaze at him, watch his sleeping face, and smile.

Patrick has stayed the night. He is stirring, his hair all messy, his face creased from the pillow. I stay as still as I can and watch him. I need to savour this moment, because for the first time in a very long time, everything worked.

It can only be Patrick. I know that beyond a doubt. Without Graham in the world, the only man for me is this one, the man who is sleeping in my bed. After all the horrible dates I have been on, after all the time I spent hating the fact that he seemed to be in love with Lucy, suddenly everything seems to have come right. We talked late into the night. I never imagined this would happen to me again.

It is half past six. Clara will be awake soon. I don't want her to come climbing into bed with me, the way she usually does, and discover Patrick sleeping there. Assuming that this does go somewhere, that last night was not a one-off, then I will need to introduce the girls to the idea gently. Finding him naked in my bed does not count as gentle.

He stirs and mutters something. He is so warm, so beautiful. I don't know enough about him, and I want to know everything. I want to know everything that has ever happened to him, all his girlfriends, all his family, his cousins, his great-aunts, everything.

I want to let him sleep. Instead, I climb over him and put on my pyjamas, lest the sight of my naked body in the cold light of day might scare him, and I stroke his hair.

He wakes up and looks at me, and smiles. I am watching carefully, in case he flinches when he sees me, but he really doesn't.

'G'morning,' he says, in a voice that is fuzzy with sleep.

'Hello,' I say, and we look into each other's eyes for a few seconds, and smile.

'I need to get up so the girls don't find me in their mum's bed?'

I nod. ''Fraid so. Coffee?'

He yawns and stretches and reaches out of the bed and takes his pants from the floor.

'Mmm. Do you always start the day this early?'

I consider lying. 'Pretty much,' I admit.

'I could get used to it, I guess,' he says, and swings his legs out of bed.

By the time Clara finds us downstairs, at five to seven, Patrick is fully dressed, and sitting at the table cradling a cup of strong coffee between his hands. I am still in my pyjamas. Clara, naturally, does not question anything.

'Hello, Patrick,' she says, and she strolls over to the fruit bowl and picks up a banana. She looks up at me. 'Can I have this banana chopped up and some yogurt and some honey and raisins on it?'

I sigh. 'Can I have this banana chopped up and some yogurt and some honey and raisins on it . . . ?'

'Please.'

'Yes you can.'

She sits at the table and concentrates on her food. Imogen is a little more suspicious when she turns up ten minutes later.

'Why are you here so early?' she demands, and I see her eyes stray to the two wine glasses beside the sink.

'I couldn't sleep,' Patrick tells her. 'So I woke up really early and came for a walk. I was walking past your house and your mum was opening the curtains downstairs and so I came and knocked very quietly at the door.'

I cover my mouth with my hand so Imogen won't see me smiling. There is no way she will believe that. She looks sceptical, but lets it pass for the moment.

Patrick stays with us for the whole morning. We walk down to the beach, which is gearing up for the surf lifesaving championships. Families are setting up tents on the sand, surfboards all around them. A stage is being erected. No one seems daunted by the mediocre weather. Falmouth is a great place to be in the summer. There is always something going on.

We walk past a family in Woolacombe Bay sweatshirts. The woman looks over at us and smiles. I see us through her eyes. We look like a family, a normal nuclear family. For a second I think of my husband, and feel that I am a traitor. Strangers will assume that Patrick is the girls' father, and that betrays Graham.

But everyone has families that are unusual. It would be more weird to have a straightforward set-up. I sigh. This is not straightforward. Nothing is straightforward. I have no idea whether any of us can handle this, so I tell myself to take it a day at a time and see what happens.

# chapter fifty-two

## Marianne

I put on the dress that Benjamin told me to wear. It is short and tight and I hate it. I do not want to have to look like this, but I tell myself that this will be the last time I have to do it, and I grit my teeth and summon some extra strength.

I stand in front of the mirror in my bedroom, the room where Mum died, and I look hard at myself. The little red dress clings to my body, there is too much leg showing, and so I put on a pair of black tights to make myself feel less like the teenage hooker that I probably am.

I tie my hair back in the demure way he likes it, and apply the minimum of make-up. A year ago, I had no clue about make-up. Now I think I am fairly good at it. I have rubbish GCSEs and a paedophile for a husband, but at least I know how to do my eyeliner.

When I've put my coat on, I pick up my two rings from the kitchen windowsill, and push them down, hard, on to my finger.

I do not want to do that. Now that I have faced the truth about him, I cannot bear the idea of the connection we have, the most intimate connection of all. He made me have sex with him when I was fifteen. When I look back on it, remember the way he held me down, laughed, assured me I would love it; recall the tears that rolled sideways down my cheekbones as I froze with terror, I know that he is not the valiant knight I wanted him to be. I try out the word. Paedophile. I find it impossible to apply it to his relationship with me, but it fits him when he is shut in his flat with the little girl.

We have packed up the house. The few things we want are in bags, in a locker at Liverpool Street station. Everything else is staying. I put my make-up bag into my handbag, and wait at the door for Finn.

Finn wanted to scrawl abuse all over the walls, but I did not let him. I don't want to leave anything that might imply that we care. I want us to vanish without a trace.

'Come on, then,' I say, as he thunders down the stairs. He takes my arm, and we leave the house for the last time.

As we slam the door, I am glad. Whatever happens next, we are moving on. I am glad to be leaving the place where she died, the place where I met him. We smile at each other, though both our smiles are forced. Finn double-locks the door, and we post both sets of keys back through the letter box.

We walk down the street together, through the autumn sunshine. We hardly talk, but Finn's presence at my side gives me the strength to keep going. We make the journey in silence.

'Good luck,' he says, as I hesitate by the buzzer.

'There's a camera here,' I tell him, suddenly jittery. 'You'd better get out of the way or he'll see you and he'll know something's up.' I am agitated, planning, hoping, terrified.

'I'll be over there,' Finn says, pointing to a low wall across the street. 'If I see him, I'll skedaddle.' We both smile. Skedaddle was something Mum used to say.

'OK.' I press the buzzer, and wait. I could use the door code, but I don't want to know it any more.

Benjamin is wary, because he knows that I saw Tricia and he knows that I am pretending not to be troubled by her. He is extra nice to me. He is waiting at the door of his penthouse when I come up the stairs.

'Hello there, my beautiful wife!' he exclaims, and he comes forward and takes me in his arms. He smells of aftershave. It is Davidoff's Cool Water. It has always been his smell but today it makes me sick. I press my face into his shoulder, inhaling the smell of him and of clean shirt, taking some comfort from his bulk in spite of myself, and hating myself for it.

He pulls back and looks hard into my face.

'Are you OK, Marianne? Hey, I've been thinking. I think you should move in. You shouldn't need to ring the bell here. Your brother's old enough to fend for himself and we'll let him keep the house, rent free. How about it? Become Mrs Burdett in earnest? Lady of the Manor?'

I do my best to look excited. 'Really?' I say, with a smile. 'I'd love that. Thank you!' I fiddle with my wedding rings. 'And Benjamin,' I say, because I really want to know the answer to this one, 'when do I get to meet your family?'

He grins, and winces very, very slightly. 'Oh, one of these days, darling. I'll have to show you off properly. After the honeymoon, perhaps. They might not understand the age gap, but who cares what people think?'

He opens a bottle of Veuve Cliquot, pours it expertly, and hands me a glass. I take a pretend sip. I walk to the window and look down. I can make out Finn's figure, sitting on the wall. When Benjamin's back is turned, I tip half my champagne into the soil of his pot plant.

He stands next to me at the window. I am not sure whether he knows that I poured my drink away. He is at my side very quickly, so perhaps he does.

'The river looks nice,' I say, randomly, looking at it, dark with a few lights reflected in it.

'Bloody water,' he says. 'I hate the stuff. Never even learned to swim. Never intend to go close enough to need to.'

'That's silly,' I say. 'It's lovely, and swimming is nice. I want to swim in the sea one day.'

'Marianne,' he says, with a laugh in his voice. 'Have you ever even been to the seaside? Have you seen the sea?'

'Not yet,' I admit. 'No.'

He puts his arm around my shoulder and pulls me close. I lean in on him.

'Well, just wait for our honeymoon,' he says. 'I might hate water, but I can manage a white sandy beach all right.'

I have to wait for ages, talking to him in a pretend-happy voice about the honeymoon that will never happen, before he goes off to the loo. I have only recently realised that when he does this, he is taking drugs of some sort. When he comes back he is always much more talkative. That must make it cocaine: one that we never tried when we were cackhandedly trying to soothe Mum's pain away.

As soon as he is gone, I take his key ring from the kitchen counter and fiddle with it until I have taken off the little key that I know opens the safe under the floor in his cupboard. I am prepared for this: I replace it with a similar key that belongs to Finn's bike lock. I put the safe key in my pocket. The first part of the task is accomplished. Then I pour the rest of my champagne down the plughole and rinse the sink, just in case he smells it there.

I am getting scared. I have a fairly good idea of the way the rest of the evening is going to go, and if I am not drinking, I am going to have to experience it properly instead of blacking out.

Benjamin comes back, and his eyes are wild, and he is talking without stopping.

'Marianne,' he says, 'you're a fucking amazing girl and I can't believe I actually get to be married to you. I think you actually *get* me, and what you did the other day – well, you accept me, and that is the most amazing thing to me – I can't tell you how much I love you. Look, Pete might bring Tricia over later – you'd be cool with that, wouldn't you? You're much more game than your mother ever was, I can tell you that much.'

'My mother?' I cannot hear this.

'Yeah. Look, you don't mind about Trish, do you? She's like you, a lovely girl. Looks younger than she is.'

'Benjamin,' I ask, because I am curious about this. 'When I'm, I don't know, twenty, or thirty, you won't want to be married to me any more, will you?'

He shakes his head. 'Oh, absolutely I'll want to be married to you! Of course I will. I'll always be however many years it is older than you. You'll always keep me on my toes.' He looks shifty.

'OK,' I say, brightly. 'Great! Can I go into your room and change?'

'No! You look great just the way you are.'

'But these tights! They're my school ones. I've got some others in your closet. Stockings. Go on. If Tim and Pete are coming over, you want me to look my best, don't you?' I hate myself for saying this. Every word is poison.

He hesitates. 'Off you go. A girl has to do what a girl has to do!'

He has a walk-in wardrobe off his bedroom. One side of it is lined with mirrors. The other has a railing with all his suits and shirts, meticulously ironed, hanging on it, and at the far end there are shelves with jumpers on them that are actually ranged in colour order. I hate this wardrobe. It completely freaks me out.

At the far end, there is a rug. I lift it quickly, unlock the metal door that is underneath, and key in the safe code, which I saw over his shoulder the other night. All the time I am alert for the sound of his approach. If he catches me now, he will be enraged. He will hate me and I will become his enemy. It will be worse than anything. I cannot think about what he would do.

The videos are piled in there. I open my bag and start to cram them in. At least two are marked 'Tricia', and there are several with 'Marianne' scrawled on the labels. I see other names, unknown names: Katie, Natalie, Sarah. I wonder how old those girls are. I feel sick, but I am certain, now, that I am doing the right thing. I fit six into my bag, which must be enough, before I hear his steps approaching. I close the metal door as fast as I can and shove the rug back on top of it.

He is right there, in the doorway, and my bag is in front of me, with the shapes of the cassettes showing through the material. My whole body is clenched and tense. He will spot it in a second. I turn to him. There is only one way to avoid him noticing all of it. I walk right up to him, press myself against him, and, hating myself, hating him, kiss him hard on the lips. I turn around, pulling him with me, and lead him towards the bed, away from my bag, away from the evidence.

I manage to escape more easily than I had expected. When the buzzer rings, I grab my bag and skip to the door.

'I'll go down and let them in,' I say, in a horrible coy voice. 'Give them a surprise. Say hello to Tricia.'

'Sure,' says Benjamin. 'Good girl. You do that. Be nice.'

I run down the stairs, open the front door, and stare in revulsion at the two men who are waiting. I hate these men, completely hate them. It is easier with them than it is with Benjamin, because these guys have no redeeming features, and Benjamin has his charm.

The girl is between them, wrapped in a big coat, looking at the ground.

'Marianne!' says Tim. He pats my bum. 'The lovely Marianne. Meet Tricia.'

'Hi,' I say to her, but she doesn't look at me. 'Come on up,' I add, and I usher them in. 'I'm just off to the chemist's for some women's stuff. I'll be back in a sec.'

Then they are in, and I am out. I hope that Benjamin is not watching his little screen, and I edge around it, just in case. Finn is beside me in a second. He takes my hand, and we run together, straight to the police.

# chapter fifty-three

I wanted to walk away and lose myself again. I wanted to go to the police. Instead, I crossed the little bridge, and stood in the shadow of a doorway, and watched. I was horror-struck, consumed by the easy way in which they had sucked me in.

Antonio and Gabriella appeared in the frame of the doorway, with all the paintings that had been adorning the gallery walls. I wondered whether any of them were by Antonio at all. They loaded them on to the motorboat, which, I could now see, had been brought there by Alberto and Delfina. All the paintings were stacked on to it, and then the desk, the box of props, even the mattress I had slept on. Finally Antonio arrived with the Americans' packages, holding them tenderly, as if they were his babies, and they all jumped on to the boat and sped away.

I was frozen. I still wanted it to be all right. I wanted there to be some mistake. I wanted Gabriella to be my friend, Antonio to be my landlord.

When they were out of sight, I shook myself back to reality, and cursed myself. I should have called the police while they were doing it. Now they had vanished, and Venice, as I knew very well, was an extremely good place into which to vanish.

I needed to keep a low profile. If I were to go to the local police, I would need to give my name and all sorts of details about myself. My involvement would make me suspicious. I had been a part of this crime, and that was the tip of my iceberg. I needed to lie low. I had told them I was called Lucia. I was the only person the Americans had met. I would be the one they would be looking for, not Antonio, not Gabriella. Just me.

I stood and stared at the building that I had, so briefly, called home. The day was hot like nothing I had ever known, and still.

I set off again, ready to vanish. Soon I was in the middle of the throng, which felt much safer. The city was slick with sweat. The crowds were everywhere, and much of the city moved at a grumpy shuffle, too densely packed for anyone to go anywhere at any speed. I used my elbows, yelled, '*Scusi!*' and walked at random, trying to focus.

In St Mark's Square, I plunged masochistically into the very worst of the crowds. I took photographs for three different groups of people. I went as close to the Basilica as I could, and watched the water oozing up through the cracks in the paving stones just in front of it. This, I felt, did not bode well for anybody's future. I wandered away, letting myself be carried around by everyone else, walking wherever the people in front of me walked. I got on a vaporetto, travelled somewhere without a ticket, and got off when I felt like it. And yet, at three o'clock, I was back outside the studio.

# chapter fifty-four

## Eliza

Patrick spends two whole days and nights with us before he declares that he had better go home. So much for introducing him gently. We talk, when the girls are asleep, about the future.

'I always liked you,' he said, last night. 'Even when Graham was still alive, I would look at you and think, lucky bugger. There was always something about you. But then he died and I just thought, keep your distance, Patrick. Wait and see if there might be a chance, when she's ready.'

I looked at him. 'I'm ready,' I said, and I knew that at last it was true. I decided to move the photographs of Graham that are still all over my bedroom. They must be disconcerting for him. I will keep them, but in a drawer, where I can look at them whenever I need to. The idea tears me apart, but I know I have to do it.

Then he goes home, and the moment he has gone, I begin to doubt it. When half a day goes by and he does not text me, I become convinced that I will never see him again, that when I bump into him at school, we will be awkward and avoid looking at each other. I think it was a foolish dream on my part, and a bit of fun on his.

'What do you think?' I ask Seth, when the girls and I go to check up on him. I am talking quietly, but I am sure that Imogen is listening. 'Have I totally blown it by being too keen?'

He shrugs. Seth is looking terrible. He is unshaven, his skin is saggy, and his eyes are ringed with bluish bags. 'Probably,' he mutters. 'How should I know? But yeah, you can be a bit full-on. You probably should have played it cool.'

I nod. I know he's right. I wish Lucy was here. She would have been able to help me out. I always wish Lucy was here. I am sick of wishing it.

'Have you heard anything?' I ask, out of habit.

Seth looks at me, and almost smiles. 'You know what?' he says. 'I almost have. Didn't expect me to say that, did you? I was on my gmail account, and suddenly there's this green spot at the side of the screen, next to her name. It means she was online. By the time I'd worked out how to send an instant message, she was gone.'

I stare at him. 'Seriously?'

'Yeah. But what can you do? I sent her another mail, in case she was checking them, but then I logged into her account, because it wasn't rocket science to guess her password, and she hasn't even opened them. Not a single one since she's been gone.'

I put my head in my hand. 'And when you were doing that, it would have looked to someone else as if she was online. Maybe it wasn't her.'

He shrugs. 'Maybe. You know what? I want to hate her for doing this. I want to get over her, email her to fuck off. But when I saw her name there, I just wanted to find her, wherever she is, and to hold her and to tell her to trust us. I want to be better than I've ever been before. I want to help her. I want her to be able to trust me with whatever's going on.' His voice cracks. 'I just miss her,' he says, quietly. 'That's all. I never thought I could feel like this.'

Later, I am in the sports shop, buying Imogen a verruca sock, when he walks up behind me. The shop is tiny and crammed with stuff, and there is nowhere for me to go.

Clara laughs. 'Look, Mummy,' she says. 'It's Patrick.'

There is nothing for it but to look around with what I imagine to be a nervous smile. I turn towards him, a pack of white rubber verruca socks in my hand.

'Hello, Clara,' Patrick says, and then he looks at me. 'Hello,

Eliza,' he adds, and he smiles at me, and everything seems to be all right again.

I don't know what to say to him, and so I just stand there, like a lemon, and I smile and try not to look too happy.

'It's nice to see you,' he adds.

'You too,' I say, and I take Clara's hand. We look into each other's eyes.

'I thought you might need some space,' he says. 'I was scared I'd come on too strong.'

I laugh in relief. 'No,' I say, but before I can say any more, Clara tugs on his trousers.

'Patrick?' she says. He looks down at her.

'Hi, there,' he says, and he crouches down.

'Patrick, we buyed a Mooncup for Mummy,' she says. I laugh in horror. The woman behind the counter sniggers.

'Oh did you?' he asks, brightly. 'And what *is* a Mooncup?'

I answer before she can, because Clara was fascinated by it and is intrigued by all the details.

'It's an eco-friendly form of sanitary protection,' I say, red-faced. 'Now, Clara, we'd better get on. I'd better pay for these.'

'It does collect the blood,' Clara tells him.

'Stop it,' I tell her. 'He doesn't want to know.' But suddenly we are all laughing, and everything feels all right again.

# chapter fifty-five

## Marianne

We have handed over the evidence. We are homeless, and London is huge. We walk through east London, towards Liverpool Street.

'That worked better than I expected,' I say. I am numb. If they don't arrest him I don't know what I will do. He is not the kind of man who would forgive what I have done. Ever. I know I am his enemy now. His enemy, and his wife. 'That poor girl,' I add.

The police were sympathetic, and they really wanted me to stay and talk to them. I could not do it. Couldn't allow the story of Mum's death to come out. I gave them the basic details, the names, the address, the fact that they needed to go there right now, and then we left.

'Yeah, she was well young. Let's hope you've saved her.'

'Now what?' I ask. I think I am actually going to be sick.

'Right,' he says. 'We're out of that bastard's house. Look, you've been distracted lately. I haven't told you what I was doing. I had a kind of a project.'

It is dark, and there are only a few people wandering around. We take a random left turn and walk along another residential street lined with brick houses.

'What project?' I ask.

He looks shy, almost overwhelmed. 'I was looking for our dads,' he says, in a quiet voice. 'It actually wasn't so difficult. To find mine. I didn't have much luck with yours because he doesn't pay us anything, does he? But mine was easy to find. His name's Alan Davidson and he's married. With three children.'

The world tilts. I whisper: 'Your brothers and sisters.'

'Brothers. Half-brothers. It's complicated, though. He says he and Mum had a one-night stand, and she never wanted him to have anything to do with me. He thinks she got pregnant on purpose, because she already had a baby and she wanted another one. She wasn't interested after she got pregnant. He met his wife at about the same time, he said, and he never told her about me.'

'But will he look after you?'

'He's going to talk to his wife. He probably already has now, I guess. But yeah, I filled him in a bit and he was like, of course you're not going to be on the streets, I've been waiting years to meet you.' Finn's voice cracks slightly. 'He said if his wife's too pissed off with him, I can live with someone else in the family for a bit.'

'In the family,' I echo. I swallow hard. We keep walking. We pass a woman in a tracksuit. 'But he's definitely not my dad . . .' I let it tail off, desperate to leave room for the possibility, the idea that there might be an escape route open to me.

'No,' he whispers. 'I wish he was.'

'Me too.'

'Where does he live?'

'Somewhere called Matlock. It's up north.'

'Finn, you should have told me you were doing this. It's such a big thing. For you on your own, I mean.'

He says nothing, and I suddenly understand that he tracked his father down so that he could get away from me. I have, after all, been unbearable. I put Benjamin before Finn, and that, I now know, was horrible of me. I see him watching me as I realise this. Neither of us addresses the point.

'What are you going to do?' he asks. 'Only I was thinking, you could come to Matlock with me, and we could find you a place to live, and maybe you could start at sixth-form college – you've only missed a bit of the courses, haven't you? And then we'd still be together, and with any luck that bastard will be locked away.'

I think about it. I think about what I am doing to Benjamin. He will know that I have set him up. He will do everything he can to get me back. He will, for instance, tell the police that we killed our mother. He will tell them where to find the body. I recall something he once said to me: 'I am the best friend you'll ever have. And I can also be the worst enemy. Don't test me on that one.' He is going to be after me. I cannot just move to a different town. It needs to be more than that.

'You'll be OK,' I tell him. 'But I have to disappear. He might not go to prison. We don't really know how these things work, do we? Maybe the evidence isn't enough or something. And he'll come after me, you know he will. And the police. You can change your name, become . . .' I hesitate before I say the new word. 'Davidson. Use one of your middle names. Patrick Davidson won't catch his eye. I don't want you to be there if he finds me. I'll head off on my own. I'm an adult now. Give me your . . .' It is a struggle to get the word out, but I manage it, in the end, in a rush. 'Give me your dad's phone number and his address. I'll contact you when I can, and we'll check we're both OK.'

Finn looks deeply unhappy. 'No. I want you with me. It's what Mum would have wanted too. The two of us against the world.'

'Mum was insane,' I remind him. 'That's what got us into this mess in the first bloody place.'

He tries to convince me. I am unmovable. I need to vanish into another city, somewhere else. I need to become someone completely different, never to talk about my life until now ever again. If it means I have to sacrifice my relationship with my brother, the only person who knows what I have been through (and it does mean that), then that is just the price I have to pay.

# chapter fifty-six

I watched from the doorway on the other side of the bridge, compelled to see it, desperate not to. At exactly three o'clock, they appeared on the pathway beside the *rio.* I watched their innocent progress towards the wooden door. The door had been propped open this morning. Now it was double-locked, and the sign that had briefly announced the presence of the Fiori Rossi gallery had vanished. They stopped in front of it. Paul had put on a straw hat since the morning, a Panama-style one. They stood there, visibly puzzled. I could hardly watch, but I could not look away either. They were much too far away for me to hear what they were saying, but I could imagine it: 'Probably they've gone for lunch. After all, they do have long lunches in Italy, don't they? Or maybe something bad has happened with his mother. We'll just wait a while.'

They could not see me, in my deep doorway. I watched them standing there, and I wondered when, exactly, they were going to begin to get worried.

Then I could stand it no longer. I drew a deep breath, steeled myself, and walked across the bridge towards them.

They saw me approaching, but I could tell that at first they did not recognise me, because I was wearing a short skirt and a T-shirt, and flip-flops, and my hair was tied up messily, still half silky and half stiff with lacquer.

'Hi there,' I said, and they looked at me again.

'Well, Lucia,' said Nancy. 'Hello. We were just wondering when you would be along.'

Paul smiled at me, still unaware that anything was amiss.

'I'm guessing you're off duty this afternoon, then,' he said, looking down at my clothes.

'Look,' I said. 'I'm really sorry.'

'What is it?' asked Nancy. 'Is he still with his mother?'

'You have to believe me, I had no idea. I had no clue about what was going on. Those prints you left at the gallery. How much are they worth?'

I watched their faces as I told them the truth. They stood and gawped at me while I went through the story. I realised how unbelievable my protestations of ignorance sounded, and I knew that I could not go to the police, because as things stood, I was the sole suspect.

'And they went where in this motorboat?' Paul demanded, almost shouting.

'I have no idea,' I said, unable to hold eye contact. 'I've been to Gabriella's flat, but there was no reply. I doubt we'd find them there. I'm so sorry. I just thought I was helping Antonio to sell his art.'

Nancy looks at me in disgust. 'It wasn't even good art. We were only there to be polite. And don't expect us to believe a word you say. What's happening now – you telling us this – this is part of the same scam, isn't it? Let me guess: you'll look after our passports for us while we go to the police?'

'No!' I told her. 'No, really. I was naïve, I admit that. I was just in a place where I needed some friends, and they were there. It made me a bit foolish.'

Paul was staring at me. 'I'll say,' he said. 'Do you have a key to this building?'

I reached into my bag. To my surprise, my keys were still there. I had assumed that Gabriella would have removed them while she and Antonio were hiding in my room.

'Yes,' I told them. 'It seems I do.'

The studio was completely empty. There was not a single painting on the walls, though the nails on which they had hung were still there. The jars of paintbrushes had gone. The tools that had been scattered around. The soap that had been beside the basin. The curtains that had been at the windows. Every single thing had been removed. I knew it would have been, but when I saw it, I felt so bleak that I thought I might as well turn myself in to the authorities. At least I would get a bed for the night. At least I would be somewhere safe.

'Well,' said Nancy, staring around. 'You sure have done us good.'

'Seriously,' I said. 'How much were those prints worth?' Paul walked to the window. I saw him getting a little phone out of his pocket.

Nancy looked at me. 'Upwards of two thousand dollars apiece,' she said, enunciating each word, furious. 'Six of them. You know, I had no qualms whatsoever about leaving them with you.'

'Neither did I.'

'Sure, honey.'

We stood in absolute silence for a while. She glared and I pretended to be oblivious. Paul was shouting into his phone, in English. Then he marched across and handed it to me.

'They don't speak much English,' he said. 'We need your Italian. You just make sure you tell them the whole truth. Tell them where we are. Tell them what happened. Tell them we need a police report for our insurance.'

At the mention of insurance, I was suddenly able to breathe again. These were rich people. They did not have everything at stake. They were going to be fine. I smiled apologetically, and did not take the phone.

'Sorry,' I said. 'I don't actually speak Italian.'

Nancy laughed, a harsh laugh.

'And I guess your name is not Lucia either?' she demanded.

The window swung open in the breeze, and a gust of warm air blew into my face.

'Oh,' I told her. 'You have no idea.'

# chapter fifty-seven

## Eliza

Patrick and I are sitting on a rug on the beach. Clara is collecting shells to decorate her somewhat haphazard sandcastle, and Imogen is kicking a ball around with some children she knows from school.

Patrick coughs a couple of times. I look up to see whether he is actually choking, whether I need to do the Heimlich manoeuvre. Then I realise that it was an attention-attracting cough. That was why it sounded strange.

'Mmm?' I respond.

'Erm,' he says. He looks as if he is going to be sick, so I give him my full attention. 'There's something we should talk about, actually. Or rather, someone.'

I know, as soon as I see the look on his face, what this is going to be about.

'Lucy?' I ask, and he nods.

'I know about you and Lucy,' I say, although I don't really. I don't know anything other than the fact that, in spite of everything he has said to me lately, he is clearly still in love with her.

He is squinting at me.

'Do you?' He begins to smile, and I look away. 'Eliza, I would love that to be true. It would save such a lot of explaining. But I really don't think so.'

I look down at the sand.

'What is it then?' I ask, and my voice sounds hard. 'I thought it was just that you adored her from afar. But is it more than that?

Did you have some sort of history together? Did you go out with each other? Or have an affair? What is it?'

He sighs. 'Nothing like that.'

'Mmm?' I cannot look at him.

'It goes a long way back.'

'Right.'

He sighs and picks up a handful of coarse sand. I can see that he is torn. He doesn't want to tell me this, whatever it is going to be. I want to stop him, to tell him that I do not need to know.

'You know how you and Seth never knew anything about her past?' he says. He clears his throat again. 'I'm really sorry we never told you. But you know how you ran up against a brick wall when you started to look for her?'

'Yes.'

'Well that's because she isn't Lucy Riddick.'

He pauses. I watch him.

'She isn't Lucy Riddick?' I ask.

He nods. 'Her name is Marianne Jenkins. She grew up in London. She had a mother and a brother. Her mother died.' He looks at me. 'Her brother's name was Finn.'

I stare at him. I cannot believe what he is saying.

An hour later, everything in the world is different. I try to make sense of what I now know. Patrick has known all about Lucy all along. He came here because of her. She was Marianne. He was Finn.

'So she's not Lucy.' I keep saying it, hoping that if I repeat it enough times, I will start to take it in. 'She's Marianne.' The name is unfamiliar on my tongue. I have, though, heard it recently. I remember: at the O2. 'Leonard Cohen has a song called "So Long Marianne",' I say. 'He sang it on the night she disappeared. That's a bit weird, isn't it?'

Patrick starts to hum it. 'No it's not. Our mother adored him. Marianne's named after that song. Her middle name's Jane, after a woman in a song called "Famous Blue Raincoat".'

I am suspicious. A part of me is not believing any of this.

'So why weren't you called Leonard?'

'She spared me. Finn Patrick Leonard.'

I don't know what to say. Patrick mentioned a nasty man, and I am sensing that this is the crux of the story.

'So what has happened to her? Do you know where she is?'

His face collapses, and I realise that I have never before seen him with his guard down. The anguish is etched on his face.

'If I knew where she was,' he says in a tight voice, 'I would be there, by her side.'

'Do you know why she had to go?'

He takes a deep breath and closes his eyes. 'Remember when she was in the papers?' he says. 'Look, let's go and find Seth. I think I'd better tell both of you together.'

'Mummy,' says Clara, sounding scared. I feel her little hand touching my back. 'Mummy, don't cry.'

I had not realised I was crying, and it makes me feel stupid and self-indulgent. I look at Patrick uncertainly. I do not know him at all. I thought I did, but I was wrong.

'Sorry,' I tell her, trying to smile. 'I'm fine. Honestly I am. Do you want an ice cream?'

We walk through town to get to Seth's house. I look at Patrick as we walk, trying to work out whether he looks like the woman I cannot really believe to be his sister. He has freckles all over his nose, and she doesn't. His skin is slightly pink from the sun, and she always turns olivey as soon as the first ray hits her. His face is wide and open, and hers is pointed with fine bone structure. They really look nothing like each other at all.

I try to think of something to say, but I cannot find the words. I stop outside the greengrocer's and pick up some blueberries, because every mother knows they are a 'superfood' and will protect one's offspring from all harm. 'You didn't hang out together,' I say. 'Or tell anyone.'

He sighs. The sun comes out from behind a cloud, and suddenly we are casting shadows. There are hordes of people in town, most of them in shorts and T-shirts, many of them holding Cornish pasties in paper bags.

'Yes,' he says. 'It's hard to explain.' He takes Clara's hand and pulls her away from the edge of the road. I look at Imogen. She is standing to the side of us, and I know that she is listening. 'I wasn't going to tell you, because it's Marianne's secret more than mine, but it suddenly seemed that I couldn't keep it secret for a moment longer. She wouldn't mind. Who knows if we'll even see her again?

'Anyway, the two of us went through such shit times when we were kids that in a way we didn't want to be that close ever again. We needed to pull away from each other, because there are so many things that only we know and only we will ever know. We could never have a fresh start together.'

He looks at me. 'But I was never happy, so far from her. I missed her too much and I worried about her *much* too much. So I decided I wanted to be near to her, so she'd always know where I was if she needed me. I didn't want to disrupt her life. We kind of settled on this – that we would see each other around, but we wouldn't be close. It seemed to work.'

I go into the shop to pay for the blueberries and a few other pieces of fruit I have randomly picked up. Clara waits outside with Patrick, and Imogen follows me in.

'Mum,' she says, as soon as we are standing in the queue.

'Yes?' I look out of the window. Patrick and Clara are talking. I see Patrick look up. Our eyes meet, and I look away.

'Who's Marianne?'

I sigh. 'I thought you were listening. Who do you think Marianne is?'

'Lucy?'

I smile at her. 'Don't tell anyone, Immy, OK? No one knows apart from us. Even Seth doesn't know yet. It's a secret.'

'But why?'

'It's complicated.'

'You always say that.'

'Well this time it really is complicated. Too complicated for me to understand, that's for sure. It's nothing to do with me.'

'When's she coming back?'

'Soon. I hope so, anyway.'

Imogen takes a blueberry, and puts it quickly into her mouth before I can stop her. 'Is she dead?' she asks.

'Of course not. Oh, Immy, did you think . . . ?'

'It's just that. Well, there was Daddy. And it felt like it was the same, and I thought you just weren't telling us because you didn't want us to be upset.'

I try to work out what to say to this. Imogen is not a little child any more. I should be treading carefully around her, giving her more credit. This parenting business is constantly shifting. It is impossible to stay on top of it.

'Imogen,' I say, as we shift forward in the queue and she takes advantage of my confusion to snaffle another blueberry. 'Darling. I'm sorry, I've shut you out a bit. I kind of forgot that you're nearly eight. I'll try to be more open with you, shall I?'

I look into her serious face. She is gazing at me with huge light brown eyes that are so much a part of Graham that I want to cry.

'OK then,' she says. 'Because I'm not a baby any more. Are you going to marry Patrick?'

I laugh. 'No,' I say. 'Not any time soon, anyway. And Lucy's not dead, Immy. Honestly, we're sure she's not. We know she's not. She just needed to get away for a while and she'll be in touch with us when she can.'

'So it's like a holiday?'

We have reached the front of the queue.

'Yes,' I say with some relief. 'It's like a long holiday.'

# chapter fifty-eight

## Marianne

We go to Liverpool Street station and retrieve our bags from the lockers where we left them.

I hardly have anything now. We have given away all of Mum's clothes, every single thing that ever belonged to her. I have kept her Leonard Cohen albums, and Finn took a leather necklace with a polished stone on it. All the clothes Benjamin ever bought me are gone, will finally be put to good use as they generate some money for Cancer Research. All the shoes. Even the school uniform he used to like me wearing, the disgusting pervert.

It doesn't seem disgusting, when it's to do with me, because I threw myself into his arms, and I thought I knew what I was doing. I thought my relationship with him was my salvation. But when I think of that girl, of that little Tricia, standing in the dark between two scumbags, I see the man for what he is. I am glad I never got to watch the tapes. I am fighting with myself, trying not to imagine what is on the ones with my name on them. I never had any idea that anyone was filming me; but I never had any idea what was happening at all.

I will still be married to him, and I suppose I really will be married to him until one of us dies, because I am sure I would never be able to ask for a divorce without letting him know where to find me. Our marriage might not be valid, since we faked Mum's consent, but, again, I don't think I'll be able to get it cancelled without giving myself away. I will just pretend not to be married. It's not as if I'm going to be wanting to do it again, ever in my whole life.

With our backpacks on our backs, we go back to Benjamin's flat, and we stand in the shadows as far away as we can, and we wait.

I look up at the windows. They are lit. That is all I can see. We stand for a long time and wonder what is happening.

'You've got nothing at all,' Finn says, looking at my bag. I look at it too. It's true. All I have brought for my new life are a few clothes, a couple of books, and a Walkman with the Leonard Cohen tapes. That, and all the cash I could get my hands on. I was going to split it equally with Finn, but he refused, and only took a hundred pounds to get him to his dad's. We still don't quite know where Matlock is, but apparently you get there from St Pancras. That is all Finn needs to know. St Pancras will be our next stop.

'I don't need much,' I tell him, 'apart from money. I'll be fine. I'll get a job and stuff. People do it. It's not exactly breaking new ground.'

I have to be so brave to do this. I am pretending it's not scary, but it is. I have never been alone like this.

'I wish you'd come with me.' A car approaches. We both step behind the little urban tree, but it doesn't slow down.

'If we'd had any leads at all about my dad . . .' I stop. I cannot follow that train of thought, cannot allow myself even to daydream about the non-existent happy ending. I tried to look for him, but I did not try very hard. I knew that if I found him, he would be a huge disappointment, a disaster. To imagine anything else is fantasy. I need to face my reality. I must make my own future.

Finn's rucksack is bursting at the seams. He has clothes, including school uniform, and all his books. He has brought back everything from school, including textbooks that he has no right removing from the place. He has his football kit, his teddy bear. He has a life in that bag.

We stand absolutely still for what feels like hours, and we wait. There is a constant hum of London in the background, but nothing actually happens. I want to put my Walkman on, but I cannot risk missing anything. I stand closer to Finn, so we are shoulder to shoulder.

When the police car approaches, I start to feel dizzy, and my vision goes blotchy, and I have to grab Finn's arm for support. We are transfixed. It stops outside his building, and two policemen get out. We cannot hear what they are saying, but we watch them open the door using the code we gave them.

We stand there, petrified, watching the thing that I have done. It takes for ever. I am sick to the stomach when I picture him being plausible, explaining it all away, rationalising things. If cornered, he will be pinning the blame on Pete and Tim. I hope they all go down. I hope they are locked up for ever.

The police have the tapes. They know where to find the rest of them. That has to be something that even Benjamin Burdett, my husband, will not be able to explain. If, that is, he is there. If he is not, at this moment, at our little house, going through the rooms, realising the extent of my betrayal.

At last, it happens. A police van pulls up. All three men are brought out, in handcuffs. I see him, lit in the orangey light of the street lamp. He is defiant, talking loudly to the police, blustering about it being ridiculous, about suing their fucking arses off.

Tricia comes out with a policewoman.

They open the door of the van.

He looks across the road. Although we thought we were hidden, he looks straight at me. Our eyes lock together. I can hardly hear him, but I see his lips move, and I know what he is saying.

'I will find you,' he mouths.

And I know that he means it, and that however many years may pass, I will never be free of this man, because I also know that even when he is in chains in a police van, he is strong, and even though I am setting off, free from him, to start a new life, I am not.

# chapter fifty-nine

Nancy and Paul were exchanging glances when they thought I wasn't looking. I knew what they were doing. They were trying to work out how to turn me in, when calling the police had not worked, and when they did not quite know how to get anywhere from this obscure alley by the tiny *rio*.

There was no way I was going anywhere near the police. Gabriella and her friends must have banked on that when they slotted me into their plot. I could not identify myself to any officials, and I had seen the Venetian police around the city with their intimidating uniforms and ferocious weapons clipped to their belts. They looked as official and as unyielding as it got.

Besides, I had committed a crime. I had knowingly deceived the naïve American couple, had welcomed them into a gallery that did not exist, had specifically asked them for the packages they were carrying, and had written out a meaningless receipt to give them a bogus sense of security.

Still, I started walking with them. I was not sure where we were going, because I had nowhere to go. There was a police station at San Zaccaria, so I would make sure we stayed away from there. They positioned themselves one on either side of me, as if they could possibly stop me from escaping. I looked up at Nancy. Her mouth was made up with brown lipstick, and set in a straight line.

She sensed me watching her.

'I guess we were naïve,' she said.

'We were goddam stupid,' said Paul.

'You weren't. I trusted them too. I thought I was just helping them to get more money for Antonio's paintings.' I thought about it. 'Which he probably didn't even paint,' I added.

'Sure. You were duped too,' said Nancy, and she stared at me with hard, unbelieving eyes.

'How did they know you had those prints?' I asked. We were getting closer to the centre. Soon we would run into a police officer. I knew we would.

'Oh, that would be because we told them,' said Nancy, with a little laugh. 'We're not exactly big-time collectors. But we adore Italy, and while we were in Europe we thought we'd pick up a few pieces to take home. We were here earlier in the summer for the Biennale, and that was where we met a woman called Francesca.'

She looked at me, the question in her eyes.

'I've never met a Francesca,' I said.

'She was about forty, spoke excellent English. She said she had studied in London and she always looked out for English speakers. She was very friendly. We got into conversation in the French pavilion. I'd just fallen in love with those prints in a gallery off the Zattere. I told her all about them. Anyway we swapped details and the next thing I know, she's emailing me. We're coming back to Venice to pick up the prints before we fly home, I told her. She said we had to see the work of an artist called Antonio Bellini, that was the next big thing and that now was the time to make an investment. She linked to the website, which was full of amazing quotes from critics. She told us to come by right after picking up the prints.'

She sighed. I saw them exchange glances, around me.

'Were you there,' asked Paul. 'At the Biennale?'

'No!' I told them. 'I met the same woman in a church; she told me she was called Gabriella. She recruited me, I guess.'

'They're not stupid,' Paul muttered. 'Those prints were valuable, but not so very, very valuable that we wouldn't be OK leaving them at what seemed like a trustworthy place. They pitched it just right, and they'll also be able to sell them on without much trouble because they're not unique. And they'll be twelve thousand dollars the richer, which is not bad for a morning's work.'

'Yeah. Look.' I looked straight ahead. 'I'm really sorry about what's happened, but you must know there's no way I'm turning myself in. So all I can say to you is sorry again, and good luck.'

Before they could react, I took off, running down a side street. I heard Paul shouting, cursing me. I heard Nancy's footsteps clipping along behind me. I ran around a corner, and saw a courtyard door ajar, so I stepped through it and closed it. It was a metal door, painted light green, and there was a small hole under the handle. I pressed my eye to the hole. After a few seconds, they came past. I watched them stop and look around.

'We'll never find her and that's a fact,' said Nancy.

'She could be anywhere in the city by now,' huffed Paul.

'Probably picked up by her friends on the motorboat.'

'You bet.'

They were walking away. I watched them, feeling scummy. I hoped their insurance would pay out, that they would get all their money back. I was sure that a better person than me would help them get their police report.

I waited until they were out of sight, then turned around. I had not even looked at my hiding place.

It was a tiny yard, with a large pot of geraniums at the centre of it, wilting in the afternoon sun. A wicker chair stood in the shade of the building, and an old woman was sitting in it, dressed in a black nylon dress, staring at me.

I raised a hand and waved.

'*Buongiorno*,' I said. She raised a hand back, half smiling, and I left.

I wandered around Venice, trying to figure out a plan. Everywhere I went, I felt people watching me. I spun around, expecting Nancy, Paul, the police, but there was never anyone there. Or rather, there were hordes of people there, and the eyes I felt on me melted away into the masses. I tried to stay away from the main tourist areas. I had nowhere to sleep – all the hotel rooms in the city were booked – and all my possessions were in the two bags on my shoulders. There was a hostel across the water from the Gabrielli. I might try that. But when I arrived at the mouth of the Grand Canal, ready to fare-dodge across the Giudecca, I saw that it was almost next door to the Cipriani, which, as the most exclusive address in Venice, was probably the very hotel in which American art collectors stayed.

It was after five o'clock. The bars were filling up with people having aperitifs. I needed somewhere to go.

I looked around. There, just down the canal bank, was the Hotel Gabrielli Sandwirth.

Luigi was on reception. He beamed at my approach.

'Lucia!' he said. 'Are you all right?'

I tried to smile. I tried to say yes, I was fine. I tried to play it cool. When I looked at him, however, I could not do any of it. I stood in front of him, and fought back the tears. I could not do this any more. I was incapable of looking after myself. I could not carry on, and this man was the only friend I had.

I opened my mouth to say something, but I was incoherent. He was beside me in a moment, his arm around my shoulder, trying to comfort me.

'Is OK,' he said, and he ushered me over to the bar. He made me sit on a high stool, and he ordered me a shot of something yellow. 'You drink, then you tell me what you need.'

# chapter sixty

## Marianne

I wave Finn off on the train to the mysterious Matlock. I try not to cry.

The platform at St Pancras is busy. I get on to the train with him and help him find a seat. I don't need to do that, but it is probably going to be the last big-sisterish thing I will get to do for him. It is, I know, too late for that: I could have looked after him if I hadn't gone off with Benjamin. I missed my chance, and something broke between us that will never be fixed.

Still, I try to put his backpack on the rack above his seat, but I can't reach, and he takes it from me and laughs and slides it easily into its place. We stand together for a while, blocking the aisle, without anything to say.

'You've got my address,' says my big, tall baby brother, in his newly deep voice.

'Yes,' I tell him. 'Look, if you have any trouble with your dad or your family or anything . . .'

'But I can't contact you,' he says. 'Because we don't know where you'll be.'

'Yes you can,' I say and I make a decision on the spur of the moment. 'I'm going to Bristol,' I say quietly. I have heard of Bristol; it's far enough from London, and Mum said once that she'd lived there. Bristol, of all the cities in the United Kingdom, has a pull for me. 'You can write to me. At the poste restante. I looked it up. That's how you get letters when you don't know where you're going to be living. Just write on the envelope, Marianne Jenkins, Poste Restante, Bristol, and I'll get it.'

He nods. 'OK.'

Then I give him the carrier bag I have been holding. Someone says, 'Is this seat taken?' and I shake my head. There is an interminable announcement about the many places where the train is going to stop.

'Good luck,' I whisper, and I don't want to hug him, so I just kiss his springy, dirty hair and turn and walk away.

I stand by the window and wave him off. He waves back. I walk down the platform, next to his face, desperately wishing him a better life. He waves and waves, and then I stop and stand still, and watch his face becoming part of the blur of the windows, watch the train snaking away from the station, away from London, away from all our trouble.

Then I turn and start to walk to Paddington.

# chapter sixty-one

I woke early, as the sun rose. That was inevitable, and in spite of everything I gasped at my surroundings. Above me the sky was pink and orange and red, and at the other side blue and slightly misty. Birds glided, high and free. The city stretched away in every direction, below me and around me.

I stretched and yawned and sat up and swung my legs off the sun lounger. I pulled the blanket around my shoulders and walked to the edge of the roof terrace. I leaned on the metal barrier, and stared down.

This was the perfect city. This was the perfect view of it: very early in the morning, absolutely quiet. But for a few modern details, I could have been looking at Canaletto's Venice, at Vivaldi's Venice. The church of San Giorgio was in front of me, perfect, white and dignified. I followed the canal with my eyes as it meandered gently in the direction of the train station, past palaces and churches, hotels and markets and bridges. The place was so different, so pure, when it was empty and cool.

Luigi had put his job on the line by letting me sleep up here. The roof terrace was locked every night at eleven. As soon as he saw the pitiful state I was in, he brought me up here, giving me a blanket and locking the door behind me. I had weighed up the chances of Nancy and Paul scaling the building or making a running leap from the one next door, and decided that this was quite secure enough for me, at the moment.

The cool breeze caressed my face and blew my hair off my neck.

I took the bottle of water from beside the sun lounger where I had slept, and dripped some of it over my head. It refreshed me, though not in the way that a night's sleep would have done. I found some clean underwear in my bag, and the dress I had bought in Paris, and got changed. I put some moisturiser on my face and scrubbed at my dirty feet. I ran a brush through my hair, then sat, cross-legged, by the railing and tried to decide where to go from here.

Gabriella and her friends had not helped my plans for a new life in Venice. However, I had nowhere else to go. My plan had always been to settle here, and for a few deluded days I had thought I was succeeding. That had fallen apart. I was exhausted at the thought of having to go somewhere else, be someone new, start all over again, yet again.

However, Nancy and Paul would leave Italy soon, and in the meantime I could dodge them if ever I happened to see them. It might be easier to stay still and make no ripples than it would be to vanish without leaving a trace.

I sat and stared at the perfect city. When someone unlocked the terrace, I would go out and get some coffee. For the moment, I could not plan beyond that.

At eight o'clock, I heard footsteps on the metal stairs. Luigi had told me that he would not be on duty to let me out, and had instructed me carefully on what to do when this happened. My bags and blanket were already stashed, so I ran on tiptoes to the alcove behind the little building that housed the lift machinery, and crouched there, out of sight of the terrace, with just a narrow strip of roof between me and the railing. I heard whoever it was walking around. Everything was in order, I knew that: I had made sure the sun loungers were perfectly aligned. I just hoped that the person did not decide, for any reason, to stroll around the back of the lift machinery. I screwed my eyes tight shut, and willed them to go away.

There was the determined click of a cigarette lighter, the barely audible whoosh of a flame. I edged out of my niche, and risked a quick look around the lift block. A woman in the black and white hotel uniform was standing exactly where I had just been, leaning over the railing, looking at the view. She was about my age. She blew a luxuriant stream of smoke out of her nose. I watched her back for a few seconds, then retreated.

I left a few minutes after she did. I went down the hotel stairs to avoid the walk from the lift through the breakfast room, and strode confidently through the foyer without looking right or left. I stood on the bank of the canal, feeling eyes on me again, and wondered where to go for coffee.

Every cafe seemed to be full of tourists, inside and out. I chose one in a small square, and took a table indoors, at the far corner, next to the loo. I ordered a cappuccino, and sat back. I watched the other customers. Indoors, most patrons were locals, or at least most of them were talking Italian. Outside, they were all foreign.

*I am safe here*. I muttered it, wanting to hear my voice say the words. Safe, and alone. I had no friend in this city beyond Luigi. All the same, there was no better place to hide than Venice in the summer.

Vivaldi was playing on the stereo: Venice's most celebrated musical son. I wondered how long you had to work in a place like this before you started to hate the sound of the Four Seasons.

The barman smiled at me. I smiled back. He went into the back room and returned with his arms full of cartons of UHT milk.

'For the tourists,' he said, holding one up. I looked into my milky coffee.

'Guilty as charged,' I said, and he nodded, looking slightly confused, probably by my courtroom phrase. If I was staying here, I was going to have to learn to drink my coffee black, the way I had drunk it with Gabriella and Antonio.

A man came and stood by the bar, and the barista took his order. The espresso machine spluttered into life with a sudden, noisy swoosh. I stared into my cup. Luigi was coming to work at midday. I would go and talk to him then, and find out whether he was able to give me work as a chambermaid. The other chambermaids would point me in the direction of a cheap place to live. There was even a university here. If I stayed, if I could support myself, I might be able, at long last, to finish my education.

When I was settled, when I was feeling more secure, I would get in touch with everyone in Falmouth, starting with my poor, ignored brother, who I knew would be quietly frantic. Meanwhile, I would trust no one. I would make my own way in life. If something seemed too good to be true (for example, if someone offered me a studio to live in in exchange for my working in an impromptu gallery), then it probably was.

It was not clear, but a path was there. I could do this. There was a table of young Italians near to me, talking and laughing. I understood the odd word. A couple of tourists were at the table nearest to the door, and when I caught a glimpse of raw sunburned necks, I knew why they were inside.

The music on the stereo abruptly stopped. I looked up, but the barman had gone. I guessed that the stereo was in a back room. Presumably he had finally reached saturation point with Vivaldi and was changing it for something else.

When the next track came on, I was surprised. I frowned, and looked around. I was always happy to hear Leonard Cohen's voice, but this was too incongruous. If it had been 'Hallelujah', I would have understood, but he was singing 'Tower of Song', which is not a song that you ever hear on a cafe stereo. The song that was playing when my mother died. The song that had reduced me to jelly when he played it in London, with his synthesiser in front of him. The song that cut through me like a knife: the song that told me I would always be Marianne.

The barista emerged from the back room, shaking his head, looking like someone who could not quite believe what he had done. The young Italians were too involved in conversation to have noticed that the music had changed. The sunburned couple had not reacted. I heard the cafe man speak to the man who was standing with his back to me at the counter.

'Is OK?' he said. 'This one?'

'Oh yes,' said the man, raising his voice enough for me to hear him. I stared at the back of his neck. His hair was half grey. He stood tall and proud. He should be stooped and defeated, ashamed of himself. He should not be here, like this, playing Leonard Cohen to me. 'This,' he said slowly, 'is the one.'

He turned around and smiled at me.

# chapter sixty-two

## Eliza

Seth is too shocked to react. He looks dazed.

'All along,' he says. 'You were her brother?'

'I was,' says Patrick. 'I am. And I'm sorry.'

'And anyway, Seth,' I say, because everything Patrick has just told us is beginning to sink in. 'Forget about the brother and sister part. Listen to the rest of it. Lucy was got by a *paedophile*. He made her *marry* him. None of the rest of it matters.'

'I wish she'd fucking told me,' says Seth. I know how hurt he is by that, because I am too, although I am trying not to be. 'I would have stood right next to her and waited for him. Let him fucking try to lay a hand on my girlfriend.'

Patrick takes my hand. He is blinking hard. Seth looks worse than he has ever looked.

'And I wish . . .' Seth continues. He bites his lip and puts his head in his hands. 'I wish I could have made her happier. Properly happy. I wish I could have done something to make it better.'

Patrick touches Seth on the shoulder. 'Seth. Mate. You did. Believe me, you really, really did.'

We all go and sit in Seth's garden. I have not asked him about the woman who was here, and he has not mentioned her either. He gets out the deckchairs. It is still just about sunny enough to be outside. I wonder where Lucy is, what the weather is like with her. Above all, though, I hope she has escaped from that man.

I cannot bear to think about what he did to her. Yet I cannot think about anything else.

I turn to Patrick.

'Did she run away from Falmouth because she knew he was after her, or just because she was afraid he might be?'

'This,' he says, 'is the key. I knew she was jumpy after she was in the papers. She always said she's bland-looking so that she could blend in anywhere, but it's not true – she's much more striking than she thinks she is, and she looks the same as she did when she was in her teens. If he saw her, he would have come after her without a doubt.'

'So do you think he did come for her?'

Patrick leans back in his deckchair. I look quickly at the girls. Both of them are absorbed in what they are doing.

'That's the question that haunts me,' he says. 'I can never switch that question off. Did he actually come? Or did she run pre-emptively? I have no idea. I thought she'd contact me, but she hasn't. She will. At some point.'

'She won't have just . . . cut all ties and run?'

'No. Well, she will for a while, but she'll come back to us. If she's all right. She knows that if I found out where she is, I'd be there instantly.'

After a while I try to change the subject slightly.

'Now tell us about you,' I say. 'I mean, we know the basics, but let's have the details. You were fourteen and you were on a train to go and live with your dad. Then what?'

Patrick sighs. 'I've never told anyone this story,' he says. 'I hoped that one day I would. I stopped being Finn Jenkins, and I became Patrick Davidson. I never spoke about what had happened before. I never told anyone what had happened to Mum, and you know what? No one even asked. My dad believed me when I said she'd gone travelling, and that was it. I discovered that no one really gives a shit if it's something that doesn't involve them. You can tell people anything.'

'But you stayed in touch with your sister.'

'I landed on my feet with my dad. It wasn't perfect, and there was a hell of a lot missing, but I had a roof and clothes and I went to school, and I only had to stay for a couple of years. It was what I needed. I didn't care that I wasn't a part of the family; I just treated it like a foster home or something. And my stepmother, Ruth, she was fine, considering. She applied the same rules to me as she did to the rest of them and I just got on with it. I felt I'd seen things they would never see, and that kept me apart, but it was cool. *Apart* suited me.'

Imogen and Clara are crouched together on the grass, going through the bucket of shells that Clara brought back from the beach. I am sure that Imogen is listening.

'So,' he continues. 'I tried to get on with life, and I would hear from her occasionally. I wrote to her all the time. But I wanted to be closer to her, like I said. It took her ages, but in the end, when she was settled here, she said I could come and visit. It was before she met Seth, and she was living this timid little life, shut away in a one-bedroom flat, never doing anything and terrified of shadows. I decided to stay.'

'And so you did.'

'Yes. I was teaching in Mansfield, so my skills were fairly transferable. I applied for jobs at schools down here until I got one. Like I said before, she insisted we didn't tell anyone and didn't act like brother and sister. I liked it that I was keeping an eye on her, although as events have shown, I didn't do a great job.'

I reach out to him.

'Nothing's straightforward, is it?' I say. He takes my hand again and we grip each other tightly.

'I'll say,' says Seth, who still looks dazed.

'Look!' Clara shouts. She runs over to us. 'I found a butterfly shell!'

It is a mussel shell, the two halves still stuck together. I hold out my arms and she runs to me. I hold her tight, and wonder what her future will hold. The sun lights up her hair, and makes her baby skin glow. I want to protect her from everything.

# chapter sixty-three

He walked to my table, smiling broadly, and took the other seat.

I was frozen. I could not speak to him, could not move. Even my face was paralysed into what must have been a stupid-looking expression of shock.

He was twenty years older, but he had barely changed. He was dressed as a tourist, in knee-length shorts, a polo shirt, and a money belt. His hairline had receded slightly.

He was still handsome, still overflowing with charisma. I felt his eyes burning into me, and focused on a spot above his shoulder, where there was a bad oil painting of a gondola on the wall.

I tried to move. I wanted to stand up, to do something. Yet now that I most needed to, I did not seem able to move. He had said he would find me, and here he was, and I had always known that it would happen. I half stood up, wondering whether I could run away. But I had run this far, and he had caught up with me.

I had always wondered how he would be, when I saw him again. I wanted him to be a harmless man heading towards sixty. I wanted him to have seen the error of his ways, to be looking at me with something like shame and regret. I wanted him to be sorry, but he was not.

I remembered his last words: 'I will find you.' Twenty years had passed, but it might as well have been yesterday. Everything I had done, ever since, had been motivated by him.

Then he spoke: 'Marianne Burdett.'

I kept my gaze on the painting. My heart was thumping, and my legs had turned to jelly. I told myself I had to be brave. This was the moment I had never wanted to happen, but now it had, and although I knew he would have no compunction, no mercy now that he had got me, I had to go down fighting.

'That is not my name,' I said. My voice came out small and pathetic. I could not look into his face.

'It's not easy to keep up with you and your aliases.' He said it in the old companionable voice, and his familiar charm made me gasp for breath at the horror of it all. 'And technically, Marianne Burdett *is* your name, no matter what your moniker of the day may be.'

The song ended and no new music came on. I wanted to say that I had never taken his surname, even during that brief period when I might have wanted to.

'How did you get him to play Leonard?' I said, instead.

'Paid him.'

'Of course you did.'

We sat in silence for a few seconds.

'It's good to see you again,' he said. His smile was engaging and I hated it. We both knew that he was toying with me. He was being charming because he could do whatever he wanted.

'How did you find me?' I asked.

'Oh, I've been around for a while,' he said, his voice light, casual. 'It's been lovely. You know, just watching. My lovely Marianne, all grown up.'

'You haven't been watching me.' I try to sound as if I mean it. All those times when I felt eyes on me, when I looked around and caught a blurred glimpse of a figure merging into a crowd. All those times I had told myself I was being paranoid, perhaps it had been him after all.

'How did you know I was here?'

He smiled. Anyone watching would have thought we were the best of friends.

'Easily,' he said, with a laugh. 'You caught the train to Paris, and the train to Venice, and you used your Lucy Riddick passport both times, so you appeared on the passenger lists.' He spread his hands, his point made. 'Besides, the Venice trains were the first ones I looked at. Your old mum had that poster in her room. I thought it might hold some sentimental attraction.'

He knew I would be here, because he knew me, inside and out. He knew me in a way that Seth could never have known me. He knew everything: the murky depths, the bad things, all of it. I was staring my demons in the face, and they were smiling right back.

*Be brave.*

I took a deep breath and forced myself to get up. I put a five-euro note on the table.

*Go down fighting.*

'Anyway,' I said, 'I have to go now.'

'Right,' he replied, with an appreciative chuckle. 'Come on then. Let's go. Let me show you the hidden Venice.'

The part of me that was still a fifteen-year-old girl wanted to do exactly as I was told. But I was an adult now. I had got away from him once, and I had to try, at least, to do it again. I walked casually out of the café, with Benjamin so close behind me that I thought I could feel his breath on the back of my neck. I could smell his cologne. It was still Davidoff's Cool Water.

I tried to shake the idea that I belonged to him, that he had come to Venice to claim what was rightfully his.

Outside, we were in a little square that had a church, two cafés, and a couple of stalls selling trashy souvenirs. It was thick with people, heavy with heat and sweat. Without looking down, I stepped out of my flip-flops, hoping that he might not notice.

I drew a breath, and looked at him. I wanted to say something, but I knew that no words could change any of this. The only thing to do was the only thing I had ever done.

I ran as fast as I could, glad that I had kept myself fit, for this very eventuality. I pushed my way through groups and around people. I dodged down alleys and around corners and kept on and on running, losing myself, losing him, my own bags bumping on my shoulders.

Sweat dripped into my eyes. I could feel wet patches spreading from under my arms. The ground was warm and smooth beneath my bare feet. I ran up humpbacked bridges and down the other side. I could outrun Benjamin, I was sure of that. But I had no idea where I was going. I did not have a plan; and he did.

I found myself in Santa Maria Formosa, beside the church in which I had first met Gabriella. I slowed down, my chest burning, my throat parched. I leaned on the wall of the church and closed my eyes. I must have lost him, but I had no idea what to do now. If I went to the station, he would be there, and if I went to the airport, then somehow he would be there too.

I would hide in the church, for the moment. I paid my two and a half euros, and skulked around in the shadows. I remembered how inspired I had been by St Barbara, and I sat in a pew close to her. I put my head down on the pew in front of me, as if I were doing some particularly devout praying, and tried to order my thoughts. My sweaty dress dried in the cooler air, but my heartbeat did not calm down.

I needed to get out of Venice. I needed to get away again, further away. I needed to keep running.

I looked over at the saint. St Barbara would never have run from a man, the way I was doing. She would have turned around and fought him off. I tried to channel some of her strength and wisdom.

She was serene, strong, a lone brave female amongst the men, with her chest puffed out, her red cloak hanging casually off her shoulders, her face calm and confident.

My only option was to find my way to the station, and if he was there, I would skulk in the shadows and hide from him. If I bought a ticket to somewhere else in Italy, I would not have to show my passport so I would not appear on any of the lists that had given me away last time.

I would take the main tourist drag to the station and use the camouflage of the crowds. I would jump on any old train and go somewhere, and when I got there, I would think of the next part.

Half an hour had passed since I went into the church. I stepped out into the square, and scoped out which alley to take. I would run, and I would try to look as if I were a recreational, though barefoot, jogger.

'I think you dropped these,' he said, falling into place next to me. He was holding up my flip-flops, and before I could react, he gripped the top of my arm tightly. His fingers hurt. He had held me like that before, plenty of times.

I looked up, into his eyes. I saw at once that he was more ruthless than he had ever been, and I knew there was no point. Everything died around him. The pigeons fell from the sky when he passed. The leaves withered on the trees. Flowers shrivelled before they had even unfurled.

He saw the defeat in my face.

'Excellent,' he said. 'You were always trouble. Always.' He led me, by the arm, out of the square, down an alley between two buildings. I did not speak to him, because there was nothing to say. One of my toes was bleeding where I stubbed it when I was running, and I hoped I was leaving bloody footprints. Any sort of trail would be a good thing. I was clutching at straws.

I kept my pace as slow as I could. He was taking me somewhere. He yanked the top of my arm from time to time.

'That was annoying,' he said, as we turned a corner into a little street that was devoid of any shade at all. 'Running away like that. Lucky you looked so – well, so distinctive. Not a hard trail to follow.'

'Fuck off,' I said. I had never said anything like that to him before. He laughed, and this time his laugh was hard.

'With all due respect,' he said, '*you* fuck off. You sent me to prison. You fuck off.'

The sun was unrelenting. The paving stones were smooth and warm, and the alleys we were following were small. He knew his way around this city. We passed tourists, people strolling carelessly around with guide books and cameras. I looked at them, using my eyes to try to convey my desperate need for help, but no one could have cared less. We were just a sweaty woman and an older man, walking arm in arm in Venice in the summer.

Every time we came to an intersection, I tried to jerk my arm free. He held me tighter each time. I knew there would be finger-shaped bruises on my upper arm in the morning, but I also knew that this was a purely academic concern.

We ended up at the mouth of the smallest of alleys. It was dark, with bare walls stretching upwards on both sides. He pushed me into it. I could see water glinting in the sun at the far end. He walked behind me. All I could smell was dank, stale urine, and the same cologne he had always worn.

We were halfway down when he stopped me. The walls were so close together above us that it felt as if they were touching one another, that it was all closing in, that we were about to be crushed to death. I gasped for breath.

Be brave, I told myself. Remember St Barbara.

'Nice spot,' I said. I glanced at the shiny water at the end. He took my bags, and put them on the ground with exaggerated care.

Then he looked at me with malice. 'I thought you'd like it.' He took both my wrists and jerked them up above my head, pinning me to the wall. We were pressed up against each other.

I tried to smile.

'I'm too old for you now.'

'Yes, I'm afraid you are.'

I asked him something I had always wanted to know.

'All those girls you had,' I said. 'Why did you marry *me*?'

He shrugged. 'Because you were so madly in love with me. It was sweet.'

I looked from side to side. I even looked up, but the buildings were storeys high, and there was no way I could scramble out vertically.

I took some deep breaths. There was no clean air, no comfort.

'Let me go,' I said. He shook his head. He stayed calm. I was completely at his mercy.

His power was elusive. He had controlled me when I was a girl, and after everything, he could control me still.

'You knew,' he said, in his real voice, which was different from the one he used when he was pretending to be friendly. I had only heard his real voice once before. 'You knew all along, didn't you, that when you double-crossed me you wouldn't get away with it.'

'You destroyed me,' I said, and the years fell away, and I remembered myself exactly as I had been. 'I was a child. I'm glad I sent you to prison. I would do it again.'

'You were no child,' he said. 'You were willing and you know it. But it's so much easier to be the victim, isn't it? Poor little Marianne. Your mother was tougher than you. She'd be disappointed if she could see you.'

I was not breathing. It didn't matter. I stared at him. I wasn't going to ask him. He was going to tell me anyway.

'Remember her?' he said. 'Your mother? Woman who used to look after you? You poisoned her? So you've killed someone, and I haven't, yet. In my book, that makes *you* the criminal.' He waited for my response. I turned my head back towards the water. He put a hand on my face, and yanked my chin back so I had to look at him. The wall scraped the back of my head.

I glanced sideways, keeping my eyes away from his gaze.

'How did you know her?' I asked, because I knew I had to. I did not want to know the answer.

'I was her pimp,' he said. I closed my eyes. 'Well, kind of her pimp,' he amended. 'I managed an establishment. She was one of my dancers. Officially it was just about dancing and looking. But, well, things happened in private rooms that were none of my business.'

I wished he would get on and kill me, rather than tell me this. For my whole life I had felt I was failing her, failing the high standards she had upheld against the odds. In my mind, she was a paragon.

'And when she got up the duff,' he continued, 'after a particularly friendly meeting with one of her favourite clients – well, I obviously had to let her go, but I liked her, you know? Mary always had something about her. I was young. She was young enough. I thought I might use her again one day, so I let her have the house. At a very reasonable rate. I was going to get her back to work after she had you, but she wasn't up for it. Had another kid soon afterwards, just to keep herself out of the workplace.' He chuckled. 'I always wanted to tell your brother that, you know, when he was being a pain in the arse. That your mother conceived you purely because she didn't want to go back on the game. Because when she had two babies, I wasn't interested any more. She was too old and she came with too much baggage. You know my tastes. But I was always fond of her, so I let her keep the house.'

And this was Benjamin's mistake. I pictured her, so determined, working in school canteens, cleaning offices and doing everything she could to give us a life that was different from the one she had led. I thought of the lengths she went to to keep him away from me, because she knew what he would do if he got his hands on me. I could not fail her now. I thought of St Barbara, and I thought of my mother, and I looked right into his eyes.

It was a lightning strike. I saw a man who chose victims who were not in a position to fight back. I realised that I had beaten him before. I had sent him to prison. I had gone on to build a life for myself, to meet a man I loved.

'This must be a first,' I said conversationally.

He gripped both of my wrists, harder. 'What?' he said, suspiciously.

'You. Picking on someone who can fight you.'

I raised my leg suddenly and kneed him in the groin as hard as I could. It was something I should have done a very long time ago. He let go, involuntarily, but put his body between me and the rest of Venice, so I could not pass. I grabbed my bags and ran, instead, the only way I could: towards the water.

The alley ended in a tiny, half-rotten wooden platform that stuck out a little way into a wide *rio*. The water was far below us, and I was afraid that the platform's supports might be too rotten to hold me. There was a bridge, too far away to reach. The water was lapping against the stone. Opposite, there were a couple of small windows in the wall of a house, but they were high up and no use.

I looked around. This was Venice in August. There had to be somebody nearby. In one direction, the *rio* turned a corner. In the other, a couple of distant figures were heading this way, but the path on which they were walking would twist around and lead them away from me, so I was inaccessible. There was nowhere for me to go but into the water. The drop was surprisingly big.

I turned. He was right behind me.

'I'm not scared of you,' I said, and it was a revelation. 'You're pathetic and you're scum.'

I put my bags down, and I jumped. I had no idea how deep the *rio* was, or how polluted. My feet did not reach the bottom, and my face was briefly underwater. The water was warm, salty, dirty. I pushed it out of my face, rubbed my eyes, and looked up at my evil husband.

The look in his eyes made me shiver through the hot air and the warm water. 'Come on then,' I said. I tried to taunt him, to encourage him. I tried to imagine him learning to swim, over the past twenty years. He was probably, I thought, lying when he'd told me that he couldn't swim, anyway. He would not have brought me here, to an alley with water at the end, had he not been able to swim. All the same, it was the only chance I had.

He did not choose Venice. I chose Venice. I trod water, looking up at him. I saw him dither, newly fallible. I looked into his eyes, and I laughed. I had never done that before. I was laughing at myself, as much as at him: I was laughing at my own stupidity, at the way I had spent twenty years cowering away from him as if I were a pathetic flower incapable of standing up for myself.

I saw him suspended in the air, frozen in time for a fraction of a second. Then he splashed down, almost on top of me.

I started to swim away. He grabbed me by the top of my arm, as he always had. His face was contorted, and then my head went under the water, and my eyes and nose filled with sewagey salty liquid. He held me down. I reached for any part of him that I could, and my fingers touched his torso. I grabbed it with both arms, tugging him in a perverse hug, and he came down, under the water with me. I felt him letting it happen. We were in this together: each of us prepared to sacrifice anything to destroy the other.

It was a different sort of reality. The world was brown and it seeped into my ears and my mouth and up my nose. We were going to die in each other's arms at the bottom of the water: it was a fitting end to our marriage. My lungs burned to take a breath, but I was curiously calm. If we did this together, then at least he would not exist. No other girls would be vulnerable to his charms. I was not surprised it had ended this way.

The seconds ticked by.

His grip loosened, just a tiny bit, but it loosened. For a second, I could have stayed with Benjamin, or I could have gone back into the world. I wanted to stay, but, for one instant, my survival instinct won out, and I pulled myself up, pushed down on him so hard that I propelled myself to the surface.

And then, my head was above the water, and I was filling my lungs with scalding, wonderful air. For a second I thought I was free. I tipped my head up, and felt the sun on my face. There was still nobody around. I started to swim away.

Somewhere below the water, his hands found me. They had always been hard, insistent, and I had never been able to get away. He grabbed my leg, encircled it, and tugged. I kicked and kicked at him. He hung on. I kicked again. And suddenly, he was gone.

I bobbed in the water. It might have been an hour, or ten seconds. Nothing happened. Hallucinatory time passed, and still nothing happened. There were no bubbles, and no submarine fingers reached for me.

When I realised that it had stopped, I swam to the side, pulled myself up on the spongey platform, and picked up my bags. I stopped and looked at the water, but it just looked like a normal *rio*. I half-wondered whether I had imagined all of it.

I walked back down the tiny alleyway and rejoined the city. I did not look back.

# chapter sixty-four

## Marianne

I follow his trial in the press with satisfaction and trepidation. He, Tim and Pete are all sentenced to eight years in prison. When they were raided, the police didn't just find a twelve-year-old girl. They didn't just have the six videos I gave them. They found an enormous number of videos of child porn stashed in various places, and ample photographic evidence of their crimes. It seems to me that their sentence is rather more lenient than it should be.

Once he is in prison, I begin to feel safe. I send a card to Patrick Davidson, celebrating the fact. He writes back at the poste restante, a chatty, scrawled letter all about his new family, his school, his life. He sounds wistful, but I am glad it is more or less working out for him.

I move out of the hostel I've been living in, into a room in a scummy shared flat in St Paul's. I find work as a barmaid. I try to be strong. I want to go back to college to finish my education, prepare myself to get a proper job of some sort. I tell myself that I am pulling pints as a means to an end, while I save up to take some A levels. It is not true. I could study at the same time as working, but I don't want to. I don't have any confidence at all. I meet people but I cannot get to know them, because if I did, I would have to tell them, sooner or later, that I was married, that I had got married when I was just sixteen, to a man who is now in jail for abusing children. I am still a part of Benjamin, still tied to him. I am ashamed of myself. So I keep a low profile, move from pub to bar, make up different stories about my life every time anyone asks. I meet a girl called Rebecca at one of the pubs, and one day I start to tell her, but then I stop myself, because I cannot bear to say it. All the same, she becomes a friend, for a while. We go on holiday together. I start to remember what it is to feel normal.

I stay well away from men. Sex is a horrible thing. It is not something I will ever do again. I live a tiny, scared life, and I flinch at shadows.

Slowly I pull myself out of it. I begin to see that I need to create a life in which I can be comfortable. I move away from the city, further and further west until I find myself in Falmouth. Falmouth fits, so I stay. I think I will grow old here, a spinster living an unremarkable life.

Benjamin and his friends are released from prison, but by this point I have a new name and a new life. As long as I can keep out of any kind of spotlight, I will be safe. He will never come looking for me here.

Finn comes to visit; both of us have new names now. He likes it in Falmouth. He wants to stick around. It seems like a risk. I still feel we should not be together. He agrees, reluctantly, not to tell anyone that we are related. It is an enormous source of comfort to me just to see him around town, to stop and chat with him and to know that we have shared unspeakable experiences, but that now we are both all right.

And then, one day, at a party, I meet a man who loves me, and I desperately want to love him too. He has no idea that he is the first man who has treated me like this. I never tell him that I am married. I cannot risk letting him know the truth.

My life settles down. It goes smoothly, for a while. And then, one day, Imogen dares Clara to climb a cliff, and everything comes tumbling down.

# chapter sixty-five

The air was perfectly still and the whole world was different. I heard footsteps and chatter in what I thought was Dutch, descending the staircase. The voices died away, and I was on my own.

I stood at the railing and looked out. I was used to the dense crowds of Venice, and now I could see expanses of space: grey water, a few boats, deep blue sky, long grass. This was the lagoon, the way it had been before the unlikely city was constructed, just over the horizon.

My hair and clothes had dried quickly, but I knew that the smell of the *rio* water was clinging to me. My dress was slightly discoloured. I looked around, checked again that I was alone, and unpacked some of the clothes from the top of my bag. I changed quickly, praying that no one would appear at the crucial moment and find a naked woman at the top of the bell tower.

I was high above it all. Torcello was the smallest of the islands that were on the tourist trail. After I'd walked away from Benjamin, I had found myself at the Fondamenta Nuove. There was a ferry about to leave for Murano, so I got on it. Murano was indeed, as I remembered a hotel guest saying, a tourist-infested hellhole. There were far too many people there for me and I wanted to stop every one of them and tell them what I had done. I thought I saw Nancy and Paul at a distance, though I did not look for long enough to find out for sure. I took another ferry and went to Burano, and from there I took yet another and ended up finding solitude at the top of the campanile in Torcello.

This island was mosquito-infested and swampy, and there were very few buildings here. One of them was a Cipriani restaurant, and one of the houses, I could see from my vantage point, had a helipad, but there were no other signs of opulence. There was simply a path that led from the boat stop to the basilica, taking in a shop and a couple of cafés on the way.

The basilica was a tonic. Once I was inside, I stared at the mosaic of the Last Judgement, and caught my breath. I made a conscious effort, and put my shoulders back, and took deep breaths. No one knew what I had done. I stared at the mosaic figures on the right, the ones who were heading for eternal damnation. One figure in particular, I thought, looked like Benjamin.

The basilica was older than the Venetian churches, its lines plain, and everything felt simple here. Outside there was a stone chair that was allegedly the throne of Attila the Hun. Visitors were queuing up to have their photographs taken sitting in it. I watched a group of Australian backpackers taking a picture of something from their lunch bag in it, and shouting: 'Attila the Bun.' I watched them through a filter, amazed by their cheerful normality.

I climbed hundreds of steps to reach the top of the bell tower. It was a peaceful place, a calm place. I could breathe here. This was where I needed to be. The space was dominated by the bell itself. It was enormous, brown with green tinges, held up by a complex structure of wooden beams. The walls of the building were red brick, with arches and niches.

A cool breeze reached my face, through the security fence that meant I saw the outside world cut up by squares of metal.

Benjamin was gone. Technically I was now a widow. And I was free. As I stared at the green grass of the island, I felt a smile spreading across my face. Perhaps I had done a bad thing, but I could never regret it. I wanted to shout, but I contented myself with smiling. I was using smile muscles that I had not used for years.

I rejoiced at his death, and I did not care how callous that made me. He was gone, and I was certain that a few more teenage girls had been saved. And I had reclaimed my real identity. I was free, now, to be Marianne again.

There were footsteps on the stairs. I looked around, unable

to shake my wariness straight away. It was a group of young people, French I thought. I smiled at them, waited for them to reach the top of the stairs, and then set off downwards, ready to rejoin the real world.

There was a payphone in front of one of the cafes. I stood there listening to the birdsong above my head, smelling the salty water and the dried-out grass. Then I picked up the receiver and punched in 112.

When I got through to the police, I refused to give my name. I just said the imperfect Italian phrase I had rehearsed, in my head, for the past couple of hours.

'*Uomo in* rio,' I said, three times, to be sure they understood. I said the name of the nearest alley. Then I hung up. I wanted his body to be pulled out of the water, and I wanted to see it in the paper, because only then would I be completely certain that he had gone.

I looked at the world of possibilities that was spread out before me, and took my phone out of my handbag.

I wrote a text to Finn.

*Sorry to vanish*, I typed. *Everything taken care of. Meet me in London in a couple of days? Am coming home.*

# chapter sixty-six

A week later, Finn and I stepped out of the police station, and looked at each other. We smiled. He touched my shoulder.

'Now there's something we ought to have done a hell of a long time ago,' he said.

'It wasn't as bad as I expected,' I said. The world still felt new. Everything was miraculous.

'Not least because she didn't believe us,' he said. 'About Mum.'

'True.'

'I thought we'd be arrested or something.'

'But they think we're time-wasters. We worry about it all that time, and no one actually believes us.'

'Which is fine.'

It was the end of August, and it felt like the first day of autumn. There were leaves dancing round our ankles. When I turned around, the wind blew straight into my face, fresh and crisp.

'So,' said my brother. 'Where are you going now?'

I looked down the street. One way was Venice. The other was Cornwall. I turned and looked at him.

'This way,' I said, and set off towards Cornwall. I had no idea what the future would hold down there, but it felt like the right direction. It felt like the place where I needed to be.

# chapter sixty-seven

We were sitting at a small table by the window in Pizza Express, looking out at the rain falling into the harbour, and we were not speaking. There was an enormous cruise ship out there in the background, and a lot of small sailing and motorboats in the foreground. Drops of rain slid down the window panes, and the mist was so low that we could hardly see the Maritime Museum, although it was just across the square.

'You came back,' he said, eventually.

I looked at him. This was the first time I had ever been myself.

'Kind of.'

He nodded. I wondered whether he actually knew what I meant.

'Lucy went away, and Marianne came back?' he said.

'Yes.'

'I don't blame you for not telling me,' he said. 'Just in case you thought I might.'

'Thanks.'

'I'm glad you saw off the fucker.'

I smiled. 'Me too. It's a bit monstrous, isn't it?'

He put his hand over mine. 'A lot of things are monstrous. You doing what you did is not one of them.'

I looked at him. It had never occurred to me for a second that Seth and I might still have a life together, after all of this. I felt tentative about it. There were a lot of things I was not going to be able to talk about. I hoped he would understand that.

'So,' he said. 'What did you actually do in Venice?' I looked at him, not sure what he meant. 'Tell me the day-to-day stuff. I want to know where you've been and what it's been like. Was it like you wanted it to be?'

I thought about it. 'I looked at churches. I walked through crowds. One night I slept on a roof. I met a bunch of tricksters and helped them steal some prints from some Americans.'

He smiled and pushed my drink towards me. 'That sounds like a good place to start,' he said. 'Why don't we forget all the rest of it for a moment? Why don't you tell me about that?'

I looked at the rain, which was easing off and becoming the Cornish drizzle that I'd missed so much. I watched the fog thinning out slightly, so I could see the shape of the museum through it. I turned to Seth, the man who still seemed to love me, the man I knew I had loved all along, and for the first time, I started to tell him the truth.